STARLIGHT 3

STARLIGHT 3

EDITED BY

PATRICK

NIELSEN

HAYDEN

TOR®

A TOM DOHERTY
ASSOCIATES
BOOK

NEW YORK

STARLIGHT 3

Edited by Claire Eddy

A Tor Book
Published by Tom Doherty Associates, LLC
175 Fifth Avenue
New York, NY 10010

www.tor.com

Tor® is a registered trademark of Tom Doherty Associates, LLC.

Library of Congress Cataloging-in-Publication Data

Starlight 3 / Patrick Nielsen Hayden, ed.—1st ed.
    p. cm.
  "A Tom Doherty Associates book."
  ISBN 0-312-86780-8 (acid-free paper)
    1. Science fiction, American. 2. American fiction—20th century.
I. Title: Starlight three. II. Nielsen Hayden, Patrick.

PS648.S3 S657 2001
813'.0876208'09049—dc21

2001027118

First Edition: July 2001

Printed in the United States of America

     0 9 8 7 6 5 4 3 2 1

For Jenna Felice, 1976–2001
Editor, writer, friend of short fiction

CONTENTS

INTRODUCTION

WELCOME BACK TO *STARLIGHT*. NOT IN THE YEAR 2000, AS promised in *Starlight 2*, but in the even more science-fictional year of 2001.

Science fiction isn't futurism, of course, nor does it have an especially good record of forecasting the actual future, notwithstanding such subcultural folktales as the FBI's visit to John W. Campbell during World War II. Science fiction in 2001, just like science fiction in 1984, 1968, 1941, or 1926, is about the present.

Despite this, it's hard for SF writers and editors to resist the temptation to play the forecasting game—and the even more interesting game of reassessing old forecasts. And of course the dual millennial years of 2000 and 2001—during the transitions to which, even the most unreflective citizens of our society must have experienced at least a few minutes of science-fictional holy-cow-I'm-living-in-the-Future *frisson*—offer us endless opportunities to play both games. (As Arwel Parry has pointed out, millennia are like buses: you wait a thousand years for one, then two come along at once.)

So when we look around in the actual Year of Arthur C. Clarke's 2001, how much does it look like the 2001 of our beloved machine dreams?

Not much, of course. Not a Pan Am orbital shuttle, research moonbase, or manned mission to Jupiter in sight. (To say nothing of mysterious rectangular artifacts left by unfathomably powerful aliens.) Indeed, the actual world of 2001—like the actual worlds of 1984, 1968, 1941, and 1926—is composed of fewer such broad chiliastic simplicities, and of far more annoying complexities, unintended consequences, and insurmountable opportunities. The ostensible futures that science fiction stories postulate are simpler, more "one-note" than the actual world of lived experience. At its most extreme, in SF works of insufficient thoughtfulness, this becomes the syndrome nailed down by James Blish with the sentence "It was raining on the planet Mongo on Thursday."

And yet, isn't this (by now commonplace) observation something of an oversimplification itself? Science fiction isn't futurism, but then, with a record of prognostication as bad as ours, neither is futurism. And while the visions provided by SF and by conventional academic, think-tank, and public-intellectual "futurism" don't ever line up with the actual future, wouldn't it be extraordinarily disquieting if they did?

Meanwhile, all these visions do indeed affect the world, by affecting how the world imagines where it's going. In a sense, the historical accident by which our genre got called "science" fiction has made this less clear than it might otherwise be. Although much great science fiction is powerfully rooted in actual science, much fine SF is not, and feels no less than SF for that. What is really at the core of our genre is *argument*, is a method for looking at the world by imagining the world if it were slightly different—or a lot different. This is what fancier critics mean when they talk about "estrangement." It is a method of engaging consequentially with a world in a state of seemingly permanent rapid change.

I write these words on the 14th floor of a skyscraper—a steel-frame skyscraper, one of the first—that is almost a hundred years old. I write by typing into an amazingly powerful device that saves my work in editable form. Using the same device, I can browse the day's news, and commentary on that news, from sources all over the planet, with just a few simple commands. I read about an unexpectedly successful attempt to soft-land an unmanned probe on an asteroid 196 million miles away. I read that a rough but substantially-complete map of the human genome is now available to anyone in the world. I read headlines that remind me of the "Crazy Years" in Robert A. Heinlein's "future history" . . . and other headlines that make me think of the American religious tyranny that Heinlein has happening next.

I reflect on how broad historic changes actually happen: sometimes with a great clangor, sometimes like a thief in the night. I look at the events of November and December 2000 in my own country, and I reflect on what a truly science-fictional experience it is to be living under an authentically illegitimate American government, born of force and fraud. I think about Ray Bradbury's "A Sound of Thunder." And about Nehemiah Scudder.

And I fear for us. But I'm glad to be living in a world that still—for now, at least—has science fiction in it. Keep arguing.

—Patrick Nielsen Hayden
February 2001

HELL IS THE ABSENCE OF GOD

THIS IS THE STORY OF A MAN NAMED NEIL FISK, AND HOW he came to love God. The pivotal event in Neil's life was an occurrence both terrible and ordinary: the death of his wife Sarah. Neil was consumed with grief after she died, a grief that was excruciating not only because of its intrinsic magnitude, but because it also renewed and emphasized the previous pains of his life. Her death forced him to reexamine his relationship with God, and in doing so he began a journey that would change him forever.

Neil was born with a congenital abnormality that caused his left thigh to be externally rotated and several inches shorter than his right; the medical term for it was proximal femoral focus deficiency. Most people he met assumed God was responsible for this, but Neil's mother hadn't witnessed any visitations while carrying him; his condition was the result of improper limb development during the sixth week of gestation, nothing more. In fact, as far as Neil's mother was concerned, blame rested with his absent father, whose income might have made corrective surgery a possibility, although she never expressed this sentiment aloud.

As a child Neil had occasionally wondered if he were being punished by God, but most of the time he blamed his classmates in school for his unhappiness. Their nonchalant cruelty, their instinctive ability to locate the weaknesses in a victim's emotional armor, the way their own friendships were reinforced by their sadism: he recognized these as examples of human behavior, not divine. And although his classmates often used God's name in their taunts, Neil knew better than to blame Him for their actions.

But while Neil avoided the pitfall of blaming God, he never made the jump to loving Him; nothing in his upbringing or his personality led him to pray to God for strength or for relief. The assorted trials he faced growing up were accidental or human in origin, and he relied on strictly human resources to counter them. He became an adult who—like so many others—viewed God's actions in the abstract until they impinged upon his own life. Angelic visitations were events that befell other people, reaching him only via reports on the nightly news. His own life was entirely mundane; he worked as a superintendent for an upscale apartment building, collecting rent and performing repairs, and as far as he was concerned, circumstances were fully capable of unfolding, happily or not, without intervention from above.

This remained his experience until the death of his wife.

It was an unexceptional visitation, smaller in magnitude than most but no different in kind, bringing blessings to some and disaster to others. In this instance the angel was Nathanael, making an appearance in a downtown shopping district. Four miracle cures were effected: the elimination of carcinomas in two individuals, the regeneration of the spinal cord in a paraplegic, and the restoration of sight to a recently blinded person. There were also two miracles that were not cures: a delivery van, whose driver had fainted at the sight of the angel, was halted before it could overrun a busy sidewalk; another man was caught in a shaft of Heaven's light when the angel departed, erasing his eyes but ensuring his devotion.

Neil's wife Sarah Fisk had been one of the eight casualties. She was hit by flying glass when the angel's billowing curtain of flame shattered the storefront window of the café in which she was eating. She bled to death within minutes, and the other customers in the café—none of whom suffered even superficial injuries—could do nothing but listen to her cries of pain and fear, and eventually witness her soul's ascension toward Heaven.

Nathanael hadn't delivered any specific message; the angel's parting words, which had boomed out across the entire visitation site, were the typical *Behold the power of the Lord*. Of the eight casualties that day, three souls were accepted into heaven and five were not, a closer ratio than the average for deaths by all causes. Sixty-two people received medical treatment for injuries ranging from slight concussions to ruptured eardrums to burns requiring skin grafts. Total property damage was estimated at 8.1 million dollars, all of it excluded by private insurance companies due to the cause. Scores of people became devout worshippers in the wake of the visitation, either out of gratitude or terror.

Alas, Neil Fisk was not one of them.

After a visitation, it's common for all the witnesses to meet as a group and discuss how their common experience has affected their lives. The witnesses of Nathanael's latest visitation arranged such group meetings, and family members of those who had died were welcome, so Neil began attending. The meetings were held once a month in a basement room of a large church downtown; there were metal folding chairs arranged in rows, and in the back of the room was a table holding coffee and doughnuts. Everyone wore adhesive name tags made out in felt-tip pen.

While waiting for the meetings to start, people would stand around, drinking coffee, talking casually. Most people Neil spoke to assumed his leg was a result of the visitation, and he had to explain that he wasn't a witness, but rather the husband of one of the casualties. This didn't bother him particularly; he was used to explaining about his leg. What did bother him was the tone of the meetings themselves, when participants spoke about their reaction to the visitation: most of them talked about their newfound devotion to God, and they tried to persuade the bereaved that they should feel the same.

Neil's reaction to such attempts at persuasion depended on who was making it. When it was an ordinary witness, he found it merely irritating. When someone who'd received a miracle cure told him to love God, he had to restrain an impulse to strangle the person. But what he found most disquieting of all was hearing the same suggestion from a man named Tony Crane; Tony's wife had died in the visitation too, and he now projected an air of groveling with his every movement. In hushed, tearful tones he explained how he had accepted his role as one of God's subjects, and he advised Neil to do likewise.

Neil didn't stop attending the meetings—he felt that he somehow owed it to Sarah to stick with them—but he found another group to go to as well, one more compatible with his own feelings: a support group devoted to those who'd lost a loved one during a visitation, and were angry at God because of it. They met every other week in a room at the local community center, and talked about the grief and rage that boiled inside of them.

All the attendees were generally sympathetic to one another, despite differences in their various attitudes toward God. Of those who'd been devout before their loss, some struggled with the task of remaining so, while others gave up their devotion without a second glance. Of those who'd never been devout, some felt their position had been validated, while others were faced with the near-impossible task of becoming devout now. Neil found himself, to his consternation, in this last category.

Like every other nondevout person, Neil had never expended much energy on where his soul would end up; he'd always assumed his destination was Hell, and he accepted that. That was the way of things, and Hell, after all, was not physically worse than the mortal plane.

It meant permanent exile from God, no more and no less; the truth of this was plain for anyone to see on those occasions when Hell manifested itself. These happened on a regular basis; the ground seemed to become transparent, and you could see Hell as if you were looking through a hole in the floor. The lost souls looked no different from the living, their eternal bodies resembling mortal ones. You couldn't communicate with them—their exile from God meant that they couldn't apprehend the mortal plane where His actions were still felt—but as long as the manifestation lasted you could hear them talk, laugh, or cry, just as they had when they were alive.

People varied widely in their reactions to these manifestations. Most devout people were galvanized, not by the sight of anything frightening, but at being reminded that eternity outside paradise was a possibility. Neil, by contrast, was one of those who were unmoved; as far as he could tell, the lost souls as a group were no unhappier than he was, their existence no worse than his in the mortal plane, and in some ways better: his eternal body would be unhampered by congenital abnormalities.

Of course, everyone knew that Heaven was incomparably superior, but to Neil it had always seemed too remote to consider, like wealth or fame or glamour. For people like him, Hell was where you went when you died, and he saw no point in restructuring his life in hopes of avoiding that. And since God hadn't previously played a role in Neil's life, he wasn't afraid of being exiled from God. The prospect of living without interference, living in a world where windfalls and misfortunes were never by design, held no terror for him.

Now that Sarah was in Heaven, his situation had changed. Neil wanted more than anything to be reunited with her, and the only way to get to Heaven was to love God with all his heart.

This is Neil's story, but telling it properly requires telling the stories of two other individuals whose paths became entwined with his. The first of these is Janice Reilly.

What people assumed about Neil had in fact happened to Janice. When Janice's mother was eight months pregnant with her, she lost control of the car she was driving and collided with a telephone pole during a sudden hailstorm, fists of ice dropping out of a clear blue sky and littering the road like a spill of giant ball bearings. She was sitting in her car, shaken but unhurt, when she saw a knot of silver flames—later identified as the angel Bardiel—float across the sky. The sight petrified her, but not so much that she didn't notice the peculiar settling sensation in her womb. A subsequent ultrasound revealed that the unborn Janice Reilly no longer had legs; flipperlike feet grew directly from her hip sockets.

Janice's life might have gone the way of Neil's, if not for what happened two days after the ultrasound. Janice's parents were sitting at their kitchen table, crying and asking what they had done to deserve this, when they received a vision: the saved souls of four deceased relatives appeared before them, suffusing the kitchen with a golden glow. The saved never spoke, but their beatific smiles induced a feeling of serenity in whoever saw them. From that moment on, the Reillys were certain that their daughter's condition was not a punishment.

As a result, Janice grew up thinking of her legless condition as a gift; her parents explained that God had given her a special assignment because He considered her equal to the task, and she vowed that she would not let Him down. Without pride or defiance, she saw it as her responsibility to show others that her condition did not indicate weakness, but rather strength.

As a child, she was fully accepted by her schoolmates; when you're as pretty, confident, and charismatic as she was, children don't even notice that you're in a wheelchair. It was when she was a teenager that she realized that the able-bodied people in her school were not the ones who most needed convincing. It was more important for her to set an example for other handicapped individuals, whether they had been touched by God or not, no matter where they lived. Janice began speaking before audiences, telling those with disabilities that they had the strength God required of them.

Over time she developed a reputation, and a following. She made a living writing and speaking, and established a nonprofit organization dedicated to promoting her message. People sent her letters thanking her for changing their lives, and receiving those gave her a sense of fulfillment of a sort that Neil had never experienced.

This was Janice's life up until she herself witnessed a visitation by the angel Rashiel. She was letting herself into her house when the tremors began; at first she thought they were of natural origin, although she didn't live in a geologically active area, and waited in the doorway for them to subside. Several seconds later she caught a glimpse of silver in the sky and realized it was an angel, just before she lost consciousness.

Janice awoke to the biggest surprise of her life: the sight of her two new legs, long, muscular, and fully functional.

She was startled the first time she stood up: she was taller than she expected. Balancing at such a height without the use of her arms was unnerving, and simultaneously feeling the texture of the ground through the soles of her feet made it positively bizarre. Rescue workers, finding her wandering down the street dazedly, thought she was in shock until she— marveling at her ability to face them at eye level—explained to them what had happened.

When statistics were gathered for the visitation, the restoration of Janice's legs was recorded as a blessing, and she was humbly grateful for her good fortune. It was at the first of the support group meetings that a feeling of guilt began to creep in. There Janice met two individuals with cancer who'd witnessed Rashiel's visitation, thought their cure was at hand, and been bitterly disappointed when they realized they'd been passed over. Janice found herself wondering, why had she received a blessing when they had not?

Janice's family and friends considered the restoration of her legs a reward for excelling at the task God had set for her, but for Janice, this interpretation raised another question. Did He intend for her to stop? Surely not; evangelism provided the central direction of her life, and there was no limit to the number of people who needed to hear her message. Her continuing to preach was the best action she could take, both for herself and for others.

Her reservations grew during her first speaking engagement after the visitation, before an audience of people recently paralyzed and now wheelchair-bound. Janice delivered her usual words of inspiration, assuring them that they had the strength needed for the challenges ahead; it was during the Q&A that she was asked if the restoration of her legs meant she had passed her test. Janice didn't know what to say; she could hardly promise them that one day their marks would be erased. In fact, she realized, any implication that she'd been rewarded could be interpreted as criticism of others who remained afflicted, and she didn't want that. All she could tell them was that she didn't know why she'd been cured, but it was obvious they found that an unsatisfying answer.

Janice returned home disquieted. She still believed in her message, but as far as her audiences were concerned, she'd lost her greatest source of credibility. How could she inspire others who were touched by God to see their condition as a badge of strength, when she no longer shared their condition?

She considered whether this might be a challenge, a test of her ability to spread His word. Clearly God had made her task more difficult than it was before; perhaps the restoration of her legs was an obstacle for her to overcome, just as their earlier removal had been.

This interpretation failed her at her next scheduled engagement. The audience was a group of witnesses to a visitation by Nathanael; she was often invited to speak to such groups in the hopes that those who suffered might draw encouragement from her. Rather than sidestep the issue, she began with an account of the visitation she herself had recently experienced. She explained that while it might appear she was a beneficiary, she was in fact facing her own challenge: like them, she was being forced to draw on resources previously untapped.

She realized, too late, that she had said the wrong thing. A man in the audience with a misshapen leg stood up and challenged her: was she seriously suggesting that the restoration of her legs was comparable to the loss of his wife? Could she really be equating her trials with his own?

Janice immediately assured him that she wasn't, and that she couldn't imagine the pain he was experiencing. But, she said, it wasn't God's intention that everyone be subjected to the same kind of trial, but only that each person face his or her own trial, whatever it might be. The difficulty of any trial was subjective, and there was no way to compare two individuals' experiences. And just as those whose suffering seemed greater than his should have compassion for him, so should he have compassion for those whose suffering seemed less.

The man was having none of it. She had received what anyone else would have considered a fantastic blessing, and she was complaining about it. He stormed out of the meeting while Janice was still trying to explain.

That man, of course, was Neil Fisk. Neil had had Janice Reilly's name mentioned to him for much of his life, most often by people who were convinced his misshapen leg was a sign from God. These people cited her as an example he should follow, telling him that her attitude was the proper response to a physical handicap. Neil couldn't deny that her leglessness was a far worse condition than his distorted femur. Unfortunately, he found her attitude so foreign that, even in the best of times, he'd never been able to learn anything from her. Now, in the depths of his grief and mystified as to why she had received a gift she didn't need, Neil found her words offensive.

In the days that followed, Janice found herself more and more plagued by doubts, unable to decide what the restoration of her legs meant. Was she being ungrateful for a gift she'd received? Was it both a blessing and a test? Perhaps it was a punishment, an indication that she had not performed her duty well enough. There were many possibilities, and she didn't know which one to believe.

There is one other person who played an important role in Neil's story, even though he and Neil did not meet until Neil's journey was nearly over. That person's name is Ethan Mead.

Ethan had been raised in a family that was devout, but not profoundly so. His parents credited God with their above-average health and their comfortable economic status, although they hadn't witnessed any visitations or received any visions; they simply trusted that God was, directly or indirectly, responsible for their good fortune. Their devotion had never been put to any serious test, and might not have withstood one; their love for God was based in their satisfaction with the status quo.

Ethan was not like his parents, though. Ever since childhood he'd felt certain that God had a special role for him to play, and he waited for a sign telling him what that role was. He'd have liked to become a preacher, but felt he hadn't any compelling testimony to offer; his vague feelings of expectation weren't enough. He longed for an encounter with the divine to provide him with direction.

He could have gone to one of the holy sites, those places where—for reasons unknown—angelic visitations occurred on a regular basis, but he felt that such an action would be presumptuous of him. The holy sites were usually the last resort of the desperate, those people seeking either a miracle cure to repair their bodies or a glimpse of Heaven's light to repair their souls, and Ethan was not desperate. He decided that he'd been set along his own course, and in time the reason for it would become clear. While waiting for that day, he lived his life as best he could: he worked as a librarian, married a woman named Claire, raised two children. All the while, he remained watchful for signs of a greater destiny.

Ethan was certain his time had come when he became witness to a visitation of Rashiel, the same one that—miles away—restored Janice Reilly's legs. Ethan was alone when it happened, walking toward his car in the center of a parking lot, when the ground began to shudder. Instinctively he knew it was a visitation, and he assumed a kneeling position, feeling no fear, only exhilaration and awe at the prospect of learning his calling.

The ground became still after a minute, and Ethan looked around, but didn't otherwise move. Only after waiting for several more minutes did he rise to his feet. There was a large crack in the asphalt, beginning directly in front of him and following a meandering path down the street. The crack seemed to be pointing him in a specific direction, so he ran alongside it for several blocks until he encountered other survivors, a man and a woman climbing out of a modest fissure that had opened up directly beneath them. He waited with the two of them until rescuers arrived and brought them to a shelter.

Ethan attended the support group meetings that followed and met the other witnesses to Rashiel's visitation. Over the course of a few meetings, he became aware of certain patterns among the witnesses. Of course there were those who'd been injured and those who'd received miracle cures. But there were also those whose lives were changed in other ways: the man and woman he'd first met fell in love and were soon engaged; a woman who'd been pinned beneath a collapsed wall was inspired to become an EMT after being rescued. One business owner formed an alliance that averted her impending bankruptcy, while another whose business was destroyed saw it as a message that he change his ways. It seemed that everyone except Ethan had found a way to understand what had happened to them.

He hadn't been cursed or blessed in any obvious way, and he didn't know what message he was intended to receive. His wife, Claire, suggested that he consider the visitation a reminder that he appreciate what he had, but Ethan found that unsatisfying, reasoning that *every* visitation—no matter where it occurred—served that function, and the fact that he'd witnessed a visitation firsthand had to have greater significance. His mind was preyed upon by the idea that he'd missed an opportunity, that there was a fellow witness whom he was intended to meet but hadn't. This visitation had to be the sign he'd been waiting for; he couldn't just disregard it. But that didn't tell him what he was supposed to do.

Ethan eventually resorted to the process of elimination: he got hold of a list of all the witnesses, and crossed off those who had a clear interpretation of their experience, reasoning that one of those remaining must be the person whose fate was somehow intertwined with his. Among those who were confused or uncertain about the visitation's meaning would be the one he was intended to meet.

When he had finished crossing names off his list, there was only one left: JANICE REILLY.

In public Neil was able to mask his grief as adults are expected to, but in the privacy of his apartment, the floodgates of emotion burst open. The awareness of Sarah's absence would overwhelm him, and then he'd collapse on the floor and weep. He'd curl up into a ball, his body racked by hiccuping sobs, tears and mucus streaming down his face, the anguish coming in ever-increasing waves until it was more than he could bear, more intense than he'd have believed possible. Minutes or hours later it would leave, and he would fall asleep, exhausted. And the next day he would wake up and face the prospect of another day without Sarah.

An elderly woman in Neil's apartment building tried to comfort him by telling him that the pain would lessen in time, and while he would never forget his wife, he would at least be able to move on. Then he would meet someone else one day and find happiness with her, and he would learn to love God and thus ascend to Heaven when his time came.

This woman's intentions were good, but Neil was in no position to find any comfort in her words. Sarah's absence felt like an open wound, and the prospect that someday he would no longer feel pain at her loss seemed not just remote, but a physical impossibility. If suicide would have ended his pain, he'd have done it without hesitation, but that would only ensure that his separation from Sarah was permanent.

The topic of suicide regularly came up at the support group meetings, and inevitably led to someone mentioning Robin Pearson, a woman who used to come to the meetings several months before Neil began attending. Robin's husband had been afflicted with stomach cancer during a visitation of the angel Makatiel. She stayed in his hospital room for days at a stretch, only for him to die unexpectedly when she was home doing laundry. A nurse who'd been present told Robin that his soul had ascended, and so Robin had begun attending the support group meetings.

Many months later, Robin came to the meeting shaking with rage. There'd been a manifestation of Hell near her house, and she'd seen her husband among the lost souls. She'd confronted the nurse, who admitted to lying in the hopes that Robin would learn to love God, so that at least she would be saved even if her husband hadn't been. Robin wasn't at the next meeting, and at the meeting after that the group learned she had committed suicide to rejoin her husband.

None of them knew the status of Robin's and her husband's relationship in the afterlife, but successes were known to happen; some couples had indeed been happily reunited through suicide. The support group had attendees whose spouses had descended to Hell, and they talked about being torn between wanting to remain alive and wanting to rejoin their spouses. Neil wasn't in their situation, but his first response when listening to them had been envy: if Sarah had gone to Hell, suicide would be the solution to all his problems.

This led to a shameful self-knowledge for Neil. He realized that if he had to choose between going to Hell while Sarah went to Heaven, or having both of them go to Hell together, he would choose the latter: he would rather she be exiled from God than separated from him. He knew it was selfish, but he couldn't change how he felt: he believed Sarah could be happy in either place, but he could only be happy with her.

Neil's previous experiences with women had never been good. All too often he'd begin flirting with a woman while sitting at a bar, only to have her remember an appointment elsewhere the moment he stood up and his shortened leg came into view. Once, a woman he'd been dating for several weeks broke off their relationship, explaining that while she herself didn't consider his leg a defect, whenever they were seen in public together other people assumed there must be something wrong with her for being with him, and surely he could understand how unfair that was to her?

Sarah had been the first woman Neil met whose demeanor hadn't changed one bit, whose expression hadn't flickered toward pity or horror or even surprise when she first saw his leg. For that reason alone it was predictable that Neil would become infatuated with her; by the time he saw all the sides of her personality, he'd completely fallen in love with her. And because his best qualities came out when he was with her, she fell in love with him too.

Neil had been surprised when Sarah told him she was devout. There weren't many signs of her devotion—she didn't go to church, sharing Neil's dislike for the attitudes of most people who attended—but in her own quiet way she was grateful to God for her life. She never tried to convert Neil, saying that devotion would come from within or not at all. They rarely had any cause to mention God, and most of the time it would've been easy for Neil to imagine that Sarah's views on God matched his own.

This is not to say that Sarah's devotion had no effect on Neil. On the contrary, Sarah was far and away the best argument for loving God that he had ever encountered. If love of God had contributed to making her the person she was, then perhaps it did make sense. During the years that the two of them were married, his outlook on life improved, and it probably would have reached the point where he was thankful to God, if he and Sarah had grown old together.

Sarah's death removed that particular possibility, but it needn't have closed the door on Neil's loving God. Neil could have taken it as a reminder that no one can count on having decades left. He could have been moved by the realization that, had he died with her, his soul would've been lost and the two of them separated for eternity. He could have seen Sarah's death as a wake-up call, telling him to love God while he still had the chance.

Instead Neil became actively resentful of God. Sarah had been the greatest blessing of his life, and God had taken her away. Now he was expected to love Him for it? For Neil, it was like having a kidnapper demand love as ransom for his wife's return. Obedience he might have managed, but sincere, heartfelt love? That was a ransom he couldn't pay.

This paradox confronted several people in the support group. One of the attendees, a man named Phil Soames, correctly pointed out that thinking of it as a condition to be met would guarantee failure. You couldn't love God as a means to an end, you had to love Him for Himself. If your ultimate goal in loving God was a reunion with your spouse, you weren't demonstrating true devotion at all.

A woman in the support group named Valerie Tommasino said they shouldn't even try. She'd been reading a book published by the humanist movement; its members considered it wrong to love a God who inflicted such pain, and advocated that people act according to their own moral sense instead of being guided by the carrot and the stick. These were people who, when they died, descended to Hell in proud defiance of God.

Neil himself had read a pamphlet of the humanist movement; what he most remembered was that it had quoted the fallen angels. Visitations of fallen angels were infrequent, and caused neither good fortune nor bad; they weren't acting under God's direction but just passing through the mortal plane as they went about their unimaginable business. On the occasions they appeared, people would ask them questions: did they know God's intentions? Why had they rebelled? The fallen angels' reply was always the same: *Decide for yourselves. That is what we did. We advise you to do the same.*

Those in the humanist movement had decided, and if it weren't for Sarah, Neil would've made the identical choice. But he wanted her back, and the only way was to find a reason to love God.

Looking for any footing on which to build their devotion, some attendees of the support group took comfort in the fact that their loved ones hadn't suffered when God took them but instead died instantly. Neil didn't even have that; Sarah had received horrific lacerations when the glass hit her. Of course, it could have been worse. One couple's teenage son had been trapped in a fire ignited by an angel's visitation, and received full-thickness burns over eighty percent of his body before rescue workers could free him; his eventual death was a mercy. Sarah had been fortunate by comparison, but not enough to make Neil love God.

Neil could think of only one thing that would make him give thanks to God, and that was if He allowed Sarah to appear before him. It would give him immeasurable comfort just to see her smile again; he'd never been visited by a saved soul before, and a vision now would have meant more to him than at any other point in his life.

But visions don't appear just because a person needs one, and none ever came to Neil. He had to find his own way toward God.

The next time he attended the support group meeting for witnesses of Nathanael's visitation, Neil sought out Benny Vasquez, the man whose eyes had been erased by Heaven's light. Benny didn't always attend because he was now being invited to speak at other meetings; few visitations resulted in an eyeless person, since Heaven's light entered the mortal plane only in the brief moments that an angel emerged from or reentered Heaven, so the eyeless were minor celebrities, and in demand as speakers to church groups.

Benny was now as sightless as any burrowing worm: not only were his eyes and sockets missing, his skull lacked even the space for such features, the cheekbones now abutting the forehead. The light that had brought his soul as close to perfection as was possible in the mortal plane had also deformed his body; it was commonly held that this illustrated the superfluity of physical bodies in Heaven. With the limited expressive capacity his face retained, Benny always wore a blissful, rapturous smile.

Neil hoped Benny could say something to help him love God. Benny described Heaven's light as infinitely beautiful, a sight of such compelling majesty that it vanquished all doubts. It constituted incontrovertible proof that God should be loved, an explanation that made it as obvious as $1+1=2$. Unfortunately, while Benny could offer many analogies for the effect of Heaven's light, he couldn't duplicate that effect with his own words. Those who were already devout found Benny's descriptions thrilling, but to Neil, they seemed frustratingly vague. So he looked elsewhere for counsel.

Accept the mystery, said the minister of the local church. If you can love God even though your questions go unanswered, you'll be the better for it.

Admit that you need Him, said the popular book of spiritual advice he bought. When you realize that self-sufficiency is an illusion, you'll be ready.

Submit yourself completely and utterly, said the preacher on the television. Receiving torment is how you prove your love. Acceptance may not bring you relief in this life, but resistance will only worsen your punishment.

All of these strategies have proven successful for different individuals; any one of them, once internalized, can bring a person to devotion. But these are not always easy to adopt, and Neil was one who found them impossible.

Neil finally tried talking to Sarah's parents, which was an indication of how desperate he was: his relationship with them had always been tense. While they loved Sarah, they often chided her for not being demonstrative enough in her devotion, and they'd been shocked when she married a man who wasn't devout at all. For her part, Sarah had always considered her parents too judgmental, and their disapproval of Neil only reinforced her opinion. But now Neil felt he had something in common with them—after all, they were all mourning Sarah's loss—and so he visited them in their suburban colonial, hoping they could help him in his grief.

How wrong he was. Instead of sympathy, what Neil got from Sarah's parents was blame for her death. They'd come to this conclusion in the weeks after Sarah's funeral; they reasoned that she'd been taken to send him a message, and that they were forced to endure her loss solely because he hadn't been devout. They were now convinced that, his previous explanations notwithstanding, Neil's deformed leg was in fact

God's doing, and if only he'd been properly chastened by it, Sarah might still be alive.

Their reaction shouldn't have come as a surprise: throughout Neil's life, people had attributed moral significance to his leg even though God wasn't responsible for it. Now that he'd suffered a misfortune for which God was unambiguously responsible, it was inevitable that someone would assume he deserved it. It was purely by chance that Neil heard this sentiment when he was at his most vulnerable, and it could have the greatest impact on him.

Neil didn't think his in-laws were right, but he began to wonder if he might not be better off if he did. Perhaps, he thought, it'd be better to live in a story where the righteous were rewarded and the sinners were punished, even if the criteria for righteousness and sinfulness eluded him, than to live in a reality where there was no justice at all. It would mean casting himself in the role of sinner, so it was hardly a comforting lie, but it offered one reward that his own ethics couldn't: believing it would reunite him with Sarah.

Sometimes even bad advice can point a man in the right direction. It was in this manner that his in-laws' accusations ultimately pushed Neil closer to God.

More than once when she was evangelizing, Janice had been asked if she ever wished she had legs, and she had always answered—honestly—no, she didn't. She was content as she was. Sometimes her questioner would point out that she couldn't miss what she'd never known, and she might feel differently if she'd been born with legs and lost them later on. Janice never denied that. But she could truthfully say that she felt no sense of being incomplete, no envy for people with legs; being legless was part of her identity. She'd never bothered with prosthetics, and had a surgical procedure been available to provide her with legs, she'd have turned it down.

She had never considered the possibility that God might restore her legs.

One of the unexpected side effects of having legs was the increased attention she received from men. In the past she'd mostly attracted men with amputee fetishes or sainthood complexes; now all sorts of men seemed drawn to her. So when she first noticed Ethan Mead's interest in her, she thought it was romantic in nature; this possibility was particularly distressing since he was obviously married.

Ethan had begun talking to Janice at the support group meetings, and then began attending her public speaking engagements. It was when he suggested they have lunch together that Janice asked him about his intentions, and he explained his theory. He didn't know *how* his fate was intertwined with hers; he knew only that it was. She was skeptical, but she didn't reject his theory outright. Ethan admitted that he didn't have answers for her own questions, but he was eager to do anything he could to help her find them. Janice cautiously agreed to help him in his search for meaning, and Ethan promised that he wouldn't be a burden. They met on a regular basis and talked about the significance of visitations.

Meanwhile Ethan's wife Claire grew worried. Ethan assured her that he had no romantic feelings toward Janice, but that didn't alleviate her concerns. She knew that extreme circumstances could create a bond between individuals, and she feared that Ethan's relationship with Janice—romantic or not—would threaten their marriage.

Ethan suggested to Janice that he, as a librarian, could help her do some research. Neither of them had ever heard of a previous instance where God had left His mark on a person in one visitation and removed it in another. Ethan looked for previous examples in hopes that they might shed some light on Janice's situation. There were a few instances of individuals receiving multiple miracle cures over their lifetimes, but their illnesses or disabilities had always been of natural origin, not given to them in a visitation. There was one anecdotal report of a man being struck blind for his sins, changing his ways, and later having his sight restored, but it was classified as an urban legend.

Even if that account had a basis in truth, it didn't provide a useful precedent for Janice's situation: her legs had been removed before her birth, and so couldn't have been a punishment for anything she'd done. Was it possible that Janice's condition had been a punishment for something her mother or father had done? Could her restoration mean they had finally earned her cure? She couldn't believe that.

If her deceased relatives were to appear in a vision, Janice would've been reassured about the restoration of her legs. The fact that they didn't made her suspect something was amiss, but she didn't believe that it was a punishment. Perhaps it had been a mistake, and she'd received a miracle meant for someone else; perhaps it was a test, to see how she would respond to being given too much. In either case, there seemed only one course of action: she would, with utmost gratitude and humility, offer to return her gift. To do so, she would go on a pilgrimage.

Pilgrims traveled great distances to visit the holy sites and wait for a visitation, hoping for a miracle cure. Whereas in most of the world one could wait an entire lifetime and never experience a visitation, at a holy site one might only wait months, sometimes weeks. Pilgrims knew that the odds of being cured were still poor; of those who stayed long enough to witness a visitation, the majority did not receive a cure. But they were often happy just to have seen an angel, and they returned home better able to face what awaited them, whether it be imminent death or life with a crippling disability. And of course, just living through a visitation made many people appreciate their situations; invariably, a small number of pilgrims were killed during each visitation.

Janice was willing to accept the outcome, whatever it was. If God saw fit to take her, she was ready. If God removed her legs again, she would resume the work she'd always done.

If God let her legs remain, she hoped she would receive the epiphany she needed to speak with conviction about her gift.

She hoped, however, that her miracle would be taken back and given to someone who truly needed it. She didn't suggest to anyone that they accompany her in hopes of receiving the miracle she was returning, feeling that that would've been presumptuous, but she privately considered her pilgrimage a request on behalf of those who were in need.

Her friends and family were confused at Janice's decision, seeing it as questioning God. As word spread, she received many letters from followers, variously expressing dismay, bafflement, or admiration for her willingness to make such a sacrifice.

As for Ethan, he was completely supportive of Janice's decision, and excited for himself. He now understood the significance of Rashiel's visitation for him: it indicated that the time had come for him to act. His wife Claire strenuously opposed his leaving, pointing out that he had no idea how long he might be away, and that she and their children needed him too. It grieved him to go without her support, but he had no choice. Ethan would go on a pilgrimage, and at the next visitation, he would learn what God intended for him.

Neil's visit to Sarah's parents caused him to give further thought to his conversation with Benny Vasquez. While he hadn't gotten a lot out of Benny's words, he'd been impressed by the absoluteness of Benny's devotion. No matter what misfortune befell him in the future, Benny's love of God would never waver, and he would ascend to Heaven when he died. That fact offered Neil a very slim opportunity, one that had seemed so unattractive he hadn't considered it before; but now, as he was growing more desperate, it was beginning to look expedient.

Every holy site had its pilgrims who, rather than looking for a miracle cure, deliberately sought out Heaven's light.

Those who saw it were always accepted into Heaven when they died, no matter how selfish their motives had been; there were some who wished to have their ambivalence removed so they could be reunited with their loved ones, and others who'd always lived a sinful life and wanted to escape the consequences.

In the past there'd been some doubt as to whether Heaven's light could indeed overcome *all* the spiritual obstacles to becoming saved. The debate ended after the case of Barry Larsen, a serial rapist and murderer who, while disposing of the body of his latest victim, witnessed an angel's visitation and saw Heaven's light. At Larsen's execution, his soul was seen ascending to Heaven, much to the outrage of his victims' families. Priests tried to console them, assuring them—on the basis of no evidence whatsoever—that Heaven's light must have subjected Larsen to many lifetimes' worth of penance in a moment, but their words provided little comfort.

For Neil this offered a loophole, an answer to Phil Soames's objection; it was the one way that he could love Sarah more than he loved God, and still be reunited with her. It was how he could be selfish and still get into Heaven. Others had done it; perhaps he could too. It might not be just, but at least it was predictable.

At an instinctual level, Neil was averse to the idea: it sounded like undergoing brainwashing as a cure for depression. He couldn't help but think that it would change his personality so drastically that he'd cease to be himself. Then he remembered that everyone in Heaven had undergone a similar transformation; the saved were just like the eyeless except that they no longer had bodies. This gave Neil a clearer image of what he was working toward: no matter whether he became devout by seeing Heaven's light or by a lifetime of effort, any ultimate reunion with Sarah couldn't recreate what they'd shared in the mortal plane. In Heaven, they would both be different, and their love for each other would be mixed with the love that all the saved felt for everything.

This realization didn't diminish Neil's longing for a reunion with Sarah. In fact it sharpened his desire, because it meant that the reward would be the same no matter what means he used to achieve it; the shortcut led to precisely the same destination as the conventional path.

On the other hand, seeking Heaven's light was far more difficult than an ordinary pilgrimage, and far more dangerous. Heaven's light leaked through only when an angel entered or left the mortal plane, and since there was no way to predict where an angel would first appear, light-seekers had to converge on the angel after its arrival and follow it until its departure. To maximize their chances of being in the narrow shaft of Heaven's light, they followed the angel as closely as possible during its visitation; depending on the angel involved, this might mean staying alongside the funnel of a tornado, the wavefront of a flash flood, or the expanding tip of a chasm as it split apart the landscape. Far more light-seekers died in the attempt than succeeded.

Statistics about the souls of failed light-seekers were difficult to compile, since there were few witnesses to such expeditions, but the numbers so far were not encouraging. In sharp contrast to ordinary pilgrims who died without receiving their sought-after cure, of which roughly half were admitted into Heaven, every single failed light-seeker had descended to Hell. Perhaps only people who were already lost ever considered seeking Heaven's light, or perhaps death in such circumstances was considered suicide. In any case, it was clear to Neil that he needed to be ready to accept the consequences of embarking on such an attempt.

The entire idea had an all-or-nothing quality to it that Neil found both frightening and attractive. He found the prospect of going on with his life, trying to love God, increasingly maddening. He might try for decades and not succeed. He might not even have that long; as he'd been reminded so often lately, visitations served as a warning to prepare one's soul, because death might come at any time. He could die tomorrow, and there was no chance of his becoming devout in the near future by conventional means.

It's perhaps ironic that, given his history of not following Janice Reilly's example, Neil took notice when she reversed her position. He was eating breakfast when he happened to see an item in the newspaper about her plans for a pilgrimage, and his immediate reaction was anger: how many blessings would it take to satisfy that woman? After considering it more, he decided that if she, having received a blessing, deemed it appropriate to seek God's assistance in coming to terms with it, then there was no reason that he, having received such terrible misfortune, shouldn't do the same. And that was enough to tip him over the edge.

Holy sites were invariably in inhospitable places: one was an atoll in the middle of the ocean, while another was in the mountains at an elevation of 20,000 ft. The one that Neil traveled to was in a desert, an expanse of cracked mud reaching miles in every direction; it was desolate, but it was relatively accessible and thus popular among pilgrims. The appearance of the holy site was an object lesson in what happened when the celestial and terrestrial realms touched: the landscape was variously scarred by lava flows, gaping fissures, and impact craters. Vegetation was scarce and ephemeral, restricted to growing in the interval after soil was deposited by floodwaters or whirlwinds and before it was scoured away again.

Pilgrims took up residence all over the site, forming temporary villages with their tents and camper vans; they all made guesses as to what location would maximize their chances of seeing the angel while minimizing the risk of injury or death. Some protection was offered by curved banks of sandbags, left over from years past and rebuilt as needed. A site-specific paramedic and fire department ensured that paths were kept clear so rescue vehicles could go where they were needed. Pilgrims either brought their own food and water or purchased them from vendors charging exorbitant prices; everyone paid a fee to cover the cost of waste removal.

Light-seekers always had off-road vehicles to better cross rough terrain when it came time to follow the angel. Those who could afford it drove alone; those who couldn't formed groups of two or three or four. Neil didn't want to be a passenger reliant on another person, nor did he want the responsibility of driving anyone else. This might be his final act on earth, and he felt he should do it alone. The cost of Sarah's funeral had depleted their savings, so Neil sold all his possessions in order to purchase a suitable vehicle: a pickup truck equipped with aggressively knurled tires and heavy-duty shock absorbers.

As soon as he arrived, Neil started doing what all the other light-seekers did: crisscrossing the site in his vehicle, trying to familiarize himself with its topography. It was on one of his drives around the site's perimeter that he met Ethan; Ethan flagged him down after his own car had stalled on his return from the nearest grocery store, eighty miles away. Neil helped him get his car started again, and then, at Ethan's insistence, followed him back to his campsite for dinner. Janice wasn't there when they arrived, having gone to visit some pilgrims several tents over; Neil listened politely while Ethan—heating prepackaged meals over a bottle of propane—began describing the events that had brought him to the holy site.

When Ethan mentioned Janice Reilly's name, Neil couldn't mask his surprise. He had no desire to speak with her again, and immediately excused himself to leave. He was explaining to a puzzled Ethan that he'd forgotten a previous engagement when Janice arrived.

She was startled to see Neil there, but asked him to stay. Ethan explained why he'd invited Neil to dinner, and Janice told him where she and Neil had met. Then she asked Neil what had brought him to the holy site. When he told them he was a light-seeker, Ethan and Janice immediately tried to persuade him to reconsider his plans. He might be committing suicide, said Ethan, and there were always better alternatives than suicide. Seeing Heaven's light was not the answer, said Janice; that wasn't what God wanted. Neil stiffly thanked them for their concern, and left.

During the weeks of waiting, Neil spent every day driving around the site; maps were available, and were updated after each visitation, but they were no substitute for driving the terrain yourself. On occasion he would see a light-seeker who was obviously experienced in off-road driving, and ask him— the vast majority of the light-seekers were men—for tips on negotiating a specific type of terrain. Some had been at the site for several visitations, having neither succeeded nor failed at their previous attempts. They were glad to share tips on how best to pursue an angel, but never offered any personal information about themselves. Neil found the tone of their conversation peculiar, simultaneously hopeful and hopeless, and wondered if he sounded the same.

Ethan and Janice passed the time by getting to know some of the other pilgrims. Their reactions to Janice's situation were mixed: some thought her ungrateful, while others thought her generous. Most found Ethan's story interesting, since he was one of the very few pilgrims seeking something other than a miracle cure. For the most part, there was a feeling of camaraderie that sustained them during the long wait.

Neil was driving around in his truck when dark clouds began coalescing in the southeast, and the word came over the CB radio that a visitation had begun. He stopped the vehicle to insert earplugs into his ears and don his helmet; by the time he was finished, flashes of lightning were visible, and a light-seeker near the angel reported that it was Barakiel, and it appeared to be moving due north. Neil turned his truck east in anticipation and began driving at full speed.

There was no rain or wind, only dark clouds from which

lightning emerged. Over the radio other light-seekers relayed estimates of the angel's direction and speed, and Neil headed northeast to get in front of it. At first he could gauge his distance from the storm by counting how long it took for the thunder to arrive, but soon the lightning bolts were striking so frequently that he couldn't match up the sounds with the individual strikes.

He saw the vehicles of two other light-seekers converging. They began driving in parallel, heading north, over a heavily cratered section of ground, bouncing over small ones and swerving to avoid the larger ones. Bolts of lightning were striking the ground everywhere, but they appeared to be radiating from a point south of Neil's position; the angel was directly behind him, and closing.

Even through his earplugs, the roar was deafening. Neil could feel his hair rising from his skin as the electric charge built up around him. He kept glancing in his rearview mirror, trying to ascertain where the angel was while wondering how close he ought to get.

His vision grew so crowded with afterimages that it became difficult to distinguish actual bolts of lightning among them. Squinting at the dazzle in his mirror, he realized he was looking at a continuous bolt of lightning, undulating but uninterrupted. He tilted the driver's-side mirror upward to get a better look, and saw the source of the lightning bolt, a seething, writhing mass of flames, silver against the dusky clouds: the angel Barakiel.

It was then, while Neil was transfixed and paralyzed by what he saw, that his pickup truck crested a sharp outcropping of rock and became airborne. The truck smashed into a boulder, the entire force of the impact concentrated on the vehicle's left front end, crumpling it like foil. The intrusion into the driver's compartment fractured both of Neil's legs and nicked his left femoral artery. Neil began, slowly but surely, bleeding to death.

He didn't try to move; he wasn't in physical pain at the

moment, but he somehow knew that the slightest movement would be excruciating. It was obvious that he was pinned in the truck, and there was no way he could pursue Barakiel even if he weren't. Helplessly, he watched the lightning storm move further and further away.

As he watched it, Neil began crying. He was filled with a mixture of regret and self-contempt, cursing himself for ever thinking that such a scheme could succeed. He would have begged for the opportunity to do it over again, promised to spend the rest of his days learning to love God, if only he could live, but he knew that no bargaining was possible and he had only himself to blame. He apologized to Sarah for losing his chance at being reunited with her, for throwing his life away on a gamble instead of playing it safe. He prayed that she understood that he'd been motivated by his love for her, and that she would forgive him.

Through his tears he saw a woman running toward him, and recognized her as Janice Reilly. He realized his truck had crashed no more than a hundred yards from her and Ethan's campsite. There was nothing she could do, though; he could feel the blood draining out of him, and knew that he wouldn't live long enough for a rescue vehicle to arrive. He thought Janice was calling to him, but his ears were ringing too badly for him to hear anything. He could see Ethan Mead behind her, also starting to run toward him.

Then there was a flash of light and Janice was knocked off her feet as if she'd been struck by a sledgehammer. At first he thought she'd been hit by lightning, but then he realized that the lightning had already ceased. It was when she stood up again that he saw her face, steam rising from newly featureless skin, and he realized that Janice had been struck by Heaven's light.

Neil looked up, but all he saw were clouds; the shaft of light was gone. It seemed as if God were taunting him, not only by showing him the prize he'd lost his life trying to acquire while still holding it out of reach, but also by giving it to someone who didn't need it or even want it. God had already wasted a miracle on Janice, and now He was doing it again.

It was at that moment that another beam of Heaven's light penetrated the cloud cover and struck Neil, trapped in his vehicle.

Like a thousand hypodermic needles the light punctured his flesh and scraped across his bones. The light unmade his eyes, turning him into not a formerly sighted being, but a being never intended to possess vision. And in doing so the light revealed to Neil all the reasons he should love God.

He loved Him with an utterness beyond what humans can experience for one another. To say it was unconditional was inadequate, because even the word "unconditional" required the concept of a condition and such an idea was no longer comprehensible to him: every phenomenon in the universe was nothing less than an explicit reason to love Him. No circumstance could be an obstacle or even an irrelevancy, but only another reason to be grateful, a further inducement to love. Neil thought of the grief that had driven him to suicidal recklessness, and the pain and terror that Sarah had experienced before she died, and still he loved God, not in spite of their suffering, but because of it.

He renounced all his previous anger and ambivalence and desire for answers. He was grateful for all the pain he'd endured, contrite for not previously recognizing it as the gift it was, euphoric that he was now being granted this insight into his true purpose. He understood how life was an undeserved bounty, how even the most virtuous were not worthy of the glories of the mortal plane.

For him the mystery was solved, because he understood that everything in life is love, even pain, especially pain.

So minutes later, when Neil finally bled to death, he was truly worthy of salvation.

And God sent him to Hell anyway.

Ethan saw all of this. He saw Neil and Janice remade by Heaven's light, and he saw the pious love on their eyeless faces. He saw the skies become clear and the sunlight return. He was holding Neil's hand, waiting for the paramedics, when Neil died, and he saw Neil's soul leave his body and rise toward Heaven, only to descend into Hell.

Janice didn't see it, for by then her eyes were already gone. Ethan was the sole witness, and he realized that this was God's purpose for him: to follow Janice Reilly to this point and to see what she could not.

When statistics were compiled for Barakiel's visitation, it turned out that there had been a total of ten casualties, six among light-seekers and four among ordinary pilgrims. Nine pilgrims received miracle cures; the only individuals to see Heaven's light were Janice and Neil. There were no statistics regarding how many pilgrims had felt their lives changed by the visitation, but Ethan counted himself among them.

Upon returning home, Janice resumed her evangelism, but the topic of her speeches has changed. She no longer speaks about how the physically handicapped have the resources to overcome their limitations; instead she, like the other eyeless, speaks about the unbearable beauty of God's creation. Many who used to draw inspiration from her are disappointed, feeling they've lost a spiritual leader. When Janice had spoken of the strength she had as an afflicted person, her message was rare, but now that she's eyeless, her message is commonplace. She doesn't worry about the reduction in her audience, though, because she has complete conviction in what she evangelizes.

Ethan quit his job and became a preacher so that he too could speak about his experiences. His wife Claire couldn't accept his new mission and ultimately left him, taking their children with her, but Ethan was willing to continue alone. He's developed a substantial following by telling people what happened to Neil Fisk. He tells people that they can no more expect justice in the afterlife than in the mortal plane, but he doesn't do this to dissuade them from worshipping God; on the contrary, he encourages them to do so. What he insists on is that they not love God under a misapprehension, that if they wish to love God, they be prepared to do so no matter what His intentions. God is not just, God is not kind, God is not merciful, and understanding that is essential to true devotion.

As for Neil, although he is unaware of any of Ethan's sermons, he would understand their message perfectly. His lost soul is the embodiment of Ethan's teachings.

For most of its inhabitants, Hell is not that different from Earth; its principal punishment is the regret of not having loved God enough when alive, and for many that's easily endured. For Neil, however, Hell bears no resemblance whatsoever to the mortal plane. His eternal body has well-formed legs, but he's scarcely aware of them; his eyes have been restored, but he can't bear to open them. Just as seeing Heaven's light gave him an awareness of God's presence in all things in the mortal plane, so it has made him aware of God's absence in all things in Hell. Everything Neil sees, hears, or touches causes him distress, and unlike in the mortal plane this pain is not a form of God's love, but a consequence of His absence. Neil is experiencing more anguish than was possible when he was alive, but his only response is to love God.

Neil still loves Sarah, and misses her as much as he ever did, and the knowledge that he came so close to rejoining her only makes it worse. He knows his being sent to Hell was not a result of anything he did; he knows there was no reason for it, no higher purpose being served. None of this diminishes his love for God. If there were a possibility that he could be admitted to Heaven and his suffering would end, he would not hope for it; such desires no longer occur to him.

Neil even knows that by being beyond God's awareness,

he is not loved by God in return. This doesn't affect his feelings either, because unconditional love asks nothing, not even that it be returned.

And though it's been many years that he has been in Hell, beyond the awareness of God, he loves Him still. That is the nature of true devotion.

STEPHEN BAXTER

SUN-CLOUD

To human eyes, the system would have been extra-ordinary:

The single, giant Sun was so vast that its crimson flesh would have embraced all of Sol's scattered planets. Across its surface, glistening vacuoles swarmed, each larger than Sol itself.

There was a planet.

It was a ball of rock no larger than a small asteroid. It skimmed the Sun's immense photosphere, bathed in ruddy warmth. It was coated with air, a thick sea.

The world-ocean teemed with life.

Beyond the Sun's dim glow, the sky was utterly dark.

She rose to the Surface. Thick water slid smoothly from her carapace.

She let her impeller-corpuscles dissociate briefly; they

swam free of her main corpus in a fast, darting shoal, feeding eagerly, reveling in their brief liberty.

She lifted optically sensitive corpuscles to the smoky sky. The Sun was a roof over the world, its surface pocked by huge dark pits.

She was called Sun-Cloud: for, at her Coalescence, a cloud of brilliant white light had been observed, blossoming over the Sun's huge, scarred face.

Sun-Cloud was seeking her sister, the one called Orange-Dawn.

Sun-Cloud raised a lantern-corpuscle. The subordinate creature soon tired and began sending quiet chemical complaints through her corpus; but she ignored them and waited, patiently, as her sphere of lantern light rolled out, spreading like a liquid over the oleaginous Surface.

The light moved slowly enough for a human eye to follow.

Sun-Cloud's people were not like humans.

Here, people assembled from specialized schools of corpuscles: mentalizers, impellers, lanterns, structurals, others. Obeying their own miniature imperatives of life and death, individual corpuscles would leave the aggregate corpus and return to their fish-like shoals, to feed, breed, die. But others would join, and the pattern of the whole could persist, for a time.

Still, Sun-Cloud's lifespan was finite. As the cycle of corpuscle renewal wore on, her pattern would degrade, mutate.

Like most sentient races, Sun-Cloud's people sustained comforting myths of immortality.

And, like most races, there was a minority who rejected such myths.

Sun-Cloud returned to the Ocean's deep belly.

The light here was complex and uncertain. Above Sun-Cloud the daylight was already dimming. And below her, from the Deep at the heart of the world, the glow of a billion lantern-corpuscles glimmered up, white and pure.

Sun-Cloud watched as Cold-Current ascended toward her.

They were going to discuss Sun-Cloud's sister, Orange-Dawn. Orange-Dawn was a problem.

Cold-Current was a lenticular assemblage of corpuscles twice Sun-Cloud's size, who nevertheless rose with an awesome unity. The ranks of impellers at Cold-Current's rim churned at the thick waters of the Ocean, their small cilia vibrating so rapidly that they were blue-shifted.

The Song suffused the waters around Sun-Cloud, as it always did; but as Cold-Current lifted away from the Deep the complex harmonics of the Song changed, subtly.

Sun-Cloud, awed, shrank in on herself, her structural corpuscles pushing in toward their sisters at her swarming core. Sun-Cloud knew that she herself contributed but little, a few minor overtones, to the rich assonance of the Song. How must it be to be so grand, so powerful, that one's absence left the Song—the huge, world-girdling Song itself—audibly lacking in richness?

Cold-Current hovered; a bank of optic-corpuscles swiveled, focusing on Sun-Cloud. "You know why I asked to meet you," she said.

"Orange-Dawn."

"Yes. Orange-Dawn. I am very disturbed, Sun-Cloud. Orange-Dawn is long overdue for Dissolution. And yet she persists; she prowls the rim of the Song, even the Surface, intact, obsessed. Even to the extent of injuring her corpuscles."

"I know that Orange-Dawn wants to see out another hundred Cycles," Sun-Cloud said. "Orange-Dawn has theories. That in a hundred Cycles' time—"

"I know," Cold-Current said. "She believes she has Coalesced with ancient wisdom. Somehow, in a hundred Cycles, the world will be transformed, and Orange-Dawn will be affirmed."

"But it's impossible," Sun-Cloud said. "I know that; Orange-Dawn must see that."

But Cold-Current said, absently: "But it *may* be possible, to postpone Dissolution so long." Sun-Cloud, intrigued, saw a tight, cubical pattern of corpuscles move through Cold-Current's corpus; individual corpuscles swam to and fro, but the pattern persisted. "Possible," Cold-Current said. "There *is* old wisdom. But such a thing would be—ugly. Discordant." Perhaps that cubical pattern contained the fragment of old knowledge to which Cold-Current hinted.

Cold-Current rotated grandly. "I want you to go and talk to her. Perhaps you can say something. . . . Nobody knows Orange-Dawn as well as you."

That was true. Orange-Dawn had helped Sun-Cloud in her earliest Coalescence, as Sun-Cloud struggled toward sentience. Orange-Dawn had hunted combinations of healthy corpuscles for her sister, helped her coax the corpuscles into an orderly shoal. Together the sisters had run across the Surface of the Ocean, their out-thrust optic corpuscles blue-tinged with their exhilarating velocity. . . .

Cold-Current began to sink back into the glimmering depths of the Ocean, her disciplined impellers beating resolutely. "You must help her, Sun-Cloud. You must help her put aside these foolish shards of knowledge and speculation, and learn to embrace true beauty. . . ."

As Cold-Current faded from view, the light at the heart of the world brightened, as if in welcome, and the Song's harmonies deepened joyously.

The world was very old. Sun-Cloud's people were very old.

They had accreted many fragments of knowledge, of philosophy and science.

A person, on Dissolution, could leave behind fragments of insight, of wisdom, in the partial, semi-sentient assemblies called sub-corpora. Before dissolving in their turn into the general corpuscle shoals, the sub-corpora could be absorbed into a new individual, the knowledge saved.

Or perhaps not.

If they were not incorporated quickly, the remnant sub-corpora would break up. Their component mentation-corpuscles would descend, and become lost in the anaerobic Deep at the heart of the world.

Sun-Cloud returned to the Surface of the Ocean.

She saw that the Sun had almost set; a last sliver of crimson light spanned one horizon, which curved sharply. Above her the sky was clear and utterly black, desolately so.

Her corpuscles transmitted their agitation to each other.

She raised a lantern; cold light bloomed slowly across the sea's oily meniscus.

She roamed the Ocean, seeking Orange-Dawn.

At last the creeping lantern light brought echoes of distant motion to her optic corpuscles: a small form thrashing at the Surface in lonely unhappiness.

With a rare sense of urgency Sun-Cloud ordered her impeller-corpuscles into motion. It didn't take long for her to accelerate to a significant fraction of lightspeed; the impellers groaned as they strained at relativity's tangible barrier, and the image of the lonely one ahead was stained with blue shift.

Wavelets lapped at her and air stroked her hide; she felt exhilarated by her velocity.

She slowed. She called softly: "Orange-Dawn?"

Listlessly Orange-Dawn raised optic corpuscles. Orange-Dawn was barely a quarter Sun-Cloud's size. She was withered, her corpus depleted. Her corpuscles lay passively over each other, tiny mouths gaping with obvious hunger.

"Do I shock you, Sun-Cloud?"

Sun-Cloud sent small batches of corpuscles as probes into Orange-Dawn's tattered carcass. "Orange-Dawn. Your corpuscles are suffering. Some of them are dying. Cold-Current is concerned for you—"

"She sent you to summon me to my Dissolution."

Sun-Cloud said, "I don't like to see you like this. You're introducing a harshness into the Song."

"The Song, the damnable Song," Orange-Dawn muttered. Moodily she began to spin in the water. The corpuscles' decay had so damaged her corpus's circular symmetry that she whipped up frothy waves which lapped over her upper carapace, the squirming corpuscles there. She poked optic corpuscles upwards, but the night sky was blind. "The Song drowns thought."

"What will happen in a hundred Cycles, Orange-Dawn?"

Orange-Dawn thrashed at the water. "The data is partial. . . ." She focused wistful optic corpuscles on her sister. "I don't know. But it will be—"

"What?"

"Unimaginable. *Wonderful.*"

Sun-Cloud wanted to understand. "What *data*?"

"There are some extraordinary speculations, developed in the past, still extant here and there. . . . Did you know, for instance, that the Cycle is actually a tide, raised in our Ocean-world during its passage around the Sun? It took many individuals a long time to observe, speculate, calculate, obtain that fragment of information. And yet we are prepared to throw it away, into the great bottomless well of the Song. . . .

"I've tried to assemble some of this. It's taken so long, and the fragments don't fit more often than not, but—"

"Integrate? Like a Song?"

"Yes." Orange-Dawn focused her optic corpuscles. "Yes Like a Song. But not the comforting mush they intone below. That's a Song of death, Sun-Cloud. A Song to guide you into nonbeing."

Sun-Cloud shuddered; little groups of her corpuscles broke away, agitated. "We don't die."

"Of course not." Orange-Dawn rotated and drifted towards her. "Watch this," she said.

Quickly, she budded off a whole series of sub-corpora,

each tiny body consisting of a few hundred corpuscles. Instantly the sub-corpora squirmed about the Surface, leaping and breaking the meniscus, blue-shifted as they pushed into lightspeed's intangible membrane.

Sun-Cloud felt uneasy. "Those sub-corpora are big enough to be semi-sentient, Orange-Dawn."

"But do you see?" said Orange-Dawn testily.

"See what?"

"*Blue shift*. The sub-corpora—see how, instinctively, they strain against the walls of the prison of lightspeed. Even in the moment of their Coalescing. Light imprisons us all. Light isolates us. . . ."

Her words filtered through Sun-Cloud, jarring and strange, reinforced by bizarre chemical signals.

"Why are you doing this, Orange-Dawn?"

"Watch." Now Orange-Dawn sent out a swarm of busy impeller-corpuscles; they prodded the independent sub-corpora back towards Orange-Dawn's corpus. Sun-Cloud, uneasy, watched how the sub-corpora resisted their tiny Dissolutions, feebly.

"See?" Orange-Dawn said. "See how they struggle against their immersion, in the overwhelming Ocean of my personality? See how they struggle to *live*?"

Sun-Cloud's own corpuscles sensed the suffering of their fellows, and shifted uneasily. She flooded her circulatory system with soothing chemicals. In her distress she felt a primal need for the Song. She sent sensor-corpuscles stretching into the Ocean beneath her, seeking out the comfort of its distant, endless surging; its harmony was borne through the Ocean to her by chemical traces.

. . . But would *she* struggle so, when it came time for her to Dissolve, in her turn, into the eternal wash of the Song?

It was, she realized, a question she had never even framed before.

Now, gathering her corpuscles closely around her,

Orange-Dawn turned from Sun-Cloud, and began to beat across the Surface with a new determination.

"You must come with me, Orange-Dawn," Sun-Cloud warned.

"No. I will see out my hundred Cycles."

"But you cannot. . . ." *Unless,* she found herself thinking, *unless Cold-Current is right. Unless there is some lost way to extend consciousness.*

"If I submit to Dissolution, I will lose my sense of self, Sun-Cloud. My individuality. The corpus of knowledge and understanding I've spent so long assembling. What is that but death? What is the Song but a comfort, an anaesthetic illusion to hide that fact? . . ."

"You are damaging the unity of the Song, Orange-Dawn. You are—discordant."

Orange-Dawn was receding now; she raised up a little batch of acoustic corpuscles. "Good!" she called.

"I won't be able to protect you!" cried Sun-Cloud.

But she was gone.

Sun-Cloud raised lantern-corpuscles, sending pulses of slow light out across the Ocean's swelling surface. She called for her sister, until her corpuscles were exhausted.

In some ways, Sun-Cloud's people resembled humans.

Sun-Cloud's component corpuscles were of very different ancestry.

Mentation-corpuscles—the neuronlike creatures that carried consciousness in tiny packets of molecules—were an ancient, anaerobic race. The other main class, the impellers and structure-corpuscles, were oxygen breathers: faster moving, more vigorous.

Human muscles usually burned glucose aerobically, using sugars from the air. But during strenuous activity, the muscles would ferment glucose in the anaerobic way evolved by the earliest bacteria. Thus human bodies, too, bore echoes of the earliest biosphere of Earth.

But, unlike a human body, Sun-Cloud's corpus was modular.

Despite their antique enmity, the two phyla within Sun-Cloud would cooperate, in the interests of the higher creature in which they were incorporated.

Until Sun-Cloud weakened.

A mass of corpora, sub-corpora, and shoals of trained impeller-corpuscles rose from the Deep in a great ring.

Not five Cycles had passed since Sun-Cloud's failed attempt to bring Orange-Dawn home. Now they had come for Orange-Dawn.

Sun-Cloud found her sister at the center of the hunt. She was shrunken, already fragmented, her corpuscles pulsing with fear.

"I don't want to die, Sun-Cloud."

Anguish for her sister stabbed at Sun-Cloud. She sent soothing chemical half words soaking through the Ocean. "Come with me," she said gently.

Exhausted, Orange-Dawn allowed herself to be enfolded in Sun-Cloud's chemical caresses.

Commingled, the sisters sank into the Ocean. Their ovoid bodies twisted slowly into the depths; light shells from curious individuals washed over them as they passed.

The light faded rapidly as they descended. Soon there were few free sub-corpora; and of the people they saw most were linked by corpuscle streams with at least one other, and often in groups of three, four, or more.

The Song was a distant, strengthening pulse from the heart of the Ocean beneath them.

Now Cold-Current rose up to meet them, huge and intimidating, her complex hide pulsing with lantern-corpuscles. The rim of her slowly rotating corpus became diffuse, blurred, as her corpuscles swam tentatively toward Orange-Dawn.

Cold-Current murmured, "You are old, yet very young, Orange-Dawn. Your unhappiness is caused by ignorance.

There is no other Ocean. Only this one. There is no change and never has been. These facts are part of what we are. That's why your speculations are damaging you.

"You have to forget your dreams, Orange-Dawn. . . ."

Orange-Dawn hardened, drawing her corpuscles into a tight little fortress. But Cold-Current was strong, and she forced compact biochemical packets into Orange-Dawn's corpus. Sun-Cloud, huddling close, picked up remote chemical echoes of the messages Cold-Current offered.

. . . *Hear the Song,* Cold-Current's corpuscles called. *Open up to the Song.*

Their bodies joined, her impeller-corpuscles herding Orange-Dawn tightly, Cold-Current began to guide Orange-Dawn deeper into the lattice of mingled persons.

Sun-Cloud followed, struggling to stay close to her sister. Orange-Dawn's pain suffused the waters around her with clouds of chemicals; Sun-Cloud suffered for her and with her.

As they descended, individuals became less and less distinct, and free corpuscles swam through the lattice's closing gaps. At last they were falling through a sea of corpuscles which, with endless intelligent grace, swam over and around each other. Sun-Cloud's structurals and impellers felt enfeebled here, in this choking water; the effort of forcing her way downwards seemed to multiply.

Perhaps this was like Dissolution, she thought.

At last there was only one entity, a complex of mingled bodies that filled the Ocean. The living lattice vibrated with the Song, which boomed around them, joyous and vibrant.

"The Deep," Cold-Current whispered to Orange-Dawn. "The Song. Now you will join this, Orange-Dawn. Uncountable billions of minds, endless thoughts straddling the world eternally. The Song will sustain your soul, after Dissolution, merged with everyone who has ever lived. You'll never be alone again—"

Suddenly, at the last, Orange-Dawn resisted. "No! I could not bear it. I could not bear—"

She was struggling. Jagged images filled Sun-Cloud's mind, of being crushed, swamped, stultified.

Immediately a host of sub-corpora and corpuscles, jagged masses of them, hurled themselves into Orange-Dawn's corpus. Sun-Cloud heard a single, agonized, chemical scream, which echoed through the water. And then the structure of the corpus was broken up.

Corpuscles, many of them wounded, came hailing out of the cloud of Dissolution; some of them spiraled away into the darkness, and others rained down towards the glowing Deep.

Sub-corpora formed, almost at random, and wriggled through the water. They were semi-sentient: bewildered and broken images of Orange-Dawn.

Sun-Cloud could only watch. Loss stabbed at her; her grief was violent.

Cold-Current was huge, complex, brilliantly illuminated. "It is over. It is better," she said.

Sun-Cloud's anger surged. "How can you say that? She's *dead*. She died in fear and agony."

"No. She'll live forever, through the Song. As will we all."

"Show me what you know," Sun-Cloud said savagely. "Show me how Orange-Dawn might have extended her life, through another ninety Cycles."

"It is artificial. Discordant. It is not appropriate—"

"Show me!"

With huge reluctance, Cold-Current budded a tight, compact sub-corpora. It bore the cubical pattern Sun-Cloud had observed earlier. "Knowledge is dangerous," Cold-Current said sadly. "It makes us unstable. That is the moral of Orange-Dawn's story. You must not—"

Sun-Cloud hurled herself at the pattern, and forcibly integrated it into her own corpus. Then—following impulses she barely recognized—she rose upwards, away from the bright-glowing Deep.

She passed through the cloud of Orange-Dawn's corpuscles, and called to them.

The Song boomed from the Deep, massive, alluring, stultifying; and Cold-Current's huge form glistened as she called her. Sun-Cloud ignored it all.

She ascended towards the Surface, as rapidly as she could. Orange-Dawn's fragmentary sub-corpora followed her, bewildered, uncertain.

The place Sun-Cloud called the Deep was an anaerobic environment. Only mentation-corpuscles could survive here. They lay over each other in complex, pulsing swarms, with neural energy flickering desultorily between them.

The Song was a complex, evolving sound-structure, maintained by the dense shoals of mentation-corpuscles which inhabited the heart of the world, and with grace notes added by the Coalesced individuals of the higher, oxygen-rich layers of the Ocean.

At the end of their lives, the mentation structures of billions of individuals had dissolved into the Deep's corpuscle shoals. The Song, they believed, was a form of immortality.

Embracing this idea, most people welcomed Dissolution. Others rejected it.

Sun-Cloud gathered around her central corpus the cubical pattern of Cold-Current, and Orange-Dawn's sad remnants, integrating them crudely. She grew huge, bloated, powerful.

And now, as she broke the thick Surface of the Ocean, she made ready.

She wondered briefly if she had gone mad. Perhaps Orange-Dawn had infected her.

But if it were so, let it be. She must know the answer to Orange-Dawn's questions for herself, before she submitted to—as she saw it now, as if through her sister's perception—the sinister embrace of the Song.

She enfolded Cold-Current's compact data pattern, and let its new wisdom flow through her. . . .

Of course. It is simple.

She began to forge forward, across the Ocean.

A bow wave built up before her, thick and resisting. But she assembled her impellers and drove through it. At last the wave became a shock, sharp-edged, traveling through the water as a crest.

And now, quickly, she began to sense the resistance of lightspeed's soft membrane. The water turned softly blue before her, and when she looked back, the world was stained red.

At length she passed into daylight.

The day seemed short. She continued to gather her pace.

Determined, she abandoned that which she did not need: lantern-corpuscles, manipulators, even some mentation-components: any excess mass which her impellers need not drag with her.

A bow, of speed-scattered light, began to coalesce around her.

The day-night cycle was passing so quickly now it was flickering. And she could sense the Cycles themselves, the grand, slow heaving of the Ocean as her world tracked around its Sun.

The light ahead of her passed beyond blue and into a milky invisibility, while behind her a dark spot gathered in the redness and reached out to embrace half the world.

Time-dilated, she forged across the Surface of her Ocean and into the future; and ninety-five Cycles wore away around her.

Light's crawl was embedded, a subtle scaling law, in every force governing the structure of Sun-Cloud's world.

The Sun was much larger than Sol—ten thousand times more so—for the fusion fires at its heart were much less vigorous than Sol's. And Sun-Cloud's world was a thousand times smaller than Earth, for the electrostatic and degeneracy pressures, which resisted gravitational collapse, were greatly weaker.

Lightspeed dominated Sun-Cloud's structure, too. If she had been a single entity, complete and entire, it would have taken too long for light—or any other signal—to crawl through her structure. So she was a composite creature; her mind was broken down into modules of thought, speculation, and awareness. She was a creature of parallel processing, scattered over a thousand fragile corpuscles.

And Sun-Cloud's body was constrained to be small enough that her gravitational potential could not fracture the flimsy molecular bonds that held her corpus together.

Sun-Cloud, forging across the Surface of her Ocean, was just two millimeters across.

At last, a new light erupted in the bow that embraced her world.

With an effort, she slowed. The light-bow expanded rapidly, as if the world were unfolding back into its proper morphology. She allowed some of her impeller-corpuscles to run free, and she saw their tiny wakes running across the Surface, determined, red-shifted.

Now that her monumental effort was done she was exhausted, depleted, her impellers dead, lost, or dying; unless new impellers joined her, she would scarcely be able to move again.

Ninety-five Cycles.

Everybody she had known—Cold-Current and the rest—all of them must be gone, now, absorbed into the Song's unending pulse.

It remained only for her to learn what mystery awaited, here in the remoteness of the future, and then she could Dissolve into the Song herself.

. . . From the darkling sky, the new light washed over her.

Her optic corpuscles swiveled upwards. She cried out.

Sun-Cloud felt her world shrink beneath her from infinity to a frail mote; the Song decayed from the thoughts of a god to the crooning of a damaged sub-corpus.

Above her, utterly silently—and for the first time in all history—the stars were coming out.

To human eyes, the skies of this cosmos would have seemed strange indeed:

The stars spawned from gas clouds, huge and cold. Hundreds of them formed in a cluster, companions to Sun-Cloud's Sun. Heat crept from each embryonic star, dispersing the remnant wisps of the birthing cloud.

It took five billion human years for the light to cross the gulf between the stars.

And at last—and as one speculative thinker among Sun-Cloud's people had predicted, long ago—the scattered light of those remote Suns washed over an unremarkable world, which orbited a little above the photosphere of their companion. . . .

The stars were immense globes, glowing red and white, jostling in a complex sky; and sheets and lanes of gas writhed between them.

Orange-Dawn had been right. This *was* wonderful, beyond her imagining—but crushing, terrifying.

Pain tore at her. Jagged molecules flooded her system; her corpuscles broke apart, and began at last their ancestral war.

She struggled to retain her core of rationality, just a little longer. Exhausted, she hastily assembled sub-corpora, and loaded packets of information into them, pale images of the astonishing sky. She sent them hailing down into the Ocean, into the Deep, into the belly of the Song itself.

Soon a new voice would join the Song: a merger of her own and Orange-Dawn's. And it would sing of Suns, countless, beyond imagining.

Everything would be different now.

She fell, gladly, into the warm emptiness of Dissolution.

MAUREEN F. McHUGH

INTERVIEW: ON ANY GIVEN DAY

(Pullout quote at top of site.)

EMMA: I had this virus, and it was inside me, and it could have been causing all these weird kinds of cancers—

INTERVIEWER: What kind of cancers?

EMMA: All sorts of weird stuff I'd never heard of like hairy-cell leukemia, and cancerous lesions in parts of your bones and cancer in your pancreas. But I wasn't sick. I mean I didn't feel sick. And now, even after all the antivirals, now I worry about it all the time. Now I'm always thinking I'm sick. It's like something was stolen from me that I never knew I had.

(The following is a transcript from an interview for the *On Any Given Day* presentation of 4/12/2021. This transcript does not represent the full presentation, and more interviews and information are present on the site. *On Any Given Day*

is made possible by the National Public Internet, by NPI-
Boston.org affiliate, and by a grant from the Carrol-Johnson
Charitable Family Trust. For information on how to purchase
this or any other full-site presentation on CDM, please check
NPIboston.org.)

> Pop-up quotes and site notes in the interview are
> included with this transcript.

The following interview was conducted with Emma Chi-
check. In the summer of 2018, a fifteen-year-old student came
into a health clinic in the suburban town of Charlotte, outside
Cleveland, Ohio, with a sexually transmitted version of a pro-
tovirus called pv414, which had been recently identified as
originating in contaminated batches of genetic material asso-
ciated with the telemerase therapy used in rejuvenation. The
virus had only been seen previously in rejuvenated elders, and
the presence of the virus in teenagers was at first seen as
possible evidence that the virus had changed vectors. The
medical detective work done to trace the virus, and the picture of teenage behavior that emerged was the basis of the
site documentary, called "The Abandoned Children." Emma
was one of the students identified with the virus.

> The Site map provides links to a description of the proto-
> virus, a map of the transmission of the virus from Terry
> Sydnowski through three girls to a total of eleven other
> people, and interviews with state health officials.

EMMA: I was fourteen when I lost my virginity. I was drunk,
and there was this guy named Luis, he was giving me these
drinks that taste like melon, this green stuff that everybody
was drinking when they could get it. He said he really liked
all my Egyptian stuff and he kept playing with my slave
bracelet. The bracelet has chains that go to rings you wear

on your thumb, your middle finger and your ring finger. "Can you be my slave?" he kept asking, and at first I thought that was funny because he was the one bringing *me* drinks, you know? But we kept kissing and then we went into the bedroom and he felt my breasts and then he wanted to have sex. I felt as if I'd led him on, you know? So I didn't say no.

I saw him again a couple of times after that, but he didn't pay much attention to me. He was older and he didn't go to my school. I regret it. I wish it had been a little more special and I was really too young. Sometimes I thought that if I were a boy I'd be one of those boys who goes into school one day and starts shooting people. (Music—"Poor Little Rich Girl" by Tony Bennett.)

INTERVIEWER: What's a culture freak?

EMMA: You're kidding, right? This is for the interview? Okay, in my own words.

A culture freak is a person who really likes other cultures, and listens to culture freak bands and doesn't conform to the usual sort of jumpsuit or Louis Vuitton wardrobe thing. So I'm into Egyptian a lot, in a spiritual way, too. I tell Tarot cards. They're really Egyptian, people think they're Gypsy but I read about how they're actually way older than that and I have an Egyptian deck. My friend Lindsey is like me, but my other friend, Denise, is more into Indian stuff. Lindsey and I like Indian, too, and sometimes we'll all henna our hands.

INTERVIEWER: Do you listen to culture freak music?

EMMA: I like a lot of music, not just culture music. I like Black Helicopters, I really like their *New World Order* CDM, because it's really retro and paranoid. I like some of the stuff my mom and dad like, too, Tupac and Lauryn Hill. I like the band Shondonay Shaka Zulu. It's got a lot of drone. I like that.

(Music—"My Favorite Things" by John Coltrane.)

I'm seventeen. I'll be eighteen in April. I went to kinder-garten when I was only four. I've already been accepted at Northeastern. I wanted to go to Bard but my parents said they didn't want me going to school in New York City.

My dad's in telecommunications. He's in Hong Kong for six weeks. He's trying to get funding for a sweep satellite. They're really cool. The satellites are really small, but they have this huge like net in front of them, like miles in front and miles across. The net like spins itself. See, if space debris hits something hard it will drill right through it, but when it hits this big net, the net gives and just lets the chunk of metal or whatever slide away so it doesn't hit the satellite. That way it won't be like that satellite in '07 that caused the chain re-action so half the United States couldn't use their phones.

My mom is a teacher. She's taking a night class two nights a week to recertify. She's always having to take classes, and she's always gone one night a week for that. Then there's after-school stuff. She never gets home before six. When I was little she took summers off, but now she does bookkeep-ing and office work in the summer for a landscaper because my older brother and sister are in college already.

The landscaper is one of those babyboomers on rejuve-nation. He's a pain in the ass. Like my dad says, they're all so selfish. Why won't they let anyone else have a life? I mean, the sixties are over, and they're trying to have them all over again. I hate when we're out and we see a bunch of baby-boomers all hopped up on hormones acting like teenagers. But then they go back and go to work and won't let people like my dad get promoted because they won't retire.

They want to have it both ways. My mom says when we're all through school, she's going to retire and start a whole dif-ferent life. A less materialistic life. She says she's going to get out of the way and let us have our lives. People have to learn how to go on to the next part of their lives. Like the Chinese. They had five stages of life, and after you were successful you were supposed to retire and write poetry and be an artist. Of course, how successful can you consider a high school teacher?

(Music—"When I'm Sixty-Four" by the Beatles.)

Okay, we were out this one Saturday hanging outside the bowling alley because the cops had thrown us out. The cops here are the worst. They discriminate against teenagers. Everybody discriminates against teenagers. Like the pizza place has this sign that says only six people under eighteen are allowed in at a time—which means teenagers. If they had a sign that only six people *over* eighteen or six *black* people were allowed in at a time everybody would be screaming their heads off, right? We rented shoes and everything but we weren't bowling yet, we were just hanging out, because we hadn't decided if we were going to bowl, and they threw us out.

We went over to the grocery store and the CVS to hang out on the steps and there was this boomer there. He was trying to dress like a regular kid. See, most boomers dress in flared jeans and black and stuff and they all have long hair, especially the men, I guess because so many of them were like, bald before the treatments. This guy had long hair, too, pulled back in a dorky ponytail, but he was wearing a camo jumpsuit. He'd have looked stupid in county orange, like he was trying too hard, but the camo jumpsuit was okay.

> In 2018, Terry Sydnowski was seventy-one years old.
> Click here for information on <u>telemerase repair,</u>
> <u>endocripnological therapy</u> and <u>cosmetic surgery</u>
> <u>techniques</u> of rejuvenation.

We were ignoring him. It was me and Denise and Lindsey, and this older black guy named Kamar and these two guys from school, DC and Matt. Kamar had bought a bunch of forty-fives. You know, malt liquor. I was kind of nervous around Kamar. Kamar seemed so grown up, in a lot of ways. He'd been arrested twice as a juvenile. Once for shoplifting and once, I think, for possession. He always called me 'little girl'. Like when he saw me, he said, "What you doing, little girl?" and smiled at me.

> Interview with Kamar Wilson, conducted in the Summit County jail where Wilson is serving eighteen months for possession of narcotics.

I was feeling pretty drunk and I started feeling sorry for this dorky boomer who was just standing over by the wall watching us. I told Denise he looked really sad.

Denise didn't really care. I remember she had a blue caste mark right in the middle of her forehead and it was the kind that glowed under streetlights. When she moved her head it kind of bobbed around. She thought Boomers were creeps.

I said he probably had money and ID. But she didn't really care because DC always had money and this other guy, Kamar, he had ID.

I know that Boomers already had childhoods and all that, but this guy looked really sad. And maybe he didn't have a childhood. Maybe his mom was an alcoholic and he had to watch his brothers and sisters. Just looking at him I felt like there was this real sadness to him. I don't know why. Maybe because he wasn't being pushy. He sure wasn't like the guy my mom worked for, who was kind of a jerk. He wasn't getting in our faces or anything. Boomers usually hang out with each other, you know?

Then DC sort of noticed him. DC is really kind of crazy, and I was afraid he and Kamar would decide to mess him up or something.

I said something about how I felt sorry for him.

And DC said something like, "You want him to be really sorry?" Kamar laughed.

I told them to leave him alone. DC is crazy. He'll do anything. Anything anybody does, DC has to be badder.

INTERVIEWER: Tell me about DC.

EMMA: DC always had a lot of money, he lived with this guy who was his godfather because his parents were divorced and his mom was really depressed or something and just laid around all the time. His godfather was always giving him anything. Kamar was nineteen and he had a fake phone ID, so he'd order stuff and they'd do a check against his phone ID and then he'd just pick it up and pay for it.

DC did all kind of crazy things. DC and Matt decided they were going to kill a bunch of kids. Just because they were mad. They were going to do a Columbine. So they drank like one of those fifths of Popov vodka, you know the kind I mean? They were going to get guns from some guy Kamar knew, but instead DC just took a baseball bat and started beating on this kid, Kevin, who he really hated.

INTERVIEWER: Why did he hate Kevin?

EMMA: I don't know, Kevin was just annoying, you know? He was this dweeby kid who was always bad-mouthing people. He used to get in a fight with this black kid, Stan, at the beginning of every school year. Stan wasn't even that good at fighting, but he'd punch Kevin a couple of times and that would be it until Kevin started bad-mouthing him the next year. It's like everything Kevin said got on DC's nerves. So DC is totally wasted, driving around with a bunch of kids, and he sees Kevin hanging out in front of Wendy's and he screams, "Stop the car!" and he jumps out with this baseball bat and goes running up to Kevin and swings at him and Kevin raises his arm and gets his arm broken and then some other people haul DC off.

No, I wasn't there. I heard all about it the next day, though. And Kevin's arm was in a cast. Kevin was real proud of it, actually. He's that kind of a dork.

No, Kevin's parents were going to go to court, but they never did. I don't know why.

No charges were ever filed. Kevin and his parents declined to be interviewed.

Anyway, that's why I was really worried about DC and this boomer. Luckily, Lindsey had a real thing about DC that night and they went off to walk back down to the bowling alley to look for this other girl whose parents were gone for the weekend. We were all going to that girl's house for a party.

INTERVIEWER: Where were your parents?

EMMA: My parents? They were home. I had to be in by midnight, but if it was a really good party I'd just go home at midnight and my parents would already be in bed, so I'd tell them I was home and then sneak back out through the side door in the basement and go back to the party.

INTERVIEWER: Do you think your parents should have kept closer watch on you?

EMMA: No. I mean, they couldn't. I mean, like, Denise has a PDA with a minder. They caught her this one time she went to Rick's in the Flats using Lindsey's sister's ID—

An industry has developed around the arsenal of monitoring devices used to track teenagers, pagers, minders, snitch packs and chips, as well as the variety of tricks teenagers use to subvert them.

INTERVIEWER: Can you describe a minder?

EMMA: It's like a chip or something, and it's supposed to tell your parents where you are. Denise walked into the club and now all the clubs have these things wired into the door or something that sets off the minder, and then this company calls your home and tells your parents where you are. But Kamar downloaded this program for Denise and put it on her PDA, and when she runs it, it tells her minder that she's somewhere else. Like, she puts my phone number in, and then it tells her minder that she's at my house.

So it was me and Denise and Kamar and this guy, Matt, and Kamar went somewhere . . . I don't remember where. Denise starts kidding me about talking to the Boomer

I was kind of drunk by then, and when I got drunk I used to think everything was funny. Oh, yeah, Kamar had gone to look for some other kids we knew, but anyway. We were kind of goofin'. You know? And Denise kept saying that she didn't think I would talk to the guy. So finally I did. I just went up to him and said hi.

And he said hi.

Up close he had that kind of funny look that geezers—I mean, boomers do. You know, like their noses and their chins and their ears are too big for their faces or something. I was pretty drunk and I didn't know what to say so I just started laughing, because I was kind of nervous and when I'm nervous, sometimes I laugh.

He asked me what I was doing, but nice. Smiling. And I told him, "Talking to you." I thought it was funny.

He said I seemed a little drunk. He said "tipsy" which was funny because it sounded so old-fashioned.

For a minute I thought he might be a cop or something. But then I decided he wasn't because he could have busted us a long time ago, and besides, we weren't doing anything but drinking. So I introduced him to Denise and Matt. He said his name was Terry, which seemed like a real geezer name, you know? He was really nice, though. Quiet.

INTERVIEWER: Do you know any rejuvenated people?

EMMA: No, I didn't know any boomers, I mean, not any rejuvenated ones, except the guy my mom works for, and I don't really know him. My grandmother is going to do it next year but she has to wait until some kind of stock retirement thing happens.

I think I asked him if he was a cop, but I didn't really mean it. I was laughing because I knew he really wasn't.

He said he was just looking for someone to hang out with.

I asked him why he didn't hang out with other people like him? I mean now it sounds kind of rude, but really, it was weird, you know?

He said that they were all old, and he wanted to be young. He didn't want to hang around with a bunch of old people who thought they were young. He said that he didn't really enjoy being a kid so he was going to try it again.

That made me think I was right about what I'd thought before about his not having a childhood or something. I liked the idea of his having one now, so I asked if he wanted to go to the party.

Denise thought it was stupid, I could see from her face, but I knew once I explained about the childhood thing she'd feel bad for him, too.

He asked where the party was and we told him it was at this girl's house but we needed to wait for DC and Lindsey and Kamar to come back. Then I started worrying about DC.

Then he said he'd go get beer, which was the coolest thing, because that would convince a lot of people he was okay. He asked us what kind of beer we wanted.

Denise really liked that lemon beer, what's it called, squash, so we told him to get that. He got in this all-gasoline car—really nice. No batteries, a real muscle car like a Mercury or something. I told Denise my theory about him not having a childhood.

She was worried DC might be crazy but I thought that if Terry had beer, DC wouldn't care. Denise kept saying that DC was going to be really cranked.

Matt kept saying DC wouldn't care if Terry had beer, but I was getting really nervous about DC, because if he decided he wanted to be a pain in the ass—I'm sorry, I shouldn't swear, but that's the way we talk when it's just us. Is that okay?

Well, I was afraid DC would be a pain in the ass, just because you never know with DC. I was kind of hoping maybe Kamar and DC and Lindsey would get back before the geezer did so we could just go on to the party and forget about it. Kamar got back. But then Terry got back before DC and Lindsey.

But when DC and Lindsey got back, DC didn't even pay any attention to Terry. They told us that Brenda had already gone to her house so we all went to the party. (Music—"Downtown" by Petula Clark.)

So the next time I saw Terry was with Kamar at another party. I was really surprised. Just because of the way Kamar was. But he and Terry were like good friends, which I figured really pissed DC off. Kamar liked DC, but part of the reason was because DC always had money, and Terry always had money. Terry was always buying beer and stuff. I thought Terry would ignore me because that's what guys do, they're nice to you one night and ignore you the next. But Terry was really nice and brought me a squash because he thought it was what I liked.

It's Denise that really likes it but I thought it was neat that he remembered.

He hung around with me for a while. He was cute, for a geezer. I bet when he was a kid he was really cute. I just forgot that he was different. He just seemed like a regular kid, only really nice. Then all the sudden I'd look at him and I think about how odd he looked, you know, just the way his face was different, and his knuckles were thick. I mean his hands and face were smooth. He told me once that he was self-conscious about it, and that some people, people in movies and stuff, have the cartilage on their nose and chin shaved. After a while though, I got so used to it I didn't even notice it anymore.

So I hung out with him and after a while we started kissing and stuff. He got really turned on, really fast. It was already maybe ten-thirty and I was drunk, so we went upstairs and Matt and Lindsey were in the bedroom, so we kind of snuck in. They were on the bed, but we spread out some coats. It's really embarrassing to talk about.

(Music—"Days of Wine and Roses" by Frank Sinatra.)

EMMA: Oh my God! I just thought of something. I shouldn't say it.

INTERVIEWER: You don't have to unless you want to.

EMMA: You won't put it on tape if I don't want you to, will you? (Laughing.) Oh my God, my face is so red. He was a mushroom.

INTERVIEWER: What?

EMMA: You know, a mushroom. I can't believe I'm saying this. He was cut. I don't remember the word for it.

INTERVIEWER: Circumcised?

> More than 90 percent of all men born between 1945 and 1963 were circumcised.

EMMA: Yeah. I'd never seen a boy like that before. Denise had sex with a guy who was, but I never had before. It was weird. I know my face is so red. I guess you can leave it in. A lot of boomers are circumcised, right?

Oh my God. (Covers face with hands, laughing.) It's such a stupid thing to remember.

(Music—More of "Days of Wine and Roses by Frank Sinatra, which has been playing underneath this portion of the interview.)

INTERVIEWER: How many people have you had sex with?

EMMA: Four. I've had sex with four guys. Yeah, including Terry and Luis.

INTERVIEWER: Do you have any regrets?

EMMA: Sure I wish I hadn't. The antivirals made me sick. I missed almost a month of school that year because every time I had a treatment I'd be sick for three days. And everybody knew why I was missing school, which was so embarrassing. There were seventeen of us who had it.

They think that the antivirals took care of it, and we won't get cancer, but they don't know because it's so new. So I've got to have blood tests and checkups every year. I hate it because I never thought about being sick before, not really, and now, every time I feel weird I'm thinking, is it a tumor? Every headache, I'm thinking, is this a brain tumor?

Sometimes I'm so mad, because Terry got to be rejuvenated, he gets like forty extra years, and I may not even get to be old because of him. Most of the time I think the antivirals took care of it, and like my mom says, all the checkups mean if I ever do get sick, it will get caught a lot faster than it would in another person, so in a way, I might be lucky.

I usually believe that the antivirals did it, but sometimes, like when I'm getting blood drawn, I'm really aware of how I feel and I'm afraid I've got cancer, and right then I don't believe it. I was unlucky enough to have this happen, so why would I be lucky about it working? I know that doesn't make any sense.

Terry and DC were arguing one time. DC was saying that when he was old he wouldn't get rejuvenated. He'd let someone else have a chance. But Terry said he'd change his mind once he got old. And Terry was right. I always thought I wouldn't want to be rejuvenated, but every time I think I'm sick, I really want to live and I don't think I'll feel different when I'm old.

Terry didn't know he had the virus. It wasn't really his fault or anything. But sometimes I still get really mad at him.

That's kind of why I'm doing this. So that maybe someone else won't have to go through what I did.

INTERVIEWER: Have you kept in touch with Terry?

EMMA: No. I haven't seen him for three years.

INTERVIEWER: Your parents wanted to file statutory rape charges, didn't they?

EMMA: Yeah, but I thought it would be stupid. It wasn't like that.

INTERVIEWER: Why not?

EMMA: Statutory rape is stupid. He didn't rape me. He was nice, nicer than a lot of other guys.

INTERVIEWER: But Terry is an adult. Terry is in his seventies.

EMMA: I know. But it's not like a guy who looks seventy years old. . . . It's different. I mean, in a way it's not, I know, but it is, because Terry was sort of being one of us, you know? I mean, he wasn't all that different from Kamar. It would have been statutory rape with Kamar, too, but nobody says anything about that. I didn't sleep with Kamar, but I know a lot of girls who did, and nobody is trying to pin that on Kamar.

They're trying to pin everything else on Kamar. They said he was dealing drugs to us and he was the ring leader, but you can get drugs anywhere. You can get them at school. And he wasn't the ring leader. There wasn't any ring leader. We didn't need to be led to do all those things.

INTERVIEWER: Was Terry one of you?

EMMA: Yeah . . . no. No. Not really. He wanted to be. I mean, I wish I had known stuff before, I wish I had known not to get involved with Terry and all this stuff—but I wish I could have been a kid longer.

(Music—"The Kids Are Alright" by The Who.)

The last time I saw Terry? It was before I got tested, before anyone knew about the virus. Before all these people said to me, "You're lucky it's not AIDS, then you'd have to take medicine your whole life."

We went together for four months, I think. From November to March because we broke up right after Denise's birthday. We didn't break up, really, so much as decide that maybe we should see other people, that we shouldn't get serious. Terry was weird to talk to. I never knew what he was thinking. I knew a little bit about him. He was retired and he'd had some kind of office job. I found out that he hadn't had a rotten childhood, he just hadn't liked it. He said he didn't have many friends and he was too serious before.

INTERVIEWER: Why did you break if off?

EMMA: We weren't in sync. He liked all that Boomer music, rock and roll and Frank Sinatra and stuff. And we couldn't exactly fall in love, because he was so different.

He was always nice to me afterwards. He wasn't one of those guys who just ignores you.

We were all hanging out at the park next to the library after school. It was the end of the year, school was almost over. Kamar was hanging out with Brenda. He wasn't exactly her boyfriend because she was also hanging out with this other guy named Anthony and one weekend she'd be with Kamar and the next weekend she'd be with Anthony.

Everybody was talking and something Terry said made DC really mad. I don't know what it was. It really surprised me because DC always acted like Terry didn't even exist. When Terry was around, he'd ignore him. When he wasn't around, DC would hang with Kamar. But DC started screaming, stuff like, why don't you have any friends! You loser! You fucking loser! You have to hang around with us because you don't have any friends! Well, we don't want you, either! So why don't you just go die!

Terry had this funny look on his face.

A couple of guys pulled DC away and calmed him down. But everyone was looking at Terry, like it was his fault. I don't know why, I mean, he didn't do anything.

That evening I was supposed to stay at Denise's house, for real, not like when I told my mom I would be at Denise's and then went out. So I took my stuff over to her house, and then my brother, who was home from Duke, took us and dropped us off at Pizza Hut so we could get something to eat and then we wandered over to the steps outside the CVS because we saw people hanging out there.

Lindsey was there and she told me that DC was looking for Terry. That DC said he was going to kill Terry. Kamar got arrested, she said. Which meant that there was nobody to calm down DC.

Kamar had gotten arrested before, for shoplifting, but he got probation. But this time he got arrested for possession. Partly it was because Kamar is black.

Everybody was talking about Kamar getting busted and DC going off the deep end.

Lindsey kept saying, "Oh my God." It really got on my nerves. I mean, I knew DC hated Terry. DC just hated Terry. He said Terry was a poser and was just using people.

INTERVIEWER: Were you friends with DC?

EMMA: I knew DC, but we never really talked, but Lindsey had been seeing him for a couple of months so she knew him better than Denise and me.

Lindsey thought DC and Kamar were really friends. I thought Kamar just hung around with DC because he had money. Kamar was something like three years older than DC. But Lindsey said Kamar was just using Terry, but he and DC were really close.

I don't know what was true.

After a while Terry showed up. I didn't know what we should do, if we should tell him or not, but finally I thought I should. Terry was sitting with his car door open, talking to some people.

I told him Kamar got arrested for possession.

He wanted to know what happened, and I didn't know anything but what Lindsey had told me

Terry wanted to know if he had a lawyer.

I never thought about a lawyer. Like I said before, mostly it was easy to forget that Terry wasn't just a kid like everyone else.

Terry called the police station on his cellphone. Just punched up the information and called. He said, he was a friend of Kamar Wilson's. They wouldn't tell him anything on the phone, so he hung up and said he was going to go down.

I felt really weird suddenly talking to him, because he sounded so much like an adult. But I told him DC was looking for him.

"Fuck DC," Terry said.

I thought Terry would take off right then and there to go to the police station. But he kept talking to people about Kamar and about what might have happened, so I gave up and I went back to sit on the steps with Denise and Lindsey. We were working on our tans because it would make us look more Egyptian and Indian. Not that I would even think of doing that now, even though skin cancer isn't one of the types of cancer.

So finally DC came walking from over towards the hardware store and Denise saw him and said, "Oh shit."

I just sat there because Terry was an adult and he could just deal with it, I figured. I'd tried to tell him. And I was kind of pissed at him, too, I don't know why.

DC started shouting that Terry was a loser.

I don't remember if anybody said anything, but Terry didn't get out of the car. So DC came up and kicked the car, really hard. That didn't do anything so he jumped up on the hood.

Terry told him to get off the car, but DC wanted him to get out of the car and talk to him. After a while Terry got out of the car and DC said something like, "I'm going to kill you, man."

DC had a knife.

Denise wanted us to go inside the CVS. But we were pretty far away. And the people inside the CVS are creeps anyway. They were calling the police, right then. Terry stood right by the door of his car, kind of half in and half out.

Lindsey was going, "Oh my God. Oh my God." She was really getting on my nerves.

I didn't think anything was really going to happen.

Terry kept saying stuff like, "Calm down, man."

DC was ranting and raving that Terry thought that just because he was older he could do anything he wanted.

Terry finally got in his car and closed the door.

But DC didn't get off the hood. He jumped up and down on it and the hood made this funny kind of splintery noise.

Terry must have gotten mad, he drove the car forward, like, gunned it, and DC fell off, really hard.

Terry stopped to see if DC was okay. He got out of his car and DC was lying there on his side, kind of curled up. Terry bent over DC and DC said something. . . . I couldn't see because Terry was between me and DC, Matt was one of the kids up there and he said that Terry pulled open his jacket and he had a gun. He took the gun out in his hand, and showed it to DC and said to fuck off. A bunch of kids saw it. Matt said that Terry called DC a fucking rich kid.

INTERVIEWER: Have you ever seen a gun?

EMMA I saw one at a party once. This kid I didn't know had it. He was showing it to everyone. I thought he was a creep.

INTERVIEWER: When did you see Terry next?

EMMA: I never saw Terry after that, although I told the clinic about him, so I'm sure they contacted him. He was where the disease came from.

I wasn't the only one to have sex with him. Brenda had sex with him, and this girl I don't know very well, JaneAnne. JaneAnne had sex with some other people, and I had sex with my boyfriend after that. I don't know about Brenda.

JaneAnne and Brenda's interviews. JaneAnne was interviewed from her home in Georgetown, MD, where her family moved six months ago. Brenda is still living in Charlotte with her mother.

It taught me something. Adults are different. I don't know if I want to be one.

INTERVIEWER: Why not?

EMMA: Because DC was acting stupid, you know? But DC was a kid. And Terry really wasn't, no matter how bad he wanted to be. So why would he do that to a kid?

INTERVIEWER: So it was Terry's fault?

EMMA: Not his fault, not exactly. But he was putting himself in the wrong place at the wrong time.

INTERVIEWER: Should he have known better?

EMMA: Yeah. No, I mean, he couldn't know better. It was my fault in a way. Because most of the time if, like, we're at the bowling alley and a couple of geezers come in trying to be young, we just ignore them and they just ignore us. It's just instinct or something. If I hadn't talked to Terry, none of this would have happened.

Terry has different rules than us. I'm not saying kids don't hurt each other. But Terry was always thinking, you know?

INTERVIEWER: What do you mean?

EMMA: I don't know. Just that he was always thinking. Even when he wasn't supposed to be, even when he was mad, he was always thinking.

(Music—"Solitude" by Duke Ellington.)

EMMA: When my parents found out they were really shocked. It's like they were in complete denial. My dad cried. It was scary.

   We're closer now. We still don't talk about a lot of things, though. We're just not that kind of family.

INTERVIEWER: Do you still go to parties? Still drink?

EMMA: No, I don't party like I used to. When I was getting the antivirals, I was so sick, I just stopped hanging out. My parents got me a PDA with a minder, like Denise's. But I wasn't doing anything anymore. Lindsey still sees everyone. She tells me what's going on. But it feels different, now. I don't want to be an adult. That must have been what Terry felt like. Funny, to think I'm like him.

   (Music—"My Old School" by Steely Dan.)

COLIN GREENLAND

WINGS

ONE DAY STANDS OUT IN MY MEMORY, ONE GREEN AND golden afternoon in Colorado. It must be May, or June. We are on a back road, returning from somewhere; going back to Bear Creek and Cathy's house on the mountain.

Cathy is talking about her landlord, who disappeared some time after she moved in, leaving her checks uncashed. "Now I get a letter from the county," she says. "It's not even his house."

A sign goes by. *Feldspar, Pop. 1,102. Home of the Frosties All-Girl Formation Skaters*. There are bullet holes in the sign, with blue sky shining through them.

"I thought he built it," I say. I always lose track of the details between visits.

Cathy laughs mirthlessly.

The only window in her bedroom is a narrow glazed slot at the top of one wall. You can't open it. There's an electrical socket that leaks water when it rains. The kitchen sink drains straight onto the lawn.

"He built it all right," she says.

Main Street, Feldspar. Men in caps and overalls drinking sodas. Dick's Antiques. The Silver Dollar Diner. A kid in a baseball shirt runs across the road.

Cathy puts her foot down.

"Asshole," she says. Her speech has become markedly more American since she moved back over. I don't know if she means the kid, the absconded landlord, or me.

We race past the Feldspar Drugstore. The plate-glass windows are plastered with dayglo enticements. *Two for One. Triple Coupons Friday.* In the parking lot a dog on the back of a pickup barks at something overhead.

"It's nice, sitting on this side of the car," I remark. "It's like when you dream you're driving. You don't have to do anything. You just sit in the car and it goes."

"*You* don't have to do anything anyway," Cathy says.

It's a point. I'm enjoying myself too much to acknowledge it. "Maybe you don't get that dream," I say. "Maybe if you can drive, you don't."

She doesn't answer.

She was born in Massachusetts, educated at Roedean and studied at Oxford, where we met. She taught classical Greek at the University of Hull for a while before retraining as a computer programmer and moving to Colorado, where she slept on the couch of a childhood friend. Before the month was out she had the ramshackle house on Eglantine Road, two large dogs, and a Hyundai 4×4 for the commuter trudge every morning into Denver.

Cathy was in Colorado. The rest of the world arranged itself accordingly, including me.

The road climbs out of Feldspar. I can hear all the dogs barking now. I wind down the window and look up through the green spires of the spruce, into the warm blue sky.

The dogs have never got used to them. They spook the horses too.

Cathy seems to misunderstand why I looked out. "Do you know where we are yet?" she says. She wants me to learn my way around so I can be less dependent on her when I'm over.

In Colorado, everyone knows their way around. I always used to astound Cathy with my complete lack of a sense of direction.

"You should take up hang-gliding, Colin," she told me once. "Hang-gliding is the best way to learn about space."

We take another bend, at speed. "You'll recognize it in a minute," Cathy says.

"I know," I say. "We keep going up here to that big road."

That amuses her. "The big road!"

I persevere. "The one that goes through the cutting. Where the radio mast is."

"I-25," says Cathy, firmly.

If she'd chosen another route home that day, things might have worked out differently for us, for her.

Perhaps there's a universe where they did. Perhaps there's one where the angels never came at all and we were left alone to muddle through, the way we used to.

Instead, a mile beyond Feldspar, an angel flags us down.

"Shit," says Cathy, who hates being stopped by anyone at any time, in the car or anywhere else. "Shit."

The angel hovers, twenty feet up. His wings gleam white in the sun.

Cathy pulls over on the dusty yellow verge, where he's pointing. She winds down her window.

Courteously the angel floats down to the ground. The speed gun he's holding looks like some futuristic space weapon.

Cathy doesn't look at him. "I know," she says at once. "I'm sorry." She sounds more English now: rigid, curt.

He's a young one, fresh-faced. His teeth are very straight and white.

"Good morning, ma'am," he says. "My name is Officer Benjamin. At this time I need to see your license and registration, please."

Officer Benjamin wears silvered aviator glasses and the insignia of half a dozen affiliations and initiatives. They love things like that.

The traffic zooms by. I look around for the other one. They go about in pairs, like Jehovah's Witnesses.

"Catherine Jefferson," reads Officer Benjamin. "Are you aware you were doing seventy-five on the bend there, Catherine?" He speaks the way they all do, with deepest sympathy for the human condition and the scrapes into which winglessness continually leads us.

Cathy sits upright, holding on to the wheel. She speaks as if she's reading it off an autocue. "I had some bad news," she tells the angel. "I just heard my company's folding."

I hold my breath.

Officer Benjamin is patient and methodical. "I'm sorry to hear that, Catherine," he says. "But taking the lowest reading, which you probably know is the way they have us do it, you were making a good seventy-two when you entered the bend there. The reason we're contacting you today, Catherine, is to remind you that's ten percent in excess of the legal limit."

His partner appears then, dropping out of the sun. "A shade over ten percent," he says, touching down on my side of the car. "If you're interested in the math."

Like Jehovah's Witnesses, or Mormons, there's always a smart one and one who may be not so bright but is all heart. This is the smart one. He smiles in at us as he stoops to check the tires.

They want you to know they have a sense of humor.

Officer Benjamin finishes writing the ticket and tears it out of his little book. He tells Cathy what she has to do about the fine, and when, and where. "Yes," she says, her face still empty of expression. "Right. Uh-huh. Okay."

Officer Benjamin's partner rests his hand on the hood of

the Hyundai. His wings occlude the afternoon traffic. His glasses flare in the sunlight.

"We'd like to draw a line under this incident, Catherine," he confides. "I'm sure that's what you'd like too."

Their voices are the same: high-pitched, dreamy, condescending. Across America half the ads on the radio are angel voices, actors imitating angels, that is. British actors, many of them. British actors do them best.

As we pull back onto the road, I give my own angel impersonation, the only token of revenge I can offer. I hunch my shoulders and speak through my nose. *"The reason we're contacting you today . . ."*

"Wee wee wee," Cathy concurs irritably. She wants me to shut up.

I put my hand on the back of her neck. She shrugs it off as if it were an angel's hand.

"Don't *touch* me."

It was true, about her job. Cathy had been working for Copacetic Gas and Oil, in their billing department. Oil prices had been climbing since the angels came, and one day everyone at Copacetic turned up to discover the company had been sold out from under them, to Exxon; or Mobil, I forget. To hear Cathy cite that as a mitigating circumstance was a surprise. The truth was, she didn't care. It was something they'd all been expecting for weeks.

"It's not a problem," she'd said on the phone, when I'd called to tell her my flight number. "I can renegotiate the financing."

I barely understood. *Redundancy. Unemployment.* To my mind, she might as well have been saying *Famine, Pestilence, War,* and *Death.*

"But what are you going to do?"

The transatlantic wind soughed down the telephone. "I'm investigating opportunities," she said.

Americans like to make declarations. "Beer makes you short of breath," they say. They say: "Hang-gliding is the best way to learn about space." They say, "I'm researching that," meaning they saw something about it in a magazine the other day.

It's not a question of facts. It's a question of staking your claim.

I'd known Cathy Jefferson for four years, on and off. I'd endured the three-hour ride by coach to visit her in Hull, in the freezing flat upstairs from the dental practice. She knew all about opportunities and claims. In the general elation when the angels came, she threw in her stake in academia and took to the hills. "I asked myself," she told everyone, "where in the world would I like to be? And the answer was Colorado."

Colorado, I realized as soon as I went to see her, is a state for the young. In Colorado, everyone is going to own their own business. Maybe not today, says the smile on the face of the checkout clerk as he asks which you prefer, paper bags or plastic. Maybe tomorrow, though.

The angels themselves, when they came, could not enlighten us on the subject of destiny. "We should get one thing perfectly straight here," they told Larry King. "We really don't have any better understanding in that area than you people do."

They sipped mineral water. The dumb one grinned.

"God is okay, though, don't you think? I mean, the universe, wow. That's neat."

After an initial flurry of excitement, Britain was beginning to find the appearance of beautiful, healthy people with wings rather depressing. Our inferiority to everyone else (the Germans, the Japanese, the Americans themselves) was a fact to which we'd grown accustomed. There was no need, we felt, to be so *blatant* about it.

The response of the Americans was just the opposite. This

was *proof*. Creation was organized vertically, just as the various Good Books said. There was a *career structure*.

Both those attitudes Larry's guests sought to discourage.

"We're so impressed by your resourcefulness." The clever one leaned forward in sincerity. The studio had given them chairs with low backs, to accommodate their dorsal appendages. "Really, we had no idea what it must be like for you."

"You're an inspiration," said the other one. "The way you get around. Your cars. Your airplanes!"

The simplest ladder fascinates them. The youngsters hang around tall buildings, watching the elevators.

They do try to spare our feelings. An entire species disabled in the third dimension, deprived by some primordial genetic mishap of the advantages bestowed on the merest sparrow, the merest fly.

They want you to know they are on our side.

"Now we're here," the clever angel promised, "we're going to do all we can to help."

"We should get *on* with it!" said his friend, beaming into the camera like a quarterback. That shot of his muscles bulging as his great wings opened was on every teenager's bedroom wall before the month was out.

"Didn't you have that picture?" a young man asks me. "I sure did."

The man is called Adam. He's twenty years old. He's wearing a black T-shirt with a skeleton on it; blue jeans, neatly pressed; and handmade shoes. It must be the next year, the year after the speeding ticket. We're in someone's backyard, Roberta's, is it? A neighbor of Cathy's, up the road. Cathy sits on the ground with some of the other women. Everyone's drinking Bud and Beck's, eating chips. Children scramble up and down the bank, dragging a big pink kite.

Adam is a CAD engineer specializing in airline seating. He earns more each year than I've ever earned altogether. He rides the highways of the west in a black Porsche playing the Grateful Dead at ear-bruising volume.

"That picture was what America had been looking for since 1903."

America is what Americans like most to make declarations about. They flourish her name like a flag. "America thinks Africa and China ought to shape up." "America always chooses freedom of worship over freedom of speech." "America puts twenty-four percent more sugar in beverages and on breakfast cereal than the next most sugar-loving nation." Occasionally I might rouse myself to ask, "Is that by volume or by weight?" They would always know.

Adam hands me a fresh beer. The skeleton on his T-shirt wears a chaplet of roses and plays an electric guitar.

I say, "1903?"

"December seventeenth, 1903," says Adam, promptly. He looks at me as if I were a long way away. "Orville and Wilbur Wright," he reminds me.

I open the beer. I've learned to twist the cap off with my hand, the way the locals do.

Adam's making a list, counting on his fingers. "John Glenn. Neil Armstrong."

"Yuri Gargarin," I suggest.

Adam looks up at the sky, tilting his head to one side as if assessing the chance of rain. "Russia had the hardware," he says. "They didn't have the theory. They thought it was something to do with communism."

He laughs and swigs his beer. Avid, high-pitched, the cries of the children pierce the afternoon.

There are no angels at the party. An angel at a party would be quite a coup, though more likely in Bear Creek than in many other places. They like Colorado. They like the clear air, the mountain optimism.

In a while Cathy has to go home to feed the dogs. I go with her, back down Eglantine. The wind whispers in the pines. A chipmunk sits on a log, occupied with its business of nuts and seeds. Cathy has a new job, working for a local company that makes and sells vitamin supplements. She is glad, she says, to be doing something worthwhile.

The house is hers now. Though mountain property is at a premium, the county was only too pleased to have that one off its hands.

We sit on the porch in our shorts and sandals, catching the last of the sinking sun. Somnolent with grass and beer, we talk about us, and Colorado. I remind her what she'd said in Hull. "If I go and live in Colorado, would you come and see me?" When I came, the first time, she'd paid my fare.

"I kind of hoped you'd like it," she says.

I spread my arms, embracing the mountains, the trees, the sunshine, the chipmunk on its log.

"I do," I say. "I love it."

She glances at me, and away again.

"You could move over," she says. "We could get you a job."

"On the radio," I say. We've talked about it before.

Ricky and Wanda come bustling round from the back. They've finished their dinner and are in search of some affection. We scratch their heads and rub their ears.

"You'd be really good," Cathy says. There's a pleading tone in her voice now, as if convincing me were the only obstacle to my immigration. "You could have your own show."

I do my angel impersonation. *"Drive Time here on KLMN and we're here playing all your cruising favorites . . ."*

Cathy shivers. I ask if she needs her sweater. She turns away as if she hasn't heard.

I gaze across the valley, thinking of England: proper tea, public transport, BBC Radio 4. After three weeks in Bear Creek I would always feel homesick for Essex, and vice versa. Whichever side of the Atlantic I was, I was always wishing I had wings to carry me to the other.

"Triple coupons at the downtown Super Saver . . ." I say, in my angel voice.

She hears me that time. "Don't," she says, quite sharply.

I ask her what the matter is.

"Making fun of the way they speak," she says. "You wouldn't make fun of an Indian."

I don't know if she means an American Indian, or one of ours. I suppose it doesn't make any difference.

I put my hands behind my head.

"I'm too hesitant for radio," I say. "I think too much."

Cathy makes a soft noise like the start of a scornful laugh. She puts her feet up on her chair and wraps her arms around her knees. Wanda noses her ankles. Ricky lies in the dirt, his chin on his paws, dreaming of jackrabbits.

"Typical Brit," says Cathy, in her most ironic, most British voice. "You always disqualify yourself from everything."

The next thing I remember is· the following spring. Twilight at the lake. Boats bobbing at their moorings, swimsuits hanging from branches. The scent of barbecues all around.

It must be the company picnic. Picnics and parties were the only times I ever met anyone, in Colorado, unless they were a checkout clerk. Home from work, in her cabin with her dogs, Cathy rarely wanted to go out again.

Around the lakeshore the darkness is clotted beneath the trees. Little lights shine out: the windows of RV's; picnic lanterns; candles in wine bottles. The water has the sheen of molten zinc.

Dot and Rudy's table is a shadowy clutter of beer cans, paper plates of corncob stalks, charred ribs in smears of sauce. Dot is speaking quietly about Aspen. "That's where Rudy and me had some of our best sex," she says. "Up there in Aspen."

The four of us have been out all afternoon in Rudy's boat. Cathy took a turn on the skis and did noticeably better than Rudy or Dot, though they go every weekend, every year between May and October. Now Dot's comparing waterskiing to downhill skiing, which she obviously prefers.

"You get up early, pull on a load of clothes, go out on the

slopes and throw yourself around all day in the snow. Then you crawl back in and eat a huge meal someone else has cooked for you and drink a couple of brandies. Then you just fall into this major king-size bed together, as relaxed as you've ever been in your life. It's a real aphrodisiac."

Soft laughter ripples through the dark.

Dot is Cathy's best friend at work. Cathy and I have been out with them on the boat once before. The first time they offered me a turn on the skis. I declined, of course. "Colin can't swim," Cathy told them, with a weariness audible despite her efforts.

At the tables around the lake people have started getting to their feet. They are gazing up into the sky. We can hear cheers, whoops of excitement.

The sky is a wide low dome of peach and lilac, holding the last of the light. A company of angels is passing, high overhead. White wings and blue uniforms, splendid in formation. Park rangers on patrol, or maybe a mountain rescue team. A smatter of applause echoes off the water.

Rudy, a strong and patient man, says humorously, "Didn't Sigmund Freud say if you dream about flying, that's really about sex? So what's it mean when you dream about sex?"

That's for my benefit: the visiting Englishman, the bespectacled intellectual. It's something I've heard a thousand times, from my own mouth as often as not. Still I'm grateful for the gesture.

Before I can muster a reply, Dot does.

"Everybody has flying dreams. Human beings everywhere have those dreams. You ever think about that? You don't dream about burrowing through the earth or swimming under the sea. You dream about flying. Something no human has ever done."

Dot can't swim either, Rudy told us, though I wondered at the time if that too was for my benefit. On waterskis Dot wears a life jacket, like everyone else. My place is in the stern with a beer and the little flag they give you to hold up when there's someone in the water.

"Something inside us," Dot concludes, "knows we ought to be able to fly."

Beside me at the table Cathy stirs. The idea appeals to her.

"It's a glitch in the programming," she says. "A genetic flaw."

Dot doodles in spilled sauce with the end of a rib. "God got it wrong."

Cathy's hand reaches for mine in the dark and squeezes it. In two days' time she will tell me she's having an affair. His name is Zachary, she met him at the courthouse, the day she went to pay her fine. He asked her about living on Eglantine, about the price of property up there. He flattered her with his attentions. I don't know, I don't really understand. It's none of my business anyway. Cathy let me know it isn't.

Dot knew, of course. I sometimes wonder whether, in some obscure way, she might have been trying to warn me, that night by the lake, with the boats rocking gently in the dark.

The last time I saw Cathy Jefferson was in the autumn of 1989. For years we'd been down to Christmas cards. *Festive greetings from Bear Creek.* Then one evening, out of the blue, she rang me to tell me she was coming over.

"My mother's there," she says. "In London."

The voice in my ear is as easy and familiar as when we shared a pillow.

"It would be nice to see you," she says.

Mrs. Jefferson, Cynthia, is visiting the Natural History Museum, apparently, doing some research. She's renting a tiny flat in Kensington.

Cathy is making a plan. Coffee on Sunday morning, maybe some lunch, a walk in the park if it stays fine.

Cathy says: "Wiggy wants to see you too."

Wiggy is her grandmother, Cynthia's mother. They all call her that, for some reason I don't think I ever knew.

"Wiggy's here too?" I say.

I like Wiggy. She was always sweet on me. She was sorry Cathy hadn't married the nice English boy.

"She's along for the ride."

Cathy doesn't seem to think it extraordinary, a woman in her eighties taking her first trip abroad, a flight across the Atlantic.

I say: "And what about the baby?"

My throat feels tight, my head full of a strange pressing darkness. I can't, at that moment, think of the baby's name.

"She's coming too," Cathy says, as if I might have taken that for granted. But her tone is more than casual now. I can hear the pride in it.

Downstairs my housemates are watching TV. Distorted comedy voices and gusty laughter filter up through the floor. I say something about looking forward to seeing Cathy's baby.

"And what about Zac?" I say at last.

"He has to work."

Salt moisture prickles in my nose. I blink. I can feel my lungs expand.

"Oh, well," I say.

She hadn't put his name on the Christmas card either, I remember. It had a host of angels on the front, proper ones in white nightshirts, frightening a gaggle of shepherds.

On Sunday I get up early and catch a series of trains. The address is a massive Victorian terrace, four floors of red brick, ornate gables, iron-railed areas, a parade of glossy front doors: coal black, bottle green, pillar-box red. The flat is half of a basement, partitioned off. It has an entrance hall, two rooms, a shower, and a kitchen the size of a shoebox. "It's a squeeze," Cynthia admits, "but we manage."

She's in jogging pants, a pale blue polo-neck top and pink-framed spectacles on a string of beads. Her touch is as smooth and light as a piece of paper. Graciously she accepts the flowers I picked up on impulse at a stall outside the Underground: a cellophane trumpet of Michaelmas daisies and shaggy golden chrysanthemums. I see Cathy in a doorway, Wiggy on a sofa. "They're for all of you," I say, in my confusion, indicating the flowers.

Cathy steps forward. I think she isn't going to hug me, but then she does, clumsily. Expressing affection still makes her awkward.

"Colin!" calls Wiggy across the room. "It's good to see you!"

I go to kiss her dry cheek. The room is piled with books and folders. Pictures of birds hang Blu-tacked from the mantelpiece: X rays of wing bones; photocopied plates from Audubon.

I ask: "So where's Columba?"

I've remembered her name.

"She's sleeping," her mother warns me, and she points to the door of the bedroom.

At that moment it seems perfectly appropriate that Cathy should have a baby. A baby is as suitable and logical for her as two large dogs, or the dingy little house in the wood.

Columba is one and a half years old. She didn't think much of the flight over, Cathy says. She wouldn't go to sleep. She kept pawing the window, as if she wanted to go outside.

Cynthia makes coffee for everyone: regular for me, decaf for them. Wiggy wants to hear about my work. She says what she always says. "It must be such a thrill, to see your own name in print!"

I agree politely, but she doesn't let it go at that. "I always look whenever I go in a bookstore," she says, "to see if you're there." She doesn't say whether I am or not, which means I'm not.

Wiggy is politeness itself, old New England. Her hair is white as bone, immaculately curled. She wears a woolen skirt and stockings. Her skinny throat is decorated with a scarf of apricot silk.

"So nice of you to bring those lovely flowers!" she says. I feel an obscure mixture of relief, that I thought to buy them at all, and shame, that I hadn't thought of something more special, more personal.

I ask Cynthia about her investigations into wing structure. Seven years after their advent, the angels remain an aerodynamic and anatomical mystery. They submit cheerfully enough to examination, but no corpses are available for dissection. When they die they disintegrate in a silent blast of golden light.

Speaking to Cynthia, not for the first time, an odd flirtatiousness comes over me. It's almost as if, having lost her daughter, I'm compelled to move my attentions up a generation.

"What you ought to do is kidnap one," I say. "Ask him in, then lock the door."

Cynthia laughs. Cathy keeps smiling, but behind her eyes she's gone away. Wiggy just looks puzzled.

"For the good of science," I say.

The old lady is shocked. She knows I'm joking, but she doesn't like it a bit. "The way people talk today!" she protests breathlessly. "Not a bit grateful."

To Wiggy, our airborne cousins are as good as royalty. Any honor they do us poor earthbound cripples is too much.

A bus goes by the window, a big red double-decker. The windows tremble. From the next room comes a small thin cry.

"There's Columba!" says Wiggy, with satisfaction. "I'm so forgetful these days, I always want to say *Columbine*," she tells me. "That's the girl in the pantomime, you know, that loves the clown."

I nod encouragingly. I haven't the first idea what she's talking about.

Everyone listens for the crying to stop. It proceeds, weak but persistent. Together, Cathy and Cynthia give in. They get up and start moving things around, preparing for a diaper change and feed.

Wiggy continues to entertain me. "I thought they might call her Angela. Don't you think that's a nice name?"

"The most popular girl's name in Britain now," I tell her. It's news to her, of course. I'm glad to have that much to contribute.

Cathy and Cynthia start speaking at the same time, Cathy saying Angela's a horrible name, and Cynthia saying she thinks Columba's a perfect one. There is a strange, almost theatrical moment when I realize I am sitting in a room with three generations of women, talking about the fourth.

Cathy raises her eyebrows then. "Do you want to see her?" It's a demand, a challenge, almost as if she genuinely believes I might decline.

"Certainly I do," I say, rising to my feet. My voice sounds elderly and pedantic, as if I were the biologist here, come to examine a specimen.

The room smells of air freshener, and faintly of baby shit. Between the bed and the wall Columba Jefferson lies face-down in a folding crib. She's kicked off her covers and she's crying totally, desperately, with infant abandon.

Her mother picks her up and tries to soothe her. Her baby face is crumpled, red and cross. She rubs it with her fist, enraged at being woken. The women coo. Columba twists away from us, burying her face in Cathy's neck. Her little nightdress has a slit up the back. Her wings stick out of it.

They are tiny, fluffy baby wings, the wings of a Botticelli cherub. As the cherub cries they flex like the first tiny green leaflets of spring uncoiling.

They want you to know they are here to stay.

SUSAN PALWICK

GESTELLA

TIME'S THE PROBLEM. TIME AND ARITHMETIC. YOU'VE known from the beginning that the numbers would cause trouble, but you were much younger then—much, much younger—and far less wise. And there's culture shock, too. Where you come from, it's okay for women to have wrinkles. Where you come from, youth's not the only commodity.

You met Jonathan back home. Call it a forest somewhere, near an Alp. Call it a village on the edge of the woods. Call it old. You weren't old, then: you were fourteen on two feet and a mere two years old on four, although already fully grown. Your kind are fully grown at two years, on four feet. And experienced: oh, yes. You knew how to howl at the moon. You knew what to do when somebody howled back. If your four-footed form hadn't been sterile, you'd have had litters by then—but it was, and on two feet, you'd been just smart enough, or lucky enough, to avoid continuing your line.

But it wasn't as if you hadn't had plenty of opportunities,

enthusiastically taken. Jonathan liked that. A lot. Jonathan was older than you were: thirty-five, then. Jonathan loved fucking a girl who looked fourteen and acted older, who acted feral, who *was* feral for three to five days a month, centered on the full moon. Jonathan didn't mind the mess that went with it, either: all that fur, say, sprouting at one end of the process and shedding on the other, or the aches and pains from various joints pivoting, changing shape, redistributing weight, or your poor gums bleeding all the time from the monthly growth and recession of your fangs. "At least that's the only blood," he told you, sometime during that first year.

You remember this very clearly: you were roughly halfway through the four-to-two transition, and Jonathan was sitting next to you in bed, massaging your sore shoulder blades as you sipped mint tea with hands still nearly as clumsy as paws, hands like mittens. Jonathan had just filled two hot water bottles, one for your aching tailbone and one for your aching knees. Now you know he wanted to get you in shape for a major sportfuck—he loved sex even more than usual, after you'd just changed back—but at the time, you thought he was a real prince, the kind of prince girls like you weren't supposed to be allowed to get, and a stab of pain shot through you at his words. "I didn't kill anything," you told him, your lower lip trembling. "I didn't even hunt."

"Gestella, darling, I know. That wasn't what I meant." He stroked your hair. He'd been feeding you raw meat during the four-foot phase, but not anything you'd killed yourself. He'd taught you to eat little pieces out of his hand, gently, without biting him. He'd taught you to wag your tail, and he was teaching you to chase a ball, because that's what good four-foots did where he came from. "I was talking about—"

"Normal women," you told him. "The ones who bleed so they can have babies. You shouldn't make fun of them. They're lucky." You like children and puppies; you're good with them, gentle. You know it's unwise for you to have any of your own, but you can't help but watch them, wistfully.

"*I* don't want kids," he says. "I had that operation. I told you."

"Are you sure it took?" you ask. You're still very young. You've never known anyone who's had an operation like that, and you're worried about whether Jonathan really understands your condition. Most people don't. Most people think all kinds of crazy things. Your condition isn't communicable, for instance, by biting or any other way, but it is hereditary, which is why it's good that you've been so smart and lucky, even if you're just fourteen.

Well, no, not fourteen anymore. It's about halfway through Jonathan's year of folklore research—he's already promised not to write you up for any of the journals, and keeps assuring you he won't tell anybody, although later you'll realize that's for his protection, not yours—so that would make you, oh, seventeen or eighteen. Jonathan's still thirty-five. At the end of the year, when he flies you back to the United States with him so the two of you can get married, he'll be thirty-six. You'll be twenty-one on two feet, three years old on four.

Seven to one. That's the ratio. You've made sure Jonathan understands this. "Oh, sure," he says. "Just like for dogs. One year is seven human years. Everybody knows that. But how can it be a problem, darling, when we love each other so much?" And even though you aren't fourteen anymore, you're still young enough to believe him.

At first it's fun. The secret's a bond between you, a game. You speak in code. Jonathan splits your name in half, calling you Jessie on four feet and Stella on two. You're Stella to all his friends, and most of them don't even know that he has a dog one week a month. The two of you scrupulously avoid scheduling social commitments for the week of the full moon, but no one seems to notice the pattern, and if anyone does notice, no one cares. Occasionally someone you know sees Jessie, when you and Jonathan are out in the park playing with balls, and Jonathan always says that he's taking care of his sister's dog while she's away on business. His sister travels a lot, he explains. Oh, no, Stella doesn't mind, but she's always been a bit nervous around dogs—even though Jessie's such a *good* dog—so she stays home during the walks.

Sometimes strangers come up, shyly. "What a beautiful dog!" they say. "What a *big* dog! What kind of dog is that?"

"Husky-Wolfhound cross," Jonathan says airily. Most people accept this. Most people know as much about dogs as dogs know about the space shuttle. Some people know better, though. Some people look at you, and frown a little, and say, "Looks like a wolf to me. Is she part wolf?"

"Could be," Jonathan always says with a shrug, his tone as breezy as ever. And he spins a little story about how his sister adopted you from the pound because you were the runt of the litter and no one else wanted you, and now look at you! No one would ever take you for a runt now! And the strangers smile and look encouraged and pat you on the head, because they like stories about dogs being rescued from the pound.

You sit and down and stay during these conversations; you do whatever Jonathan says. You wag your tail and cock your head and act charming. You let people scratch you behind the ears. You're a *good* dog. The other dogs in the park, who know more about their own species than most people do, aren't fooled by any of this; you make them nervous, and they tend to avoid you, or to act supremely submissive if avoidance isn't possible. They grovel on their bellies, on their backs; they crawl away backwards, whining.

Jonathan loves this. Jonathan loves it that you're the alpha with the other dogs—and, of course, he loves it that he's your alpha. Because that's another thing people don't understand about your condition: they think you're vicious, a ravening beast, a fanged monster from hell. In fact, you're no more bloodthirsty than any dog not trained to mayhem. You haven't been trained to mayhem: you've been trained to chase balls. You're a pack animal, an animal who craves hierarchy, and you, Jessie, are a one-man dog. Your man's Jonathan. You adore him. You'd do anything for him, even let strangers who wouldn't know a wolf from a wolfhound scratch you behind the ears.

The only fight you and Jonathan have, that first year in the States, is about the collar. Jonathan insists that Jessie wear a collar. Otherwise, he says, he could be fined. There are policemen in the park. Jessie needs a collar and an ID tag and rabies shots.

Jessie, you say on two feet, needs so such thing. You, Stella, are bristling as you say this, even though you don't have fur at the moment. "Jonathan," you tell him, "ID tags are for dogs who wander. Jessie will never leave your side, unless you throw a ball for her. And I'm not going to get rabies. All I eat is Alpo, not dead raccoons: how am I going to get rabies?"

"It's the law," he says gently. "It's not worth the risk, Stella."

And then he comes and rubs your head and shoulders *that* way, the way you've never been able to resist, and soon the two of you are in bed having a lovely sportfuck, and somehow by the end of the evening, Jonathan's won. Well, of course he has: he's the alpha.

So the next time you're on four feet, Jonathan puts a strong chain choke collar and an ID tag around your neck, and then you go to the vet and get your shots. You don't like the vet's office much, because it smells of too much fear and pain, but the people there pat you and give you milk bones and tell you how beautiful you are, and the vet's hands are gentle and kind.

The vet likes dogs. She also knows wolves from wolfhounds. She looks at you, hard, and then looks at Jonathan. "Gray wolf?" she asks.

"I don't know," says Jonathan. "She could be a hybrid."

"She doesn't look like a hybrid to me." So Jonathan launches into his breezy story about how you were the runt of the litter at the pound: you wag your tail and lick the vet's hand and act utterly adoring.

The vet's not having any of it. She strokes your head; her hands are kind, but she smells disgusted. "Mr. Argent, gray wolves are endangered."

"At least one of her parents was a dog," Jonathan says. He's starting to sweat. "Now, *she* doesn't look endangered, does she?"

"There are laws about keeping exotics as pets," the vet says. She's still stroking your head; you're still wagging your tail, but now you start to whine, because the vet smells angry and Jonathan smells afraid. "Especially endangered exotics."

"She's a dog," Jonathan says.

"If she's a dog," the vet says, "may I ask why you haven't had her spayed?"

Jonathan splutters. "Ex*cuse* me?"

"You got her from the pound. Do you know how animals wind up at the pound, Mr. Argent? They land there because people breed them and then don't want to take care of all those puppies or kittens. They land there—"

"We're here for a rabies shot," Jonathan says. "Can we get our rabies shot, please?"

"Mr. Argent, there are regulations about breeding endangered species—"

"I understand that," Jonathan says. "There are also regulations about rabies shots. If you don't give my *dog* her rabies shot—"

The vet shakes her head, but she gives you the rabies shot, and then Jonathan gets you out of there, fast. "Bitch," he says on the way home. He's shaking. "Animal-rights fascist bitch! Who the hell does she think she is?"

She thinks she's a vet. She thinks she's somebody who's supposed to take care of animals. You can't say any of this, because you're on four legs. You lie in the back seat of the car, on the special sheepskin cover Jonathan bought to protect the upholstery from your fur, and whine. You're scared. You liked the vet, but you're afraid of what she might do. She doesn't understand your condition; how could she?

The following week, after you're fully changed back, there's a knock at the door while Jonathan's at work. You put down your copy of *Elle* and pad, barefooted, over to the door. You open it to find a woman in uniform; a white truck with "Animal Control" written on it is parked in the driveway.

"Good morning," the officer says. "We've received a report that there may be an exotic animal on this property. May I come in, please?"

"Of course," you tell her. You let her in. You offer her coffee, which she doesn't want, and you tell her that there aren't any exotic animals here. You invite her to look around and see for herself.

Of course there's no sign of a dog, but she's not satisfied. "According to our records, Jonathan Argent of this address had a dog vaccinated last Saturday. We've been told that the dog looked very much like a wolf. Can you tell me where that dog is now?"

"We don't have her anymore," you say. "She got loose and jumped the fence on Monday. It's a shame; she was a lovely animal."

The animal-control lady scowls. "Did she have ID?"

"Of course," you say. "A collar with tags. If you find her, you'll call us, won't you?"

She's looking at you, hard, as hard as the vet did. "Of course. We recommend that you check the pound at least every few days, too. And you might want to put up flyers, put an ad in the paper."

"Thank you," you tell her. "We'll do that." She leaves; you go back to reading *Elle*, secure in the knowledge that your collar's tucked into your underwear drawer upstairs and that Jessie will never show up at the pound.

Jonathan's incensed when he hears about this. He reels off a string of curses about the vet. "Do you think you could rip her throat out?" he asks.

"No," you say, annoyed. "I don't want to, Jonathan. I liked her. She's doing her job. Wolves don't just attack people: you know better than that. And it wouldn't be smart even if I wanted to: it would just mean people would have to track me down and kill me. Now, look, relax. We'll go to a different vet next time, that's all."

"We'll do better than that," Jonathan says. "We'll move."

So you move to the next county over, to a larger house with a larger yard. There's even some wild land nearby, forest and meadows, and that's where you and Jonathan go for walks now. When it's time for your rabies shot the following year, you go to a male vet, an older man who's been recommended by some friends of friends of Jonathan's, people who do a lot of hunting. This vet raises his eyebrows when he sees you. "She's quite large," he says pleasantly. "Fish and Wildlife might be interested in such a large dog. Her size will add another, oh, hundred dollars to the bill, Johnny."

"I see." Jonathan's voice is icy. You growl, and the vet laughs.

"Loyal, isn't she? You're planning to breed her, of course."

"Of course," Jonathan snaps.

"Lucrative business, that. Her pups will pay for her rabies shot, believe me. Do you have a sire lined up?"

"Not yet." Jonathan sounds like he's strangling.

The vet strokes your shoulders. You don't like his hands. You don't like the way he touches you. You growl again, and again the vet laughs. "Well, give me a call when she goes into heat. I know some people who might be interested."

"Slimy bastard," Jonathan says when you're back home again. "You didn't like him, Jessie, did you? I'm sorry."

You lick his hand. The important thing is that you have your rabies shot, that your license is up to date, that this vet won't be reporting you to Animal Control. You're legal. You're a *good* dog.

You're a good wife, too. As Stella, you cook for Jonathan, clean for him, shop. You practice your English while devouring *Cosmopolitan* and *Martha Stewart Living*, in addition to *Elle*. You can't work or go to school, because the week of the full moon would keep getting in the way, but you keep yourself busy. You learn to drive and you learn to entertain; you learn to shave your legs and pluck your eyebrows, to mask your natural odor with harsh chemicals, to walk in high heels. You learn the artful uses of cosmetics and clothing, so that you'll be even more beautiful than you are *au naturel*. You're stunning, everyone says so: tall and slim with long silver hair and pale, piercing blue eyes. Your skin's smooth, your complexion flawless, your muscles lean and taut: you're a good cook, a great fuck, the perfect trophy wife. But of course, during that first year, while Jonathan's thirty-six going on thirty-seven, you're only twenty-one going on twenty-eight. You can keep the accelerated aging from showing: you eat right, get plenty of exercise, become even more skillful with the cosmetics. You and Jonathan are blissfully happy, and his colleagues, the old fogies in the Anthropology Department, are jealous. They stare at you when they think no one's looking. "They'd all love to fuck you," Jonathan gloats after every party, and after every party, he does just that.

Most of Jonathan's colleagues are men. Most of their wives don't like you, although a few make resolute efforts to be friendly, to ask you to lunch. Twenty-one going on twenty-eight, you wonder if they somehow sense that you aren't one of them, that there's another side to you, one with four feet. Later you'll realize that even if they knew about Jessie, they couldn't hate and fear you any more than they already do. They fear you because you're young, because you're beautiful and speak English with an exotic accent, because their husbands can't stop staring at you. They know their husbands want to fuck you. The wives may not be young and beautiful any more, but they're no fools. They lost the luxury of innocence when they lost their smooth skin and flawless complexions.

The only person who asks you to lunch and seems to mean

it is Diane Harvey. She's forty-five, with thin grey hair and a
wide face that's always smiling. She runs her own computer
repair business, and she doesn't hate you. This may be related
to the fact that her husband Glen never stares at you, never
gets too close to you during conversation; he seems to have
no desire to fuck you at all. He looks at Diane the way all the
other men look at you: as if she's the most desirable creature
on earth, as if just being in the same room with her renders
him scarcely able to breathe. He adores his wife, even though
they've been married for fifteen years, even though he's five
years younger than she is and handsome enough to seduce a
younger, more beautiful woman. Jonathan says that Glen must
stay with Diane for her salary, which is considerably more
than his. You think Jonathan's wrong; you think Glen stays
with Diane for herself.

Over lunch, as you gnaw an overcooked steak in a bland
fern bar, all glass and wood, Diane asks you kindly when you
last saw your family, if you're homesick, whether you and Jonathan have any plans to visit Europe again soon. These questions bring a lump to your throat, because Diane's the only
one who's ever asked them. You don't, in fact, miss your family—the parents who taught you to hunt, who taught you the
dangers of continuing the line, or the siblings with whom you
tussled and fought over scraps of meat—because you've trans-
ferred all your loyalty to Jonathan. But two is an awfully small
pack, and you're starting to wish Jonathan hadn't had that
operation. You're starting to wish you could continue the line,
even though you know it would be a foolish thing to do. You
wonder if that's why your parents mated, even though they
knew the dangers.

"I miss the smells back home," you tell Diane, and immediately you blush, because it seems like such a strange
thing to say, and you desperately want this kind woman to
like you. As much as you love Jonathan, you yearn for someone else to talk to.

But Diane doesn't think it's strange. "Yes," she says, nodding, and tells you about how homesick she still gets for her grandmother's kitchen, which had a signature smell for each season: basil and tomatoes in the summer, apples in the fall, nutmeg and cinnamon in winter, thyme and lavender in the spring. She tells you that she's growing thyme and lavender in her own garden; she tells you about her tomatoes.

She asks you if you garden. You say no. In truth, you're not a big fan of vegetables, although you enjoy the smell of flowers, because you enjoy the smell of almost anything. Even on two legs, you have a far better sense of smell than most people do; you live in a world rich with aroma, and even the scents most people consider noxious are interesting to you. As you sit in the sterile fern bar, which smells only of burned meat and rancid grease and the harsh chemicals the people around you have put on their skin and hair, you realize that you really do miss the smells of home, where even the gardens smell older and wilder than the woods and meadows here.

You tell Diane, shyly, that you'd like to learn to garden. Could she teach you?

So she does. One Saturday afternoon, much to Jonathan's bemusement, Diane comes over with topsoil and trowels and flower seeds, and the two of you measure out a plot in the backyard, and plant and water and get dirt under your nails, and it's quite wonderful, really, about the best fun you've had on two legs, aside from sportfucks with Jonathan. Over dinner, after Diane's left, you try to tell Jonathan how much fun it was, but he doesn't seem particularly interested. He's glad you had a good time, but really, he doesn't want to hear about seeds. He wants to go upstairs and have sex.

So you do.

Afterwards, you go through all of your old issues of *Martha Stewart Living*, looking for gardening tips.

You're ecstatic. You have a hobby now, something you can talk to the other wives about. Surely some of them garden. Maybe, now, they won't hate you. So at the next party, you chatter brightly about gardening, but somehow all the wives are still across the room, huddled around a table, occasionally glaring in your direction, while the men cluster around you, their eyes bright, nodding eagerly at your descriptions of weeds and aphids.

You know something's wrong here. Men don't like gardening, do they? Jonathan certainly doesn't. Finally one of the wives, a tall blonde with a tennis tan and good bones, stalks over and pulls her husband away by the sleeve. "Time to go home now," she tells him, and curls her lip at you.

You know that look. You know a snarl when you see it, even if the wife's too civilized to produce an actual growl.

You ask Diane about this the following week, while you're in her garden, admiring her tomato plants. "Why do they hate me?" you ask Diane.

"Oh, Stella," she says, and sighs. "You really don't know, do you?" You shake your head, and she goes on. "They hate you because you're young and beautiful, even though that's not your fault. The ones who have to work hate you because you don't, and the ones who don't have to work, whose husbands support them, hate you because they're afraid their husbands will leave them for younger, more beautiful women. Do you understand?"

You don't, not really, even though you're now twenty-eight going on thirty-five. "Their husbands can't leave them for me," you tell Diane. "I'm married to Jonathan. I don't *want* any of their husbands." But even as you say it, you know that's not the point.

A few weeks later, you learn that the tall blonde's husband has indeed left her, for an aerobics instructor twenty years his junior. "He showed me a picture," Jonathan says, laughing. "She's a big-hair bimbo. She's not *half* as beautiful as you are."

"What does that have to do with it?" you ask him. You're angry, and you aren't sure why. You barely know the blonde, and it's not as if she's been nice to you. "His poor wife! That was a terrible thing for him to do!"

"Of course it was," Jonathan says soothingly.

"Would you leave me if I wasn't beautiful anymore?" you ask him.

"Nonsense, Stella. You'll always be beautiful."

But that's when Jonathan's going on thirty-eight and you're going on thirty-five. The following year, the balance begins to shift. He's going on thirty-nine; you're going on forty-two. You take exquisite care of yourself, and really, you're as beautiful as ever, but there are a few wrinkles now, and it takes hours of crunches to keep your stomach as flat as it used to be.

Doing crunches, weeding in the garden, you have plenty of time to think. In a year, two at the most, you'll be old enough to be Jonathan's mother, and you're starting to think he might not like that. And you've already gotten wind of catty faculty-wife gossip about how quickly you're showing your age. The faculty wives see every wrinkle, even through artfully applied cosmetics.

During that thirty-five to forty-two year, Diane and her husband move away, so now you have no one with whom to discuss your wrinkles or the catty faculty wives. You don't want to talk to Jonathan about any of it. He still tells you how beautiful you are, and you still have satisfying sportfucks. You don't want to give him any ideas about declining desirability.

You do a lot of gardening that year: flowers—especially roses—and herbs, and some tomatoes in honor of Diane, and because Jonathan likes them. Your best times are the two-foot times in the garden and the four-foot times in the forest, and you think it's no coincidence that both of these involve digging around in the dirt. You write long letters to Diane, on e-mail or, sometimes, when you're saying something you don't want Jonathan to find on the computer, on old-fashioned paper. Diane doesn't have much time to write back, but does send the occasional e-mail note, the even rarer postcard. You read a lot, too, everything you can find: newspapers and novels and political analysis, literary criticism, true crime, ethnographic studies. You startle some of Jonathan's colleagues by casually dropping odd bits of information about their field, about other fields, about fields they've never heard of: forensic geography, agricultural ethics, poststructuralist mining. You think it's no coincidence that the obscure disciplines you're most inter-ested in involve digging around in the dirt.

Some of Jonathan's colleagues begin to comment not only on your beauty but on your intelligence. Some of them back away a little bit. Some of the wives, although not many, be-come a little friendlier, and you start going out to lunch again, although not with anyone you like as much as Diane.

The following year, the trouble starts. Jonathan's going on forty; you're going on forty-nine. You both work out a lot; you both eat right. But Jonathan's hardly wrinkled at all yet, and your wrinkles are getting harder to hide. Your stomach refuses to stay completely flat no matter how many crunches you do; you've developed the merest hint of cottage-cheese thighs. You forgo your old look, the slinky, skintight look, for long flowing skirts and dresses, accented with plenty of silver. You're going for exotic, elegant, and you're getting there just fine; heads still turn to follow you in the supermarket. But the sportfucks are less frequent, and you don't know how much of this is normal aging and how much is lack of interest on Jonathan's part. He doesn't seem quite as enthusiastic as he once did. He no longer brings you herbal tea and hot water bottles during your transitions; the walks in the woods are a little shorter than they used to be, the ball-throwing sessions in the meadows more perfunctory.

And then one of your new friends, over lunch, asks you tactfully if anything's wrong, if you're ill, because, well, you don't look quite yourself. Even as you assure her that you're fine, you know she means that you look a lot older than you did last year.

At home, you try to discuss this with Jonathan. "We knew it would be a problem eventually," you tell him. "I'm afraid that other people are going to notice, that someone's going to figure it out—"

"Stella, sweetheart, no one's going to figure it out." He's

annoyed, impatient. "Even if they think you're aging unusually quickly, they won't make the leap to Jessie. It's not in their worldview. It wouldn't occur to them even if you were aging a hundred years for every one of theirs. They'd just think you had some unfortunate metabolic condition, that's all."

Which, in a manner of speaking, you do. You wince. It's been five weeks since the last sportfuck. "Does it bother you that I look older?" you ask Jonathan.

"Of *course* not, Stella!" But since he rolls his eyes when he says this, you're not reassured. You can tell from his voice that he doesn't want to be having this conversation, that he wants to be somewhere else, maybe watching TV. You recognize that tone. You've heard Jonathan's colleagues use it on their wives, usually while staring at you.

You get through the year. You increase your workout schedule, mine *Cosmo* for bedroom tricks to pique Jonathan's flagging interest, consider and reject liposuction for your thighs. You wish you could have a facelift, but the recovery period's a bit too long, and you're not sure how it would work with your transitions. You read and read and read, and command an increasingly subtle grasp of the implications of, the interconnections between, different areas of knowledge: ecotourism, Third World famine relief, art history, automobile design. Your lunchtime conversations become richer, your friendships with the faculty wives more genuine.

You know that your growing wisdom is the benefit of aging, the compensation for your wrinkles and for your fading— although fading slowly, as yet—beauty.

You also know that Jonathan didn't marry you for wisdom.

And now it's the following year, the year you're old enough to be Jonathan's mother, although an unwed teenage one: you're going on fifty-six while he's going on forty-one. Your silver hair's losing its luster, becoming merely gray. Sportfucks coincide, more or less, with major national holidays. Your thighs begin to jiggle when you walk, so you go ahead and

have the liposuction, but Jonathan doesn't seem to notice anything but the outrageous cost of the procedure.

You redecorate the house. You take up painting, with
enough success to sell some pieces in a local gallery. You start
writing a book about gardening as a cure for ecotourism and
agricultural abuses, and you negotiate a contract with a pres-
tigious university press. Jonathan doesn't pay much attention
to any of this. You're starting to think that Jonathan would
only pay attention to a full-fledged Lon Chaney imitation,
complete with bloody fangs, but if that was ever in your nature, it certainly isn't now. Jonathan and Martha Stewart have
civilized you.

On four legs, you're still magnificent, eliciting exclamations
of wonder from other pet owners when you meet them in the
woods. But Jonathan hardly ever plays ball in the meadow
with you anymore; sometimes he doesn't even take you to the
forest. Your walks, once measured in hours and miles, now
clock in at minutes and suburban blocks. Sometimes Jonathan
doesn't even walk you. Sometimes he just shoos you out into
the backyard to do your business. He never cleans up after
you, either. You have to do that yourself, scooping old poop
after you've returned to two legs.

A few times you yell at Jonathan about this, but he just
walks away, even more annoyed than usual. You know you
have to do something to remind him that he loves you, or
loved you once; you know you have to do something to rein-
sert yourself into his field of vision. But you can't imagine
what. You've already tried everything you can think of.

There are nights when you cry yourself to sleep. Once,
Jonathan would have held you; now he rolls over, turning his
back to you, and scoots to the farthest edge of the mattress.

During that terrible time, the two of you go to a faculty
party. There's a new professor there, a female professor, the
first one the Anthropology Department has hired in ten years.
She's in her twenties, with long black hair and perfect skin,

and the men cluster around her the way they used to cluster around you.

Jonathan's one of them.

Standing with the other wives, pretending to talk about new films, you watch Jonathan's face. He's rapt, attentive, totally focused on the lovely young woman, who's talking about her research into ritual scarification in New Guinea. You see Jonathan's eyes stray surreptitiously, when he thinks no one will notice, to her breasts, her thighs, her ass.

You know Jonathan wants to fuck her. And you know it's not her fault, any more than it was ever yours. She can't help being young and pretty. But you hate her anyway. Over the next few days, you discover that what you hate most, hate even more than Jonathan wanting to fuck this young woman, is what your hate is doing to you: to your dreams, to your insides. The hate's your problem, you know; it's not Jonathan's fault, any more than his lust for the young professor is hers. But you can't seem to get rid of it, and you can sense it making your wrinkles deeper, shriveling you as if you're a piece of newspaper thrown into a fire.

You write Diane a long, anguished letter about as much of this as you can safely tell her. Of course, since she hasn't been around for a few years, she doesn't know how much older you look, so you simply say that you think Jonathan's fallen out of love with you since you're over forty now. You write the letter on paper, and send it through the mail.

Diane writes back, and not a postcard this time: she sends five single-spaced pages. She says that Jonathan's probably going through a midlife crisis. She agrees that his treatment of you is, in her words, "barbaric." "Stella, you're a beautiful, brilliant, accomplished woman. I've never known anyone who's grown so much, or in such interesting ways, in such a short time. If Jonathan doesn't appreciate that, then he's an ass, and maybe it's time to ask yourself if you'd be happier elsewhere. I hate to recommend divorce, but I also hate to see you suffering so much. The problem, of course, is economic: can you support yourself if you leave? Is Jonathan likely to be reliable with alimony? At least—small comfort, I know—there are no children who need to be considered in all this. I'm assuming that you've already tried couples therapy. If you haven't, you should."

This letter plunges you into despair. No, Jonathan isn't likely to be reliable with alimony. Jonathan isn't likely to agree to couples therapy, either. Some of your lunchtime friends have gone that route, and the only way they ever got their husbands into the therapist's office was by threatening divorce on the spot. If you tried this, it would be a hollow threat. Your unfortunate metabolic condition won't allow you to hold any kind of normal job, and your writing and painting income won't support you, and Jonathan knows all that as well as you do. And your continued safety's in his hands. If he exposed you—

You shudder. In the old country, the stories ran to peasants with torches. Here, you know, laboratories and scalpels would be more likely. Neither option's attractive.

You go to the art museum, because the bright, high, echoing rooms have always made it easier for you to think. You wander among abstract sculpture and Impressionist paintings, among still lifes and landscapes, among portraits. One of the portraits is of an old woman. She has white hair and many wrinkles; her shoulders stoop as she pours a cup of tea. The flowers on the china are the same pale, luminous blue as her eyes, which are, you realize, the same blue as your own.

The painting takes your breath away. This old woman is beautiful. You know the painter, a nineteenth-century English duke, thought so too.

You know Jonathan wouldn't.

You decide, once again, to try to talk to Jonathan. You make him his favorite meal, serve him his favorite wine, wear your most becoming outfit, gray silk with heavy silver jewelry. Your silver hair and blue eyes gleam in the candlelight, and the candlelight, you know, hides your wrinkles.

This kind of production, at least, Jonathan still notices. When he comes into the dining room for dinner, he looks at you and raises his eyebrows. "What's the occasion?"

"The occasion's that I'm worried," you tell him. You tell him how much it hurts you when he turns away from your tears. You tell him how much you miss the sportfucks. You tell him that since you clean up his messes more than three weeks out of every month, he can damn well clean up yours when you're on four legs. And you tell him that if he doesn't love you any more, doesn't want you any more, you'll leave. You'll go back home, to the village on the edge of the forest near an Alp, and try to make a life for yourself.

"Oh, Stella," he says. "Of course I still love you!" You can't tell if he sounds impatient or contrite, and it terrifies you that you might not know the difference. "How could you even *think* of leaving me? After everything I've given you, everything I've done for you—"

"That's been changing," you tell him, your throat raw. "The changes are the *problem*. Jonathan—"

"I can't believe you'd try to hurt me like this! I can't believe—"

"Jonathan, I'm *not* trying to hurt you! I'm reacting to the fact that you're hurting me! Are you going to stop hurting me, or not?"

He glares at you, pouting, and it strikes you that after all, he's very young, much younger than you are. "Do you have any idea how ungrateful you're being? Not many men would put up with a woman like you!"

"*Jonathan!*"

"I mean, do you have any idea how hard it's been for *me*? All the secrecy, all the lying, having to walk the damn dog—"

"You used to enjoy walking the damn dog." You struggle to control your breathing, struggle not to cry. "All right, look, you've made yourself clear. I'll leave. I'll go home."

"You'll do no such thing!"

You close your eyes. "Then what do you want me to do? Stay here, knowing you hate me?"

"I don't hate you! You hate me! If you didn't hate me, you wouldn't be threatening to leave!" He gets up and throws his napkin down on the table; it lands in the gravy boat. Before leaving the room, he turns and says, "I'm sleeping in the guestroom tonight."

"Fine," you tell him dully. He leaves, and you discover that you're trembling, shaking the way a terrier would, or a poodle. Not a wolf.

Well. He's made himself very plain. You get up, clear away the uneaten dinner you spent all afternoon cooking, and go upstairs to your bedroom. Yours, now: not Jonathan's anymore. You change into jeans and a sweatshirt. You think about taking a hot bath, because all your bones ache, but if you allow yourself to relax into warm water, you'll fall apart; you'll dissolve into tears, and there are things you have to do. Your bones aren't aching just because your marriage has ended; they're aching because the transition is coming up, and you need to make plans before it starts.

So you go into your study, turn on the computer, call up an Internet travel agency. You book a flight back home for ten days from today, when you'll definitely be back on two feet again. You charge the ticket to your credit card. The bill will arrive here in another month, but by then you'll be long gone. Let Jonathan pay it.

Money. You have to think about how you'll make money, how much money you'll take with you—but you can't think about it now. Booking the flight has hit you like a blow. Tomorrow, when Jonathan's at work, you'll call Diane and ask her advice on all of this. You'll tell her you're going home. She'll probably ask you to come stay with her, but you can't, because of the transitions. Diane, of all the people you know, might understand, but you can't imagine summoning the energy to explain.

It takes all the energy you have to get yourself out of the

study, back into your bedroom. You cry yourself to sleep, and this time Jonathan's not even across the mattress from you. You find yourself wondering if you should have handled the dinner conversation differently, if you should have kept yourself from yelling at him about the turds in the yard, if you should have tried to seduce him first, if—

The ifs could go on forever. You know that. You think about going home. You wonder if you'll still know anyone there. You realize how much you'll miss your garden, and you start crying again.

Tomorrow, first thing, you'll call Diane.

But when tomorrow comes, you can barely get out of bed. The transition has arrived early, and it's a horrible one, the worst ever. You're in so much pain you can hardly move. You're in so much pain that you moan aloud, but if Jonathan hears, he doesn't come in. During the brief pain-free intervals when you can think lucidly, you're grateful that you booked your flight as soon as you did. And then you realize that the bedroom door is closed, and that Jessie won't be able to open it herself. You need to get out of bed. You need to open the door.

You can't. The transition's too far advanced. It's never been this fast; that must be why it hurts so much. But the pain, paradoxically, makes the transition seem longer than a normal one, rather than shorter. You moan, and whimper, and lose all track of time, and finally howl, and then, blessedly, the transition's over. You're on four feet.

You can get out of bed now, and you do, but you can't leave the room. You howl, but if Jonathan's here, if he hears you, he doesn't come.

There's no food in the room. You left the master bathroom toilet seat up, by chance, so there's water, full of interesting smells. That's good. And there are shoes to chew on, but they offer neither nourishment nor any real comfort. You're hungry. You're lonely. You're afraid. You can smell Jonathan in the room—in the shoes, in the sheets, in the clothing in the closet—but Jonathan himself won't come, no matter how much you howl.

And then, finally, the door opens. It's Jonathan. "Jessie," he says. "Poor Jessie. You must be so hungry; I'm sorry." He's carrying your leash; he takes your collar out of your underwear drawer and puts it on you and attaches the leash, and you think you're going for a walk now. You're ecstatic. Jonathan's going to walk you again. Jonathan still loves you.

"Let's go outside, Jess," he says, and you dutifully trot down the stairs to the front door. But instead he says, "Jessie, this way. Come on, girl," and leads you on your leash to the family room at the back of the house, to the sliding glass doors that open onto the back yard. You're confused, but you do what Jonathan says. You're desperate to please him. Even if he's no longer quite Stella's husband, he's still Jessie's alpha.

He leads you into the backyard. There's a metal pole in the middle of the backyard. That didn't used to be there. Your canine mind wonders if it's a new toy. You trot up and sniff it, cautiously, and as you do, Jonathan clips one end of your leash onto a ring in the top of the pole.

You yip in alarm. You can't move far; it's not that long a leash. You strain against the pole, the leash, the collar, but none of them give; the harder you pull, the harder the choke collar makes it for you to breathe. Jonathan's still next to you, stroking you, calm, reassuring. "It's okay, Jess. I'll bring you food and water, all right? You'll be fine out here. It's just for tonight. Tomorrow we'll go for a nice long walk, I promise."

Your ears perk up at "walk," but you still whimper. Jonathan brings your food and water bowls outside and puts them within reach.

You're so glad to have the food that you can't think about being lonely or afraid. You gobble your Alpo, and Jonathan strokes your fur and tells you what a good dog you are, what a beautiful dog, and you think maybe everything's going to be all right, because he hasn't stroked you this much in months, hasn't spent so much time talking to you, admiring you.

Then he goes inside again. You strain towards the house, as much as the choke collar will let you. You catch occasional glimpses of Jonathan, who seems to be cleaning. Here he is dusting the picture frames: here he is running the vacuum cleaner. Now he's cooking—beef stroganoff, you can smell it—and now he's lighting candles in the dining room.

You start to whimper. You whimper even more loudly when a car pulls into the driveway on the other side of the house, but you stop when you hear a female voice, because you want to hear what it says.

"So terrible that your wife left you. You must be devastated."

"Yes, I am. But I'm sure she's back in Europe now, with her family. Here, let me show you the house." And when he shows her the family room, you see her: in her twenties, with long black hair and perfect skin. And you see how Jonathan looks at her, and you start to howl in earnest.

"*Jesus,*" Jonathan's guest says, peering out at you through the dusk. "What the hell *is* that? A wolf?"

"My sister's dog," Jonathan says. "Husky-Wolfhound mix. I'm taking care of her while my sister's away on business. She can't hurt you: don't be afraid." And he touches the woman's shoulder to silence her fear, and she turns towards him, and they walk into the dining room. And then, after a while, the bedroom light flicks on, and you hear laughter and other noises, and you start to howl again.

You howl all night, but Jonathan doesn't come outside. The neighbors yell at Jonathan a few times—*Shut that dog up, goddammit!*—but Jonathan will never come outside again. You're going to die here, tethered to this stake.

But you don't. Towards dawn you finally stop howling; you curl up and sleep, exhausted, and when you wake up the sun's higher and Jonathan's coming through the open glass doors. He's carrying another dish of Alpo, and he smells of soap and shampoo. You can't smell the woman on him.

You growl anyway, because you're hurt and confused. "Jessie," he says. "Jessie, it's all right. Poor beautiful Jessie. I've been mean to you, haven't I? I'm so sorry."

He does sound sorry, truly sorry. You eat the Alpo, and he strokes you, the same way he did last night, and then he unsnaps your leash from the pole and says, "Okay, Jess, through the gate into the driveway, okay? We're going for a ride."

You don't want to go for a ride. You want to go for a walk. Jonathan promised you a walk. You growl.

"Jessie! Into the car, *now*! We're going to another meadow, Jess. It's farther away than our old one, but someone told me he saw rabbits there, and he said it's really big. You'd like to explore a new place, wouldn't you?"

You don't want to go to a new meadow. You want to go to the old meadow, the one where you know the smell of every tree and rock. You growl again.

"Jessie, you're being a *very bad dog*! Now get in the car. Don't make me call Animal Control."

You whine. You're scared of Animal Control, the people who wanted to take you away so long ago, when you lived in that other county. You know that Animal Control kills a lot of animals, in that county and in this one, and if you die as a wolf, you'll stay a wolf. They'd never know about Stella. As Jessie, you'd have no way to protect yourself except your teeth, and that would only get you killed faster.

So you get into the car, although you're trembling.

In the car, Jonathan seems more cheerful. "Good Jessie. Good girl. We'll go to the new meadow and chase balls now, eh? It's a big meadow. You'll be able to run a long way." And he tosses a new tennis ball into the backseat, and you chew on it, happily, and the car drives along, traffic whizzing past it. When you lift your head from chewing on the ball, you can see trees, so you put your head back down, satisfied, and resume chewing. And then the car stops, and Jonathan opens the door for you, and you hop out, holding your ball in your mouth.

This isn't a meadow. You're in the parking lot of a low concrete building that reeks of excrement and disinfectant and fear, fear, and from the building you hear barking and howling, screams of misery, and in the parking lot are parked two white Animal Control trucks.

You panic. You drop your tennis ball and try to run, but Jonathan has the leash, and he starts dragging you inside the building, and you can't breathe because of the choke collar. You cough, gasping, trying to howl. "Don't fight, Jessie. Don't fight me. Everything's all right."

Everything's not all right. You can smell Jonathan's desperation, can taste your own, and you should be stronger than he is but you can't breathe, and he's saying "Jessie, don't bite me, it will be worse if you bite me, Jessie," and the screams of horror still swirl from the building and you're at the door now, someone's opened the door for Jonathan, someone says, "Let me help you with that dog," and you're scrabbling on the concrete, trying to dig your claws into the sidewalk just outside the door, but there's no purchase, and they've dragged you inside, onto the linoleum, and everywhere are the smells and sounds of terror. Above your own whimpering you hear Jonathan saying, "She jumped the fence and threatened my girlfriend, and then she tried to bite me, so I have no choice, it's such a shame, she's always been such a good dog, but in good conscience I can't—"

You start to howl, because he's lying, *lying*, you never did any of that!

Now you're surrounded by people, a man and two women, all wearing colorful cotton smocks that smell, although faintly, of dog shit and cat pee. They're putting a muzzle on you, and even though you can hardly think through your fear—and your pain, because Jonathan's walked back out the door, gotten into the car and driven away, Jonathan's *left* you here—even with all of that, you know you don't dare bite or snap. You know your only hope is in being a good dog, in acting as submissive as possible. So you whimper, crawl along on your stomach, try to roll over on your back to show your belly, but you can't, because of the leash.

"Hey," one of the women says. The man's left. She bends down to stroke you. "Oh, God, she's so scared. Look at her."

"Poor thing," the other woman says. "She's *beautiful*."

"I know."

"Looks like a wolf mix."

"I know." The first woman sighs and scratches your ears, and you whimper and wag your tail and try to lick her hand through the muzzle. Take me home, you'd tell her if you could talk. Take me home with you. You'll be my alpha, and I'll love you forever. I'm a *good* dog.

The woman who's scratching you says wistfully, "We could adopt her out in a minute, I bet."

"Not with that history. Not if she's a biter. Not even if we had room. You know that."

"I know." The voice is very quiet. "Wish I could take her myself, though."

"Take home a biter? Lily, you have kids!"

Lily sighs. "Yeah, I know. Makes me sick, that's all."

"You don't need to tell me that. Come on, let's get this over with. Did Mark go to get the room ready?"

"Yeah."

"Okay. What'd the owner say her name was?"

"Stella."

"Okay. Here, give me the leash. Stella, come. Come on, Stella."

The voice is sad, gentle, loving, and you want to follow it, but you fight every step, anyway, until Lily and her friend have to drag you past the cages of other dogs, who start barking and howling again, whose cries are pure terror, pure loss. You can hear cats grieving, somewhere else in the building, and you can smell the room at the end of the hall, the room to which you're getting inexorably closer. You smell the man named Mark behind the door, and you smell medicine, and you smell the fear of the animals who've been taken to that room before you. But overpowering everything else is the worst smell, the smell that makes you bare your teeth in the muzzle and pull against the choke collar and scrabble again, helplessly, for a purchase you can't get on the concrete floor: the pervasive, metallic stench of death.

JANE YOLEN

❦

THE BARBARIAN AND THE QUEEN: THIRTEEN VIEWS

1.

DAX SAT ON THE EDGE OF HIS CHAIR, UNEASY WITH THE cushion at the back. His people always said that "Comfort is the enemy of the warrior." He was always most careful when he felt most at ease.

He clutched the porcelain cup with one of his death grips. It was only by chance that he did not break the cup and spill the contents—a special blend of Angoran and Basilien tea flavored with tasmairn seeds—down his leather pants. They were his best leather, sewn by his favorite wife. He did not want to stain them.

This queen of the New People who invited him to drink, this old woman with the face of a frog. Did she mean him to come and discuss peace? Or did she mean to threaten more war?

He looked into the cup and saw the black leaves thick as bog at the bottom.

She meant him to die, then.

I will not, he thought—slowly drawing out his long blade—*go to the dark lands alone.*

2.

Prince Henry sat next to his mother and stared at the barbarian who perched on the edge of his seat, one enormous hairy hand wrapped around a teacup.

Rather like a vulture on a cliff's edge, Prince Henry thought. *Except, of course, for the teacup.*

"Excuse me, sir," Prince Henry said, "but why don't you lean back in the chair. You look terribly uncomfortable."

The barbarian grunted, a sound quite like the sound Prince Henry's prize pig made in labor.

"Comfortable warrior," the barbarian said in his grunt voice, "dead warrior."

"Yes, of course. But no one here is actually trying to kill you," Prince Henry said sensibly.

The barbarian stood up suddenly and looked about with hooded eyes. His muscles bunched alarmingly.

"He means," Prince Henry's mother put in tactfully, "that he must at all times be on his guard so as not to get into bad habits. And Henry—you do know about bad habits, don't you?"

Satisfied that no enemies were coming up from behind, the barbarian sat again. On the edge of the chair.

The queen smiled and poured some of the tasmairn-laced tea into the cup. She never showed—even for a moment—that she feared the barbarian might crush the cup, and it one of an important set sent to her by her godmother, the Sultana.

"Sugar?"

Prince Henry was too young to be impressed with his mother's calm demeanor. But he knew better than to say anything more. Bad habits was a subject best left unexplored.

3.

She crossed and uncrossed her legs three times just to hear the stockings squeak. She'd never actually owned a pair before, having to make due with drawing lines down the back of her legs. But then all the girls did that. At least they'd done it through the war. No one had ever known the difference. And since she had the best-looking legs in her little town, she'd never actually felt the need for the real thing.

Before now, that is.

She made the squeak again.

Catching a glimpse of herself in the full-length mirror, she checked her shoulder-length blonde hair.

"Looking good, Babs," she said, and winked at the reflection and took a sip of tea from the little pink flower cup. God, how she could have used a slug of something stronger.

Just then the queen came into the room and Babs stood at once. They had taught her well, all those nameless servants. And she was a fast learner, as long as it wasn't school stuff.

She wobbled ever so slightly on the high heels. Those were new for her, too, the height of them. But with the money the servants had doled out, she knew she had to have them. It made her taller than the prince, but then he didn't seem to mind.

The queen stood at the door waiting for something. A bow maybe. But Babs knew her rights. She was an American and they didn't need to bow to any old queen. Still she gave a quick little bob just in case.

"So you are this Barbie character," the queen said, looking down her long nose. "The girl my son has been seeing. The girl everyone is talking about." She said the word *everyone* as if it were dirty somehow. But necessary.

"I'm called Babs, your majesty."

"Babs? Don't be ridiculous. Babs is a cow's name." The queen signaled for her tea to be served. "I shall call you Barbie." She sat down on a chair that was covered with a fine raw silk the color of old milk.

Babs caught another glimpse of herself in the mirror before sitting. Every golden hair was in place and her mouth was drawn on perfectly. On the other hand, the queen—with her long nose and bulging eyes, her dowdy dress and her blue hair—the queen was a mess.

And who's the cow here? Babs thought, crossing her legs slowly so that the queen could hear every little squeak.

4.

Queen Victoria stared over the flowered teacup at her new Prime Minister. Her nose twitched but she did not sniff at him. It would not do. *He* was the barbarian, not she. All Jews were barbarians. Eastern, oily, brilliant, full of dark unpronounceable magic. However long they lived in England, they remained different, apart, unknowable. She did not trust him. She *could* not trust him. But she would never say so.

"More tea, Mr. Disraeli?"

Disraeli smiled an alarmingly brilliant smile, and nodded. His lips moved but no words—no English words—could be heard. Across the rosewood table the queen slowly melted like butter on a hot skillet. A few more cabalistic phrases and she reformed into a toad.

"Yes, please, ma'am," Disraeli answered.

The toad, wearing a single crown jewel in her head, poured the tea.

"Ribbet," she said clearly.

"I agree, ma'am," said Disraeli. "I entirely agree." With a single word he turned her back. It was not an improvement. Such small distractions amused him on these state visits. He could not say as much for the queen.

5.

The queen had turned three that morning and had not gotten what she wanted for her birthday. At the moment she was lying on the floor and holding her royal breath and turning quite blue.

In any other household, Nanny Brown would have paddled her charge swiftly on her lovely pink bottom. Such a tempting target right now, on the Caucasian Dragon carpet. But one does not paddle a royal bottom whatever the cause.

Nanny Brown sighed and, holding the dimity cup filled with tasmairn tea—the best thing for her headaches—leaned back against the rocker waiting for the tantrum to wear itself out.

"I . . . want . . . a . . . barbarian," the little queen had screamed before flinging herself down.

Nanny Brown knew that tame barbarians from the Eastern Steppes were all the rage these days. Most castles had one or two. But the regent had said no.

And when that piece of "ordure" ("Best say shite where one means shite," Mr. Livermore, the butler, had told her, but she could never let such a word pass her lips) said no to something that the little queen wanted . . .

"Well, he does not have to deal with her tantrums," Nanny Brown said under her breath.

The tantrum finally passed, of course. They always did. The queen sat up, her face the color of one of her dear dead mother's prize roses. Her golden ringlets, so lovingly twirled around Nanny Brown's finger not an hour since, were now wet little yellow tangles. The lower lip stuck out more than was strictly necessary.

"Oh, Nanny," she cried. "My tummy hurts. I think I am going to swallow up again."

"Come to Nanny," Nanny Brown said. She put down the cup, the tasmairn having once again worked wonders, and held her arms out wide. "And I shall tell you a story about a big bad wolf. So much better than any old smelly barbarian, don't you think?" That was safe. They had a wolf down in the private zoo and she could spin out the tale till the little queen fell asleep and they could visit it after her nap. Wolves always went down well with this one.

The little queen stood up and wriggled into Nanny Brown's ample lap, her big, blue eyes still pooling.

"A story, Nanny," she said, "I want my story."

"And so you shall have it, my dove," said Nanny Brown, setting the rocker into motion.

The queen put her thumb in her mouth, like a stopper in a perfume bottle.

The barbarian was forgotten.

6.

The Barbarian, waist a solid 44, pecs nicely sculpted by recent days at the Uptown Gym, this week's special at $25 if you sign up the full year and use the coupons from Safeway, wrapped his hamfist around the dimity cup of tea carefully because the cup was frigging hot. He could smell the mint leaves and something else as well, maybe a touch of tasmairn? Good for what ails you and then some, as his old aunt used to say, his mother's sister still in the old country or cuntry as Cappy put it. He'd always drink tasmairn tea. As long as there was nothing else added. Nothing—you know—illegal. Like some guys always wanted you to try. They tested you these days after every match. He couldn't afford to be ruled off. Not with the house payment coming due. And wanting to buy Jolie a real ring for putting up with him without complaints or at least not a lot for so many years.

But this Queen dame who was fronting money for his training was—Cappy said—an angel come from somewhere real far away, Connecticut maybe, or Maine. Wanting to be part of the action. And he had to see her for tea. She said a drink but Cappy said not during training though he longed for a single malt something from Scotland where his mother— God Rest her—had come from and even eighty years later had a brogue could flay the skin off your cheeks. The ones both sides of your nose and the other ones as well.

This Queen character wanted to know what she was buy-ing for her cash, touch the bod a bit, he guessed, the dames who came to watch him always wanted that. Jolie didn't mind; she was used to it as long as it wasn't anywhere seri-ous. An arm, a calf, maybe even a thigh, though not higher or Jolie really would kill him and if she left what would be-come of him he didn't know but probably like some old cau-liflower fighter just hang around the gym not knowing his ass from . . . from a teacup.

He smiled, glad he'd put in the new bridge so the spaces between his teeth didn't show. And the colored lenses which he wore out of the ring but not in since a good blow to the head could lose them and them worth a small fortune being colored and all not like glasses which were twelve bucks at Safeway if you could find one to fit. Turned his head slightly to look at her, the Queen character, out of the corner of his eye. Jolie liked that, said it was cute which given he weighed in at 388 was something he supposed.

And the Queen smiled back, only her teeth were odd— even pointed like, even filed if he didn't know better. Not Connecticut then, or Maine. Somewhere across the pond maybe. Her accent was strange. Maybe Brooklyn, maybe fur-ther away. And he didn't or wouldn't ever know better be-cause she leaned into him, over him, those teeth in his throat and razoring down to his belly, slitting him open, the hot intestines falling out like so many sausages, her eyes glittering, and he never laid a hand, Jolie, he swore. Or a hold. Nothing serious at all, so who was the barbarian now?

7.

Since coming from East Jersey, the barbarian had been forced to be tea-total, and never more so than when he had drinks with the Queen. She, poor mad thing, was once again AA-ed and—he knew—that meant T. Really, things were better be-fore alphabet soup had been invented. He remembered fondly his illiterate days on the steppes and the fermented yak dung. It was why he liked Lapsang Souchong, it had the same slightly smoky, yakky taste. Not this tasmairn stuff. Crap with a capital K.

"Drink up, Queenie," he said to her, lifting the cup, the one with all the letters on it.

She raised her flower-sprigged cup back at him. It did— he thought—suit her to a T.

8.

Boobs the Barbarian sat and spread her thighs to let in a little breeze. Leather was hot this time of year, but the customers demanded it.

She'd been weeks without a paying gig, and this one— dancing for Randy Queen's birthday party—was easily a C-note, not counting tips, and could pay off her week's rent and with some over. Maybe get some new hardware. Her sword was looking a bit thin. The costumer who'd made it for her three years ago was out of business now. But a new place had opened up just down the street, promising fine edges and light-weights. She could do with a lighter blade.

The tea in her floral cup had gone cold, but she drank it anyway. Then she swirled her finger in the sugar at the bottom and sucked on the finger. A good sugar high right now was what she needed to get through the next couple of hours.

Behind the door the music started.

Usually she liked to dance to *Carmina Burana*, but this was a strictly bump-and-grind crowd, the men already well oiled and eager for some hot stuff. Which she could do, of course.

Hot.

The leather.

The tea.

And me, she thought.

Flinging the cup over her shoulder for luck—she hated those little sprigged flowers anyway—she stood and started for the kitchen door. As she walked, already swaying to the music, she began to loosen the strings on her jerkin.

When she strode into the room, the roar of the men was nearly overpowering. But with a smile, she drew her sword and quieted them all.

9.

The sky over Venice was the deep blue of a glass bead. No stars. No moon.

Ned Robertson shrugged his shoulders, and the costume he was wearing felt heavy and ill-fitting. *Like an old boot*, he thought.

When he had complained, the costumer had smiled a gap-tooth smile and said, "All barbarian costumes fit like dis, signor. Otherwise they would not be barbary. You capice?" Though of course his English was atrocious and Ned had had to talk rather more loudly to make him understand.

I should have worn a Pierrot, he thought. *Chalk to cheese.* Instead he had let Sofia talk him into the leather. She'd run her hand over his shoulder, down his back, and whispered in his ear, "I love the feel of this stuff."

He should have let *her* wear the leather.

Venice was too hot for such a costume on a man.

Sofia, of course, was dressed like Marie Antoinette, in a wig that made her almost as tall as he was. She was such a pretty little thing, a pocket Venus as his mother used to say.

He cursed the leather costume, the heat of Venice, his new wife's towering wig.

But what's a man to do?

He put on the mask with its permanent smile and went downstairs.

There were at least ten Marie Antoinettes in the milling tour group, and a dozen Pierrots. He could not see Sofia in the crowd.

But evidently all the Marie Antoinettes could see him. Or

some part of him, anyway. For suddenly they were all laughing behind their fans and pointing and the Pierrots made a series of awful jokes at his expense.

Bugger this, he thought, and ran back upstairs where he shed the leather skins and swore he would not go back down there again.

Not for all the tasmairn tea in China.

10.

Dar sat uneasily by the northern queen and stared at the black spot high up on her cheekbone. It was not a god-spot, which all his wives had. It looked like a bit of a petal stuck there. He wondered if he should point it out to her. He wondered if such things mattered to these brittle creatures from the north.

She lowered one eyelid at him.

Among his people, such a thing meant she wanted to fuck. But did it mean the same here? He did not want to offend. Not now. Not when his people and hers were deep in negotiations for the passage across the Great River. The cattle were unsettled and lowing their misery. As were his wives. He had to be certain.

There. She did it again.

Dar hesitated.

But then her unshod foot touched his under the table, the toes slowly rubbing up his leg, past the calf, along the inside of the thigh.

There was no mistaking her desire.

Dar stood up quickly, upended the table, teapot, flowered cups, and sachets of tea. Reaching the queen in a single step, he grabbed her up, flipped her over, slammed her onto the ground, and raised the massive skirts over her head. Momentarily flummoxed by the thing that hid her bum, he solved that problem by ripping the soft material apart.

Then he entered her.

She was harder than his wives, harder than any of his

sheep. But she opened to him at last and let out only one stifled cry.

Dar was sure it was a cry of pleasure.

11.

EXT: HAMPTON COURT, day, 17th century

A COACH comes up the drive, driven by two HORSES. FOOTMEN run out and open the door. TWO COURTIERS in capes descend. They help out a YOUNG WOMAN dressed in the latest Elizabethan fashion. She is dark skinned. Her black hair is in braids. The COURTIERS, of course, are powdered whiter than white and wear wigs. The COURTIERS and YOUNG WOMAN all enter the building.

INT: PRESENCE ROOM. Even though it is day, there are torches and candles everywhere. QUEEN ELIZABETH I, well past middle age, her face whitened with powder, sits on a high carved chair on a dais, a large goblet decorated with flowers in her hand. She is speaking to SIR ROBERT CECIL, a middle-aged scribe/politician.

ELIZABETH

Is she a barbarian?

CECIL
(Cautiously)
How does one measure barbarity, Majesty?

ELIZABETH
(Testily)
Do not play words with me, Cecil. You will not win the game. Does she wear skins? Does she have a bone through her nose? Does she eat her enemies?

CECIL
(Bowing slowly, languidly)
She wears skins in her own home, Majesty. Here she is dressed in the latest fashion. There is no bone through her nose. And as far as I know, she does not cannibalize her neighbors.

ELIZABETH
(She sighs, looks bored, takes a sip from the cup)

CECIL
She does, however, use bear grease in her hair.

ELIZABETH
(Looking up eagerly)
Does she smell?

DOOR bursts open and TWO COURTIERS from the carriage march in, stop, bow. FIRST COURTIER waves in the dark-skinned YOUNG WOMAN to stand by him. He takes her by the hand and forces her to bow.

ELIZABETH
(Looking interested, leans forward)
Come here. Come here, child.

FIRST COURTIER pushes the young woman forward. The SECOND COURTIER with a flourish and bow, speaks.

SECOND COURTIER
She is a princess in her own country, Majesty.

ELIZABETH
(Aside to Cecil)

Better and better, Cecil. You did not tell me she was a barbarian *princess*.

CECIL
(Recovering quickly; clearly this is news to him)

It was meant to be a surprise, Majesty. I see we have been
successful.

ELIZABETH
(Putting the goblet down on a side table)

What is your name, my lady?

YOUNG WOMAN
(Turns and looks at the two men for translation)

FIRST COURTIER
(He speaks in her own language a quick sentence)

YOUNG WOMAN
(Speaking directly to Elizabeth)

Pocahontas.

ELIZABETH
(Bringing a pomander ball to her nose)

Have her come closer. I would smell her.

FIRST COURTIER
(Speaking to Young Woman)

Go. Forward. Now.

YOUNG WOMAN goes reluctantly up to the steps of
the dais and when signaled by ELIZABETH, goes up
the three steps to stand by the queen.

ELIZABETH takes the pomander from her nose for a moment, then sniffs YOUNG WOMAN, who, in turn, sniffs her.

Young Woman
(Turns and speaks to the First Courtier)
Feh! Feh! Feh!

Elizabeth
What did she say? What did she say?

Cecil
(Trying hard not to laugh)
Oh, I think she was perfectly clear, Majesty. She says you smell!

<Note to Producer—Pocahontas was actually brought to England during the reign of King James I, several years after Elizabeth died. But I doubt the public will know this. Or care.>

12.

Do not, I beg thee, make me wait too long.
True love should yield the ground with little fight.
We stand here taking count of what is wrong,
When all but sense and reason have ta'en flight.
Then send them off, thy soldiers standing guard,
That all unrobed, thy beauty might be seen,
Till crying pax I come across your sward,
Barbarian to his unresisting queen.
Fling now the castle gates full open wide,
And with your fingers, offer up the store
That others have all cautioned you to hide;
Your royal jewels I richly will adore.
Pray let me roam your countryside full free
So that by love alone I ravage thee.

13.

Grax sat uneasily on the synth-hide stool waiting for the queen. He drank tea because, after a night of bar-hopping, from the Wet End to the White Horse, his stomach was tied up, knotted as neatly as a sailor's rope.

Running his fingers over the tensed muscles, he groaned. He could hear the tea gurgling inside, complaining like the river Dee in full flood. In the diner's mirror, his face was reflected back with a green tinge.

The queen would notice such things. *Mean and green*, she'd probably say. If he was lucky she wouldn't sing.

He took another sip out of the chipped white cup with the flower decals all along the rim. By-the-Powers-Tetley, he could have used something stronger. Blackberry maybe. He whispered to himself:

> "Blackberry,
> Bayberry,
> Thistle and thorn.
> You'll rue the day
> That you were born."

But she'd smell it on him and say something. Her word alone could make his stomachache last a full month.

When he took his third sip, she was there, sitting on a stool next to him as if it were a throne. Her hair was gold today and piled in a high crown, her lips rowanberry red.

"New in town, sailor?" she asked lightly. "What's a nice barbarian like you doing in a place like this?"

He knew she didn't expect an answer. Not from a barbarian.

"Give us a kiss."

He did what was expected, on the cheek. But her cheek was rough, the beard already beginning to show through the rouge. It surprised him. She never used to be so careless.

"By the Green, Mab!" he said, incautiously. "I thought you could do a better job than that."

She smiled sadly at him. "The grid is going, Grax. The Magic is failing. An old queen just doesn't have the power to fool anymore."

He put down his cup and held her hands. "It doesn't matter," he said, and meant it. "It doesn't matter to me."

But of course it did matter, which is why Mab had come to him.

"You shall put the grid aright," she said. "A day's work."

A week at least, he knew. *And an eternity if I get it wrong.* But he didn't say it aloud. Some things were best left unsaid, lest the wrong ears hear them. He said only what was expected. "I will go, my queen."

She smiled at him. There was a gap between her top front teeth that hadn't been there before. And a pimple on the side of her nose.

Oh-oh, mused Grax, *the grid is in worse shape than I thought.* He stood, bowed quickly, and was gone.

Mab watched him till he was no more than a point on the horizon, then sighed.

The counterman leaned over and said, "Mab, he's not the best any more."

She turned and raised an eyebrow. "He's all there is, Sil."

The counterman ran a nervous hand through his shaggy locks and rubbed one of his button horns. "What about Dar? What about Babs? What about . . ."

"Gone," she said with an awful sigh that fluttered the wings of three pigeons in a nearby park. "All gone." Then she put her head on the counter and cried, her tears making deep runnels in her makeup, for once something was gone from her, it was gone from all the world.

GREG VAN EEKHOUT

WOLVES TILL THE WORLD GOES DOWN

My brother and I flew recon over the gray Santa
Monica beach, half-frozen rain striking our black feathers. Below, a skater swaddled in Gore-Tex swished around the curves
of the bike path, while surfers in wetsuits bobbed in the dark
waters.

It was the coldest winter on record in southern California.
It was the coldest winter everywhere.

"Hey," said my brother. "Down there." Without waiting,
he dove toward the sand where a dead Rottweiler rolled in
the white foam. It had been a long flight and we were both
ravenous. I angled in to follow, and soon we were absorbed
in our feast.

A big gray gull challenged our salvage rights, screaming
and beating us with his wings, but we tore him to shreds, ate
him, then returned to the dog.

Later, my brother would be able to report every little detail of the incident. He'd describe the precise markings on

the gull's bill, the way he favored his left foot over his right, the iron and salt taste of his blood.

But he wouldn't be able to say *why* we'd killed him. He's expert at the *whats* and *whens* and *wheres*, but he leaves the *whys* to me.

His name is Munin, Memory. I'm Hugin, Thought.

Our hunger satisfied, we took to the skies again and continued south over the T-shirt shops and sunglass stands of Venice Boardwalk. When we reached the storm-shattered pier, we turned seaward, onward, away and beyond.

We heard a blue whale sing its last song before dying of old age. We watched an undiscovered species of fish go extinct. And we saw something enormous on the ocean floor, slithering on its belly and churning waves hundreds of fathoms above.

We flew and flew, carefully observing and cataloguing so that later we could give our boss, Odin, an accurate report. But first we had a special appointment to keep.

Well past the horizons of Midgard we came upon the shores of the dead. Hel is a dry place. It's a land of gray plains and twigs and dust. And in the center of this land there lived a pair of slain gods. We found them reclining atop the roof of a great timber hall, passing a cup back and forth.

The poets used to say that Baldr was so good and pure he radiated white light, a sun compressed into human form. There used to be something about him, something that, when he walked by, made a man put down his drinking horn or stop hammering trolls for a second and just be glad he was alive to witness the moment. You knew that Baldr, somehow, was what the whole thing was about.

He was still beautiful, but not the same. Now he was cold and magisterial, a god of glaciers and dark stone mountains. He rose to his feet and announced our arrival to his brother.

Höd was a much humbler creature, thinner in the shoulder, longer in the face, his shriveled eyes lost in dark sockets.

You really didn't want to look into those sockets. They went a long way down.

We landed on Baldr's outstretched forearms and dug our talons in a little to see if he'd flinch. He didn't, of course. Even exiled from the realms of the living, he was still a god. "Just when I was thinking you wouldn't come," he said. "I'm glad to see you. Let's go inside."

Getting welcomed to Hel isn't such an enormous thrill, but I politely thanked him anyway.

His hall was cold and dimly lit. Pale flames wavered in the hearth, their light barely pushing back the shadows. A long table bore a modest feast—a few loaves of bread, a pair of emaciated roast pigs.

Munin perched on the edge of the table and appraised the fare. "I guess it's a good thing we already ate."

Höd's jaw muscles clenched. "If you'd like to contribute to the meal, I can start plucking feathers right now."

Baldr laughed. "Brother," he said in his gentle voice, "we observe hospitality in my house."

I think Höd would have rolled his eyes had he been capable.

At the end of the table sat a plump old woman in a purple sweatshirt. The shopping cart beside her was filled with empty soup cans, magazines, rotting batteries, a sword hilt, a broken car antenna. Over her matted gray hair she wore a Minnesota Vikings cap. She clutched a long twig in her left hand.

"Sibyl," I said, nodding respectfully. I hadn't seen the witch-prophetess in a long time. Not since the world was younger and greener, when, in exchange for a meal, she'd told Odin how the world would end.

"There is an ash tree," she said now. "Its name is Yggdrasil. Lofty Yggdrasil, the Ash Tree, trembles, ancient wood groaning."

Not knowing if she was uttering an incantation or just making conversation, I indicated the twig with my wing. "Is that part of Yggdrasil?"

She shook the stick. "The world tree's an ash. Does this look like ash? Stupid bird."

Same old sibyl.

We sat around the table and picked at the skinny pigs for a while before Baldr asked us about affairs back in the land of men. Normally we report only to Odin, but how often do you get invited to Baldr's house? So Munin spoke of the weather on Midgard. Three winters, each colder and longer than the previous one, with little summer between. Floods, bad crops, people freezing in the streets, hoarding and price gouging and rioting and looting.

But Munin didn't say the *word*.

He didn't have to.

We all knew where this was heading: Ragnarök. The great monsters would do battle with the gods, and most of the gods would be slain. Heimdall. Hermod. Frey. Thor. Even Odin. A world without Odin. And the world itself would burn and crumble, and the ancient chaos that preceded us all would return. But from the ashes would rise the younger gods, and Baldr and Höd would end their exile in Hel to help them rebuild.

Munin went on and on, citing wind chill factors from CNN until Baldr put an end to his chatter. "Thank you, Munin," he said. "Most thorough. My father is lucky to have your counsel." He turned his gray eyes to me. "And you, Hugin, what will you tell Odin when next you see him?"

As if you didn't know, I almost said. But being Odin's agent has taught me to reflect before I speak. I'd play along for now. "I can tell you of two brothers," I said. "Like you and Höd, two sons of Odin." And there, in a vast dry hall situated at the center of Hel, with the sibyl worrying her twig, I told Baldr about an attempt to end the world.

Munin and I had watched the godling sons of Odin sail for many days and nights before they came to an island between worlds. As they neared the shore, Vidar threw the anchor over, jumped out and waded toward the beach. He was much like his father, lean and rangy with a voice that rarely rose above a dry whisper.

Vali was different. Forever a toddler, he scrambled over the gunwale and belly-flopped into the waves, thrashed about as he realized his feet couldn't touch the stony sea bottom, then gave a mighty kick that sent him flying through the air and onto the beach.

"Did you see?" he said, delighted. "I almost drowned!"

Vidar brushed sand off his half-brother's bottom. "I saw."

"I could have been killed!"

"Yes, you came perilously close to an untimely demise. Please follow, Vali. We have a task."

The beach sloped up sharply from the tide toward a towering wall of jagged basalt. The gods began to hike up the rise.

"Vidar, I'm hungry."

"Possibly because you didn't eat your supper?"

"Dried fish. I hate dried fish. I hate all fish."

"If I give you a piece of candy, will you be quiet?"

"No."

Vidar sighed and gave him a piece of candy anyway. All the gods in Asgard knew it was easier if you didn't anger Vali.

They reached the rock wall and began to climb.

"Vidar, tell me a story."

"Now is not the best time."

Vali pouted. "You better tell me a story, or I'll rip open your tummy and pull all the tubes out, and then I'll choke you with the tubes, and then I'll make you eat the tubes, and then I'll—"

Vidar closed his eyes. "Once upon a time there was—"

"There was a god named Baldr," Vali cut in. "And Frigg, his momma, loved him, and everybody loved him, and he was always very nice. So Frigg got everything in the world to make a promise—all the animals and flowers and birds and *every-*

thing—she asked everything to promise to never, ever, *ever* hurt Baldr."

A gust of wind picked up an unpleasant scent. Fur. Damp animal fur. Vidar continued the tale. "As you said, Vali, Mother Frigg exacted an oath from fire and water and metal and stones, and from earth and trees and beasts, from ailments and birds and poisons and serpents. She wrung a promise from every conceivable thing that it would do Baldr no harm. All except a young plant growing on the very skirts of Asgard, a small sprig of mistletoe. She felt it too small to be of any consequence."

Vali's grip slipped and he tumbled until a rock broke his fall. Vidar climbed down and retrieved him. "We don't have time for this," he said. "Climb on my back." They renewed the ascent, Vali riding piggyback.

"And so a game arose around Baldr's invulnerability," said Vidar. "He would stand at the highseat during assemblies, and the gods would hurl objects at him. Stones, spears, cauldrons of boiling water, wasp nests—all bounced off him and did no harm."

"But then Loki got all mad!" interrupted Vali. "And he put on ladies' clothes and tricked Frigg into telling him about the mistletoe. And there was Höd, and he was blind, and he couldn't play along, and Loki said, 'How come you're not playing?' And Höd said, 'I'm blind! They won't let me play.' And Loki said, 'That's not fair.' And he gave Höd the mistletoe, and said, 'Throw it! Throw it!' And Höd goes, 'I'm blind! I can't aim good.' But Loki helped him throw, and . . . and . . .'"

"Catch your breath, brother. And try not to choke me."

"Your turn!"

Vidar crested the wall and peered over the summit. In the center of the island loomed a great, dark shape. The son of Odin swallowed and began his descent down the other side of the wall. Vali leaped off his back and scrambled after him.

"I said it's your turn, Vidar."

Vidar's mouth set in a grim line. "The mistletoe pierced

Baldr's breast," he said. "And it was . . . it was horrible. How can I tell you what it was like? You never saw him, brother. The skalds say he was beautiful, but it was more than that. You know how when you look at Thor, he's like a great dark thundercloud stepped down from the sky to assume human shape. And Njord, he's like the sea itself, tidal waves crashing in his eyes. Baldr was like that. Only he personified everything that was . . . I don't know, good? Worthwhile?" Vidar paused there, hanging off the side of the rock wall, his face haunted. Even Vali took notice and preserved the silence. Then, finally, Vidar said, "He died. Right there in front of all of us. You could almost see the world change color. Nobody knew what to say or what to do. And the next day, we put him in his ship and sent him off to Hel. That's the last any of us saw of him. And ever since we've been living out the sibyl's prophecy. We, the great and mighty Aesir. Puppets."

Something at the foot of the wall made a noise. A low growl, a clank of metal.

"Come on," said Vidar. "Let's cut some strings." They jumped the last twenty feet to the ground. Vidar drew his sword and led the way to a shadowy, massive form chained to a boulder. It turned its blue, liquid eyes to the brothers and watched them approach.

"But you didn't tell the good part of the story," Vali wailed. "The part when All-Father Odin got mad at Höd for killing Baldr, because he loved Baldr best of anybody, so he and my momma had me, and when I was just one day old I jumped on Höd's chest and I put my arms around his throat and squeezed and squeezed and squeezed, and then he was dead and he had to go to Hel, too. You didn't tell that part."

"You told it very well, Vali. Now let's finish our job."

"Was she pretty?"

"Was *who* pretty?"

"My momma. Was she pretty?"

"Vali, she was a giant."

Vali stopped walking, his lip curling into a snarl.

Vidar sighed. "All right. All right. Words are insufficient to describe her gigantic beauty. She was the most lovely giantess that ever was. Yes? Will that do?"

That satisfied Vali. The little god squared his shoulders, puffed out his chest, and took the lead toward the monster at the center of the island.

Viewed head-on, the wolf was merely the size of an adult grizzly bear. But if you squinted just so and looked at it through the corner of your eye, it was larger. Larger than the island that contained it, large enough to dwarf the mountains, to swallow the sun and the moon.

Vidar put a hand on his brother's shoulder, holding him firm. "This is Fenrir Lokisson, the wolf. He and I are destined to do battle at Ragnarök. And I will kill him. But not before he destroys the sky."

The wolf's jaws were propped open by a sword, and its legs were bound by a silk ribbon connected by a chain to a boulder.

Vidar raised his sword high in the air. The wolf stared at him placidly, his slow breaths sending clouds of steam into the gloom.

The ribbon binding him was made of six true things, from the roots of a mountain to the breath of a fish.

But Vidar's sword was made of seven.

He brought the sword down, parting the air with a thunderclap and sending up a shower of sparks as the blade cut through the ribbon. Then he gingerly removed the sword gag from the wolf's mouth. One day, Fenrir would devour Vidar's own father. And now he was free.

"Kill him!" screamed Vali. "Give me the sword!" The child god lunged at the wolf, but Vidar grabbed him by the arms, restraining him.

Fenrir bowed his great back, stretched his forelegs out and yawned. He shook dust from his tail, then turned to Vidar. His mouth formed something of a smile. "That was unexpected. Why set me loose?"

Vidar shrugged. "We're tired of sitting around waiting for Ragnarök to happen."

"Ah," said the wolf. "I think I get it. Why wait for the fulfillment of the prophecy when you can ignite it yourself? Hasten the destruction of several billion men, trolls, elves, giants, gods, horses, dogs, what have you. Usher in a sea of blood and fire and pain the likes of which not even Odin can fully imagine. Just so you and your brother and the other little godlings can step out of the wings and take charge of the remains now. A plot worthy of Loki."

"Actually," said Vidar, "I was just anxious to get to the part of the story where I kill you."

"I'll see you later, then," said Fenrir with a laugh. He leaped into the sky, momentarily eclipsing the moon, before vanishing into the dark.

The gods started back to the boat, and Munin and I circled overhead for a time, watching them.

"Well," I said to Munin. "What do you think about that?"

He flapped his wings twice to gain altitude. "Thinking's your department."

With the shadows deepening in Baldr's hall, Höd picked at the scant remains of the pig on his platter and shook his head. "It seems entirely unacceptable to me that a psychopathic little toddler is due to inherit the world after the Great Battle."

"Is that an objective opinion?" I asked. "That has nothing to do with the fact that Vali slew you?"

"It has *everything* to do with the fact that he slew me! If I wrung your feathered neck today, would you want to sit in council with me tomorrow? What kind of working relationship would that be?"

I turned to Baldr. "Maybe you could answer that question. What do you make of it when Aesir try to bring about the end of one world, just so they can hurry up and start ruling over the next?" I so badly wanted Baldr to say he found it reprehensible. I wanted him to be angry with the young gods. I wanted him to tell me he wasn't like them at all.

He regarded me with an almost cynical smile. On his face, it was a sad thing to see. "Those gods are Odin's progeny. The same as Thor or Höd or myself. They're doing what we're all doing, what we've done for thousands of years—playing their role in this hideous prophecy. Only they realized it was possible to accelerate the process. I admire their initiative. It's something we've lacked for too long."

My feathers bristled. "They should be patient," I argued. "All they have to do is wait and they'll get what they want. Let things happen in the way they were meant to happen. The world ends, the gods and monsters fight, and the young gods inherit a new earth. They don't appreciate what a privilege that will be, to rule over something new and fresh and green. They don't appreciate what an honor that is." And now I looked hard into Baldr's gray eyes. "It's wrong to interfere with the prophecy."

The corners of Baldr's mouth curved up in a small smile. Folding his ice white hands on the table before him, he said, "What do you do, Hugin?"

I shifted my weight from one foot to the other and cocked my head sideways. "What do you mean?"

"I mean what do you *do*? You fly around and watch and analyze and calculate, and you whisper intelligence in Odin's ear. But do you actually *do* anything?" The hall had grown colder by many degrees as Baldr spoke. "Why do you judge those who have the courage to act, when you, Thought, have only the courage to think?"

Before I could devise a response, he turned his attention away from me and spoke to Munin. "Do you remember my funeral?"

"Of course. I'm Memory. I remember everything. Odin came with his Valkyries, and Frey came in a chariot drawn by a boar, and Freyja was there with her cats. Her dress was very pretty. And there were the trolls and elves, the mountain-giants and frost-giants. Everyone showed up. The Aesir wept. Thor kept blowing his nose, and it made a great *schnoork* sound that shook the leaves from the trees."

Leave it to Munin to remember the thunder of Thor clearing his nostrils. I remembered something else.

Odin the All-Father frightened me. In the dark hole left behind by his sacrificed eye, I saw his fear. He remembered the sibyl's prophecy from so long ago. She'd told him that Baldr would die, that his death would be the first step towards the doom of everything Odin had ever known. He'd always hoped that somehow the sibyl would be wrong. Sometimes witch babble is just witch babble. But now there was the shocking white corpse of Baldr, whom Odin loved not in the way a war god loves a warrior, but in the way a father loves a son.

That day, everything started to die.

I thought about some of the things Munin and I had seen recently. The world-spanning serpent who churned the waters and brewed tidal waves and hurricanes. Thor's son, Modi, had loosed him a week ago. And there was the Ship of Dead Men's Nails, freed of its moorings by the young god Magni. I thought of the bloodbath Midgard was becoming, with people killing each other over a can of ravioli. All the portents were coming true.

Bent over her twig, the sibyl muttered softly to herself. "And the serpent rises, and children drown in its wake, and the blood-beaked eagle rends corpses, screaming. Ragnarök, doom of the gods, doom of all. Battle-axe and sword rule, and an age of wolves, till the world goes down."

She spat upon the twig, and now it wasn't a twig at all, but a spear with smoking runes burned down its side. I didn't recognize them. She put the spear in Höd's hands.

Baldr nodded. "Tell me what Odin did at my funeral, Munin." He wasn't looking at Munin. He was looking at me.

"He laid the gold ring Draupnir on your chest," Munin

said. "And then he knelt at your side, brushed the hair off your forehead, just like he used to do when you were a boy. He whispered something in your ear."

"What did he whisper?"

Munin opened his beak, paused, shut it. He looked at me, and I shrugged. I didn't know either. On that awful day, Odin used his cunning and spoke in a voice not even I could hear.

The sibyl snorted. "I know what he said. I'm the one who gave him the words. And he had to say them, too. Didn't want to, but he had to. No choice. That was my price for giving him a heads-up about the future."

"Tell the ravens, please," said Baldr.

"This: The sibyl's magic can give you true death."

Baldr stood at the head of the table. "Now, Höd," he said.

"Wait," I squawked. "You're not really going to do this." Stupid, stupid bird. Baldr wasn't working with Vidar and Vali. He wasn't interested in freeing monsters. He wasn't trying to accelerate Ragnarök and end his days in Hel.

With a slight shudder, Höd rose to his feet. He fingered the mistletoe spear. "I don't want to do this," he said. "Not again. It's not fair. The prophecy says we get to live. That's what's supposed to happen. Not this."

Baldr's face darkened. "I thought we were agreed. Who are we to build a new world on the corpses of others?"

After a very long moment, Höd lifted the spear over his shoulder. He sighed. "I just . . . I just want to say thanks. For not ever being mad at me. Everybody else *hated* me for killing you. But you always treated me like a brother."

"It's all right," said Baldr. "You *are* my brother."

"This has all been for my benefit," I said to Baldr. "Mine and Munin's. That's why you sent for us. That's what this whole thing has been about."

Baldr nodded. "I wanted Odin to know what happened here tonight. I wanted him to know why I did it. I was always the first link in the chain. The most important link. Remove me, and the chain shatters. Send me to a true death. End my existence." Baldr closed his eyes. "Munin can tell Odin of my deed. But you, Hugin, you have to tell him . . . I don't know. You'll think of the right thing to tell him."

"I could tell him something right now," I said. "He'd never allow this. And if I don't stop to observe the world as I fly, I can be at his side before Höd lifts a finger."

"I know you can," said Baldr. "It would be very easy for you to do that."

I felt a tightness in my throat.

How often do you see a god defy the universe to save a world? How often do you realize that you can let it happen, or you can stop it? And how long do you have to think about it before you figure out the right thing to do?

Höd pulled the spear back a little farther and took a deep breath.

I took a deep breath, too.

"Your aim's too far right," I told him. "A little left. A little more. There."

Baldr smiled at me, this time with some of his old magic, and the hall seemed to warm, and I basked in him.

"Hey, wait!" said Munin. He was just now figuring it out. "Can they do this?"

I shushed him. "I think it'll be all right."

And Baldr stood there, his arms stretched out to his sides. And when the rune-burned mistletoe spear punched through his chest, he was laughing.

The world changed color again.

Munin and I left them there, Höd staring blindly at his hands, the sibyl reading her magazines. And Baldr, not just exiled from the living but truly and finally dead.

Later, after the long flight home, when we perched on Odin's shoulder and he asked us what we'd seen and heard, Munin told him everything in detail from his perfect memory. He told him of the break in the leaden clouds and the melting of the snow. He told him how we saw the great Fenrir wolf

slink back to his rock, frightened for the first time of an unknown future.

And me, Hugin, Thought, I told him that he had better
start making some plans.

Because Baldr had given us a whole new tomorrow.

And today, anything was possible.

GEOFFREY A. LANDIS

THE SECRET EGG
OF THE CLOUDS

IN THE DAWNING YEARS OF THE SECOND SPACE AGE, THE first human expedition to orbit the planet Venus gazed down on the pearl planet, and to their vast surprise, saw cities floating in the stratosphere, like swarms of sparkling jellyfish.

Quite clearly the cloud dwellers of Venus must once have possessed the means of space travel, though when the spacefarers of the second age came, they had no spaceships. The only possible explanation for the cloud dwellers' existence was that the planet had been settled by pioneers of the fabled first space age. The few surviving documents we have from the first age of spaceflight tell nothing of the founding of cities on Venus. But, writing as the ancients did in the form of magnetic impressions on fragile plastic films, much of the history of that complicated and contradictory age of wonders has been lost.

Great scholarly tomes can be written—have been written—about the floating sky cities of the clouded planet, with their transparent canopies of kilometer-wide diamond film to hold in a bubble of oxygen and nitrogen (which is a lighter-than-air mixture, considering that the atmosphere of the planet itself is carbon dioxide). The cities float in the upper atmosphere, far above the sulfurous pressure of the barren rocky surface, at a level where the atmosphere is cool, where the pressure is Earthlike, and the thinnest patina of cloud screens the too-bright sun. A hundred thousand iridescent cities float in the temperate zones of Venus, blowing around the planet with the stratospheric winds, each one a tiny human garden floating in the atmosphere of hell.

Why, indeed, would they be interested in spaceflight? If a boy should want to experience adventure, why, each city has its own culture and traditions, and it would take a thousand years to visit them all. And the landscape of the clouds has room for a thousand times more, should none of the cities be satisfactory.

It was a great disappointment to the scholars of Earth to find that the study of history was a concept alien to the cloud denizens. Much of our own history had been lost in the chaos and wars that followed the first space age, and scholars had hoped that the cloud denizens might have preserved a pristine history of those years.

The only hints come from two Earth anthropologists, Haafiza and Obaidullah Majumdar. When they asked what stories were told told by the people of the sky cities, they were answered that no, the people of the sky do not tell stories. But they persisted in asking about stories, even if they were only for children, and at last, the oldest of the old men admitted to knowing a story, and then the others admitted, that, yes, they, too, knew that story. This is the story that the anthropologists heard.

This is the story that is told to the children of the people of the sky.

In the time before the time that is now (the old man said), in the earliest of the early times when people lived on only one earth, there lived a thousand brothers, and each of the brothers had ten thousand sons. Of all the brothers, only the youngest was without children, and he worked for all the others. He plowed and cooked, hunted and fished, he built houses for his brothers, and for their children he invented clever toys.

Unbeknownst to one another, each brother had a secret egg.

With time, the earth became stripped and barren, and it became hard to find plenty, and the youngest took longer and longer to bring for the brothers less and less. A time came when one of the brothers grew greedy. This brother came to believe that he was wiser than the others, and his sons more deserving, and he decided that it was his right and his duty to rule over all the others. So he raised his secret egg over his head, and smashed it upon the ground. Out from the egg sprang a vast and terrible army, an army of beasts in the shape of men, with claws like curved swords, that would fight with no care of any wounds, for they were but beasts. And so this brother ruled the others.

He ruled for a long time, and the youngest served them all, but now served this one first of them all. Then another of the brothers thought, why should my brother rule me, and be served first, when it is I who am wiser than the others, and my children more deserving? And so this brother took his secret egg, and raised it over his head, and smashed it upon the ground. Out from the egg sprang a vast and terrible army, an army of machines in the shapes of men, with faceted eyes like glowing jewels, that could fight without tiring, for they had no souls. And so this brother's army fought the other brother's army, and, although the destruction was fearsome, in the end his army vanquished them, and so he ruled.

A third one among the brothers thought to himself, why should this brother rule, and not myself? And so he took his own secret egg, and smashed it, and out from the egg sprang a vast and terrible army, an army of insects with bright flashing wings. And another brother smashed his egg, and out from the egg sprang a vast and terrible army, an army of tornadoes in the shapes of men, with a huge singing roar. And another brother smashed his egg, and then yet another, and it came to pass that many brothers fought, and their armies were the more terrible because they had not souls, and had nothing to lose, and no way to ask or offer quarter.

The destruction made the youngest of the brothers sorrowful, for each army was more terrible than the last, and wherever they had fought, the earth was blasted and arid. In time even he, who had always been of cheerful disposition, grew to despair, and he took from its hiding place in his vest (for he always carried it with him) his own secret egg. The egg was beautiful and precious, for it was all that he had ever had of his own. But he raised it over his head and smashed it on the ground, and with a sound like a thousand thunderbolts, there sprang forth a vast and terrible army, too terrible even to describe. And the army, trembling with their eagerness for battle, waited for his orders, to tell them what they should destroy. He saw his army, and knew that with it he could destroy his brothers and their sons and their armies together. But instead he collected the broken pieces of the eggshell carefully, and then he told his army, lift me into the sky.

And so the army took him up and raised him to the sky, and when he was in the sky he took his army and folded them carefully back into the eggshell.

In the sky the clouds surrounded him, and cloud-monsters roared and threatened, but he was not fearful, for he knew that they were only air, and could do him no harm. He watched the clouds, and by careful study he winkled out their secrets. Using nothing but air to build with—for I told you that he was very clever—he made a city, to float in the air with the secret that is known by the clouds. But the city was empty.

One day, in his empty city, who should come to him but Grandmother Sky. Grandmother Sky was a daughter of those who went before. Now, it happened that the thousand brothers had never told the youngest how it was that their sons had come to them, and they were careful never to let any women near to him, for fear that if the youngest had his own sons, he would stop serving them. They would marry two and even three wives, and keep them hidden to make sure that the youngest would never meet them. Grandmother Sky instantly saw that he knew nothing of the way of a man with a woman, and said, it is right for the older to take the younger in marriage, to teach him, that much of ancient knowledge shall not be forgotten. And so the youngest son married Grandmother Sky, and she taught him much of ancient knowledge, both of the paths of secret pleasure, and also of the knowledge of the sky.

From their children are descended all who dwell in the clouds, far from the battles and the hatreds of men. Hidden away but never forgotten, the last secret egg yet waits with power and patience, and within it a vast and terrible army.

When the old man fell silent, no one spoke. After a while, Haafiza Majumdar asked, and what then?

There is no more, the old man said. This is the story.

And why are you now so serious and sad, Obaidullah Majumdar asked? It is but a story.

No, it is true, the old man said, and all the old men nodded and agreed, it is true, this is the way it happened, long ago.

But perhaps, one of them added, your stories tell something different. The two anthropologists looked around them at the circle of old men, and they saw that the faces that they had taken for hospitality were masks that hid contempt. And so they gathered no more data, and shortly afterwards they left. They never returned to the floating cities of Venus.

The ruins of the first space age hide many secrets, and the cities in the clouds are, perhaps, not the most mysterious of the relics from that distant age.

But none of the other relics tell stories.

BRENDA W. CLOUGH

HOME IS THE SAILOR

HIS CREW HAD LASHED SPARS AND OARS TOGETHER INTO A crude stretcher. Swearing and stumbling in the autumn downpour, they hauled their captain up the steep rocky road to Ithaka's humble acropolis. Odysseus clutched the slanting poles, making no unseemly outcry, his face turned skyward so that the sweat of agony was cleansed by the rain.

A shrill clamor of women's voices, and the stretcher leveled out so he could lie more easy. He looked along his body, past his upturned toes, to where the sodden brown back of a sailor steamed softly as the cold rain pelted the hot exhausted muscles. Brave fellows, they had borne him home as swift as Hermes. Now Itheus the mate babbled the story piecemeal, inexpertly, talking across him as if his captain and king was a foundered cow: "—never got to the country of the Thesproti. The rain pissing down all the way, rough seas, and then a wave caught an oar just wrong. The butt end knocked the king ass over tip, like he was tossed by a bull—"

Galled beyond endurance, Odysseus raised his head. "The gods rot you, have you no sense? Get us in out of this rain!"

The movement drove dull knives into his chest, and he sank back gasping. His people seemed to wheel and flutter around him, mewling gulls preparing to pick over his carcass. But then he came to himself again. He lay warm and dry in the royal bedchamber, in the big bed he had built with his own clever hands, under a familiar coverlet woven of fine wool. A woman sat in a wooden chair beside the bed, her fingers busy with roving and spindle. "Penelope . . ."

"No, it's Polykaste, sir."

Of course—Penelope was in her tomb these past five years and more. He squinted in the dim lamplight at the newcomer. How could it be night? He must have dozed the day away. Her hair was pinned up like a woman's, but she was little more than a girl, muffled against the chill in a big brown shawl. Polykaste . . . He couldn't place her. With feeble cunning he said, "Who is your father, child?"

"Oh, for heaven's love! I'm your daughter-in-law."

"Of course—lovely Polykaste, youngest of the daughters of Nestor son of Neleus." Gods, how had he forgotten? "Where's Telemachos, then?"

"Gone to Mykenae, at the behest of the high king. A messenger has gone to fetch him back."

"Oh, no need. A minor injury . . ." His son did all the stodgy diplomatic chores. "No flair for roaming or raiding, that boy."

He hadn't wanted to say that out loud, but her ears were young and sharp. "He swore he'd be home in time for the birth," she said. When she stood up he saw the bulk of her pregnant body, misshapen against the mellow glow of the clay lamp. The things that happened, when you left home for a year or so!

The physician came at her call and laid his cold thin fingers against the horrible black bruises on his right side and chest. "Look how he can feel it, when I do this." Odysseus snarled wordlessly at him. "The ribs are broken. Let him lie perfectly still as I have propped him, and we shall see if they knit. If the lung within has sustained no puncture, there is good hope of his recovery."

"Vulture! You talk *to* me, not *over* me." But the physician only held out a medicine cup. Odysseus took one swallow and gagged on the bitter brew, turning his head away. The cup followed, forcing itself upon him, and he had to drink. There must have been poppy juice in the dose, because he tumbled into a deep blank hole of sleep.

Doggedly, slowly, he climbed back out of the dark into another gray day. Rain thrummed on the roof tiles above his head, and water plashed from the eaves onto the terrace overlooking the harbor far below. If he could fling off the coverlet and stride to the parapet, he might see his ship. But he was too wise to do that yet. Heal up first, and then return to the sea. . . .

The girl was there again, spinning the creamy fluff of wool into an even thread. She had been a pretty piece at the wedding, indeed the loveliest of old Nestor's daughters—it must have been Aphrodite's mercy, that a king with a face like the butt end of a cow could sire princesses with the grace of Naiads. But now with her puffy face and swollen ankles she was plainer than a mud hut. "Klotho," he said. "Don't measure and cut the thread yet."

She frowned at him, shifting her weight awkwardly in the wooden chair. "Polykaste," she reminded him.

"Joke," he said, and her mouth thinned into a sour line. What a humorless child! But then it came to him that she was unhappy. Weren't increasing women supposed to be content? Perhaps she was missing the boy. "Telemachos is a solemn one too."

The spindle didn't pause in its twirl. She seemed to be thinking of other things, listening with only half an ear to a sick man's mutterings. The thought was like the prick of a goad. Was he not much-enduring Odysseus, beguiler of kings, favored of gray-eyed Athene, as full of stories as an egg is of meat? He spoke up more strongly. "Don't worry about me. I'm sure to recover."

Her indifferent gaze didn't shift from the thread. "Indeed?"

"Yes. Because, on my last voyage—have you heard the story? Ah! I was on my way to the Paphlagonians, where the cattle are snow-white and as tall as a man. The milk they give is of such virtue that one sup can add a handspan's growth to a child, or keep a man on his feet for a day of hard labor. We thought to steal us some of those fine cows. But contrary winds blew us ashore in Etruria. . . ."

He had her now. Her sullen blue eyes took on a soft shine of interest, and she leaned forward to ask, "Are there people in Etruria? Is it far?"

"Oh, a long voyage! But there are fields and olives, sheep and cattle, men and maids, just like us." Hastily he abridged a bit. A princess of Pylos ought not to hear sailor stories of Etrurian maidens and their charms. "And I met there a seer, a poet all in red, who read my future for me in a pool of ink and rendered it into triple rhyme. He lived in a cave on the bluff above the river Arno, and I gifted him with two sheep, a silver armlet, and a bronze cauldron as wide as a shield, in return for the story of my death."

The dangling spindle had slowed to a stop. The wool was now slowly unwinding itself, forgotten. "Your death!" She made an avert sign. "How can such a vision be worth treasure?"

He hitched himself higher on his pillows, ignoring the fierce twinge in his side. "Hah. Don't think this old salt hasn't had more than one. Once, a trouble-making prophet tried to turn me against the boy, saying that my own begotten son would kill me. That ploy's older than Perseus. And there was the dull one, where I was supposed to go inland, to where oars could be mistaken for winnowing fans, and be murdered by the barbarians there. But this last one was the best, a treasure of a death—beautiful! He sang of my final voyage past the Pillars of Herakles into the World Ocean. I shall see the far side of the world, before I sink within sight of the Isle of the Blest. My heart could ask for no better. That's the death for me."

It was growing difficult to breathe properly, and to get the rest of the words out he had to struggle like a fish on the gaff. "So you see, I'm sure to get better. Not going to die in my bed . . . at home. Not I."

She rearranged the cushions, propping him to lie on the wounded side as the physician had ordered. Curiously, this gave him some relief. If he could get her to talk, he could rest a while without betraying weakness. "You must have gone to the seer yourself." He nodded at her belly.

Immediately he sensed that it was the wrong thing to say. She pulled the shawl close around her shoulders, and set the spindle twirling again. "We sacrificed a black goat to Artemis. The priestess said it will be a boy. And the delivery will go well."

"That's a good seeing. Is it not?"

"Only if you believe."

He said nothing, taking canny refuge in weakness, and after a time she went on. "There are different omens in my family."

"Ah." He nodded wisely.

"My mother died in childbed. And my older sister too."

Again he nodded, though he knew nothing of midwives' work. At last she said, "I dread the trial to come. I'm afraid."

It seemed to him that Polykaste's mother must have been brought successfully to bed at least twice. Else how did Polykaste herself come to be here? And an older sister too. But the reasoning would be a waste of his short breath to voice. Frightened girls did not hear wisdom. Instead he beckoned her closer. There were other ways to hearten and encourage. He knew them all. "May I?"

He laid his hand on the firm dome of her belly. The life

within bumped suddenly under the layers of shawl and hi-
mation and womb, strong as a piglet in a market sack. He
counted each painful word out like a grain of gold. "Heroes
know. We have our lore. Shall I tell you our biggest secret?"
He waited for her nod. "Don't tell anyone, then. But we know
fear too."

She stared. "Mighty Odysseus, leader of men, wily and
wise? Truly?"

"In the Trojan Horse we were puking with fright. Child,
if you're wise, you know fear. The trick is to not give it free
rein. Great treasure is not won without great travail."

He had done some good. A ghostly little smile brushed
past the corners of her mouth. But it weighed on him, that
he had not spoken with his old persuasion and power. Where
are you, Athene, with your wisdom? And his side hurt un-
bearably. The physician came in, fussing and prodding, and
he was glad to take his dose and sleep again.

With the next day came fever, a scorching heat that racked
him without mercy. He knew this was bad, but would not
admit it. Instead he battled the physician, who wanted to cup
him and administer a purge. The girl Polykaste was nowhere
to be seen, and he had not the breath to ask for her aid. He
contrived to kick over the physician's brazier and to spit out
most of the medicine, but he couldn't upbraid the old fraud
as he deserved. Resourceful Odysseus, speechless! It disgusted him.

And over the steady roar of the rain on the tiles came
another sound, the mutter and tramp of men. He could hear
them pass out in the great hall, men enough to throng the
place. More men than his one ship could hold. For a moment
he was lost in memory, the feasting suitors filling the hall and
the mighty bow in his hand. Then the physician stooped
nearer. "Your sailors are here, lord," he said. "Itheus, and
Lykon, and Ainios, and the others. They want to come in."

"What for?" He had to mouth it.

The physician rolled his eyes, collecting the approval of
the other sickroom attendants. "Lord, to say goodbye."

He shook his head. "Not going. Not I. Tell them—fettle
the ship, caulk her. We sail in the spring." In this cursed
downpour there would be little enough work they could do,
but it was important for a ship's captain to keep the men busy
and out of trouble.

Then it was night, and he was too weak to resist any more.
They worked their will on him far into the evening, cupping
him and bleeding him and plastering his feet and head with
herbs pounded into a slimy paste and spread on linen.

He lay still, struggling for every breath, and recited to
himself all the perils he had escaped: Scylla and hungry Cha-
rybdis, the Cyclops, angry Ajax, Hector with his bright bronze
sword, kingly Priam and bright doomed Achilles. I, Odysseus,
I survived all these. I came alive out of Troy. I returned home
safe after ten years' journeying. And I will live to laugh at this
stupid injury. Heroes cannot die in sickbed, with slaves and
women weeping all around. How could a poet make a decent
song of an end like that? We die in the bitter clash of armor
and swords on the plains of windy Troy, leaving a corpse to
be fought over by gods and men. Or we yell brass-lunged
defiance and go down in a wallow of cold water as the bronze-
headed rams cleave the ship into planks and floating rags. . . .

The air and his head grew clear, as if the rain had washed
both clean together. The storm had passed, and a clear yellow
morning lay long and bright on the pavement outside the bedchamber. Beyond, above the terrace parapet, the sky was ten
thousand leagues deep, that clear high Aegean blue fit to be
set in the bezel of the ring of a god. Perfect traveling weather!
It was a day for departures—a day to pour the libations of
wine and oil to Poseidon, and cast off the lines, and haul the
sail high with singing and joy!

He leaned back on his pillows and drank the sweet air in
tiny sips, not fighting for gulps of breath any longer. The
morning shimmered with expectancy. Some great good was

approaching, casting its glow before—a sure forerunner of the divine. He was not surprised to see a slim figure in flowing white pace slowly along the terrace towards him: Athene. The tears prickled in his eyes. At last!

But no—this woman wore no helm and bore neither spear nor shield. Instead she carried something close-wrapped in a brown shawl, something small and fragile. With enormous dignity, she came in to the bedside and folded back the edge of the shawl for him to see. "King Odysseus, may I present your grandson?"

"Polykaste!" he breathed. She smiled down at him, and at the pink wriggling newborn in her arms. He wanted to burst out with congratulations and good-luck words, but all he could do was grin up at her. In his weakness he didn't even dare to hold the infant. But he put his hand on the tiny head. The downy tender scalp was dented and discolored from the long battle to reach the light. A lively lad, a fighter already! And new, so very new. Against the baby head his hand looked like an old tree root scoured and bleached by the sea and cast up, driftwood, on the beach. He blessed the boy silently: See new things and make new things, my lad. Travel far. Drink every cup to the lees, and sink within sight of the Isle of the Blest.

"As soon as I stopped fighting the pangs, the birth went well," Polykaste was saying. "It was just like your adventures: I passed through great travail to win a mighty treasure."

Brave child, he wanted to tell her. Worthy descendant of a line of kings!

He had been certain her eyes were blue. But now in the golden morning, they looked gray, gray as rain. And she said, "There is a time to fight nature, and a time to be her friend."

For an instant he held his breath, though he had no breath to spare. Athene, bright lady, he prayed silently. Never have you failed me. Thank you.

The girl beamed down at her baby with doting pride. Then she glanced at him, and her mouth dropped open with alarm. "Sir, are you well? Shall I call the physician?"

He shook his head. She was right. Death indeed came as no foe, but a friend. But one last task lay before him. He crooked a kingly finger, beckoning her closer. "My men," he croaked. He could no longer hear them out there in the great hall, but he knew they had waited, the brave hearts, faithful as Argos. Let them come in, he wanted to say. I can stay a little for them. To say goodbye.

SUSANNA CLARKE

TOM BRIGHTWIND, OR, HOW THE FAIRY BRIDGE WAS BUILT AT THORESBY

THE FRIENDSHIP BETWEEN THE EIGHTEENTH-CENTURY JEW-ish physician David Montefiore and the fairy Tom Brightwind is remarkably well documented. In addition to Montefiore's own journals and family papers, we have numerous descriptions of encounters with Montefiore and Brightwind by eighteenth- and early nineteenth-century letter writers, diarists and essayists. Montefiore and Brightwind seem, at one time or another, to have met most of the great men of the period. They discussed slavery with Boswell and Johnson, played dominoes with Diderot, got drunk with Richard Brinsley Sheridan and, upon one famous occasion, surprized Thomas Jefferson in his garden at Monticello.[1]

---

[1]Poor David Montefiore was entirely mortified to be discovered trespassing upon another gentleman's property and could scarcely apologise enough. He told Thomas Jefferson that they had heard so much of the beauty of Monticello that they had been entirely unable to resist coming to see it for themselves. This polite explanation went a good way towards pacifying the President (who was inclined to be angry). Unfortunately Tom Brightwind immediately began to describe the many ways in which his own gardens were superior to Thomas Jefferson's. Thomas Jefferson promptly had them both turned off his property.

Yet, fascinating as these contemporary accounts are, our most vivid portrait of this unusual friendship comes from the plays, stories and songs which it inspired. In the early nineteenth century "Tom and David" stories were immensely popular both here and in Faerie Minor, but in the latter half of the century they fell out of favour in Europe and the United States. It became fashionable among Europeans and Americans to picture fairies as small, defenceless creatures. Tom Brightwind—loud, egotistical, and six feet tall—was most emphatically not the sort of fairy that Arthur Conan Doyle and Charles Dodgson hoped to find at the bottom of their gardens.

The following story first appeared in Blackwood's Maga-*zine (Edinburgh: September 1820) and was reprinted in* Si-*lenus's* Review *(Faerie Minor: April 1821). Considered as literature it is deeply unremarkable. It suffers from all the usual defects of second-rate early nineteenth-century writing. Nevertheless, if read with proper attention, it uncovers a great many facts about this enigmatic race and is particularly enlightening on the troublesome relationship between fairies and their children.*

Professor James Sutherland
Research Institute of Sidhe Studies
University of Aberdeen
October 1999

How the Fairy Bridge was Built at Thoresby

For most of its length Shoe-lane in the City of London follows a gentle curve and it never occurs to most people to wonder why. Yet if they were only to look up (and they never do) they would see the ancient wall of an immense round tower and it would immediately become apparent how the lane curves to accommodate the tower.

This is only one of the towers that guard Tom Brightwind's

house. From his earliest youth Tom was fond of traveling about and seeing everything and, in order that he might do this more conveniently, he had placed each tower in a different part of the world. From one tower you step out into Shoe-lane; another occupies the greater part of a small island in the middle of a Scottish loch; a third looks out upon the dismal beauty of an Algerian desert; a fourth stands upon Drying-Green-street in a city in *Faerie Minor*; and so on. With characteristic exuberance Tom named this curiously constructed house *Castel des Tours saunz Nowmbre*, which means the Castle of Innumerable Towers. David Montefiore had counted the innumerable towers in 1764. There were fourteen of them.

On a morning in June in 1780 David Montefiore knocked upon the door of the Shoe-lane tower. He inquired of the porter where Tom might be found and was told that the master was in his library.

As David walked along dim, echoing corridors and trotted up immense stone staircases, he bade a cheerful "Good Morning! Good Morning!" to everyone he passed. But the only answers that he got were doubtful nods and curious stares, for no matter how often he visited the house, the inhabitants could never get used to him. His face was neither dazzlingly handsome nor twisted and repulsive. His figure was similarly undistinguished. His countenance expressed neither withering scorn, nor irresistible fascination, but only good humour and a disposition to think well of everyone. It was a mystery to the fairy inhabitants of *Castel des Tours saunz Nowmbre* why anyone should wish to wear such an expression upon his face.

Tom was not in the library. The room was occupied by nine fairy princesses. Nine exquisite heads turned in perfect unison to stare at David. Nine silk gowns bewildered the eye with their different colors. Nine different perfumes mingled in the air and made thinking difficult.

They were a few of Tom Brightwind's grand-daughters.

Princess Caritas, Princess Bellona, Princess Alba Perfecta, Princess Lachrima and Princess Flammifera were one set of sisters; Princess Honey-of-the-Wild-Bees, Princess Lament-from-over-the-Water, Princess Kiss-upon-a-True-Love's-Grave and Princess Bird-in-the-Hand were another.

"O David ben Israel!" said Princess Caritas, "How completely charming!" and offered him her hand.

"You are busy, Highnesses," he said, "I fear I disturb you."

"Not really," said Princess Caritas, "We are writing letters to our cousins. Duty letters, that is all. Be seated, O David ben Israel."

"You did not say that they are our female cousins," said Princess Honey-of-the-Wild-Bees. "You did not make that plain. I should not like the Jewish doctor to run away with the idea that we write to any other sort of cousin."

"To our female cousins *naturally*," said Princess Caritas.

"We do not know our male cousins," Princess Flammifera informed David.

"We do not even know their names," added Princess Lament-from-across-the-Water.

"And even if we did, we would not *dream* of writing to them," remarked Princess Alba Perfecta.

"Though we are told they are very handsome," said Princess Lachrima.

"Handsome?" said Princess Caritas. "Whatever gave you that idea? I am sure I do not know whether they are handsome or not. I do not care to know. I never think of such things."

"Oh now, *really* my sweet!" replied Princess Lachrima with a brittle laugh. "Tell the truth, do! You scarcely ever think of anything else."

Princess Caritas gave her sister a vicious look.

"And to which of your cousins are you writing?" asked David quickly.

"To Igraine . . ."

"Nimue . . ."

"Elaine . . ."

"And Morgana."

"Ugly girls," remarked Princess Caritas.

"Not their fault," said Princess Honey-of-the-Wild-Bees generously.

"And will they be away long?" asked David.

"Oh!" said Princess Flammifera.

"Oh!" said Princess Caritas.

"Oh!" said Princess Honey-of-the-Wild-Bees.

"They have been sent away," said Princess Bellona.

"Forever . . ." said Princess Lament-from-across-the-Water.

". . . and a day," added Princess Flammifera.

"We thought everybody knew that," said Princess Alba Perfecta.

"Grandfather sent them away," said Princess Kiss-upon-a-True-Love's-Grave.

"They offended Grandfather," said Princess Bird-in-the-Hand.

"Grandfather is most displeased with them," said Princess Lament-from-across-the-Water.

"They have been sent to live in a house," said Princess Caritas.

"Not a nice house," warned Princess Alba Perfecta.

"A nasty house!" said Princess Lachrima, with sparkling eyes. "With nothing but male servants! Nasty, dirty male servants with thick ugly fingers and hair on the knuckles! Male servants who will doubtless show them no respect!" Lachrima put on a knowing, amused look. "Though perhaps they may show them something else!" she said.

Caritas laughed. David blushed.

"The house is in a wood," continued Princess Bird-in-the-Hand.

"Not a nice wood," added Princess Bellona.

"A nasty wood!" said Princess Lachrima excitedly. "A thoroughly damp and dark wood, full of spiders and creepy, slimy, foul-smelling . . ."

"And why did your grandfather send them to this wood?" asked David quickly.

"Oh! Igraine got married," said Princess Caritas.

"Secretly," said Princess Lament-from-across-the-Water.

"We thought everyone knew that," said Princess Kiss-upon-a-True-Love's-Grave.

"She married a Christian man," explained Princess Caritas.

"Her harpsichord master!" said Princess Bellona, beginning to giggle.

"He played such beautiful concertos," said Princess Alba Perfecta.

"He had such beautiful . . ." began Princess Lachrima.

"Rima! Will you desist?" said Princess Caritas.

"Cousins," said Princess Honey-of-the-Wild-Bees sweetly, "when you are banished to a dark, damp wood, we will write to *you*."

"I did wonder, you know," said Princess Kiss-upon-a-True-Love's-Grave, "when she began to take harpsichord lessons every day. For she was never so fond of music till Mr. Cartwright came. Then they took to shutting the door—which, I may say, I was very sorry for, the harpsichord being a particular favorite of mine. And so, you know, I used to creep to the door to listen, but a quarter of an hour might go by and I would not hear a single note—except perhaps the odd discordant plink as if one of them had accidentally leaned upon the instrument. Once I thought I would go in to see what they were doing, but when I tried the handle of the door I discovered that they had turned the key in the lock . . ."

"Be quiet, Kiss!" said Princess Lament-from-across-the-Water.

"She's only called Kiss," explained Princess Lachrima to David helpfully, "she's never *actually* kissed anyone."

"But I do not quite understand," said David. "If Princess Igraine married without her grandfather's permission, then that of course is very bad. Upon important matters children ought always to consult their parents, or those who stand in the place of parents. Likewise parents—or as we have in this case, grandparents—ought to consider not only the financial aspects of a marriage and the rank of the prospective bride or bridegroom but also the child's character and likely chances of happiness with that person. The inclinations of the child's heart ought to be of paramount importance. . . ."

As David continued meditating out loud upon the various reciprocal duties and responsibilities of parents and children, Princess Honey-of-the-Wild-Bees stared at him with an expression of mingled disbelief and distaste, Princess Caritas yawned loudly, and Princess Lachrima mimed someone fainting with boredom.

". . . But even if Princess Igraine offended her grandfather in this way," said David, "Why were her sisters punished with her?"

"Because they did not stop her, of course," said Princess Alba Perfecta.

"Because they did not tell Grandfather what she was about," said Princess Lament-from-across-the-Water.

"We thought everybody knew that," said Princess Bird-in-the-Hand.

"What happened to the harpsichord master?" asked David.

Princess Lachrima opened her large violet blue eyes and leaned forward with great eagerness, but at that moment a voice was heard in the corridor.

". . . but when I had shot the third crow and plucked and skinned it, I discovered that it had a heart of solid diamond—just as the old woman had said—so, as you see, the afternoon was not entirely wasted."

Tom Brightwind had a bad habit of beginning to talk long before he entered a room, so that the people whom he addressed only ever heard the end of what he wished to say to them.

"What?" said David.

"Not entirely wasted," repeated Tom.

Tom was about six feet tall and unusually handsome even for a fairy prince (for it must be said that in fairy society the upper ranks generally make it their business to be better-looking than the commoners). His complexion gleamed with such extraordinary good health that it seemed to possess a faint opalescence, slightly unnerving to behold. He had recently put off his wig and taken to wearing his natural hair, which was long and straight and a vivid chestnut-brown color. His eyes were blue, and he looked (as he had looked for the last three or four thousand years) about thirty years of age. He glanced about him, raised one perfect fairy eyebrow, and muttered sourly, "Oak and Ash, but there are a lot of women in this room!"

There was a rustle of nine silk gowns, the slight click of door, a final exhalation of perfume, and suddenly there were no princesses at all.

"So where have you been?" said Tom, throwing himself into a chair and taking up a newspaper. "I expected you yesterday. Did you not get my message?"

"I could not come. I had to attend to my patients. Indeed I cannot stay long this morning. I am on my way to see Mr. Monkton."

Mr. Monkton was a rich old gentleman who lived in Lincoln. He wrote David letters describing a curious pain in his left side and David wrote back with advice upon medicines and treatments.

"Not that he places any faith in what I tell him," said David cheerfully. "He also corresponds with a physician in Edinburgh and a sort of sorcerer in Dublin. Then there is the apothecary in Lincoln who visits him. We all contradict one another but it does not matter because he trusts none of us.

Now he has written to say he is dying and at this crisis we are summoned to attend him in person. The Scottish physician, the Irish wizard, the English apothecary and me! I am quite looking forward to it! Nothing is so pleasant or instructive as the society and conversation of one's peers. Do not you agree?"

Tom shrugged.[2] "Is the old man really ill?" he asked.

"I do not know. I never saw him."

Tom glanced at his newspaper again, put it down again in irritation, yawned and said, "I believe I shall come with you." He waited for David to express his rapture at this news.

What in the world, wondered David, did Tom think there would be at Lincoln to amuse him? Long medical conversations in which he could take no part, a querulous sick old gentleman, and the putrid airs and hush of a sickroom! David was on the point of saying something to this effect when it occurred to him that, actually, it would be no bad thing for Tom to come to Lincoln. David was the son of a famous Venetian rabbi. From his youth he had been accustomed to debate good principles and right conduct with all sorts of grave Jewish persons. These conversations had formed his own character and he naturally supposed that a small measure of the same could not help but improve other people's. In short he had come to believe that if only one talks long enough and expresses oneself properly, it is perfectly possible to argue people into being good and happy. With this aim he generally took it upon himself to quarrel with Tom Brightwind several times a week—all without noticeable effect. But just now he had a great deal to say about the unhappy fate of the harpsichord master's bride and her sisters, and a long ride north was the perfect opportunity to say it.

So the horses were fetched from the stables, and David

[2]Fairy princes do not often trouble to seek out other fairy princes, and on the rare occasions that they do meet, it is surprising with what regularity one of them will die—suddenly, mysteriously, and in great pain.

and Tom got on them. They had not gone far before David began.

"Who?" asked Tom, not much interested.

"The Princesses Igraine, Nimue, Elaine and Morgana."

"Oh! Yes, I sent them to live in . . . What do you call that wood on the far side of Pity-Me? What is the name that you put upon it? No, it escapes me. Anyway, there."

"But eternal banishment!" cried David in horror. "Those poor girls! How can you bear the thought of them in such torment?"

"I bear it very well, as you see," said Tom. "But thank you for your concern. To own the truth, I am thankful for any measure that reduces the number of women in my house. David, I tell you, those girls talk *constantly*. Obviously I talk a great deal too. But then I am always doing things. I have my library. I am the patron of three theaters, two orchestras and a university. I have numerous interests in *Faerie Major*. I have seneschals, magistrates, and proctors in all the various lands of which I am sovereign, who are obliged to consult my pleasure constantly. I am involved in . . ." Tom counted quickly on his long, white fingers. ". . . thirteen wars which are being prosecuted in *Faerie Major*. In one particularly complicated case I have allied myself with the Millstone Beast and with his enemy, La Dame d'Aprigny, and sent armies to both of them. . . ." Tom paused here and frowned at his horse's ears. "Which means, I suppose, that I am at war with myself. Now why did I do that?" He seemed to consider a moment or two, but making no progress he shook his head and continued. "What was I saying? Oh, yes! So *naturally* I have a great deal to say. But those girls do nothing. Absolutely nothing! A little embroidery, a few music lessons. Oh! and they read English novels! David! Did you ever look into an English novel? Well, do not trouble yourself. It is nothing but a lot of nonsense about girls with fanciful names getting married."

"But this is precisely the point I wish to make," said David.

"Your children lack proper occupation. Of course they will find some mischief to get up to. What do you expect?"

David often lectured Tom upon the responsibilities of parenthood, which annoyed Tom, who considered himself to be a quite exemplary fairy parent. He provided generously for his children and grandchildren and only in exceptional circumstances had any of them put to death.[3]

"Young women must stay at home quietly until they marry," said Tom. "What else would you have?"

"I admit that I cannot imagine any other system for regulating the behavior of young Christian and Jewish women. But in their case the interval between the schoolroom and marriage is only a few years. For fairy women it may stretch into centuries. Have you no other way of managing your female relations? Must you imitate Christians in everything you do? Why! You even dress as if you were a Christian!"

"As do you," countered Tom.

"And you have trimmed your long fairy eyebrows."

"At least I still have eyebrows," retorted Tom, "Where is your beard, Jew? Did Moses wear a little grey wig?" He gave David's wig of neat curls a contemptuous flip. "I do not think so."

"You do not even speak your own language!" said David, straightening his wig.

---

[3]Fairies exceed even Christians and Jews in their enthusiasm for babies and young children, and think nothing of adding to their brood by stealing a pretty Christian child or two.

Yet in this, as in so many things, fairies rarely give much thought to the consequences of their actions. They procreate or steal other people's children, and twenty years later they are amazed to discover that they have a house full of grown men and women. The problem is how to provide for them all. Unlike the sons and daughters of Christians and Jews, fairy children do not live in confident expectation of one day inheriting all their parents' wealth, lands and power, since their parents are very unlikely ever to die.

It is a puzzle that few fairies manage to solve satisfactorily and it is unsurprising that many of their children eventually rebel. For over seven centuries Tom Brightwind had been involved in a vicious and bloody war against his own firstborn son, a person called Prince Rialobran.

"Neither do you," said Tom.

David immediately replied that Jews, unlike fairies, hon-ored their past, spoke Hebrew in their prayers and upon all sorts of ritual occasions. "But to return to the problem of your daughters and grand-daughters, what did you do when you were in the *brugh*?"

This was tactless. The word *"brugh"* was deeply offensive to Tom. No one who customarily dresses in spotless white linen and a midnight-blue coat, whose nails are exquisitely manicured, whose hair gleams like polished mahogany—in short, no one of such refined tastes and delicate habits—likes to be reminded that he spent the first two or three thousand years of his existence in a damp dark hole, wearing (when he took the trouble to wear anything at all) a kilt of coarse, un-dyed wool and a moldering rabbitskin cloak.[4]

"In the *brugh*," said Tom, lingering on the word with ironic emphasis to shew that it was a subject polite people did not mention, "the problem did not arise. Children were born and grew up in complete ignorance of their paternity. I have not the least idea who my father was. I never felt any curiosity on the matter."

By two o'clock Tom and David had reached Notting-

---

[4]The *brugh* was for countless centuries the common habitation of the fairy race. It is the original of all the fairy palaces one reads of in folktales. Indeed the tendency of Christian writers to glamorize the *brugh* seems to have increased with the cen-turies. It has been described as a "fairy palace of gold and crystal, in the heart of the hill" (Lady Wilde, *Ancient Legends, Mystic Charms and Superstitions of Ireland,* Ward & Downey, London, 1887). Another chronicler of fairy history wrote of "a steep-sided grassy hill, round as a pudding-basin . . . A small lake on its summit had a crystal floor, which served as a skylight." (Sylvia Townsend Warner, *The Kingdoms of Elfin,* Chatto & Windus, London, 1977).

The truth is that the *brugh* was a hole or series of interconnecting holes that was dug into a barrow, very like a rabbit's warren or badger's set. To paraphrase a writer of fanciful stories for children, this was not a comfortable hole, it was not even a dry, bare sandy hole; it was a nasty, dirty, wet hole.

Fairies, who are nothing if not resilient, were able to bear with equanimity the damp, the dark and the airlessness, but stolen Christian children brought to the *brugh* died, as often as not, of suffocation.

hamshire,[5] a county which is famous for the greenwood which once spread over it. Of course at this late date the forest was no longer a hundredth part of what it once had been, but there were still a number of very ancient trees and Tom was determined to pay his respects to those he considered his particular friends and to shew his disdain of those who had not behaved well towards him.[6] So long was Tom in greeting

---

[5]In the late eighteenth century a journey from London to Nottinghamshire might be expected to take two or three days. Tom and David seem to have arrived after a couple of hours: this presumably is one of the advantages of choosing as your traveling companion a powerful fairy prince.

[6]Fairies born in the last eight centuries or so—sophisticated, literate, and consorting all their lives with Christians—have no more difficulty than Christians themselves in distinguishing between the animate and the inanimate. But to members of older generations (such as Tom) the distinction is quite unintelligible.

Several magical theorists and commentators have noted that fairies who retain this old belief in the souls of stones, doors, trees, fire, clouds, etc., are more adept at magic than the younger generation and their magic is generally much stronger.

The following incident clearly shows how, given the right circumstances, fairies come to regard perfectly ordinary objects with a strange awe. In 1697 an attempt was made to kill the Old Man of the White Tower, one of the lesser princes of Faerie. The would-be assassin was a fairy called Broc (he had stripes of black and white fur upon his face). Broc had been greatly impressed by what he had heard of a wonderful new weapon which Christians had invented to kill each other. Consequently he forsook all magical means of killing the Old Man of the White Tower (which had some chance of success) and purchased instead a pistol and some shot (which had none). Poor Broc made his attempt, was captured, and the Old Man of the White Tower locked him up in a windowless stone room deep in the earth. In the next room the Old Man imprisoned the pistol, and in a third room the shot. Broc died sometime around the beginning of the twentieth century (after three centuries without a bite to eat, a drop to drink, or a sight of the sun, even fairies grow weaker). The pistol and the shot, on the other hand, are still there, still considered by the Old Man as equally culpable, still deserving punishment for their wickedness. Several other fairies who wished to kill the Old Man of the White Tower have begun by devising elaborate plans to steal the pistol and the shot, which have attained a strange significance in the minds of the Old Man's enemies. It is well known to fairies that metal, stone and wood have stubborn natures; the gun and shot were set upon killing the Old Man in 1697 and it is quite inconceivable to the fairy mind that they could have wavered in the intervening centuries. To the Old Man's enemies it is quite clear that one day the gun and the shot will achieve their purpose.

his friends, that David began to be concerned about Mr. Monkton.

"But you said he was not really ill," said Tom.

"That was not what I said at all! But whether he is or not, I have a duty to reach him as soon as I can."

"Very well! Very well! How cross you are!" said Tom. "Where are you going? The road is just over there."

"But we came from the other direction."

"No, we did not. Well, perhaps. I do not know. But both roads join up later on so it cannot matter in the least which we chuse."

Tom's road soon dwindled into a narrow and poorly marked track which led to the banks of a broad river. A small, desolate-looking town stood upon the opposite bank. The road reappeared on the other side of the town and it was odd to see how it grew broader and more confident as it left the town and traveled on to happier places.

"How peculiar!" said Tom, "Where is the bridge?"

"There does not seem to be one."

"Then how are we to get across?"

"There is a ferry," said David.

A long iron chain stretched between a stone pillar on this side of the river and another pillar on the opposite bank. Also on the other side of the river was an ancient flat-bottomed boat attached to the chain by two iron brackets. An ancient ferryman appeared and hauled the boat across the river by means of the chain. Then Tom and David led the horses onto the boat and the ancient ferryman hauled them back over.

David asked the ferryman what the town was called.

"Thoresby, sir," said the man.

Thoresby proved to be nothing more than a few streets of shabby houses with soiled, dusty windows and broken roofs. An ancient cart was abandoned in the middle of what appeared to be the principal street. There was a market cross and a marketplace of sorts—but weeds and thorns grew there in abundance, suggesting there had been no actual market for several years. There was only one gentleman's residence to be seen: a tall old-fashioned house built of grey limestone, with a great many tall gables and chimneys. This at least was a respectable-looking place though in a decidedly provincial style.

Thoresby's only inn was called the Wheel of Fortune. The sign showed a number of people bound to a great wheel which was being turned by Fortune, represented here by a bright pink lady wearing nothing but a blindfold. In keeping with the town's dejected air the artist had chosen to omit the customary figures representing good fortune and had instead shown all the people bound to Fortune's wheel in the process of being crushed to pieces or being hurled into the air to their deaths.

With such sights as these to encourage them, the Jew and the fairy rode through Thoresby at a smart trot. The open road was just in sight when David heard a cry of "Gentlemen! Gentlemen!" and the sound of rapid footsteps. So he halted his horse and turned to see what was the matter.

A man came running up.

He was a most odd-looking creature. His eyes were small and practically colorless. His nose was the shape of a small bread roll, and his ears—which were round and pink—might have been attractive on a baby, but in no way suited him. But what was most peculiar was the way in which eyes and nose huddled together at the top of his face, having presumably quarreled with his mouth, which had set up a separate establishment for itself halfway down his chin. He was very shabbily dressed and his bare head had a thin covering of pale stubble upon it.

"You have not paid the toll, sirs!" he cried.

"What toll?" asked David.

"Why! The ferry toll! The toll for crossing the river."

"Yes. Yes, we have," said David. "We paid the man who carried us across the river."

The odd-looking man smiled. "No, sir!" he said. "You paid

the fee, the ferryman's penny! But the toll is quite another thing. The toll is levied upon everyone who crosses the river. It is owed to Mr. Winstanley and I collect it. A man and a horse is sixpence. Two men and two horses is twelvepence."

"Do you mean to say," said David in astonishment, "that a person must pay *twice* to come to this miserable place?"

"There is no toll, David," said Tom airily. "This scoundrel merely wishes us to give him twelvepence."

The odd-looking man continued to smile, although the expression of his eyes had rather a malicious sparkle to it. "The gentleman may insult me if he wishes," he said, "Insults are free. But I beg leave to inform the gentleman that I am very far from being a scoundrel. I am a lawyer. Oh, yes! An attorney consulted by people as far afield as Southwell. But my chief occupation is as Mr. Winstanley's land agent and man of business. My name, sir, is Pewley Witts!"

"A lawyer?" said David. "Oh, I do beg your pardon!"

"David!" cried Tom. "When did you ever see a lawyer that looked like that? Look at him! His rascally shoes are broken all to bits. There are great holes in his vagabond's coat and he has no wig! Of *course* he is a scoundrel!" He leaned down from his tall horse. "We are leaving now, scoundrel. Good-bye!"

"These are my sloppy clothes," said Pewley Witts sullenly. "My wig and good coat are at home. I had no time to put them on when Peter Dawkins came and told me that two gentlemen had crossed by the ferry and were leaving Thoresby without paying the toll—which, by the bye, is still twelvepence, gentlemen, and I would be much obliged if you would pay it."

A devout Jew must discharge his debts promptly—however inadvertently those debts might have been incurred; a gentleman ought never to procrastinate in such matters; and, as David considered himself to be both those things, he was most anxious to pay Pewley Witts twelvepence. A fairy, on the other hand, sees things differently. Tom was determined not to pay. Tom would have endured years of torment rather than pay.

Pewley Witts watched them argue the point back and forth. Finally he shrugged. "Under the circumstances, gentlemen," he said, "I think you had better talk to Mr. Winstanley."

He led them to the tall stone house they had noticed before. A high stone wall surrounded the house and there was a little stone yard which was quite bare except for two small stone lions. They were crudely made things, with round, surprised eyes, snarls full of triangular teeth, and fanciful manes that more resembled foliage than fur.

A pretty maidservant answered the door. She glanced briefly at Pewley Witts and David Montefiore, but finding nothing to interest her there, her gaze traveled on to Tom Brightwind, who was staring down at the lions.

"Good morning, Lucy!" said Pewley Witts. "Is your master within?"

"Where else would he be?" said Lucy, still gazing at Tom.

"These two gentlemen object to paying the toll, and so I have brought them here to argue it out with Mr. Winstanley. Go and tell him that we are here. And be quick about it, Lucy. I am wanted at home. We are killing the spotted pig today."

Despite Pewley Witt's urging, it seemed that Lucy did not immediately deliver the message to her master. A few moments later from an open window above his head, David heard a sort of interrogatory murmur followed by Lucy's voice exclaiming, "A beautiful gentleman! Oh, madam! The most beautiful gentleman you ever saw in your life!"

"What is happening?" asked Tom, drifting back from his examination of the lions.

"The maid is describing me to her mistress," said David.

"Oh," said Tom, and drifted away again.

A face appeared briefly at the window.

"Oh, yes," came Lucy's voice again, "and Mr. Witts and another person are with him."

Lucy reappeared and conducted Tom, David and Pewley

Witts through a succession of remarkably empty chambers and passageways to an apartment at the back of the house. It was odd to see how, in contrast to the other rooms, this was comfortably furnished with red carpets, gilded mirrors and blue-and-white china. Yet it was still a little somber. The walls were paneled in dark wood and the curtains were half drawn across two tall windows to create a sort of twilight. The walls were hung with engravings but, far from enlivening the gloom, they only added to it. They were portraits of worthy and historical personages, all of whom appeared to have been in an extremely bad temper when they sat for their likenesses. Here were more scowls, frowns and stares than David had seen in a long time.

At the far end of the room a gentleman lay upon a sopha piled with cushions. He wore an elegant green-and-white chintz morning gown and loose Turkish slippers upon his feet. A lady, presumably Mrs. Winstanley, sat in a chair at his side.

As there was no one else to do it for them, Tom and David were obliged to introduce themselves (an awkward ceremony at the best of times). David told Mr. and Mrs. Winstanley his profession, and Tom was able to convey merely by his way of saying his name that he was someone of quite unimaginable importance.

Mr. Winstanley received them with great politeness, welcoming them to his house (which he called Mickelgrave House). They found it a little odd, however, that he did not trouble to rise from the sopha—or indeed move any of his limbs in the slightest degree. His voice was soft and his smile was gentle. He had pleasant, regular features and an unusually white complexion—the complexion of someone who hardly ever ventured out of doors.

Mrs. Winstanley (who rose and curtsied) wore a plain gown of blackberry-colored silk with the merest edging of white lace. She had dark hair and dark eyes. Had she only smiled a little, she would have been extremely lovely.

Pewley Witts explained that Mr. Brightwind refused to pay the toll.

"Oh no, Witts! No!" cried Mr. Winstanley upon the instant, "These gentlemen need pay no toll. The sublimity of their conversation will be payment enough, I am certain." He turned to Tom and David. "Gentlemen! For reasons which I will explain to you in a moment, I rarely go abroad. Truth to own I do not often leave this room and consequently my daily society is confined to men of inferior rank and education, such as Witts. I can scarcely express my pleasure at seeing you here!" He regarded David's dark, un-English face with mild interest. "Montefiore is an Italian name, I think. You are Italian, sir?"

"My father was born in Venice," said David, "but that city, sadly, has hardened its heart towards the Jews. My family is now settled in London. We hope in time to be English."

Mr. Winstanley nodded gently. There was, after all, nothing in the world so natural as people wishing to be English. "You are welcome too, sir. I am glad to say that I am completely indifferent to a man's having a different religion from mine."

Mrs. Winstanley leaned over and murmured something in her husband's ear.

"No," answered Mr. Winstanley softly, "I will not get dressed today."

"You are ill, sir?" asked David. "If there is anything I can—"

Mr. Winstanley laughed as if this were highly amusing. "No, no, physician! You cannot earn your fee quite as easily as that. You cannot persuade me that I feel unwell when I do not." He turned to Tom Brightwind with a smile. "The foreigner can never quite comprehend that there are more important considerations than money. He can never quite understand that there is a time to leave off doing business."

"I did not mean . . ." began David, coloring.

Mr. Winstanley smiled and waved his hand to indicate that

whatever David might have meant was of very little significance. "I am not offended in the least. I make allowances for you, Dottore." He leant back delicately against the cushions. "Gentlemen, I am a man who might achieve remarkable things. I have within me a capacity for greatness. But I am prevented from accomplishing even the least of my ambitions by the peculiar circumstances of this town. You have seen Thoresby. I daresay you are shocked at its wretched appearance and the astonishing idleness of the townspeople. Why, look at Witts! In other towns lawyers are respectable people. A lawyer in another town would not slaughter his own pig. A lawyer in another town would wear a velvet coat. His shirt would not be stained with gravy."

"Precisely," said Tom, looking with great disdain at the lawyer.

David was quite disgusted that anyone should speak to his inferiors in so rude a manner and he looked at Witts to see how he bore with this treatment. But Witts only smiled and David could almost have fancied he was simple, had it not been for the malice in his eyes.

"And yet," continued Mr. Winstanley, "I would not have you think that Witts is solely to blame for his slovenly appearance and lack of industry. Witts's life is blighted by Thoresby's difficulties, which are caused by what? Why, the lack of a bridge!"

Pewley Witts nudged Mr. Winstanley with his elbow. "Tell them about Julius Caesar."

"Oh!" said Mrs. Winstanley, looking up in alarm. "I do not think these gentlemen wish to be troubled with Julius Caesar. I dare say they heard enough of him in their schoolrooms."

"On the contrary, madam!" said Tom, in accents of mild reproach, "I for one can never grow tired of hearing of that illustrious and courageous gentleman. Pray go on, sir."[7] Tom

---

[7] Tom Brightwind was not the only member of his race who was passionately devoted to the memory of Julius Caesar. Many fairies claim descent from him and there was a medieval Christian legend that Oberon (the wholly fictitious king of the fairies) was Julius Caesar's son.

sat back, his head supported on his hand and his eyes fixed upon Mrs. Winstanley's elegant form and sweet face.

"You should know, gentlemen," began Mr. Winstanley, "that I have looked into the history of this town and it seems our difficulties began with the Romans—whom you may see represented in this room by Julius Caesar. His portrait hangs between the door and that pot of hyacinths. The Romans, as I daresay you know, built roads in England that were remarkable for both their excellence and their straightness. A Roman road passes very close to Thoresby. Indeed, had the Romans followed their own self-imposed principle of straightness, they ought by rights to have crossed the river here, at Thoresby. But they allowed themselves to be deterred. There was some problem—a certain marshiness of the land, I believe—and so they deviated from their course and crossed the river at Newark. At Newark they built a town with temples and markets and I do not know what else, while Thoresby remained a desolate marsh. This was the first of many occasions upon which Thoresby suffered for other people's moral failings."

"Lady Anne Lutterell," prompted Pewley Witts.

"Oh, Mr. Winstanley!" said his wife, with a little forced laugh, "I must protest. Indeed I must. Mr. Brightwind and Mr. Montefiore do not wish to concern themselves with Lady Anne. I feel certain that they do not care for history at all."

"Oh! quite, madam!" said Tom. "What passes for history these days is extraordinary. Kings who are remembered more for their long dull speeches than for anything they did upon the battlefield, governments full of fat old men with grey hair, all looking the same—who cares about such stuff? But if you are speaking of real history, true history—by which of course I mean the spirited description of heroic personages of ancient times—Why, there is nothing which delights me more!"

"Lady Anne Lutterell," said Mr. Winstanley, taking no notice of either of them, "was a rich widow who lived at Ossington." (Mrs. Winstanley looked down at her folded hands in her lap.) "There is a picture of her ladyship between that little writing table and the longcase clock. It was widely known that she intended to leave a large sum of money as an act of piety to build a bridge in this exact spot. The bridge was promised and in anticipation of this promise the town of Thoresby was built. But at the last moment she changed her mind and built a chantry instead. I dare say, Mr. Montefiore, you will not know what that is. A chantry is a sort of chapel where priests say mass for the dead. Such—though I am ashamed to admit it—were the superstitious practices of our ancestors."

"Queen Elizabeth," said Pewley Witts, winking at David and Tom. It was becoming clear how he revenged himself for all the slights and insults which he received from Mr. Winstanley. It seemed unlikely that Mr. Winstanley would have made quite so many foolish speeches without Witts to encourage him.

"Queen Elizabeth indeed, Witts," said Mr. Winstanley pleasantly.

"Queen Elizabeth!" cried Mrs. Winstanley in alarm. "Oh! But she was a most disagreeable person! If we must talk of queens, there are several more respectable examples. What do you say to Matilda? Or Anne?"

Tom leaned as closely as he conveniently could to Mrs. Winstanley. His face shewed that he had a great many opinions upon Queen Matilda and Queen Anne which he wished to communicate to her immediately, but before he could begin, Mr. Winstanley said, "You will find Elizabeth, Mr. Brightwind, between the window and the looking-glass. In Elizabeth's time the people of Thoresby earned their living by making playing cards. But the Queen granted a Royal Patent for a monopoly for the manufacture of playing cards to a young man. He had written a poem praising her beauty. She was, I believe, about sixty-five years old at the time. As a consequence no one in England was allowed to make playing-cards except for this young man. He became rich and the people of Thoresby became destitute."

Mr. Winstanley continued his little history of people who might have built a bridge at Thoresby and had not done so, or who had injured the town in some other way. His wife tried to hide his foolishness as much as was in her power by protesting vigorously at the introduction of each fresh character, but he paid her not the slightest attention.

His special contempt was reserved for Oliver Cromwell, whose picture hung in pride of place over the mantelpiece. Oliver Cromwell had contemplated fighting an important battle at Thoresby but had eventually decided against it, thereby denying Thoresby the distinction of being blown up and laid to waste by two opposing armies.

"But surely," said David at last, "your best course is to build the bridge yourself."

"Ah!" Mr. Winstanley smiled. "You would think so, wouldn't you? And I have spoken to two gentlemen who are in the habit of lending money to other gentlemen for their enterprises. A Mr. Blackwell of London and a Mr. Crumfield of Bath. Mr. Witts and I described to both men the benefits that would accrue to them were they to build my bridge, the quite extraordinary amounts of money they would make. But both ended by declining to lend me the money." Mr. Winstanley glanced up at an empty space on the wall as if he would have liked to see it graced by portraits of Mr. Blackwell and Mr. Crumfield and so complete his museum of failure.

"But it was a very great sum," said Mrs. Winstanley. "You do not tell Mr. Brightwind and Mr. Montefiore what a very great sum it was. I do not believe I ever heard such a large figure named in my life before."

"Bridges are expensive," agreed David.

Then Mrs. Winstanley, who seemed to think that the subject of bridges had been exhausted among them, asked David several questions about himself. Where had he studied medicine? How many patients had he? Did he attend ladies as well as gentlemen? From speaking of professional matters David was soon led to talk of his domestic happiness—of his wife and four little children.

"And are you married, sir?" Mrs. Winstanley asked Tom.

"Oh, no, madam!" said Tom.

"Yes," David reminded him. "You are, you know."

Tom made a motion with his hand to suggest that it was a situation susceptible to different interpretations.

The truth was that he had a Christian wife. At fifteen she had a wicked little face, almond-shaped eyes and a most capricious nature. Tom had constantly compared her to a kitten. In her twenties she had been a swan; in her thirties a vixen; and then in rapid succession a bitch, a viper, a cockatrice and, finally, a pig. What animals he might have compared her to now no one knew. She was well past ninety and for forty years or more she had been confined to a set of apartments in a distant part of the *Castel des Tours saunz Nowmbre* under strict instructions not to show herself, while her husband waited impatiently for someone to come and tell him she was dead.

By now Tom and David had given the half hour to the Winstanleys which politeness demanded and David began to think of Mr. Monkton in Lincoln and of his anxiousness to reach him. But Mr. Winstanley could not quite bring himself to accept that his two new friends were about to leave him and he made several speeches urging them to stay for a week or two. It was left to Mrs. Winstanley to bid them farewell in a more rational manner.

They were not, however, able to leave immediately. There was some delay about fetching the horses and while they were waiting in the yard Lucy came out and looked nervously from one to the other. "If you please, sir, Mrs. Winstanley wishes to speak to you privately!"

"Ah ha!" said Tom, as if he half-expected such a summons.

"No, sir! Not you, sir!" Lucy curtsied her apologies. "It is the Jewish doctor that is wanted."

Mrs. Winstanley was waiting in her bedchamber. The

room was large, but somewhat sparsely furnished. It contained nothing but a chair, a chest and a large four-poster bed with green brocade hangings. Mrs. Winstanley stood by the bed. Everything about her—rigid bearing, strained look, the way in which she continually twisted her hands together—betrayed the greatest uneasiness.

She apologized for troubling him.

"It is no trouble," said David, "Not the least in the world. There is something you wish to ask me?"

She looked down. "Mr. Winstanley and I have been married for four years, but as yet we have no children."

"Oh!" He thought for a moment. "And there is no dislike upon either side to the conjugal act?"

"No." Mrs. Winstanley sighed. "No. That is one duty at least that my husband does not shirk."

So David asked all the usual questions that a physician generally asks in such a situation and she answered without any false shame.

"There is nothing wrong as far as I can see," David told her. "There is no reason why you should not bear a child. Be in good health, Mrs. Winstanley. That is my advice to you. Be cheerful and then—"

"Oh! But I had hoped that . . ." She hesitated. "I had hoped that, as a foreign gentleman, you might know something our English doctors do not. I am not the least afraid of anything you might suggest. I can bear any pain for the sake of a child. It is all I ever think of. Lucy thinks that I ought to eat carrots and parsnips that have odd shapes, and that I ought to persuade Mr. Winstanley to eat them too."

"Why?"

"Because they look like little people."

"Oh! Yes, of course. I see. Well, I suppose it can do no harm."

David took as affectionate a leave of Mrs. Winstanley as was consistent with so brief an acquaintance. He pressed her hand warmly and told her how sincerely he hoped she might soon have everything she wished for. He was sure that no one could deserve it more.

Tom was seated upon his horse. David's horse stood at his side. "Well?" said Tom, "What did she want?"

"It is a lack of children," said David.

"What is?"

"That afflicts the lady. The reason she never smiles."

"Children are a great nuisance," said Tom, reverting immediately to his own concerns.

"To you, perhaps. But a human woman feels differently. Children are our posterity. Besides, all women, fairy, Christian, or Jew, crave a proper object to love. And I do not think she can love her husband."

David was in the act of mounting his horse as he said this, an operation which invariably cost him a little trouble. He was somewhat surprised, on arriving upon the horse's back, to discover that Tom was nowhere to be seen.

Now wherever has he gone? he wondered. *Well, if he expects me to wait for him, he will be disappointed! I have told him half a dozen times today that I must go to Lincoln!*

David set off in the direction of Lincoln, but just as he reached the end of the town he heard a sound behind him and he looked round, expecting to see Tom.

It was Pewley Witts mounted on a horse which seemed to have been chosen for its great resemblance to himself in point of gauntness, paleness, and ugliness. "Mr. Montefiore!" he said. "Mr. Winstanley is most anxious that you and Mr. Brightwind should see his property and he has appointed me your guide. I have just spoken to Mr. Brightwind, but he has something important to do in Thoresby and cannot spare the time. He says that you will go for both!"

"Oh, does he indeed?" said David.

Pewley Witts smiled confidentially. "Mr. Winstanley thinks that you will build his bridge for him!"

"Why in the world should he think that?"

"Come, come! What sort of fools do you take us for in

Thoresby? An English lord and a Jew traveling about the country together! Two of the richest devils in all creation! What can you be doing, but seeking opportunities to lengthen your long purses?"

"Well, I fear you will be disappointed. He is not an English lord and I am the wrong sort of Jew. And I am not traveling about the country, as you put it. I am going to Lincoln."

"As you wish. But it so happens that Mr. Winstanley's property lies on either side of the Lincoln road. You cannot help but see it, if you go that way." He grinned, and said helpfully, "I will come with you and point out the places of interest."

In Mr. Winstanley's fields the weeds stood as thick as the corn. A number of thin, sad-looking men, women, and children were scaring the birds away.

Poor wretches! thought David. *They do indeed suffer for other people's moral failings. How I wish that I could persuade Tom to build the bridge for their sakes! But what hope is there of that? I cannot even persuade him into loving his own children.*

While David indulged these gloomy reflections, Pewley Witts named the yields of Mr. Winstanley's lands (so many bushels per acre) and described how those yields would be doubled and tripled should Mr. Winstanley ever trouble to drain his waterlogged fields or enrich his soil with manure.

A little farther on Pewley Witts pointed out some grassy hillocks beneath which, he said, was a thick layer of clay. He described how Mr. Winstanley could, if he wished, establish a manufactory to make pots and vases out of the clay.

"I believe," said Pewley Witts, "that earthenware pots and vases are quite the thing nowadays and that some gentlemen make a great deal of money from their manufacture."

"Yes," said David with a sigh, "I have heard that."

In another place they looked at a thin wood of birch trees on a windblown, sunny hillside. Pewley Witts said that there was a rich seam of coal beneath the wood, and Mr. Winstanley could, if he felt at all inclined to it, mine the coal and sell it in Nottingham or London.

"Answer me this, then!" cried David in exasperation. "Why does he not do these things? Sell the coal! Make the pots! Grow more corn! Why does he do nothing?"

"Oh!" said Pewley Witts with his malicious smile. "I have advised him against it. I have advised him that until the bridge is built he ought not to attempt anything. For how would he carry the corn or pots or coal to the people who wanted them? He would lose half his profit to carriers and barge-owners."

The more David saw of Mr. Winstanley's neglected lands, the more he began to doubt the propriety of going to Lincoln.

After all, he thought, *Mr. Monkton already has two doctors to attend him, not counting the Irish wizard. Whereas the poor souls of Thoresby have no one at all to be their friend. Do I not perhaps have a superior duty to stay and help them if I can by convincing Tom to build the bridge? But what in the world could I say to make him do it?*

To this last question he had no answer just at present, but in the meantime: "Mr. Witts!" he cried. "We must go back. I too have something important to do in Thoresby!"

As soon as they arrived at Mickelgrave House David jumped off his horse and set about looking for Tom. He was walking down one of the empty stone passageways when he happened to notice, through an open door, Mrs. Winstanley and Lucy in the garden. They appeared to be in a state of some excitement and were exclaiming to each other in tones of amazement. David, wondering what in the world the matter could be, went out into the garden, and arrived there just as Lucy was climbing up upon a stone bench in order to look over the wall.

"It has reached Mr. Witts's house!" she said.

"What is it? What is wrong?" cried David.

"We have just had a visit from three little boys!" said Mrs. Winstanley in a wondering tone.

"They were singing," said Lucy.

"Oh! Boys like to sing," said David. "My own two little sons—Ishmael and Jonah—know a comic song about a milk-maid and a cow which—"

"Yes, I daresay," interrupted Mrs. Winstanley. "But this was quite different! These boys had wings growing out of their backs. They were sailing through the air in a tiny gilded ship rigged with silken ribbons and they were casting out rose petals on either hand."

David climbed up beside Lucy and looked over the wall. Far off in a bright blue sky, a small golden ship was just sailing out of sight behind the church tower. David made out three little figures with lutes in their hands; their heads were thrown back in song.

"What were they singing?" he asked.

"I do not know," said Mrs. Winstanley, in perplexity. "It was in a language I did not know. Italian, I think."

In the drawing room the curtains had been pulled across the windows to shut out the golden light of early evening. Mr. Winstanley was lying upon the sofa with his hand thrown across his eyes.

"Mr. Winstanley!" cried his wife. "The most extraordinary thing . . ."

Mr. Winstanley opened his eyes and smiled to see David before him. "Ah! Mr. Montefiore!" he said.

"Lucy and I were in the garden when—"

"My love," said Mr. Winstanley in tones of mild reproach, "I am trying to speak to Mr. Montefiore." He smiled at David. "And how did you enjoy your ride? I confess that I think our surroundings not unattractive. Witts said he believed you were mightily entertained."

"It was most . . . enlightening. Where is Mr. Brightwind?"

The door was suddenly flung open and Tom walked in.

"Mr. Winstanley," he said, "I have decided to build your bridge!"

Tom was always fond of amazing a roomful of people and of having everyone stare at him in speechless wonder, and upon this particular occasion he must have been peculiarly gratified.

Then Mr. Winstanley began to speak his joy and his gratitude. "I have looked into the matter," he said, "or rather Mr. Witts has done it on my account—and I believe that you can expect a return on your investment of so many percent—that is to say, Mr. Witts can tell you all about it. . . ." He began to leaf rapidly through some papers which David was quite certain he had never looked at before.

"You may spare yourself the trouble," said Tom, "I have no thought of any reward. Mr. Montefiore has been lecturing me today upon the necessity of providing useful employment for one's children and it occurs to me, Mr. Winstanley, that unless this bridge is built your descendants will have nothing to do. They will be idle. They will never achieve that greatness of spirit, that decisiveness of action which ought to be theirs."

"Oh, Indeed! Quite so!" said Mr. Winstanley. "Then all that remains is to draw up plans for the bridge. I have made sketches of my ideas. I have them somewhere in this room. Witts estimates that two years should be enough to complete the work—perhaps less!"

"Oh!" said Tom. "I have no patience for a long undertaking. I shall build the bridge tonight between midnight and sunrise. I have just one condition." He held up a long finger. "One. Mr. Winstanley, you and all your servants, and Mr. Montefiore too, must go and stand upon the riverbank tonight and witness the building of my bridge."

Mr. Winstanley eagerly assured him that not only he and Mrs. Winstanley and all their servants would be there, but the entire population of the town.

As soon as Mr. Winstanley had stopped talking, David took the opportunity to tell Tom how glad he was that Tom was going to build the bridge, but Tom (who was generally very fond of being thanked for things) did not seem greatly interested. He left the room almost immediately, pausing only to speak to Mrs. Winstanley. David heard him say in a low voice, "I hope, madam, that you liked the Italian music!"

As David was now obliged to stay in Thoresby until the following morning, Mr. Winstanley sent one of his servants to Lincoln to tell Mr. Monkton that Mr. Montefiore was on his way and would be at his house the next day.

Just before midnight the people of Thoresby gathered at the Wheel of Fortune. In honor of the occasion Mr. Winstanley had got dressed. Oddly enough he was somehow less impressive in his clothes. The air of tragedy and romance which he commonly possessed seemed to have disappeared entirely when he put his coat and breeches on. He stood upon a three-legged stool and told the wretched, ragged crowd how grateful they should be to the great, good, and generous gentleman who was going to build them a bridge. This gentleman, said Mr. Winstanley, would soon appear among them to receive their thanks.

But Tom did not appear. Nor was Mrs. Winstanley present, which made her husband very angry, and so he sent Lucy back to Mickelgrave House to fetch her.

Mr. Winstanley said to David, "I am greatly intrigued by Mr. Brightwind's proposal of building the bridge in one night. Is it to be an *iron* bridge, I wonder? I believe that someone has recently built an iron bridge in Shropshire. Quite astonishing. Perhaps an iron bridge can be erected very quickly. Or a wooden bridge? There is a wooden bridge at Cambridge. . . ."

Just then Lucy appeared, white-faced and frightened.

"Oh, there you are!" said Mr. Winstanley. "Where is your mistress?"

"What is the matter, Lucy?" asked David. "What in the world has happened to you?"

"Oh, sir!" cried Lucy. "I ran up the high street to find my mistress, but when I reached the gate of the house two lions came out and roared at me!"

"Lions?" said David.

"Yes, sir! They were running about beneath my feet and snapping at me with their sharp teeth. I thought that if they did not bite me to death they were sure to trip me up!"

"What nonsense this is!" cried Mr. Winstanley. "There are no lions in Thoresby. If your mistress chooses to absent herself from tonight's proceedings then that is her concern. Though frankly I am not at all pleased at her behavior. This is, after all, probably the most important event in Thoresby's history." He walked off.

"Lucy, how big were these lions?" asked David.

"A little larger than a spaniel, I suppose."

"Well, that is most odd. Lions are generally larger than that. Are you quite sure—"

"Oh! What does it matter what size the horrible creatures had grown to?" cried Lucy impatiently. "They had teeth enough and snarls enough for animals thrice the size! And so, Lord forgive me, I was frightened and I ran away! And supposing my poor mistress should come out of the house and the lions jump up at her! Supposing she does not see them in the dark until it is too late!" She began to cry.

"Hush, child," said David. "Do not fret. I will go and find your mistress."

"But it was not just the lions," said Lucy. "The whole town is peculiar. There are flowers everywhere and all the birds are singing."

David went out of the inn by the front door and immediately struck his head against something. It was a branch. There was a tree which stood next to the Wheel of Fortune. In the morning it had been of a reasonable size, but it had suddenly grown so large that most of the inn was hidden from sight.

"That's odd!" thought David.

The tree was heavy with apples.

"Apples in June," thought David, "That's odder still!"

He looked again.

"Apples on a horse-chestnut tree! That's oddest of all!"

In the moonlight David saw that Thoresby had become very peculiar indeed. Figs nestled among the leaves of beech-trees. Elder-trees were bowed down with pomegranates. Ivy was almost torn from walls by the weight of ripe blackberries growing upon it. Anything which had ever possessed any sort of life had sprung into fruitfulness. Ancient, dried-up window frames had become swollen with sap and were putting out twigs, leaves, blossoms and fruit.

Door-frames and doors were so distorted that bricks had been pushed out of place and some houses were in danger of collapsing altogether. The cart in the middle of the high street was a grove of silver birches. Its broken wheels put forth briar roses and nightingales sang in it.

"What in the world is Tom doing?" wondered David.

He reached Mickelgrave House and two very small lions trotted out of the gate. In the moonlight they looked more stony than ever.

"I assume," thought David, "that, as these lions are of Tom's creating, they will not harm me."

The lions opened their mouths and a rather horrible sound issued forth—not unlike blocks of marble being rent in pieces. David took a step or two towards the house. Both lions leaped at him, snarling and snapping and snatching at the air with their stone claws.

David turned and ran. As he reached the Wheel of Fortune he heard the clock strike midnight.

Eighty miles away in Cambridge an undergraduate awoke from a dream. The undergraduate (whose name was Henry Cornelius) tried to go back to sleep again, but discovered that the dream (which was of a bridge) had somehow got lodged in his head. He got out of bed, lit his candle, and sat down at a table. He tried to draw the bridge, but he could not get it exactly (though he knew he had seen it somewhere quite recently).

So he put on his breeches, boots and coat and went out into the night to think. He had not gone far when he saw a very odd sight. Edward Jackson, the bookseller, was standing in the doorway of his shop in his nightgown. There was no respectable grey wig on his head, but only a greasy old night-cap. He held a quarto volume in one hand and a brass candlestick in the other.

"Here!" he said the moment he clapped eyes upon Henry Cornelius. "This is what you are looking for!" And he pushed the book into Cornelius's hands. Cornelius was surprised because he owed Jackson money and Jackson had sworn never to let him have another book.

The moon was so bright that Cornelius was able very easily to begin examining his book. After a while he glanced up and found he was looking into the stable-yard of an inn. There, in a shaft of moonlight, was Jupiter, the handsomest and fastest horse in Cambridge. Jupiter was saddled and ready, and seemed to wait patiently for someone. So, without giving any further consideration to the matter, Cornelius got upon his back. Jupiter galloped away.

Cornelius sat calmly turning the pages of his book. Indeed, so absorbed was he in what he found there, that he did not pay a great deal of attention to the journey. Once he looked down and saw complicated patterns of silver and blue etched on the dark ground. At first he supposed them to be made by the frost, but then it occurred to him that the month was June and the air was warm. Besides, the patterns more resembled moonlit fields and farms and woods and lanes seen from very high up and very far away. But, whatever the truth of it, it did not seem to be of any great importance and so he contin-ued to examine his book. Jupiter sped on beneath the moon and the stars and his hooves made no sound whatsoever.

"Oh! Here it is," said Cornelius once.

And then, "I see."

And a little later, "But it will take a great deal of stone!"

A few minutes later Cornelius and Jupiter stood upon the riverbank opposite Thoresby.

"So!" said Cornelius softly. "Just as I supposed! It is not built yet."

The scene before Cornelius was one of the most frantic industry imaginable. Massive timbers and blocks of stones lay strewn about on the bank and teams of horses were bringing more every minute. There were workmen everywhere one looked. Some drove or pulled the horses. Others shouted orders. Yet more brought lights and stuck them in the trees. What was very extraordinary about these men was that they were dressed in the oddest assortment of nightgowns, coats, breeches, nightcaps and hats. One fellow had been in such a hurry to get to Thoresby that he had put his wife's gown and bonnet on, but he hitched up his skirts and carried on regardless.

Amidst all this activity two men were standing still, deep in conversation. "Are you the architect?" cried one of them, striding up to Cornelius. "My name is John Alfreton, master mason of Nottingham. This is Mr. Wakeley, a very famous engineer. We have been waiting for you to come and tell us what we are to build."

"I have it here," said Cornelius, showing them the book (which was Giambattista Piranesi's *Carceri d'Invenzione*).

"Oh! It's a prison, is it?"

"No, it is only the bridge that is needed," said Cornelius, pointing to a massive bridge lodged within a dreary prison. He looked up and suddenly caught sight of an eerie, silent crowd on the opposite bank. "Who are all those people?" he asked.

Mr. Alfreton shrugged. "Whenever industrious folk have work to do, idle folk are sure to gather round to watch them. You will find it best, sir, to pay them no attention."

By one o'clock a huge mass of wooden scaffolding filled the river. The scaffolding was stuffed full of torches, lanterns and candles and cast a strange, flickering light over the houses of Thoresby and the watching crowd. It was as if a firefly the size of St. Paul's Cathedral had sat down next to the town.

By two o'clock Henry Cornelius was in despair. The river was not deep enough to accommodate Piranesi's bridge. He could not build as high as he wished. But Mr. Alfreton, the master mason, was unconcerned. "Do not vex yourself, sir," he said. "Mr. Wakeley is going to make some adjustments."

Mr. Wakeley stood a few paces off. His wig was pushed over to one side so that he might more conveniently scratch his head and he scribbled frantically in a little pocket book.

"Mr. Wakeley has a great many ideas as to how we shall accomplish it," continued Alfreton. "Mr. Wakeley has built famous navigations and viaducts in the north. He has a most extraordinary talent. He is not a very talkative gentleman but he admits that he is pleased with our progress. Oh! It shall soon be done!"

By four o'clock the bridge was built. Two massive semicircular arches spanned the river. Each arch was edged with great rough-hewn blocks of stone. The effect was classical, Italianate, monumental. It would have been striking in London; in Thoresby it dominated everything. It seemed unlikely that any one would ever look at the town again; henceforth all that people would see was the bridge. Between the arches was a stone tablet with the following inscription in very large letters:

THOMAS BRIGHTWIND ME FECIT
ANNO DOMINI MDCCLXXX[8]

David had spent the night inquiring of the townspeople if any of them knew where Tom had got to. As soon as the bridge was built he crossed over and put the same question to the workmen. But an odd change had come over them. They were more than half-asleep and David could get no sense out of any of them. One man sighed and murmured sleepily, "Mary, the baby is crying." Another, a fashionably

---

[8]Thomas Brightwind made me, the year of our Lord 1780.

dressed young man, lifted his drooping head, and said, "Pass the port, Davenfield. There's a good fellow." And a third in a battered grey wig would only mutter mathematical equations and recite the lengths and heights of various bridges and viaducts in the neighborhood of Manchester.

As the first strong golden rays of the new day struck the river and turned the water all to silver, David looked up and saw Tom striding across the bridge. His hands were stuffed into his breeches pockets and he was looking about him with a self-satisfied air. "She is very fine, my bridge, is she not?" he said. "Though I was thinking that perhaps I ought to add a sort of sculpture in *alto rilievo* showing God sending zephyrs and cherubim and manticores and unicorns and lions and hypogriffs to destroy my enemies. What is your opinion?"

"No," said David, "the bridge is perfect. It wants no further embellishment. You have done a good thing for these people."

"Have I?" asked Tom, not much interested. "To own the truth, I have been thinking about what you said yesterday. My children are certainly all very foolish and most of them are good-for-nothing, but perhaps in future it would be gracious of me to provide them with responsibilities, useful occupation, etc., etc. Who knows? Perhaps they will derive some advantage from it."[9]

"It would be very gracious," said David, taking Tom's hand

[9]Despite Tom's low opinion of his offspring, some of his sons and daughters contrived to have quite successful careers without any help from him. A few years after the period of this tale, at more or less the same time, several scholarly gentlemen made a number of important discoveries about electricity. Among them was a shy, retiring sort of person who lived in the town of Dresden in Saxony. The name of this person was Prince Valentine Brightwind. Tom was most interested to learn that this person was his own son, born in 1511. Tom told Miriam Montefiore (David's wife), "This is the first instance that I recall of any of my children doing anything in the least remarkable. Several of them have spent remarkably large amounts of money and some of them have waged wars against me for remarkably long periods of time, but that is all. I could not be more delighted or surprised. Several people have tried to persuade me that I remember him—but I do not."

and kissing it. "And entirely like you. When you are ready to begin educating your sons and daughters upon this new model, let you and me sit down together and discuss what might be done."

"Oh," said Tom, "but I have begun already!"

On returning to Thoresby to fetch their horses, they learned that Mr. Winstanley's servant had returned from Lincoln with the news that Mr. Monkton had died in the night. ("There, you see," said Tom airily, "I told you he was ill.") The servant also reported that the English apothecary, the Scottish physician and the Irish wizard had not permitted Mr. Monkton's dying to interfere with a very pleasant day spent chatting, playing cards, and drinking sherry-wine together in a corner of the parlor.

"Anyway," said Tom, regarding David's disappointed countenance, "what do you say to some breakfast?"

The fairy and the Jew got on their horses and rode across the bridge. Rather to David's surprise they immediately found themselves in a long, sunlit *piazza* full of fashionably-dressed people taking the morning air and greeting each other in Italian. Houses and churches with elegant façades surrounded them. Fountains with statues representing Neptune and other allegorical persons cast bright plumes of water into marble basins. Roses tumbled delightfully out of stone urns and there was a delicious smell of coffee and freshly baked bread. But what was truly remarkable was the light, as bright as crystal and as warm as honey.

"Rome! The Piazza Navona!" cried David, delighted to find himself in his native Italy. He looked back across the bridge to Thoresby and England. It was as if a very dirty piece of glass had been interposed between one place and the other. "But will that happen to everyone who crosses the bridge?" he asked.

Tom said something in Sidhe[10], a language David did not

---

[10]The language of the fairies of the *brugh*.

know. However the extravagant shrug which accompanied the remark suggested that it might be roughly translated as "Who cares?"

After several years of pleading and arguing on David's part Tom agreed to forgive Igraine for getting married and her three sisters for concealing the fact. Igraine and Mr. Cartwright were given a house in Camden Place in Bath and a pension to live on. Two of Igraine's sisters, the Princesses Nimue and Elaine, returned to the *Castel des Tours saunz Nowmbre.* Unfortunately something had happened to Princess Morgana in the nasty house in the dark, damp wood and she was never seen again. Try as he might David was entirely unable to interest anyone in her fate. Tom could not have been more bored by the subject, and Nimue and Elaine, who were anxious not to offend their grandfather again, thought it wisest to forget that they had ever had a sister of that name.

The fairy bridge at Thoresby did not, in and of itself, bring prosperity to the town, for Mr. Winstanley still neglected to do anything that might have made money for himself or the townspeople. However two years after Tom and David's visit, Mr. Winstanley was shewing the bridge to some visitors when, very mysteriously, part of the parapet was seen to move and Mr. Winstanley fell into the river and drowned. His lands, clay and coal all became the possessions of his baby son, Lucius. Under the energetic direction first of Mrs. Winstanley and later of Lucius himself the lands were improved, the clay was dug up, and the coal was mined. Pewley Witts had the handling of a great deal of the business which went forward, and grew very rich. Unfortunately this did not suit him. The dull satisfaction of being rich himself was nothing to the vivid pleasure he had drawn from contemplating the misery and degradation of his friends and neighbors.

And so nothing remains but to make a few observations upon the character of Lucius Winstanley. I daresay the reader will not be particularly surprised to learn that he was a most unusual person, quite extraordinarily handsome and possessed of a highly peculiar temper. He behaved more like Thoresby's king than its chief landowner and ruled over the townspeople with a mixture of unreliable charm, exhausting capriciousness, and absolute tyranny which would have been entirely familiar to anyone at all acquainted with Tom Brightwind.

He had besides some quite remarkable talents. In the journal of a clergyman we find an entry for the summer of 1806. It describes how he and his companion arrived at Thoresby Bridge (as the town was now called) on horseback and found the town so still, so eerily silent that they could only suppose that every creature in the place must be either dead or gone away. In the yard of the New Bridge Inn the clergyman found an ostler and asked him why the town was as quiet as any tomb.

"Oh!" said the ostler. "Speak more softly, if you please, sir. Lucius Winstanley, a very noble and learned gentleman—you may see his house just yonder—was drunk last night and has a headache. On mornings after he has been drinking he forbids the birds to sing, the horses to bray and the dogs to bark. The pigs must eat quietly. The wind must take care not to rustle the leaves and the river must flow smoothly in its bed and not make a sound."

The clergyman noted in his journal, ". . . the entire town seems possessed of the same strange mania. All the inhabitants go in awe of Mr. Lucius Winstanley. They believe he can work wonders and does so almost every hour."[11]

But though the people of Thoresby Bridge were proud of Lucius, he made them uncomfortable. Around the middle of the nineteenth century they were forced to admit to themselves that there was something a little odd about him; although forty or so years had passed since his thirtieth birthday he did not appear to have aged a single day. As for Lucius

---

[11]Journals of the Reverend James Havers-Galsworthy, 1804–1823.

himself, it was inevitable that he should eventually get bored of Thoresby even if he did enliven it for himself by having great ladies fall in love with him, changing the weather to suit his moods and—as once he did—making all the cats and dogs talk perfect English while the townspeople could only mew and bark at each other.

On a spring morning in 1852 Lucius got on his horse, rode on to his father's bridge and was never seen again.

MADELEINE E. ROBINS

LA VIE EN RONDE

THE DESCENT BEGAN IN WINTER. VIVEY WAS PULLING A brush through her thick, graying curls and humming with the January wind outside the bathroom window. She had been working at home all day, compiling an actuarial report from stacks of printouts, still in her pajamas, with a quilt draped across her shoulders and a mug of tea cooling at her elbow. Now, getting ready for bed, she was sitting on the toilet, brushing her hair, still thinking about numbers, so that she missed the moment when the toilet, with her on it, began to sink into the floor.

It was a fast descent, but soft, pillowy, as if the toilet were dropping into cushions that were being lowered into the bathroom below hers. Only, of course, it was not. Her body was certain that this extraordinary thing was happening, but the evidence her eyes gave was that nothing moved: she blinked a couple of times and each time she was at the same height relative to the walls and sink. But she couldn't suspend the sensation of sinking. Now the toilet was tilting to one side with a slight turning motion. Vivey tried to stand and felt the floor roll to one side; she lost her balance, dropped down and lay there. The thought that if she died she'd be found, arms outspread to clutch at the base of the toilet and the pedestal of the sink, with her pants pulled down, made her giggle anxiously. Finally the sensation stopped, and Vivey got up.

She did not call the doctor, trying to talk herself out of anxiety with robust common sense. Just a cold. Or allergies, mold from the heating ducts. A perimenopausal estrogen spike. Calling her doctor would only get her a lecture, one of those "at your age" talking-tos that ended with a recommendation to take hormones and get out more. Vivey was not willing to be scolded. A good night's sleep and she would forget all about it. And she did.

Winter slid into spring, then into the hot months. Late in summer Vivey was coming back to her office after lunch with her friend Rosemary, walking through the broad carpeted hallways of the insurance company where they both worked. Vivey was laughing at something Rosemary had said when Rosemary stopped and looked her.

"Viv, why do you *do* that?" Rosemary asked.

"Do what?" Vivey turned back to look at her friend.

"Walk that way. With your right shoulder almost touching the wall, and your head to one side."

"I don't. Do I?"

Rosemary nodded; her brows were drawn together. "You've always done it a little, but it's been getting"—she paused as if she didn't want to say "worse"—"more marked lately."

Vivey thought about it. "Show me what you think I'm doing."

"I *know* you're doing it, Viv. Like this." Rosemary went to the wall and stood against it so her right shoulder was pressed to the wall and her right arm huddled against her body. She tipped her head so far over that her right ear almost touched her shoulder.

Vivey shook her head. "I don't stand like that. If I did, I'd know it."

"You do." Rosemary's voice softened a little, almost pitying. "You do, Viv. Look." She turned Vivey to one of the mirror panels which punctuated the hallway. "Look," she said again.

Vivey looked at the polished brass, and saw there a woman with her red skirt and black sweater, her own short graying-brown hair and brown eyes, leaning against the wall with her arm wrapped around her waist and her head tilted over. It looked exactly like her, Vivey thought, down to the brown sandals she had put on this morning. But she felt disconnected from that reflection; she didn't recognize it as herself.

"Not me," she said aloud. "That's not me." Tears began to roll down her cheeks.

Her doctor sent her to specialists; Vivey had never imagined there were so many parts of the body to specialize in. Each one agreed there was something wrong, but no one could tell exactly what it was. When they repositioned Vivey, put her head straight and moved her away from the wall, unwrapped her arm from her waist, she became panicky and unbalanced, as if she were about to fall over.

"This is all wrong," she told the doctors. "Don't you feel it?"

They talked to her and to each other. Tests ruled out a brain tumor, an aneurysm, an unsuspected stroke. The psychiatrist gave his opinion that while Vivey showed some neurotic symptoms, her vertigo was clearly not emotional in origin. The ENT could find nothing wrong with her ears; her eyes and hormones were fine; and while the neurologists claimed the problem for their own, they could not say exactly what it was. They tried different drugs, in different combinations, but nothing helped.

In the fall, as the cold weather began, Vivey felt the sinking again. It was different this time: now it felt as if everything, the whole world, were falling away to the right. Straight lines had begun to curve and curl. Floors could not be depended upon to stay flat, to bear the weight of one step as they had the last. Walking through the long mirrored halls at work became a torture. Elevators were the worst: getting up to her office on the forty-fourth floor made Vivey so nauseated she could barely focus on her work. She left earlier and earlier each day.

The people she worked with were sympathetic and concerned. For as long as she could, Vivey's boss distributed the bulk of her work among her co-workers. Vivey fretted that it would not be done properly, that none of them really understood her calculations. Math had not deserted her yet. Vivey could still make numbers dance, make them explain behavior and chance half a world away. But it grew harder and harder to discuss her results clearly: words got jumbled and the sense of them slid together and had to be untangled and parsed. Finally the company could not carry her any longer. She was put on medical disability and sent home for the last time with her personal effects in a box. It was as if she had died, although everyone spoke brightly of seeing her soon.

Rosemary drove her home and walked Vivey to her door.

"Will you be okay getting upstairs, hon?" Vivey had to strain to understand the words, which slid together liquidly, sounds crashing into each other. When she'd made sense of the question, she nodded.

"Ahcawdenighdeseeoowerduun." More jumble. "I'll call you tonight to see how you're doing. Viv, should you be alone? Really, isn't there anyone who could stay with you?"

"There's no one," Vivey said. "I'll be okay."

Rosemary shook her head. Vivey, watching, felt her own head moving to the right in sympathy, wanting to make the circle complete. When Rosemary leaned toward Vivey to kiss her cheek, Vivey drew back, panicked: she didn't know where her space began or ended, and Rosemary seemed to be rushing at her, ready to knock her down. Vivey knew, with old knowledge, that Rosemary was hurt by her withdrawal.

"Sorry," Vivey managed. Words were thick on her tongue; they wanted to curl and slide off one side of her tongue, or collect and jumble together and spit out all at once. "Sorry, Rose. I'll be—" She worked hard and made a smile. "I'll be okay. Thank you, Rose."

Rosemary smiled, a sad crescent. Vivey's eyes followed the path of that arc; then she remembered that Rosemary was still there. "Be okay. Bye, Rose."

Vivey let herself into the building, shuffling around the perimeter of the room toward the stairs. Climbing the stairs was hard, but it was better than taking the elevator, which was fraught with sudden lunges and rolls. Better to take an hour to walk up the four flights to her apartment, poised for the funhouse tricks the stairs played. Vivey left her cardboard box in front of the super's door and struggled to write a note in which the letters did not drip and roll off each other, puddling at the bottom of the page. She asked him to bring the box up to her.

Then she climbed the stairs. It took almost an hour and left her exhausted. Vivey went to her room and lay down, holding hard to the sides of the mattress as her bed rose and fell, rocked and fluttered. At last she slept.

She woke up a little after six that evening. The super had not brought up her box. It was hardly surprising; he never did anything when asked. She did not want to leave the box downstairs all night. She thought about the the problem for a few minutes. It might take her an hour to get downstairs, and she knew it would take two to climb back upstairs with the box.

So take the elevator. It would only be a few minutes, worth the discomfort to get her stuff and come back with it. Vivey left her apartment, slinking along the wall to the elevator.

Lately her left shoulder had begun to drop, and her left hand stretched toward the ground, her whole body leaned away from the clockwise tilt of the world. It was hard to press the call button. The elevator came, and Vivey slunk in and pressed the button for one.

Instantly the floor dropped away from her and she fell into the corner, rolling back and forth from wall to wall. She saw a circle of steel—the handrail—and tried to grasp it, but it rolled away from her. Then the floor threw her upward, until she could touch the arching ceiling of the elevator. And then it stopped, and she was crouched against the wall with her left hand grasping the wavy line of the handrail as it uncoiled itself and began to slide toward the ground.

The door rolled open. Panting, Vivey crawled out.

No one was in the lobby. She coiled upward to her feet and found the super's door, where her box and the note were still waiting. Vivey pushed the box back toward the elevator. When she got there she slumped down on the floor, white faced and sick. The floor arched away from Vivey, curving toward the ceiling; the lobby couch was sliding toward her, and she was at the bottom of a bowl, holding on to a cardboard box that melted and wavered in her arms. Vivey curled in on herself and rolled up onto her knees, long enough to reach endlessly for the elevator button that danced below the indicator light.

Only a few more minutes, she promised herself. *Just a little ride in the elevator.*

She pushed the button. The door opened. Vivey rolled in with the box. She pushed the button for four, and the door cartwheeled shut.

It was worse than it had ever been. The elevator threw her out, up into the darkness of the shaft, and spun below her as she sank down again. Her eyes insisted she was not moving but her body knew that was a lie; she was sinking into a floor that tossed, rippled, and rose. The rhythmic clicks of the elevator buzzed metallically in her head. Vivey vomited, watching the handrail spin and lash out like a Catherine wheel.

When the door arced open Vivey crawled out again, stained with vomit, dragging the box with her. Outside the elevator the hall curved upward toward a vanishing horizon. Her own door was on the right side, just past the stairs.

She sat and wept, and the tears rolled upward into her hair and eyebrows.

At last, she got up, picked up the box and put it under her left arm; her right was curved protectively around her abdomen, and she leaned into the comfortable curve of the wall. She sidled along the wall, eyes half-closed, stepping cautiously so that the floor's sudden flexes and ripples would not throw her off balance. She was doing well; then the floor bucked and tossed, and Vivey lost her balance and teetered to the right, and the stairwell curled up and took her, and she tumbled down and down and up again.

Vivey woke up in the hospital, strapped down and filled with drugs that kept the rolling and tossing of the bed to a bearable level. She had broken a leg, and her left arm. She was concussed. She would require constant care while her bones mended, and after that . . .

Vivey strained to understand what they were saying. The doctors' tact, and her own churning senses, made it hard to understand individual words, but the sense was clear: she could no longer care for herself. She would have to be institutionalized.

Arrangements were made. Vivey lay there, grateful for the drugs that kept the world from tossing and let it simply roll in a circle, all straight lines arching, all the words rolling together. Her mother and sister came to arrange things, close her apartment, sign the commitment papers. Their faces, and the doctor's and the nurses with their small round smiles, who cleaned her and fed her and chatted meaninglessly in sliding sentences, began to roll together. Everything wanted to return to the circle. Vivey was sliding further and further away.

Her mother sat at her bedside for hours, praying. Vivey dreaded her mother's voice and the demands it brought; more and more she slid away. It was restful, giving up the effort to decipher faces and words. She had fought against giving in for so long that the release, now, was overwhelming, delicious.

There were also times she felt panicked and lonely, trapped in a world that spun her away from everyone else. She lay in the bed, eyes closed, trying to remember friends from when she was little, and from college and her first job, the people she knew from work. She had always been shy, there weren't many to remember, but now there were none. The world and everyone she knew were rolling away from her, cartwheeling into the distance and leaving her behind.

A day came when she no longer understood what the people around her were saying; she could not decipher their faces or even read the meaning of the objects around her. The flush of warmth that accompanied her different medications would roll through her, and in the wake of it she sometimes briefly felt closer to understanding words and things again. Then, as the drugs ebbed, she spiraled down into incomprehension again. Only the endless rolling made sense to her. When she gave in to it, there was a beauty to living in the circle, an adventure. But it was lonely.

For a long time Vivey was just there, riding on the edge of the circle, learning to balance there. Then something began to pull her deeper in. At first it was just a brush of sound, like air skimming the surface of her skin; as it got more distinct, as she listened longer, she became sure it was language. Only it was so low, so hushed, so *round* that Vivey could not force it to make sense. It was tantalizing, like something just out of sight. For the first time she began to work *toward* something: she wanted to understand what was being whispered. She wanted to see who was whispering. When she opened her eyes she saw only the ponderous orbs of darkness against the light that were shadows from the old place, nurses or doctors or family. She strained to look beyond them. Something was out there, and Vivey wanted to know what it was.

She listened. Closed her eyes, relaxed into a circle on the bed, and ignored the hands that moved her and tended her. Vivey put all her strength into listening. It took time, more days, but she began to hear the voices clearly, to pick out words as they rolled by her, curved like eggs with unpredictable paths. She began to understand the graceful, arching sounds. They were talking about her.

". . . will be talking." one voice said, like a whispering bell.

"Not yet; soon though," another trilled.

"She hears, I think," a third.

The first one loosed a string of mocking curls of sound: laughter. "Stupid! Anyone can *hear*."

Vivey wanted to ask who they were, but her mouth wouldn't form the rolling sounds. Still, she listened *hard*, and worked her breath to form the words she began to understand.

"Where are you?" It was not speech so much as an exhalation shaped into curls of whispering sound. In the quiet of where she was, the oddly shaped words rolled away, chasing each other; but she was understood.

"She speaks!" the bell voice cried out. "Hello, girl!"

"Hello," Vivey said. "Who are you?"

"Hello, girl; hello, girl!" the other voices—four or five, at least—sang the greeting in a round that tumbled together.

"Stop, stupids!" the bell-voice commanded. "It's too much, all at once. We have to talk one at a time!"

"Who are you?" Vivey asked again. Maybe she was saying it wrong. Maybe they didn't understand her.

There was a swirl of words too rapid to understand. "We *are*." It was the trilling voice this time. The emphasis was not a hard line, but a sinking into sound, deepening the trill as it circled around its center. "You can understand us now?"

Vivey wanted to nod, but knew that wasn't right. She moved her head in a circle, hoping that would mean something to them. "Understand," she agreed. "Who are you?"

"You keep asking that! Your question makes no sense. We *are*." That was the bell-voice, impatient.

"You live here?" Vivey asked.

"We live everywhere!" the third voice assured her. "In the round places. Where are you?"

Vivey didn't understand the question. "I'm here. In—" She did not know the word in this language and tried to use English. "Hospital. We're in the hospital, right?"

There was a rolling clatter of response, as if their words had been dropped all at once onto a metal floor. The sound made Vivey feel a little sick. Finally one of the voices, the bell-voice, cut through.

"*You* are still being in that place," it said. "You must come closer to the round places." Vivey heard more whispering, as if the bell-voice were conferring with the others. "You are tired. We'll go now." And the whispering stopped, abruptly.

Vivey tried to call them back, but they were right. She slid toward sleep and slept for a long time.

Now Vivey had two lives, one sliding away into the past, the other rolling, tumbling into something new. Her body was cared for, there was sensation, feelings of pressure and hot and cold that curled into her consciousness, smells that coiled into her, the roll of medication in her blood, first cold, then hot. She must once have cared what these feelings were, but no more; her memory of them was soft and shapeless. The caretakers were dark spots on a wheel of movement and light, meaningless noises that lashed and bruised her as often as they comforted.

In her new life, Vivey was learning the language of the

round people, her new friends. When she opened her eyes she saw them, sparkles of light darting in and out between the slow dark arcs of her caretakers, speaking so quickly and liquidly it was still hard to follow them. She could not describe them—seeing them was hard enough.

At first she was all they spoke about: how they could reach her, what she could do. The bell-voiced one was the leader, or spoke as if she were. Vivey thought of them as female, perhaps because their voices were soft and high-pitched. The bell-voiced one insulted them all, Vivey included, but she also fussed over Vivey, drawing the others away when she was tired, explaining little things to her as if Vivey were a child. She began to see herself as a child, too. A student of her new world, becoming one of them.

They seemed to have no names, and no idea of names. She tried to explain, but lacked the language and at last gave up. Vivey felt slow-witted and immature, still clinging to naming, but she did not know how else to think about the new people. Privately she named them: the bell-voiced one was Bell. The one with the trilling voice, Trilby, and a third one, whose voice tumbled and leapt like a fish through whitewater, she called Dance. Others came, but these three were the ones Vivey named first. They spoke to her constantly, a rolling delicious peal of commentary. Had she ever been lonely, as she rolled so far away from human life? Not now. Now Bell and Trilby and Dance and their friends courted her and gossiped to her and surrounded her with community. Vivey did very little but listen, but they seemed delighted with that.

"Are there others like me?" she asked one day. "People who've—" She thought of how to put it. "People who've rolled into the round places?"

There was a burst of ringing clatter that she knew was their laughter. "You're not in the round places, just nearby, close enough to see and hear us. *You* can't be in the round places."

That stung, Bell's laughter as she shut Vivey out of their world. "Why can't I?"

What Bell said translated in Vivey's mind as something about square pegs and round holes. Vivey persisted. "Aren't there others like me?" she asked again.

Dance gurgled roundly. "None that come this close. Too afraid of losing the long place." That was what they called Vivey's old home: the place of the too-long arcs.

Vivey thought of a circle that bound her to the old world, then of slivers of the arc shredding into tiny coiling wisps, fraying until the circle broke and she rolled free, freely toward the round places. "Will *I* lose the long place?"

"Why would you want that place? It's *dark*. It's ugly. Here it's beautiful. You're much better off here." That was Trilby, wheeling in the air with unconcern. "Even if you cannot go farther."

"Not ever?" Vivey had hoped that as she grew more familiar, more comfortable with the round ones, they would take her with them, show her more of the round places. "Even if I wasn't afraid of losing the long places?"

Trilby wheeled around Vivey's head teasingly. "You're tied to the long places, they hold you here. You see closer, deeper, into our places, but you're still there as well. No rolling around for the girl!" She laughed with a harsh, metallic sound like marbles rolling on a tin plate.

"Hush!" Bell broke in bossily. "She's tired, she doesn't understand. We will roll away now. We can come back when she's rested." Bell circled around Vivey's head, rushing down to murmur in her ear. "We'll go now. You must rest."

"No!" Vivey said loudly. But the spinning light was gone, the warmth and the whispering were gone just like that. And she could not follow.

Bell whirled back later. It was the first time she had come without her friends.

"Tell around your home," she hummed without preamble, as if she had waited long enough. "Tell me about your place."

"Isn't this my place now?" Vivey asked.

Bell loosed a chiming sound of impatience. "Oh, of course. Now. But tell me about your old home. *Please.*"

It was not usually Bell's way to ask directly for what she wanted; more often she circled around a question and let Vivey ask it, agreeing that perhaps that would be interesting information to have. Bell asking now, alone and direct, gave the question weight Vivey could not ignore. But it was hard to answer truthfully: the words slid away from her, the concepts of *straight* and *long* and *angular* made no sense any more.

"Tell me," Bell insisted.

"It's hard," Vivey said. "I can't find the way to tell you. My place is not round," she said. "It is not filled with light, the people who live there do not shimmer or roll or slide. They move from one place to another without arc—"

Bell's light grew thin, unsatisfied and angry.

Vivey could only explain what the old world had not got, all the things it lacked. *But there must have been some good things*, Vivey thought. It was suddenly important to her that Bell understand that there had been good in that old life, but the harder she tried to tell it, the more it eluded her. "Lines do not meet their ends." Vivey closed her eyes, defeated. "Everything is far apart."

"You're not telling me everything. You're keeping things from me."

"I don't know how to tell you everything," Vivey said. "What I've told you is the truth—as much as I know how to tell you here."

"How could anyone live in such a place?" Bell challenged. "Arcs do not meet? It makes no sense!"

Vivey moved her head in the bobbing arc that meant yes.

"No softness? The heart would—" Bell's light flickered. "The heart would stop."

It seemed to Vivey that Bell must be right, but she knew that once she had lived there, that it *had* made sense.

"The heart knew how to be there," Vivey said to Bell. "And it was beautiful, its own way." Rows of numbers telling tidy stories; the warmth of tea on a cold morning; birdsong and sunrise; a rose unfolding, spangled with dew. How could she explain this to Bell? "The heart knew how to be there," she said again.

"Then how did your heart learn—" Bell sang something Vivey did not understand, but the whirling motion of her light rolled broadly around, as if to include everything. "Could you teach the heart to be there?"

"Your heart?" Vivey asked.

Bell rolled away from the question. "Could you teach?"

"I don't know," Vivey told her. "You're not made for the long place."

Bell's light was warm, cajoling. "You are not made for the round places, but *you* rolled here."

Vivey had tried to explain this before. "I am sick, broken in the long place—that's why I am here. I don't know how to get back. I don't want to go back."

The sparkle of Bell's light was cold as she spiraled away.

After that, Bell became more sarcastic, more bossy. She came, and brought the others with her, and they danced around Vivey and chimed and sang and gossiped to her. Sometimes Bell and Trilby, her lieutenant, asked about Vivey's life in the long place. But Vivey sensed that Bell, despite her anger, was listening, remembering everything she heard.

Trilby seemed offended by the idea of the place Vivey described, asking about it only for the sport of denying it. As they swung and swarmed around her, Vivey realized that Trilby was always in Bell's orbit, that Bell was the star Trilby followed, and her trilling voice was sweeter when she spoke to Bell. Vivey considered this, amused; it might explain why

Trilby dismissed Vivey's stories, afraid of anything that might lure Bell away from her. As for the others, none of them listened as closely as Bell or denied as vigorously as Trilby. Dance was amused by everything Vivey said, her laughter cascading in swells of sound which were sometimes delightful, sometimes oppressive. Vivey craved their visits and was exhausted when they rolled away.

On a day when Vivey was drifting, watching distant circles of light and color that she suspected made a village or a settlement or a gathering of some sort, Trilby wheeled toward her. Her light was sparking cold, her movements abrupt.

"She is gone."

"What?" Vivey did not understand why Trilby was upset, although she clearly was. "Who is gone?"

"Stupid girl, listen!" Trilby roared. "She is gone!"

In the inflection of Trilby's light and music Vivey heard what she had not heard before: *she* was Bell.

"She is Bell? Bell went where?"

Trilby roared at her. "Stupid girl! Stupid! She went to see the long place. You did this! It's your fault! You!"

"But how could she go to the long place? I told her she *couldn't*! I told her—"

"She does not know what she does not want to know," Trilby said. She wheeled threateningly around Vivey. "Now she is gone. You must bring her back."

"What? I don't know how to get back. I told her that, too."

"You must find Bell." Trilby did not wait. She wheeled away in a huge, angry arc. Vivey was alone, trying to think what to do. Find Bell? How would she start? How would she begin? It was not her fault, Vivey thought. She had told Bell not to, had refused to help her. What more could she do? But if she had not come here, had not told Bell and Dance and Trilby about her old world, would Bell have gone looking for it? *You must find Bell.*

Simple to say.

Vivey turned ideas over and over in circles and figure

eights, trying to imagine how she could return a little way into the long place. She had worked so hard to sink into the round place, to cut herself adrift from attachment to the long place. Now she would have to find her way back, away from the light, remembering what it had been like to really occupy her body and experience the arcs and spirals of this place as harsh and intrusive and frightening.

When she had thought and remembered enough, Vivey tried.

First she found her breathing again, respiration not in a line but a long, sighing oval. One dragged the breath up and over and down into exhalation, then rolled downward into the curve that rose, drawing breath in again. When she found the breathing, she let it reach out for her and remind her about her body. Gingerly she sensed her own perimeters, the curves of muscle, the roundness of bone, the gyration of blood through her body. For a long time she simply breathed and explored, gradually narrowing the arc of respiration until it was a pistoning line; gradually making herself remember the line of her femur and the finger's reach from the wrist. Making sense of the lines and straightness even in her own body.

It was terrifying. Vivey made herself go slowly, eyes closed. After a long time she opened her eyes and saw dark shapes. The weight of them, even at a distance, was so crushing that she closed her eyes, hoping to drift back to the light of the round places.

You must find her.

Furious, Vivey opened her eyes again, looking for Bell's darting light. She saw a landscape of grays, light and dark, unmoving or so slow it was hard to tell the difference. Bell's light should have been easy to spot. Instead, Vivey saw one of the dark shapes above her, stretching ponderously toward another shape. She had a sense that she should know why, but it was not until she felt a hot flush spear through her veins that she recognized what had happened. Medicine. The stuff that was piped into her veins to hold her in the long place, only it had never had this effect before. The gray blurs sharpened, acquired edges and weird, distorted shapes. For the first time in a long time Vivey was aware of a swooping drop under her, then a slow rising, a tilt to one side. She had been so detached from her body; now she felt its reactions to vertigo: nausea and panic. The medication spread through her body, recalling her.

From the corner of her eye Vivey thought she saw a cartwheel of light: Bell, dancing across the long place. She tried to call out to her, using Bell's language. It was unbelievably difficult, staying in the world with lines and angles, speaking the language of the world of rolling curves. Like being pulled from the inside out. She cried out to Bell again.

Bell did not turn. Vivey strained after her and called again, watching the angular landscape, breathing into rolls of fluting language. It was hopeless, she thought.

And then something new happened. For the tiniest part of a second, everything snapped together. Vivey saw both circle and line, saw how they met, what they gave each other. She saw how to describe the long place in the words of the round world. It was so beautiful she caught her breath.

It vanished.

There was no use seeking the moment again; the harder she tried, the further away it moved. The medication was ebbing, the effects gentling. The shadows' edges blurred, the world had stopped its fierce bucking. Bell's darting cartwheel of light was gone. *I don't have to stay here,* Vivey thought. *If I close my eyes I can still break away.* She looked one more time, searching for Bell's dancing light, but it was gone. She was afraid to stay longer. Vivey closed her eyes and curled and spun and sank toward the round places again.

Vivey woke and saw lights hovering near, and heard the swooping whisper of conversation just out of earshot. One of the voices was Dance's, she thought.

"What happened?" she said. The time in the long place had made it hard for her to speak; her voice came out as a stammer.

The voices came nearer, their lights subdued.

"Are you awake?" That was Dance.

"Awake," she agreed. "Bell came home?"

The lights near her moved in slow, tight circles. From behind them came another, a dark reddish light. It was Trilby. Vivey knew before she heard the words that Bell was dead.

"How?"

Trilby did not speak. In mourning she was more line than circle, rolling slowly.

"I tried to find Bell," Vivey said. *I damned near got stuck there myself*, she thought. "I told her not to go. I'm *sorry*."

The words rolled like hard little balls across the wide, empty space between Vivey and Bell's friends.

Trilby rolled away, with Dance spinning around her agitatedly. The other lights followed, in twos and threes, until Vivey was left alone.

She thought they would never come back. She wept and sulked and cried out into the pale, shifting emptiness, and finally gave up. Bell was gone, Trilby blamed her for it, there was really no reason for any of them to come back to her. She waited and gave up waiting and began to accustom herself to loneliness again, shut out of two worlds. Sometimes in the distance she saw a haze of moving lights, the round ones meeting, maybe even dancing around some other person intruding from the long places.

She was accustomed to seeing the lights far off, so she did not understand at first when the lights began to roll toward her, in twos and threes, not always the same ones. The first ones spun cautiously at a distance, then one approached, demanding bossily to know what she had seen when she went to find Bell. As she collected her thoughts Vivey felt a pang, missing Bell. She struggled to convey what she remembered: the dark, ponderous world, Bell's light briefly wheeling through it, and that tiny moment of seeing both worlds knit together in impossible, glorious beauty. She made sure to make the long place as dire as she could; Vivey did not want to be responsible for another one of Bell's folk spiraling away to die there.

Dance came once or twice, her light riper with passed time. She danced more slowly now, but the movements were so graceful they made Vivey want to cry. The movements of the youngest ones were hectic and wild, just as their lights were the brightest; they came the most often to hear, to spin around Vivey and tease her. Trilby did not come again, and Vivey did not know whether to be sad or relieved. But she was not lonely. She named, and began to know, a whole new group of them, and as they grew older, a group after that.

A word circled through Vivey's thoughts when she considered her role in the round places. Like many words from her old life it seemed to roll away from her when she sought it, but when she was still it would sometimes come to her: Grannie. She had become the grannie. She stayed where she was, where the body she barely remembered was moored to a world she had released. But she hardly noticed her stillness. They came in dozens, in swarms of circling light so thick the air sometimes buzzed with them: the young ones of the round places came to her to hear her stories, to laugh at her marvelous stories of that other world. She watched for one like Bell, with fear and hope, wondering what she would do if one of the bright cartwheeling lights stayed behind to whisper "show me." She watched for one who would be able to understand both the circle and the line. She thought it was important, that one day someone would have that gift. *But not me*, Vivey thought. *I was only almost.*

"Tell it again, tell it again!" one of the new ones sang,

wheeling among her fellows on the spark of her laughter. "Tell it again!"

Again, Vivey told the story. The curling laughter of the youngest round ones rolled over and around her and took her with it.

D. G. COMPTON

IN WHICH AVU GIDDY TRIES TO STOP DANCING

I WOULDN'T WANT YOU TO THINK THAT I'M GOING TO TELL you all this about Avu Giddy because I think he's someone special. I don't. Nobody's suggesting he was the first man to challenge the dance police, not by a long chalk, and he certainly never came up with even a half-decent new argument to face them down with. Nothing like that. I doubt if poor old Avu's been the first at anything in his whole life—he's not that sort. And as for new arguments . . . well, he's a good enough fellow and no fool, not really, but he's not exactly this great original thinker. A dull man, if I'm honest. Unimaginative. In a word, boring.

Even if he has his secrets, bits of himself he's ashamed of, and I admit that's possible, most of us do, I'm willing to bet they're boring too.

Obviously the simple fact that he tried to stop dancing shows that he's got guts of a sort, but he's hardly special in that. Let's face it, people somewhere or other are trying it all the time—government likes to vague up the figures, but it's clear enough if you read between the lines. They seldom succeed, of course. The dance police see to that. They see to that the same way they saw to Avu.

So the reason I'm telling Avu Giddy's story is not that he, or it, is unusual. In fact you could probably say that its general lack of unusualness is part of my reason: the old this-could-easily-happen-to-you bit. But that's only a small part. Mostly I'm telling this story simply because I saw it happen, and it shouldn't have, and some of it I made happen, and it makes me weep. It still makes me weep, even months after. Which is not like me. I hate admitting it. I never weep. I never weep. But I do now.

So that's why I'm telling Avu's story. I need to get it out. And I need people to know. He won't thank me, but I need people to know.

Avu and I go back. I won't say we've ever been close friends, even before all this happened—my wife used to say I went on seeing him because I thought it would help me get to heaven, like he was my good deed or something, but for god's sake, in those last months I was all he seemed to have—but we'd meet every few weeks and have a natter. After all, we'd worked at the same sort of jobs in the same sort of offices for around thirty years so we could always talk shop, compare notes, that sort of thing.

Checking the last paragraph I see that it reads as if Avu and I don't see each other any more. That isn't true. We often meet. We often bump into each other. I admit we don't have so much to talk about these days, so it's not the same, but Avu always waves, fluttering his fingers as he dances by. And he smiles, of course. And I smile back. So we're still on good terms.

But I know very well that his feet still hurt and he still can't hear the music.

What else could I have done? There has to be the law. And if the law requires dancing, and I agree with it—I vote for it every time it comes up, for heaven's sake—what else could I have done? Dancing is part of how we conduct ourselves, part of the civilized way. We can't have people just opting out. If everybody opted out, just because they felt like it, we'd be in serious trouble. If everybody opted out, just because they felt like it, that'd be the end of civilization as we know it. That's what people always say, of course, *if everybody did this, if everybody did that . . .* But that's not what I'm talking about. I'm talking about Avu Giddy. He isn't everybody, he's just Avu Giddy.

So what else could I have done?

It all began about a year ago, early in the summer. Avu and I used to meet now and then during our lunch breaks, in the park. Our offices at that time were only half a kilometer or so apart and at lunchtime on sunny days we'd take our packets of sandwiches—wholemeal for me, white for Avu, he'd never learn—and we'd meet in a park roughly midway between us, a pretty little square with grass and paths and dusty plane trees inside high black cast-iron railings. The park was nice but the area had gone down a bit. The tall redbrick houses around the square, narrow, with fancy Dutch-style gables, had once been rich people's homes, but now they were offices for advocates and small import/export businesses. Our meetings weren't regular, we both had busy lives to live, just now and then. If the weather was dry, we'd spread our coats and sit on the grass. If it had rained recently we made use of one of the park benches. They were black cast iron to match the railings, with black cast-iron arms in the shape of mythical winged beasts. Gryphons, I believe they're called.

I say it all began then because that was when I first noticed it, but it must have been stoking up for months. A man like Avu doesn't get so low, not the way he was that day in early June, just out of the blue, not the way he was that day. Avu always took his time. He didn't rush things. Still, that was the first day I'd noticed he was low so I asked him what was up, and he said, nothing much, just that his daughter had taken off, gone to live with her boyfriend, and he was finding it hard, getting used to managing alone. But I knew it wasn't just that because he'd lived alone before, before the girl had had the bust-up with her mother and landed back on his doorstep, and it hadn't bothered him then.

That's his younger daughter, of course. Karin. His older daughter, Jenna, had married and gone off seven years ago. Much too young, of course, and paying for it now, two kids and a husband never far from the nearest racetrack, but that had been before Avu and his wife had separated, and Jenna'd had her reasons. The younger daughter would have gone off too, the way things were in the home, but she'd been only twelve, so she'd stayed till the divorce. It hadn't been, shall we say, a happy household.

So what does a man say? I told him things were bound to get better, the first few weeks were always the worst, living alone really did have its advantages, think of all the girls he could have whoopi-do with now in the evenings, and we laughed and he said he was getting a bit old for that and I said, never, and we talked about the new hot drinks machine they'd installed at his office and the disgusting coffee it made. Those machines always do. Neither of us could understand how the manufacturers went on getting away with it. Wasn't this the day of consumerism, capitalism, the operation of the free market, all that stuff? Wasn't the customer always right?

Avu was fifty-three. He'd been with the same firm for most of his working life. All of his working life, actually, if you didn't count his first job, stacking supermarket shelves, straight from school. He'd done well. He had an eye for administrative detail and they valued his services. He had a nice house, a decent car, holidays abroad. Two beautiful girls, a proper success story. Except for his marriage. He'd made a mess of that, he and his wife between them.

So we talked about consumerism and capitalism, the operation of the free market, all that stuff, and then it was time for us to go back to work. I didn't see Avu again for several weeks. I was busy. I'm treasurer of my local historical society and a lot of my lunchtimes were taken up getting ready for the July AGM. There were minutes to write up and I like to do these things properly. When I did finally ring Avu's office he wasn't keen to come but I could tell he hadn't cheered up much so I persuaded him. Before he rang off he asked me straight out, over the telephone, what I thought about all this dancing, which I didn't like the sound of, but I told him we'd talk about it when we met.

It was a lovely day, bright and sunny but not too hot, which was one of the reasons why I'd suggested lunch. The little park was crowded, lots of pretty young secretaries and their boyfriends in smart striped shirts dancing by, and all the best areas of grass were taken by the time we got there, but I found us a patch under a tree, a bit on the bald side but dappled with sunlight and fairly private. I hadn't been planning a philosophical discussion on the pros and cons of dancing, more a friendly chat in the park, but what can you do? At least the phone call had warned me.

Oddly enough, when Avu arrived—he was nearly four minutes late—he seemed quite perky. He'd been having a chat with his daughter, he said, and this even before he'd opened up his sandwiches. He'd gone over to his daughter's place, he said, and he'd sounded her out and she'd told him he was a miserable old sod and he could do as he pleased.

He laughed. He seemed for some reason to find his daughter's answer cheering.

I asked him which daughter, Karin or the married one, Jenna, and he said, Jenna. It didn't matter to me all that much which daughter—I could guess which one anyway, the reply was Jenna all over—but I needed a bit of thinking time. Avu wasn't making himself clear. Sounded Jenna out? What about? Dancing? Jenna was a great little dancer, full of it, so he'd hardly have needed to sound her out about that. And anyway, what did he mean by "sounded her out"? And why was he so chirpy?

I groped a bit. What's Jenna doing these days? I said.

Avu said he wasn't sure. She and Clifton were always up to something new.

And the kids?

Avu shrugged. He hadn't asked. And that too, he said—wasn't not asking, not even thinking to ask, wasn't all that just another part of the problem?

Problem?

He was a terrible grandfather, he said. Never remembered their birthdays. And all this dancing. He was so bad at it.

Avu laughed again. He wasn't making much sense. He'd unwrapped his sandwiches by now and they were a mess too. A mess. More tuna on the paper than between the bread. And white bread, of course, totally lacking in vitamins. He wasn't looking after himself.

I suggested that he take some of the five weeks' holiday due to him as a senior staff member. He needed a break and the younger men on the staff with kiddies wouldn't be going until school was over at the end of July, so the timing was perfect.

Why won't you talk about dancing? he said.

I told him I'd talk about dancing anytime he wanted. I just didn't see the point.

No, he said. He pinched up his lips. Nor do I.

It didn't take me long to work out what he meant, that it was dancing he didn't see the point of, and I didn't like that sort of talk. But I'd known him a long time and I had to take him seriously, so I admitted that it probably wasn't much fun, dancing on your own the way he had to just then, but if that was all there was, then you did it. Most people seemed to manage. It was a question of attitude, really.

He said his feet hurt.

I told him that was just self-pity.

He said they really did, they hurt quite badly, and I told him that was no excuse.

I'm boring you, he said. I always have.

I told him that was the stupidest nonsense I'd heard in a long time. We were friends, weren't we? Of course he didn't bore me. Of course he didn't bore me.

So he sighed and asked me what was so great about dancing anyway, and I eyed his sandwiches and told him they looked pretty foul. I offered him one of mine, though I'd only the two. He was in a bad mood, I said. Maybe he wasn't sleeping properly. Had he thought of seeing a doctor?

What should I have told him? *Great? About dancing?* What sort of a question was that? I do my dancing, we all do. It's something we do. Some days it's better than others, and mostly we don't think about it. It's fine, enjoyable, the way it should be, but I'd have felt a proper fool trying to come up with some great special moment for him, some great special moment on some fancy beach, maybe at dawn, all pink and pearly. We weren't like that, him and me. Most people aren't. For god's sake, wasn't the point of it all really that if we didn't do our dancing what else did we do?

So instead I suggested that he see a doctor.

He looked down at the sandwich I was offering him then, and then back up at me, at my face, and it was a sad sort of look, not perky, not at all perky, and it told me that I'd failed him, which I'd already known. But I hadn't known how badly. He'd been begging me, begging me to come up with something. This was what "sounding out" meant. But I still didn't have anything to say, not a damn thing, at least his daughter had told him to bugger off, which was honest and maybe in a way had set him free, but I had nothing to say so he looked down again at the sandwich I was offering him and asked me if I was sure I could spare it and when I nodded and pushed it at him, he took it. Then he said something else to me very softly, so softly that I didn't hear.

I told him I hadn't heard him.

He wasn't eating the sandwich, just staring down at it. I think he was crying. Screwing up his face, it took that much effort, he spoke to me again, more clearly. He couldn't hear the music, he said. Not any more. He couldn't hear the music. People expected him to dance, he said, but he couldn't hear the music.

It shook me. If it was true, and I had no reason to suppose it wasn't, then he was in deep trouble. He really was. You know as well as I do, it's the music that keeps us going. Not all the time, maybe only now and then, but enough to keep us going. I simply couldn't imagine dancing on, not hearing the music. Every day, day after day, not hearing the music. It was dreadful. Appalling.

I slapped him encouragingly on the shoulder. I laughed. He was having a bad day, I said. A bad mood. He really should go and see a doctor.

We sat on the bald grass in the dappled sunlight under the tree and I watched the secretaries and their boyfriends while he pulled himself together. I didn't hurry him, just watched the passing crowd, and when he'd pulled himself together he cleared his throat and said that I was probably quite right, it was just a mood and maybe he'd go and see a doctor. People got these moods sometimes. It really wasn't anything to get upset about.

Then he ate my sandwich, he seemed quite hungry, and we talked about the new productivity incentive scheme his immediate boss, his snotty departmental manager, was proposing, and the way it risked reducing office staff to the level of piece workers at a conveyor belt. Avu didn't think it would work and I agreed with him.

Three days later I was rung at work by his daughter Karin. That's the younger one. She sounded furious. Really wild. She asked me if I would kindly tell her what the hell her father was up to and when I asked her what she meant she said I was his friend, wasn't I? It was disgraceful. He'd written her this letter all about maybe not keeping on dancing and what the hell did he think he was up to?

I told her to calm down. I told her stopping dancing was perfectly legal.

And so it is. Once you stop, of course, you never can start again, but that's perfectly legal too. I hadn't answered her question, though. I didn't like her question.

She didn't notice. She didn't even listen. She ranted on about how incredibly selfish her father was. And she knew perfectly well what he was up to. He was trying to make her feel bad about leaving him for her boyfriend. As if that hadn't been all his fault, anyway. Like living with a corpse. No wonder she'd pushed off as soon as Jake'd said he'd have her. And no wonder her father'd got fed up with dancing. He got fed up with everything. He'd been that way with her mum, always drizzling on. Drizzle, drizzle, drizzle. And now this letter, trying to make out it was all her fault. As if *she'd* failed *him*, rather than the other way round.

I managed to chip in there, telling her Avu never blamed her for anything. He never blamed other people. It wasn't his way.

So she went really wild. If her father was such a saint, she said, how come he didn't care what people would think about her, having a father who stopped? What her friends would say. They'd blame her, for sure. Wasn't that the most selfish thing I'd ever heard?

Frankly no, I thought. I asked her if it had occurred to her to wonder why he'd written her the letter? Had she thought of asking him if he was wanting help, maybe?

She said she hadn't needed to ask. He'd told her all about it in the letter, moaning on and on about how much his feet hurt.

Didn't that seem reasonable? I suggested. If the poor man's feet were hurting, then of course he'd—

Reasonable? Just a lot of selfish fuss. If everyone stopped dancing the first time their stupid corns gave them gyp, she asked me, what did I think would happen?

I sighed. The tired old *what if everybody* argument . . . I told her I thought it was a bit more than corns in Avu's case. I didn't mention the music, his not hearing the music, that seemed up to him, too personal, a very private matter, but I told her that maybe she should find out how bad his feet were for certain.

She said she didn't need to. She said he'd admitted in his letter that he'd been to the doctor, who'd found nothing wrong and had tried to give him tranquilizers.

Maybe he was depressed, then.

Depressed? Who wasn't depressed these days? Anyway, he didn't mean it. He just wanted to punish her for leaving. Make her feel bad. And besides, it was so insulting. Who did he think he was, setting himself up above other people? They were happy enough with their dancing, so how come he thought he was so superior?

She was having it both ways, of course. He didn't mean it, and at the same time he was thinking himself superior. Poor Avu. He couldn't win.

Ah, the things one says. *Couldn't win.* Was that really what the two of them had come to, a father and his daughter, one or other of them needing to win?

I asked her why she was calling me. What did she want me to do?

She said I must talk to him. I was his friend, wasn't I? I must talk some sense into him. It was all self, self, self. If he thought his letter would bring her scurrying back, he had another think coming. She had Jake now. That was what the trouble was. She had Jake now and her father was jealous.

I asked her if she'd done anything about the letter, other than call me, and she said she'd torn it up into tiny pieces, burned them, and blown the ashes to the four winds. And she'd called her sister Jenna. Jenna was right behind her. Jenna thought the letter completely disgusting.

She was very upset. I didn't know her well but she'd never seemed a bad sort of girl. Of course, her parents being divorced, and the messiness of it all, would account for a lot. But there were kinder ways of looking at what Avu was doing. What if he just wanted help? What if he was using this dancing threat as an excuse? I didn't think so, that sort of thing wasn't Avu, but I could be wrong.

I told her I'd give him a call. Then I'd let her know. But he might be busy, in a meeting, so she might have to wait.

He was busy. In a meeting. I left a message for him to call me back but he didn't so I tried again, around five, and he'd already gone home so I tried yet again that evening at his home number, and again several times during the evening, which he didn't answer. I thought of going round but his house was a good way off and it was getting later and my wife said I should mind my own business. I called Karin to let her know how things stood, and told her not to worry. She said she had no intention of worrying. She and Jake were having some friends in. If her father decided to stop dancing in the middle of the night, that was his problem. The dance police wouldn't like it, but that was their problem.

I rang Avu's office one more time when I got to work in the morning and he hadn't come in. And he hadn't sent word either. It wasn't like him, they said.

It's a big city. I couldn't really go looking for him. And besides, I had the day's work to get on with. I tried his home number again, but with no success.

It was a miserable day, early August but cold and rainy, the sky like the inside of one of those aluminum saucepans that stay grey no matter how hard you scrub them. I thought a lot about Avu that morning, in between meetings and some pretty important paperwork, and when lunchtime came I stuffed my sandwiches in my briefcase, put on my raincoat, took my umbrella, and went out. I had tried to imagine what I would do if I were Avu, where I would go, and the only place that kept on coming up, especially in the rain, was the park.

And here Avu is. He's sitting on one of the black cast-iron benches. Rain is falling really quite heavily and, unsurprisingly, apart from the two of us the park is empty. Beyond the railings the high redbrick houses that line the road all have steamed-up windows, office striplights behind them shining brightly. Cars pass slowly, hissing on the wet road. Nobody sees us.

Avu has one ankle up on his other knee, the shoe off, and he is massaging his stockinged foot. His umbrella leans on the ground beside him, the wrong way up, filling with water. The rain is steady, he doesn't have a coat on, and he's getting totally wet.

I've taken a pill, he says. It's a special pill. It's going to paralyse my legs. The man who sold it to me promised.

Oh, Avu. I try to hold my umbrella over both of us. What man? What man?

You shouldn't have found me, old friend. But it's my fault, this park and all. I didn't realize I was so obvious.

What man, Avu? Before I do anything I need to know if the man is reputable, if he is making a reputable promise. I need to know if his pill is going to work. What man?

The dance police won't find me, though. They aren't that clever.

What man?

Avu shakes his head. It's a secret, he says.

I decide to assume that the man *isn't* reputable. His pill isn't going to work. I ask Avu, Why are you so set on this? Dancing's not so bad. I don't dare to mention the music, him not hearing the music. I ask him, Are your feet really so sore?

He kneads his toes. I think it's working, he says. I'm sure it is. Then he looks up at me, smiling gently, and asks, How sore is *so* sore, d'you reckon?

Not really having the faintest idea, I say, It has to be pretty bad.

Whose pretty bad? Your pretty bad? My pretty bad?

He puts his shoe back on and changes legs, massaging the other foot. The trouser leg is drawn back above the edge of the sock and it shows an ugly area of bare hairy ankle. To be honest, I don't like to see this.

I avoid his question. You have to think about other people, Avu. The people your stopping will have an effect on.

I agree. They have to think about me too. He massages his foot. And you're avoiding my question. I'm sad and tired, old friend. And my feet hurt. Does it matter how much they hurt? Is it any of your business how much they hurt?

You should get out more, Avu. There are folks you could help.

No, there aren't. Not me, old friend. Not me.

That sort of talk is always irritating, yet I have to admit that in Avu's case it's probably true. You're talking like this because you're angry, Avu.

He considers. Perhaps I am. It feels as if I'm tired and sad, just tired and sad, but perhaps I'm angry. He considers some more. He asks me, Would you rather I was angry? Is that what you're saying?

The rain falls still more heavily, bouncing on the path, and I devote my entire umbrella to him. I want you to go on dancing, Avu, I tell him. And I really mean it. I'm not sure why, it's not as if he's my best friend or anything, but I really mean it.

All this will pass, I tell him. I want you to go on dancing.

So do the dance police. He frowns. But they can't be everywhere. And I don't believe how much my feet hurt matters a damn. I don't believe how much my feet hurt is anyone else's damn business.

This stuff isn't Avu. The bench is soaking wet but I sit down beside him, soaking the backs of my thighs. I hold the umbrella with one hand and touch his sleeve with the other.

I want you to go on dancing.

My feet hurt. Thank you, but my feet hurt.

I want you to. Please. Please.

It's not enough, old friend. He begins to replace his second shoe. He says, I don't hear the music. I've told you this before. I don't hear the music.

This is more than I can bear.

Please, Avu. I want you to go on, Avu. I want you to.

It's not enough.

It is now, as he is replacing his second shoe, that the leg under it collapses. The other follows and he starts to slip off the bench. I put my arm round his chest, stopping him from falling. Unless Avu is putting on a brilliant performance it seems that the man, the secret man, was reputable after all.

I cry out. I tell him, You can't do this to me. You can't do this to me.

I'll never have to dance again, he answers.

His legs are collapsing more and I find it harder to keep him on the bench. He's weeping now but it's because he's happy.

I'll never have to dance again.

Anxiously I look round the park. There is no one. Just the rain bouncing on the path. I shout and no one comes running, so I stand up and hold Avu in place with my knees while I close my umbrella and put it on the ground beside his open one, then I shove my arms under Avu, one under his shoulders and one under his two poor paralysed legs, and I lift him and carry him away.

He's heavy. Fifty-three years old, a heavy man, and I lurch about, bumping into benches and then railings and then the park gates. Our umbrellas stay behind, mine closed, leaning against the bench, his open and filling with water. Outside the park on the slippery pavement I fall. One elbow hits the pavement with Avu's full weight on it and the pain is bad. I have broken a small bone, so the doctor will tell me later, but I get up, still carrying Avu, and struggle on. People appear, going from one place to another, hurrying to get out of the rain, and they eye me suspiciously, this crazy man who is carrying some sort of corpse and shouting things. I alone can see the tears on Avu's face, quite different from the rain, as he cries happily.

Then a taxi comes along, which doesn't want to stop, but we lurch in front of it so that it has to. I drag the door open and bundle Avu in, and myself after him, and I ask the driver to take us to the nearest hospital. We're going to save Avu's now paralyzed legs.

At this point Avu stops crying. He begins to curse instead, the f-word and blasphemies, and scrabbles at the taxi door. He isn't himself. Blasphemies. The f-word. This isn't Avu, so I hug him, enveloping his arms so that he can't reach the taxi door latch, and because his legs are paralyzed there isn't much he can do, so I hug him all the way to the hospital, my elbow hurting like hell, while he struggles and swears.

He isn't himself. We're going to save Avu's legs because he isn't himself. Tomorrow he'll thank us, when he's himself again.

Porters in white coats get him out at the hospital while I pay the taxi driver, just his exact fare, he wouldn't have stopped for us if we hadn't lurched in front of him, and they carry Avu into the emergency department. I tell a nurse what has happened and she calls a doctor and they draw curtains round Avu and give him an injection. They have to hold Avu down, the doctor, the nurses and the two porters, even though his legs are paralyzed, and he shouts at them not to, please not to, please not to, all the time they are getting the needle in. I watch through a gap in the curtains. He isn't himself.

Afterwards he's quiet. The doctor comes out through the curtains and talks to me discreetly, saying that my prompt action has saved Avu Giddy's legs. Another five minutes and they'd probably have been paralyzed for good. Then he gets a hospital form and asks me if Avu has any next of kin who ought to be informed and I don't think his daughters will thank me for getting them involved so I lie and tell him no. No, I say, he's all alone. I ask the doctor if the hospital will be taking any action against Avu for what he's done, and the doctor says no. He'd like to get at the man who supplied the pill but people like Avu never tell. Then I mention my arm and the doctor takes me away and gets it x-rayed. A small bone in it is broken, not something that needs plaster, but they put my arm in a sling and I have to keep it there for the next two weeks.

Avu's legs got completely better. Nothing else changed much and his daughters never got to hear of his little adventure. They haven't yet forgiven him his letter. I believe he offered to do volunteer work in an alcoholics' hostel but the organizers turned him down. Oh, and when I went back to the park that evening for our umbrellas, they'd both disappeared. That's the way things are in this city.

Avu and I have never talked about what happened. And of course, he's never thanked me. He'll maybe try again, but I doubt if he's brave enough. We still meet. We haven't that much to say these days but we often bump into each other and Avu waves, fluttering his fingers as he dances by. He smiles, and I smile back, so we're still on good terms. But he's old now, and small and grey, and I know very well that his feet still hurt and he still can't hear the music.

And I weep. I weep for the world. After we've met, and sometimes at night, in the small hours of the morning, I feel ashamed and I weep. There aren't really any dance police, you know. Only you and me.

CORY DOCTOROW

POWER PUNCTUATION!

Hi, Mom!

Wow, you won't believe what happened today. First of all, I was nearly late for work because my new roommate is worried about the electrical and he pulled out all the plugs last night, even my alarm clock! His name is Tony, and I think he is either weird or crazy, or maybe both! He keeps saying that the Company uses the plugs to listen to our minds! He unplugged all the electricals and put tape over them in the middle of the night. When I woke up this morning, my room was totally black! I had my flashlight from work on the chair near my bed, and I used that to find the living room. Tony was sitting in his shorts on the sofa, in the dark, watching the plug behind the TV. Hey, I said, you watch the television, not the plug, and then he said some bad words and told me that he didn't want me plugging in *anything*. He is skinny like Jimmy got when he had the AIDS, but he is not sick, he is hyperkinetic, like Manny was when he went to the special school.

That is why he is management and I still work on a truck. If I have to be skinny and crazy to be management, I'll take the truck all day long!

So I got dressed and ran out of the apt and took all those stairs up to the slidewalk because there was a big lineup of people waiting for the elevators, like always, and I didn't have time to wait, because my watch was already warning me that I was going to be late as if I didn't know! I ran all the way to the garage, around all the people on the slidewalk, who don't know to walk right and stand left like you always told me. Life up here in the city is different from back home and no doubt at all.

My watch knew that I wasn't in the garage at 8:25 and it started counting down the minutes till I was late. Its voice gets higher and higher and more and more excited as I get closer to being late, and I thought it was going to bust something as I ran through the door of the garage. It told me that I'd had a close call, but I'd made it, and I felt pretty good about that.

Wendell, the day supervisor, smiled at me when I came in, which he *never* does, and I got nervous that maybe my watch was wrong about my being late, except that my watch is never wrong. Jap, he said, you're on special truck 982 today. I said what's that, and he told me that it was a great honor and then he said I'd like you to meet your pusher for today, Rhindquist.

So I shook Rhindquist's hand. He was a kind of old, fat, short guy, and his uniform was old-fashioned looking and not as smart as the one I wear, that you liked so much in the photo I sent home last month. So right away I thought that he was some kind of moron and I was being punished for being late. He said, pleased to meet you, Jasper, and he didn't sound like a moron, but more like one of those guys on your TV stories that are rich and powerful and in charge. I said call me Jap everybody else does and he said twenty years ago the All-Nippon Anti-Defamation League would have put a stop to that and I laughed even though I didn't get the joke until later. It is that Jap is also short for Japanese, which is like the Moonies but they are from Korea.

Let's roll 'em out, Rhindquist said, and hopped on the back of the truck and held on tight. I got in and did my ten-point startup safety check like they taught me. By point four, he was banging on the side of the truck and saying Let's go! and I leaned out my window and said that I wouldn't skip my safety check for nobody and he said some bad words and I said that I would have to start over again and he'd better keep quiet or we'd never get out of there. My watch said I did right, which made me feel good. I hoped that Rhindquist's watch told him off for trying to shortcut on safety!

We rolled out a little late. I drove to my first pickup, which is the side of Finance 38. Finance 38 is a very, very tall building and all no windows because they don't want spies from other cities seeing them and their money. I drove over the Severe Tire Damage yard and passed through three security gates and backed up to the shredder bay. I did my four-point shutdown safety check and Rhindquist banged on the truck again and said more bad words but I ignored him. His watch must be busy all the time, telling him not to be so mean!

I went through the metal detector and into the Finance 38 and the guard's watch and my watch talked to each other for a while and then the guard stopped pointing his gun at me and said, You're late now move this stuff out of here and I said OK and started moving the boxes. Finance 38's boxes are very heavy, and there sure are a lot of them! Every day, there are fifty boxes, as big as the big TV at the community center back home. I am getting very strong working at this job, Mom! My arms are bigger every morning.

I moved the boxes back to the truck. I left them for Rhind-quist, who started opening them and pushing the papers inside into the hopper. On my normal truck, 3528, my pusher is Vasquez, who is very fast at pushing the papers. Rhindquist was slow, so that by the time I'd moved half the boxes back to the truck, there was no more room to move the rest! I thought that for a guy who's always in a big hurry, he sure works slow!

So I went into the truck, with my flashlight. And there was Rhindquist, and do you know what he was doing? He was reading the papers before putting them into the shredder! What are you doing? I said, you aren't allowed to do that! He gave me a look, not like he was angry, but like he thought *I* was a moron or something. My watch told me that I should report him right away, and I started to go back into Finance 38 to use the guard's phone, but Rhindquist did something with his own watch and my watch stopped working! You broke my watch! I said to him!

He said, That's from the Blues Brothers, and he said, What do they do, attach the disposal baskets to the laser printers? This is all junk, none of this needs secure disposal! And I said, you broke my watch, Rhindquist, and everything in the Finance Buildings needs secure disposal, it's in the manual.

He said, I didn't break your watch, I just shut it off for a while. It will be OK, trust me. Come here, have a look at this.

Mom, I did it! I read the paper in his hand, with my flashlight. It said, Johnson, your performance review has been rescheduled for 1630h on Friday, 78th floor boardroom.

This is crap! Rhindquist said. This doesn't need secure disposal. He kept digging through the papers, and looking at them before shoving them in the shredder. Every time he looked at one, he said, Crap, and then put it in. I couldn't stop watching. I thought we were going to be fired! Or put in jail! Then he said, Aha! He showed me the paper, it said, CONFIDENTIAL at the top, and I felt like I was going to sick up, I was so scared. It said RE-ORG CHART, and it had lots of names with dotted lines connecting them to other names. Rhindquist winked at me and put it in his pocket— his old-fashioned uniform had pockets!

I thought I figured it out then. Rhindquist was a spy from another city! They talked about spies in Basic Training, and

what to do when you found one. You are supposed to make
sure they won't go anywhere, then contact security. So I ran
as quick as I could out of the truck and slammed the door
and security-locked it from the outside, and then I climbed
over all the boxes of unshredded documents from Finance 38
and ran to the security guard. I said, there's a spy in my truck,
and he's reading the papers! And he said, What? I said, My
pusher is a spy! I caught him reading the papers and putting
them in his pockets! The security guard looked like he thought
I was crazy! I said, Really! And he picked up his phone and
spoke in Securitese to the other security guards and then
there were sirens and lots of cars and guards with armor and
guns, Mom!

They surrounded the truck and unlocked it and Rhindquist stepped out with his hands in his pockets. He said, Quality Auditor, boys, radio it in. The security guards looked like
they wanted to shoot him, but one of them talked into his
phone and then shouted out at all the security guards in Securitese and they went away!

Rhindquist walked over to me and said, Jap, you aren't the
brightest bulb on the marquee, but you think fast and you
follow orders. I said, I am as smart as the next person and I
do my job. I said to the security guard from Finance 38, aren't
you going to arrest him, he's a spy!? And the security guard
said, Look, he's management. He's allowed to do this.

And Rhindquist put his arm around my shoulders and said,
You're stuck in a loop, son. New data: I'm not a spy, I'm your
boss, and you did right, even if you have blown the audit.
How'd you like a promotion?

And I said, you're management?

And then, do you know what? He said, Jap, my boy-o, I
am Rhindquist J. McBride, CEO, President, and Chairman of
the Board of the File-O-Gator Corporation, The Incorporated
Township of File-O-Gator, Ontario, and File-O-Gator International Holdings, Limited. I'm *in charge*!

Hi, Mom!

Thanks for the pictures from Buddy's wedding. He sure looks handsome in a suit! You're right, he should dress nice more!

I'm dressing nice, too. Rhindquist J. McBride has made me a Special Vice President! I'm management! Not management like my crazy roommate, Tony, who isn't my roommate anymore. They moved him and gave me the whole apt to myself, and I can plug in anything I want to, whenever I want to! I'm Real Brass! I only drive my old truck number 3528 two days a week now, and Vasquez has a different driver who I've never met the other four days. Vasquez says he is not as careful as I am, and sometimes, he makes them late! And he says, now that I'm running the show, can I make sure that his performance appraisal shows that it's the new guy's fault? I said I would look into it.

I haven't had a chance to look into it yet, because the other four days, I go to Operations 1 and sit in a beautiful office on the top floor, one hundred floors above ground! They keep me busy, Mom! Rhindquist comes into my office and sits in the chair by the door, and talks on his phone, and asks me all kinds of crazy questions, like, Do I think that the pinheads in HR know their ass from a hole in the ground? And I say Yes, and he says, What makes you think so?

So I told him about Basic Training, and how I learned the history of File-O-Gator, and memorized our Vision Statement, which is, The File-O-Gator Organization is a diverse multinational sovereign power that is a World-Class Leader in its fields of Operations, a status it has achieved through the diligence and responsibility of its Human Resources, which are the Heart of every Organization. I told him about how the HR Sergeant was always fair about our Training Appraisals, and how he always knew when someone had been goofing in the showers and made sure that they got disciplined. And I told him about how I played the Anthill Simulator and learned how the one drone doesn't know why he's moving a grain of sand, but that from the Queen's seat in the middle, it all makes sense. I told him that whenever my watch asks me to do something I didn't understand, or when something weird happens to me, like my crazy roommate Tony covering up all the plugs, that I remember the Anthill Simulator and I do my job.

Rhindquist laughed and said Jap, my bright boy, you are a treasure, a walking focus-group. I'm not paying you enough. And then he gave me a raise! He called someone on his phone and said, Give my boy a raise, and they did! I am sending home a little money as an attachment with this note, and a picture of me in my Special Vice-President's suit.

Every afternoon, Rhindquist shuts off his phone and my watch, and a pretty secretary wheels in a big TV. We watch movies! Rhindquist says he likes to unwind with a movie at the end of the day. The movies are old and funny, and I've never seen them before. Rhindquist sure has, though! He knows most of them by heart! Yesterday, we watched one called Educating Rita, and Rhindquist told me that I am like Rita. I already had that figured out, though. Rita is a dumb girl from England, Ltd., and she works as a hairdresser until someone from management teaches her all about life. I liked the movie a lot. I think that Rhindquist will teach me lots and lots about management, too.

My crazy old roommate Tony works in Operations 1, too, in the basement. I know this because this morning I saw him getting off the slidewalk and going to the basement elevators. He sure looked worried. I ran up to him and said Hi and he looked at me in my suit and his eyes bugged out and then he said Hi, too.

I told Rhindquist about him, and he said that he thought Tony had interesting prospects and he would keep an eye on him. I tried to tell him about Vasquez and the new guy but then his phone rang and he talked for a long time. He sounded angry, and he shouted that he didn't care what it took—get him Redmond! Even if you have to nuke it! I have a small TV on my desk, and I used it to look up Redmond, but it kept saying, See Microsoft. I asked Rhindquist about it and he said that Redmond is what Microsoft used to be called before they incorporated. He is always talking like that, calling things by their old names.

It was quitting time then, so I went home and wrote you this letter.

Hi Mom!

I am real sorry to hear about Buddy. I know he must feel sad. I didn't think that Carla was a spy, either, but now that she's been arrested, I guess that Buddy should feel lucky that he didn't stay married to her long enough to have little spy babies!

This is my third week as Special Vice President. I'm doing well for myself! Crazy Tony is now my assistant! He sits at a smaller desk in my office with me and Rhindquist, and Rhindquist asks him the same crazy questions he asks me, but Tony's answers are always weird. He has been in management stream since the second grade, and he has read all kinds of TV that I've never even heard of. Rhindquist doesn't know about it, either. He says that Tony is paranoid, which means that he thinks everyone is out to get him. Tony said that even paranoids have enemies, and Rhindquist laughed so much, I thought he would bust.

Some days, Rhindquist is very sad, and on those days, we just watch movies. I've seen My Fair Lady, Pygmalion, Trading Places, The Prince and the Pauper, and a whole bunch more. They are all about poor people like you and me who become rich and powerful like Rhindquist. Mom, I think it means that Rhindquist wants me to be in charge! I haven't said anything, but I am trying to get ready. I am learning Word Power at night with the TV in my apt. I am not using it yet, because I want to make sure I am very good at it before I do.

I told Rhindquist about Vasquez and the new guy, and do

you know what he did? He sat down at my desk and he opened up Vasquez's file on my TV and he gave him Excellents in all of his Appraisal Categories! Can you believe it? There's nothing he can't do! He said, You gotta give the working stiffs a Christmas present now and then, right, Jap? I said, Sure.

But I don't know. The Performance Appraisals are supposed to be *scrupulously* fair—that's one of my Power Words, it means *very*. It doesn't seem right to just treat them like a bunch of numbers. It's Vasquez's whole life! It's good that Rhindquist gave him all Excellents, because that means that he'll probably be promoted this year, maybe he'll end up a dispatcher or even a trainer. But what if Rhindquist had decided to put Needs Improvements down? It would have ruined Vasquez for the rest of his life! It's full of arbitrary—that means that it doesn't make sense.

I haven't talked to Rhindquist about this. I don't want to seem stupid. Tony and I talked about it on the slidewalk, though. He said that I was very stupid if I still believed that Performance Appraisals meant anything. He said that the only Appraisal that counts is the one they get from reading your mind. I laughed and called him paranoid. He said, I take that shit from Rhindquist but I don't have to take it from an ignorant farm-boy like you. I got scared for a second, and then I remembered that I was Tony's boss! Tony, I said, I should fire you on the spot. (That was from one of the movies we watched) Then *he* looked scared and he said Sorry, sorry! I said, What makes you think anyone could read your mind?

And he said, What makes you think they can't? I said, Well, if Rhindquist could read my mind, he would have known that I was going to call out Security the day we met, at Finance 38. Tony said, Rhindquist is just a puppet of the Ones In Charge. They pull his strings and he dances for him.

I said I didn't understand and Tony looked at me with pity. He said, The Ones In Charge are running all the cities,

Microsoft and England and BBD&O and Red Stripe. They know everything that's going on. This is all a game for them.

And I said, Boy, you don't know anything! BBD&O is our biggest enemy! File-O-Gator is locked in a death-struggle with them, it said so on the news this morning!

Jap, Tony said, we're not fighting BBD&O—File-O-Gator is. *We're* riding a slidewalk back home. Can't you tell the difference between fighting and riding a slidewalk?

And I said, of course I can! That's full of sophistry! (Another Power Word, which means cow-patties.) We're part of File-O-Gator. File-O-Gator is fighting BBD&O. That means we're fighting BBD&O, Ergo. (That means, so there!)

Tony laughed and said, That's where you're wrong! File-O-Gator is just the long arm of one of the Ones In Charge. He probably slept with the wife of the One In Charge who runs BBD&O, and now they're fighting it out.

I laughed at Tony and said, You keep talking about the Ones In Charge! Everything you say is stupid unless you believe in the Ones In Charge! What makes you think that there are any Ones In Charge?

There *has* to be, Tony said. Who else is running the show?

Rhindquist is! I said.

Tony looked at me like I was stupid. I'm pretty sick of him looking at me like that. Tony said, If Rhindquist is running the show, then how come he has time to waste on you?

I wanted to say something, but I didn't know what. Tony sure makes me angry! I got off the slidewalk and went home and wrote you this letter.

Hi Mom!

Gosh, poor Buddy! How can *he* be a spy? I played with him all my life! I never saw him being a spy! He'd have to be pretty sneaky to be a spy! I don't think he's a spy! I'm sure that the manager at his disciplinary hearing will figure out that he couldn't be a spy!

I am learning Power Punctuation now. I have been using

my Power Words with Rhindquist all week, but he doesn't seem to notice. I think that if I start sending him Written Reports that are Power Punctuated, he'll notice that I'm really making effortful progress!

Today, Rhindquist sent Tony back to his old office to bring up all their Secure Document Storage Containers. It was the first time that Rhindquist and I were alone together since Tony was made my assistant, and I had a private talk with Rhindquist.

I said, "Are you really in charge?"

Rhindquist stared at me. "What is that supposed to mean?" he asked.

I said, "Tony says that if you were 'in charge,' you wouldn't have time to squander with us. He says: 'You're just a puppet of the "Ones In Charge." ' "

Rhindquist smiled and shook his head. He said: "Tony thinks he's pretty smart—huh?"

I smiled back at him because I thought he thought Tony was crazy. "He sure does!" I said.

Rhindquist said: "Well, even 'paranoids' have enemies!"

I said, "Wow! Do you mean: 'Tony is right?'!"

He said, "Well, no one except weirdos like me would want to know what's in Tony's brain, so I don't think he really has to worry about anyone reading his mind! But he's right about one thing: even though I'm in charge of File-O-Gator, I'm not necessarily running the show. I have *investors*. Pray God you never meet them, Jap. They'd eat you alive."

I said, "But they taught me in Basic that you started File-O-Gator with just one truck and a shredder! And that you shrewdly parlayed your meager holdings into a powerful organization by strategically deploying your human resources!"

He laughed! "Strategically deploying human resources? I paid the mob to scare the s**t out of the guys driving the other trucks!"

I thought that the drivers of the other trucks must've been

pretty gutless if they let someone scare them away from their appointed responsibilities, but I didn't say so.

Rhindquist looked at me like he was sorry he'd said what he said. "Oh, I didn't *hurt* anyone. Just put the fear of God in them. Then I picked up their routes, borrowed some cash, bought some more trucks, and the rest is history. I just sort of stumbled along with it, best as I could.

"Sometimes, I wonder how it all happened. One minute, you're shredding papers in Toronto, the next, you're buying the place! I can't see that I was a whole lot smarter than any of the other guys who were doing the same thing . . . I did design the uniforms, though. They were pretty sharp—nicer than the potato-sacks you guys wear these days."

I like my uniform, Mom, and I wear it with pride. If it had been crazy Tony making fun of my uniform, I would have maybe hit him, but when Rhindquist said it, I just had to look like I understood and smile at him.

I said, "You've done a lot more than design the uniforms! You run the show! You said so!"

He looked at me like I was a little kid and shook his head. "If I was running the show, would I be amusing myself by pulling random Quality Audits on the trucks?"

Crazy Tony walked in then. He looked at us and said, "What?! What are you two talking about?"

Rhindquist said, "Jap here was just explaining to me how you don't think I'm in charge." Tony looked scared and Rhindquist winked at me.

Tony looked at me like he wanted to kill me!

Tony said, "Do you really want to discuss this? Here? In this place, with all the ears and eyes in this room?"

Rhindquist laughed and laughed and laughed. "Ears and eyes? Tony, you're beautiful, you twisty little weirdo. A real laugh riot."

Tony's face got red and he looked fit to bust. "Fine, then. Let's talk. Talk about the Calabrese and the Gnomes and the Tongs and the Masons and the Posses! How'd you like that?"

Rhindquist tried to stop laughing, but he couldn't. "Jap, there's nothing more dangerous than a little knowledge!" He didn't say it to me, though, he said it to Tony. Tony was so angry, he shook!

Just then, Rhindquist's phone rang. He said, "McBride here," which is how he always answers. Then he said, "Yes, sir! That's fabulous!" He covered the bottom of the phone and said, "Why don't you guys take the rest of the day off, huh?" And then he opened the door and sent us out!

When I got home, my TV was already on, with a Special Bulletin: BBD&O was our sister city, and the two of us were fighting a life-and-death battle with Microsoft. There was also a message from Rhindquist, and attached to it was a copy of another old movie, 1984.

It was boring.

Hi Mom!

I can't believe it! They gave Buddy life? Jeez! I'm going to talk to Rhindquist about this—this is ridiculous!

Today was Tuesday, so I was on the truck with Vasquez. I got to the garage nice and early, and my watch congratulated me. It kind of bothered me. I guess I'm just getting used to working in my office, with the watch switched off.

By the time we made our first stop, at HR 102, I was ready to throw my watch out the window! It had told me *eight times* how great I was: when I got to the garage; when I did my safety-check; when I stopped at three red lights; when I backed up to the document disposal dock; when I cleared security; and when I lifted the boxes with my legs instead of my back. To tell you the truth, it made me feel pretty stupid. I felt like I was a puppy, getting patted on the head.

By lunch, my watch had given me 57 positive feedbacks. I mentioned it to Vasquez.

He said, "I don't know what you're complaining about. It beats having it shout at you all the time. It just means you're doing all right. When I'm out with the new guy, this thing never shuts up. It just yammers on and on about how late we are, how many more pickups we have to do, what percent of our pickups we've been late for. I got so mad last week, I shouted at it: 'Don't tell me! Tell the retard who's driving!' "

We both laughed at that. I said, "Sure, it's better to get loved off than it is to get chewed out, but don't you feel like an idiot, having a machine telling you what a great job you're doing?"

My watch said that I was lowering morale and I should stop. I got so angry, Mom! I told it to mind its own business! It said that it *was* minding its own business and did I want it to connect me with a maintenance operator to evaluate its judgment?

I'd never mouthed off to my watch before. The idea of talking to a real person about it scared me, but I remembered that even though I was driving a truck, I was also a Special Vice President, and that made me almost everybody's boss. I said, "Yes!" Vasquez looked at me like I'd gone nuts!

A few seconds later, a new voice came out of my watch. "How can I help you, Mr. Whitehead?" The voice was smooth and oily, like the man from Physical Plant who used to come around to collect the rent back home.

All of a sudden, I didn't know what to say. I said, "My watch is irritating me."

The voice said, "Have you developed a rash? Is there visible chafing?"

I said, "No. It's irritating me mentally. It never shuts up."

The voice didn't say anything for a while, then it said, "Well, from my records, I see that you have a 98% positive-feedback index. In fact, your watch hasn't given you any corrective feedback in weeks, with the exception of a mild correction about antimorale speculations."

I felt stupid, like one of those guys in Basic who carped about every little thing. I said, "Well, I'm just getting tired of having a machine tell me when I'm right and when I'm wrong. I can figure that out on my own."

The voice said, "I see." And then it didn't say anything.

I tried to wait until the voice said something else, but the quiet made me very nervous. I said, "I don't mean to be rude or anything. I am very conscientious about my job. It's just that I feel like a moron or something, always having the watch tell me what I'm doing." I knew that I wasn't expressing myself very well, but I couldn't remember any of my Power Words just then. "It bugs me, you know?"

The voice said, "I'm sorry, but I'm afraid that that's not my business. I'm in Maintenance. If you have a concern about HR policy, you'll need to take it up with them."

I thought about my HR Sergeant in Basic, and tried to imagine telling him that I didn't want my watch to talk to me anymore, and nearly jumped out of my skin. "That's OK," I said. "My lunch is almost over. I'll try them after my shift."

The voice said, "Thank you for calling Maintenance! Have a nice day!" Then my watch told me it was time to get in the truck and start driving again.

Vasquez kept looking at me all day like I was some kind of crazy.

Hi Mom!

Tell Buddy he doesn't have to keep on calling me to say thanks. I'm just glad that he and Carla are all right. Tell him to enjoy his promotion!

When I got to the office this morning, I found Rhindquist wearing his old-fashioned pusher's uniform. I hadn't seen it since the day we met. I was surprised by how normal he looked in it: he could have been any pusher.

"Well, aren't you dressed for success?" I asked him ironically.

He spun around and said, "I've got something new. For three of the days that you're here, I'll be on a truck with Vasquez. You fill in for me, take any calls, handle any business. Order up some movies. We'll meet up on the fourth day here and I'll answer any questions you have. If something urgent comes up, give me a call."

I felt a little out of my depth, but I wanted to demonstrate my take-charge attitude to Rhindquist, so I smiled and said, "Can do, boss! Knock 'em dead!"

Tony came in and snorted a snide laugh at Rhindquist. Rhindquist raised an eyebrow at me, and I took the hint. "What are you smirking at, mister?" I barked, like my old Sarge. "You find something amusing about the official uniform of a representative of this organization?"

He cast his eyes down and mumbled "No."

I was enjoying myself. I said, "I can't hear you, mister!"

Tony looked at me, his eyes focused in space beside my head. "No, sir!" he said.

"Get downstairs and see what the pinheads on the third floor are shredding. Sort it, box it, and have it on my desk by lunch, hear me?"

"Yes, sir!" Tony shouted, and hustled out of my office.

Rhindquist shook his head and looked admiringly at me. "Sonny-boy, you're going to do just fine," he said.

"You know it!" I said.

Rhindquist gave me a big thumbs-up and left me alone.

So there I was, alone, in my office, in charge. Sort of.

I played with my TV for a while. The TV at the office gave me all kinds of access that I didn't have at home. I clicked on something, and there were the personnel files! I felt like a snoop, but it was too fun to stop. I opened my file, and Vasquez's, and a whole bunch more. Boy, the Company sure knows a lot about us! My file went all the way back to the Infirmary where I was born, and then I clicked on your name, and there was everything about you!

Mom, I didn't know you had your tubes tied!

I followed our family tree up and down, and I came to Buddy. His file was spotless, all the way up to the spying thing. I clicked on the name of the Security Manager who'd "caught" him, and do you know what? He was engaged to Carla last year! Carla is his ex-girlfriend!

Well, it was pretty easy to see what was going on, let me tell you. Buddy got married to Carla, and her ex-boyfriend had them locked up. I tell you, I was so angry, I felt like I would bust. But I'm smarter than that. All it took was a few minutes' typing and wham, I'd gotten Buddy and Carla out of jail, given them promotions, and had the Security Manager busted down to a janitor. I bet that confused him!

So it really wasn't much. It scares me to have that much power, Mom, but it feels good, too. I made sure that all my friends back home were set up all right, too.

You just wait till your Christmas bonus, Mom!

Tony came up at lunchtime, with three big boxes of papers. He'd sorted out the memos, personal documents and the interdepartmental communications. They were pretty interesting reading! Especially the personal documents: shopping lists, letters home, love notes and gossip. It was like being the queen ant, sitting in the middle of the hill, seeing what all the drones were up to. I sent Tony out to get some more.

It was getting on to movie time when the phone on my desk rang. I answered it, "Jasper Whitehead, Special Vice-President."

The person on the phone shouted at me, "Get me McBride now!"

I felt sick. I said, "I'm sorry, he's not available right now. I'm filling in for him. Can I be of service?"

The person laughed at me. "Well, maybe you can at that, son! Rhindquist has been promising to do something for me for months now, I guess he's just been too busy. Do you have his access codes?"

I said I did, and turned on my TV.

"Good boy," he said. "Now, I want you to find docket 09.3457. You know how to open a docket?"

I told him I did and found the docket. It was called "Microsoft," and it had a long Action-Item List attached to it. I didn't really get most of the Action Items, but they were all checked off except one.

"OK—there's an unchecked item at the bottom of that list. It's called, 'Deploy Strategic Negotiation Tool.' You see it?"

I said I did.

"Check it off," he said.

I did. The TV asked me if I was sure. I said I was. The TV asked me again. I said I was, again. I told the man I was done.

"Good kid. Thanks! Tell McBride I like his new hire."

He laughed again and hung up before I could say "You're welcome."

My phone rang again. It was a reporter from PR 43, and she wanted to know all about my dynamic leadership in handling the Microsoft Crisis. I didn't really understand the question, but they taught me what to say to the press in Basic. I said, "The File-O-Gator Organization is a diverse multinational sovereign power that is a World-Class Leader in its fields of Operations, a status it has achieved through the diligence and responsibility of its Human Resources, which are the Heart of every Organization."

The reporter sounded impressed. I thanked her and hung up and turned on the TV and flipped around. There was a reporter lady on the screen, showing satellite maps of Microsoft, like a weather map. Except that instead of lighting bolts or a smiling sun, there were tanks and soldiers and flames. The TV said that bold directives from Special Vice-President Jasper Whitehead had brought an end to the Microsoft conflict. It said that a classified number of File-O-Gator troops had occupied the conflict-zone, deploying strategic neurotoxins and nonlethal influenza vectors, resulting in an estimated 85% compliance-and-conversion rate among the Microsoftians.

Tony came in with more boxes and looked at me. He said, "God, what's eating you?"

I told him. I didn't know what else to do. I thought that maybe I could get Rhindquist on the phone, but he'd left me in charge.

Tony smiled, but it wasn't a happy smile. "Well, there you go. You've made your first executive decision."

I said, "I didn't make any decision!"

He just laughed and pointed to the TV, which was showing pictures of a city just like File-O-Gator, the buildings all collapsed and burning. He said, "Sure looks like an executive decision to me." The picture panned over an apartment building that was split down the middle, the apartments naked and exposed, the people who lived there dead and sprawled or alive and hanging over the edge, vomiting.

Oh, those poor people!

I didn't know what I was doing!

I spent all last night throwing up, and I'm not sure if I'm going to go to the office today.

Hi Mom!

Well, I didn't go to work yesterday. Instead, I got out of bed, sat on the sofa in my shorts, and turned on the movies. My watch got loud and angry, so I stuck it underneath my pillow. Then, messages started appearing on my TV. I ignored them. I ate some cereal around 11, and I threw it up right away, so I stopped trying.

Someone knocked on my door after lunch, but I was watching a good part in Wall Street, so I didn't answer it.

I fell asleep after Wall Street, and woke up after 18h, because someone was really giving my door a pounding.

I opened the door, not caring that I was wearing my shorts. It was Rhindquist. He looked sad, and beaten. You know what he did? He gave me a hug! Boy, that was weird.

He came in and sat on the sofa. I sat next to him. He didn't say anything, just picked up the remote and put on a funny movie, Blazing Saddles. When that was over, he put on The Princess Bride. I never laughed so much!

We watched movies all night. They were all funny. They took my mind off things. We both fell asleep, sitting on the sofa, but when I woke up, I was in bed, and Rhindquist had put the blanket over me. He was asleep on the sofa. His phone was on the TV, and its batteries were on the floor.

I was really hungry, so I ate three bowls of cereal and some toast and an apple, and I must've woken Rhindquist up, because he came into the kitchen.

"Little man, you had a busy day, huh?" he said.

I said, "I can't do it."

He got a GatorCola out of my fridge and drank it. It was pretty strange to have the CEO of the whole Company drinking a Goke in my kitchen for breakfast. It really made him seem like you and me, not like a powerful guy from the stories.

He burped.

He said, "I understand."

I said, "Why did you do this to me?"

He said, "You've been in my shoes now. Wouldn't you do anything to get out of them?"

I said, "But why *me*?"

He sighed. He said, "This sounds worse than I mean it. I thought you were ignorant enough to enjoy it."

I said, "Thanks a lot." Is there anyone out there who *doesn't* think I'm a retard?

He said, "I don't mean it in a bad way, really. I thought you were naive enough to just do the job, take the perks, and sleep well at night. I was wrong. You're too smart."

It didn't make me feel any better. I went back and sat on the sofa and put on a movie, Horsefeathers.

Rhindquist watched the movie with me, and when it was over, he said, "You don't have to do the job."

I said, "So what now? You pick some other poor retard and give him the old screw-job?"

He said, "I guess so."

I said, "In that case, I'll do it."

His mouth dropped. He sat down and put on a movie, Pink Flamingos. What a sick movie!

When it was over, he said, "In that case, I'll do it."

And then I had the best idea I've ever had. It was so good, I couldn't say anything for five whole minutes. Mom, you sure didn't raise any idiots!

Hi Mom!

Well, today was just *fine*. Me and Rhindquist got to the garage in the nick of time and it's a good thing that he turned our watches down because they give me a headache!

Vasquez was waiting for us when we got there and he had on his mad face for the other guys but when me and Rhindquist got on the truck, he smiled and winked at us.

I drove and Rhindquist hung onto the back and he shouted at me to go faster and I just ignored him! He kept on shouting, saying, You pinhead, my grandma drives faster than you do and she's been dead for years! And that made me laugh so hard I nearly rolled the truck and Rhindquist nearly fell off and he was pretty quiet after that!

We got to Finance 38 and I started lifting the boxes and Rhindquist as usual took too long to push them. The security guard and me both laughed at the big pile of boxes outside the truck, and he offered me a smoke, but I said no thanks.

I went inside and told Rhindquist to Get it in gear! And he just tossed me the paper he was reading. It said MEMO TO ALL EMPLOYEES REGARDING NEW SECURITY MEASURES. And underneath, it said, EFFECTIVE IMMEDIATELY ALL AC OUTLETS ARE TO BE COVERED WHEN NOT IN USE.

We laughed and laughed and laughed, and then my watch blipped back on even though Rhindquist had turned it off! It said, "Laugh it up, retards!" in Tony's voice.

Rhindquist put his arm around my shoulders and said Jap my prodigy, when you are right, you are *right*. He's the perfect man for the job.

ALEX IRVINE

THE SEA WIND OFFERS LITTLE RELIEF

HE LOOKED UP WHEN HIS JAILERS ENTERED THE CELL, imagining the aether pouring in around them, lifted in Coriolis swirls by the passage of their bodies. It was a moment of fantasy; the aether had been there before their entrance, monitoring him, streaming into his lungs with each steady inhalation, transmitting information about his vital functions. He imagined despite this a purity in his solitude, a purity at least partially real, and the presence of the jailers fractured this dear illusion. Their entrance bludgeoned him with the Assimilated world that had excommunicated him at his sentencing, one hundred and forty-seven years ago. One hundred forty-seven years. He had become an old man.

The first jailer spoke to him, and he discovered again that solitary years had not inured him to shame. To be spoken to was to feel the impact not only of sound wave against tympanum but of one's own exile against the memory of choices wrongly taken. The aether conducted thoughts to everyone but him.

I should be comfortable. My space is my own, and I am surrounded by furniture and possessions of my own choosing. I am alone, but that too is my choice, and I have had many years to acquiesce to its consequences. Alone in my room—my cell—I find the virtue of contemplation.

In contemplation, though, and in comfort, I find sadness.

I write by hand, to place myself within a matrix of relationships available to me only through mimicry. The words I produce inspire joy and gratitude, and these emotions in turn inspire my attempt at reconstruction. Reading: what must it have been like for him? I imagine and I write, a scholar of languages sketching himself into the experience of a scholar of languages. Allow me this latitude; without it I would be stifled. The story will not be told the way it happened, but if I separate myself from time to time . . . please. Allow me this latitude. The Assimilation is centuries past, but because I cannot fear it I fear its memory instead, the history-spanning shadow of its occurrence, and this fear provokes inopportune utterances. From time to time I must assert myself. My self.

He bit back his shame and listened to the words. They came quickly, in an unfamiliar accent, and it took him several moments to piece together what had been said. Like bright light after long darkness, they dazzled his mind.

"You are required to read," the first jailer had said to him.

He breathed steadily, imagining the aether streaming in and out, binding to the dead receptors in his brain. He tried to calm the sudden spasming of his heart.

"Am I not," he began, and his voice failed him. Eyes closed, he sipped water and spoke again. "Am I not imprisoned for reading?" A rhetorical question. Words without information, run across his tongue to remind it how to speak.

"Come with us," the first jailer said. Something shifted in the scholar's head and he understood that the jailer did not know how to speak the language he was using. He was reciting, a parrot-jailer squawking out words. So, the scholar thought. They have lost the habit of speech.

As, for other reasons, have I.

An image of religious intensity presented itself: the aether as a visible, faintly shining presence, inscribed with sounds. The Assimilated jailer had only to wonder how to say a thing, and his tongue would begin to form the words. Without the natural cadence of a practiced speaker, though, the words did not fall together naturally into sentences.

Understanding this, the scholar rose and followed the jailers out into the white corridor. He shuffled, and his hips ached. Through his memory passed fragmentary sensations of youth: running. Leaning with a long-dead friend into the sting of a sea wind. The ecstatic exertion of making love.

The white corridor curved gently to the left. At regular intervals the smoothness of the walls gave way to recessed doorways. Other cells, he supposed, incarcerating other prisoners much like himself. His crime was not rare.

The jailers stopped, and a door opened on their right. "Enter," the first jailer said.

The room was the same size and shape as his cell. The scholar was comforted by the sameness of the room's shape and color, but agitated by the difference of its furnishings. No bed; no toilet; no sink; no point-source of light. A chair and table, and diffuse whiteness radiating from the walls. A table occupied the greater part of its floor space, and a jailer stood between him and the table. She was blind.

"Read," said the blind jailer. The vowel went on a little too long, the final consonant punched a little too harshly between tongue and alveolar ridge.

A cruel joke, thought the scholar. It was not unheard of.

Prison duty eroded guards' humanity just as imprisonment gradually reduced inmates to automata; sometimes the only release for either was displacement of frustration and self-loathing onto the other. But to read: to track one's eyes across a field of symbols, parsing and connecting, inferring and interpreting, recreating symbol as idea, as emotion, as experience. He had no idea how long since he had done it, no idea in fact if he still could. At times he dreamed of reading, but upon waking could never be certain that his dream had authentically rendered the reality. What persisted beyond waking was a sense that the readingness of reading survived, somewhere in the dream hemisphere of his brain.

They were telling him to read. He had been imprisoned, many years ago, for his literacy. These two facts refused to accommodate each other.

Avarice overcame him, flooding from a reservoir of desire his silence had kept dammed. His hands trembled; his breath whistled in his throat; something fluttered in his stomach and he was aware that he had not moved his bowels in several days. They were telling him to read. He stepped around the blind jailer, approached the table, saw on the live part of its surface: words.

The scholar covered his face with his hands and fell to the ground. When the blind jailer touched him, he began to scream. His voice, frail from disuse, soon gave out, and by the time the jailers had taken him back to his cell, his screams lacked even the power to keep him awake. He slept as if stricken by catatonia, and his last thought was to remember his name, emerging by some graphological alchemy from the field of letters that had etched itself into his mind.

I know that he did in fact suffer a brief episode upon his first viewing of the text. This much is established in the records of the time, recovered from the aether at the end of Assimilation. What I do not know are his thoughts, but it seems to me that seeing text for the first time in one hundred and forty-seven years must have brought Edmar de Carvalho's identity crashing catastrophically down upon him. I think that he broke down not so much from seeing the words as from seeing what the loss of the words had done to him. Indeed the first question of the poem seems specifically designed to provoke such a reaction.

What is memory? The question like a low cloud
Settles in the sunset, beyond the hero's reach,
Who stands on deck, bright helm held and grey head
    bowed.

Again he asks. Sea mocks, he thinks, when it should
    teach.
But it is not up to him, who chases after
Horizons, whose quests bring him back to that same
    beach

On which he was born, on which the sea-goddess
    spread
Her legs and left him to dry in the sun until
Neyaus came upon him,

Edmar de Carvalho looked up from the words. "Neyaus?" "Nomenclature indigenous to the planet of origin," said the blind jailer, after a pause perceptible only because he knew to expect it. The phrase rolled metronomically from her tongue, carefully memorized and prepared. They knew, then, more than they were willing to tell him; else they would not have taken such care to rehearse for his questions. *Planet of origin*, he thought. Around these bits of information, a plan began to accrete.

———

Historians of language note at least two independent occurrences of the name Edmar, in German and Anglo-Saxon. Possibly Portuguese offers a third. Unlike its German homophone, a demotic form of the name Ottmar, the Anglo-Saxon name Edmar means "rich sea," or "richness of the sea." To my knowledge, Edmar de Carvalho never knew of this. Even more than irony, I prize this bit of information: it is the one thing I know that I am sure he did not.

<blockquote>
took him in, soaked his bread

In goat's milk, brushed the sand from his back, and
  laughing
Taught him to speak, to desire his name, crave
  knowledge
Of all that was forgotten. This is memory

Under whose whip rhyme falters.
</blockquote>

"Read it aloud," the blind jailer said. Edmar de Carvalho began to speak. His recitation fell into the cadence of the poem. At the last line, his voice faltered, and he bent his head to hide his tears from the aether and those who attended to its transmissions.

"Explain," said the jailer, and Edmar de Carvalho's head snapped up. His tears dried and with burning eyes he said, "I will not. You demanded reading. I have provided it." A joke after all, he thought. They probe at my desires, coerce me into a vain exercise of the talents in which I once took such pride.

Unmoved by his anger, the blind jailer said, "The poem goes on. As you explain each portion, more will be made available. The choice is yours."

It was no choice at all. Even the single fact that more lines existed was more than Edmar de Carvalho could resist. Behind it, something else: the jailers, and whoever controlled them, needed to know something, and they thought he could tell them.

Leverage. He did not yet know what it was, or how it might be exercised, but he would find out. For the first time since his imprisonment, his desire and his guilt channeled themselves into the exercise of will.

"I must think," he said, and stood to return to his cell.

In his cell he thought, and when he was done thinking, he forgot. Edmar de Carvalho had the talent of forgetting. It had kept him free as long as anything could have.

It is a talent I wish I had.

He sat in his cell. I sit in mine. He was a prisoner, looking ahead. I am imprisoned only by the specter of him: a collaborator, a traitor. The most unlikely of ancestors.

"It's an imitative epic," said Edmar de Carvalho. He looked up from the text. Its words scrolled through his mind, perfect on the table display. He wondered about the handwriting of the man who had set it down. Certainly a man, something about the language already had told him that, or perhaps just the preconceptions of one too long by himself, who recreates the world in his own image. "I would be better able to contextualize it if I could see the original manuscript artifact."

"Imitative epic," his interrogator said. "The connotation of this phrase is unclear."

"Epic in that it's a poetic story of foundations, or so I would assume from what I've read so far. A story of a hero. Generally a story of origins, of nation-building. Imitative in that it's written in hexameter terza rima. Hexameter means a line of twelve syllables, with a number of possible stress counts; terza rima describes the poem's rhyme scheme. Greek and Roman epics employed hexameters, and Dante's *Commedia* is the first epic-scale poem written in terza rima. The schemes occur throughout the history of European and American poetry, with various embellishments. Perhaps the last significant poet to ring changes on these structures was the Transmillennial Derek Walcott, who combined hexameter and terza rima as this poet has, albeit more skillfully." Edmar de Carvalho did not add that Walcott was the last because less than fifty years after his death, dactylic hexameter and poetry itself had drowned in Assimilation. And he had been a scholar of Greek plays, his knowledge of Walcott and Dante conjured from undergraduate seminars two hundred years gone. "Walcott's intent was to explore the utility of epic in constructing stories of culture and perpetuating cultural myths—"

"Enough." The interrogator pivoted to meet the opening door.

There is material for a digressive footnote here, one that I shall probably never write, delving into the reflexive nature of any text executed as an inquiry into the nature of understanding text. Words speaking of words, a scholar of languages imagining the predicament of a scholar of languages: I take my place in what seems an endlessly receding spiral of inter-reflecting intelligence. Minds gazing back at what other minds have thought, and leaning forward to imagine what later minds might make of their ruminations. An imitative epic.

> The hero has a name
> That rhymes with nothing, but even now, approaching
> The beach of his birth on the sea-wind of his fame

Memories of his name are whales at night, breaching
Amid a moon-shocked glow of foam that hides their
   shape
From the searching eyes of his mind. Blind
   beseeching

Of sea-goddess mocking: I am named like seascape,
The hero thinks, a word that slides over many scenes
Like moon-shocked foam, connotation leaving mind
   agape

At these tricks of meaning. Mind's grasping only
   gleans
Certainty of difference: Seascapes no more the same
Than sunrise and sunset. Heroic deeds are means

To the end of finding one's name. The end of fame,
The final forgetting. The mind slackens, must forgo
Futures.

I have said that I thought Edmar de Carvalho's identity
must have collapsed upon him when, for the first time in a
century and more, his gaze was allowed to fall upon written
language. It may seem at this point that, like any number of
scholars before me, I am confusing, conflating, mistaking the
text for the reader, the reader for the author. Edmar de Carvalho did not write the poem; he only read it. But removed
from both text and reader as I am, I can no longer just read
either. I must write them. This is the majesty of writing, its
wonder and its danger. It maps itself onto the topology of our
breathing interaction with the universe.

   You may assume that I am recovering a bit too much from
textual and biographical associations that are less fruitful than
I wish to make them. Whether this is true has no bearing on
the relevance of my story. Believe it if you wish.

In fact I ask you to. Please. Read me into Edmar de Carvalho, read my reading of him into his reading of the poem.

Deeds beget memories, the hero taking aim

At enemies remembers that moments ago
He was a babe on a beach. And then, the next day,
Anonymous on an anonymous sea he goes

Crying aloud, "Enough thoughts! Ocean, I will say
What I have done, not said, what my hands have
    wrought
Not my mind's eye bred. Nameless, I will not stay

So, but will speak myself though it be life's last lot
Like low clouds to see my name written on seascape.
My name, the name I would have chosen and would

Write anew, just as the sea-goddess once wrote me
In her blood on a beach for a goatherd to read.
My blood is the ocean, and on its flood I see

Mother mocking when she should teach. She knows
    my need,"
The hero cried to banded birds circling his mast,
"I will know hers, and show it her, and on it feed."

Thus saying, the hero leaned into the sea's blast
Closed his eyes, tasted salt, commanded memory
To open her doors, to show him both first and last

Of his actions that like celestial jewelry
Hung shining around the starry neck of renown.
She obeyed,

"This is fairly typical of a certain kind of hero," said Edmar de Carvalho. "A venerable strain of criticism would have it that any hero's journey is every hero's journey, and every hero's journey is undertaken in search of self. The hero here commands the ocean from whence he has come, asserting his control over both elements and origins. The rhetorical trope maps neatly onto the concern with identity. In addition, although I don't think much of the whole, some of the lines are quite fine as poetry."

"Aesthetic judgments are of no interest to us," said the blind jailer. She always stood between Edmar and the door while he read. A routine had established itself over the previous days, whether from administrative directives or the simple inertia of habit he did not know. Every day at the same time—as nearly as he, deprived of aether, timepieces, and natural light, could estimate—his jailers brought him to this room. He was more certain of the room than the time, having counted his steps on the way to it once the jailers had deemed him fit to examine the text again. Every day since then, he had taken approximately the same number of steps, and turned at approximately the same points along the way. Edmar de Carvalho was not prone to compulsive actions, but he remembered the overwhelming shock of seeing words, and he was afraid not only that it would happen again, but that if it did happen again he would be prevented from examining the words again. To exist—not live, exist—for one hundred forty-seven years without reading was horror enough; to weaken at the moment when the lexical exile was ending . . . unforgivable. Counting alleviated the worst of his nerves. He walked, counted evenly, inhaled evenly through his nose, exhaled evenly through his mouth. Did not think about what lay this or that number of steps beyond the walls of his prison.

"Aesthetic judgments," he said today, holding his voice level, "are part and parcel of the scholar's evaluative process."

How to explain that each word of a poem—of any expression—demands an aesthetic response, depends for its meaning and answer on such responses? How to explain that for this ideal he had sacrificed his friends and the best part of himself?

Edmar de Carvalho did not speak. He turned to the poem's next line.

and the hero saw the scullery

Where as a stripling boy he broke the knobby crown
Of a leering giant lifting the red-shingled roof
Of the noble house where the goatherd bowed low
    down

In fealty to a mighty lord, whose flaw was proof
That men given dominion only deserve
Such respect as demands their remaining aloof.

It did not happen overnight. Networks proliferated, absorbed each other; nanotechnology liberated them from the constraints of node and conduit; the aether began to coalesce. A slow accretion led eventually to a critical mass, and inter-cortical information transfer—Uplink, in the argot of its twenty-first-century innovators—destroyed a literate culture that had persisted for seven thousand years. Whatever the benefits, and benefits there were, this fact cannot be gainsaid. But the aether had no moral valence itself; its existence did not demand the legislative and cultural currents that churned in its wake. No teleology demanded the abolition, for security reasons, of nonaetheric communication. The Assimilation could not have happened without aether, but aether did not predetermine Assimilation.

Still, what happened, happened—and how grateful I am to be writing those words twenty-five hundred years after the events I recount (two thousand five hundred years: the distance, in another direction, between Edmar de Carvalho and the Greek plays to which he had devoted his working life). Never imprisoned, I can be objective, or at least dispassionate. I can speak of memories erased, cultures ground to blankness; but my telling assumes the hollow tone of a lecture delivered only to oneself. Edmar de Carvalho at least had auditors. This was his unmaking and his redemption.

He memorized, of course. At the end of each day, he had committed every line to memory. In a strange way, though, he had not read those lines. One hundred forty-seven years of incarceration develops peculiar properties of the mind, one of which is a dissociative sort of compartmentalization, and Edmar de Carvalho had escaped prosecution for so long because he had already possessed this faculty before his arrest.

The Assimilated Powers outlawed writing because it could be hidden, passed around to a select few friends—or conspirators. An incredible metamorphosis: writing, historically a means of disseminating information, became a tool of secrecy when employed by people who knew how to forget. Secrecy itself became treason in a civilization rebuilt upon the universal availability of human knowledge but still beholden to pre-Assimilation ideas of authority and power.

Every technological innovation is used both to consolidate power and to subvert it. The aether, sustained as it was by fantastic technological exertion, could be subverted by equally ingenious technological interference. It could be avoided, though only locally and never for very long. Thoughts could be thought and then forgotten. Even forgotten thoughts hide somewhere in the brain, but Edmar de Carvalho had developed the talent of forgetting things in places where the aether did not look. He became a node in a network of individuals, all born since the first Uplink in 2062, who quietly fought to restore the sanctity of the mind, who rejected the Assimilated axiom that all thought, because it could be shared, must be.

Each of us knows, through anecdote or experience, the power of the mind to suppress trauma, horror, even simple embarrassment. Learning to control this power, to make it an act of will instead of an infantile response, took a certain perversion of aetheric technology as well as a formidable strength. Learning to remember took still more technical and psychological acuity, and surviving for the thirty years and more of their conspiracy demanded an heroic arsenal of aetheric countermeasures in addition to an unswerving commitment: not to anything so trivial as the value of art or the beauty of beauty, but to the incorrigible truth that self and world are incomprehensible without the action of the aesthetic mind. They communicated through poetry, each verse a manifesto declaring the rebellion of the aesthetic living mind against the sublimely anaesthetic power of Assimilation. The aesthetic, perhaps, of revolution.

It was the methodology of every conspiracy in recorded history: each of them knew only what they required to advance the cause one step further. They allowed themselves to forget that they had even forgotten this information until they were called upon to use it again. In honing this skill, they developed an odd sense of distance from themselves, a consciousness that by constructing artificial barriers between parts of their minds, they were cutting themselves into pieces. Estranging themselves from themselves. They did not become precisely insane, but they sailed close enough to insanity's shore that—had there been language for it—they might have been able to speak of its contours.

They were caught, as they knew they would be, and tried, and their jury was every sentient mind on Earth. They were few enough that, after conviction, their memories were spared and their literacy called into service: at evidentiary hearings, primarily, where the apprehended literate acted as witness and defendant, one clamping down on shameful memories, the other anticipating, hoping to survive with mind intact even if the cost was witnessing at the ongoing purge of one's fellows and one's ideals. Edmar de Carvalho was one of those spared. Gradually his role as evidentiary witness had diminished, and after some decades he was left alone in his cell to ponder his betrayals. To keep his mind working, he remembered. He burnished his ability to memorize until it shone, but also until it grew dangerously thin, and he felt that he could see the glow of forgetting behind it.

Edmar de Carvalho had been a scholar of ancient literatures before he had become a conspirator, and the jailers' poem reinvigorated his mind. He knew every word of it long before he had read it carefully, and he forgot it in the way that he had nearly forgotten how to forget. It became a part of him that he did not notice, like a bone in the inner ear. He stored the poem against the possibility that it would be taken away from him, and he doled it out to himself only when he was in the presence of his jailers. At night his lips moved over stanzas he'd examined during the day, making notes on form, alliteration, allusion. His memory reawakened and grew distended with words and images; his tongue formed words, he translated stanzas of the poem into languages he hadn't spoken in more than a century.

Perhaps more importantly, he read himself the way he read the poem: a Brazilian, emigrated as a boy to Australia; a failed conspirator, son of a professor of literatures who named him for an athlete; an amateur astronomer who once wanted to marry a woman from Michigan. Slowly the feeling came over him that after a long stasis, an enforced senescence, he was living again. Thinking again. He began to fantasize escape, to imagine atonement.

"A fairly typical hero's first action," he said to the blind jailer. She did not answer. "Killing giants, rescuing women, and so on. No real surprises." He considered. "The juxtaposition of the young hero and the flawed overlord, though, is interesting, particularly if the lord's downfall is, as it seems, sexually motivated. In some traditions heroes are quite promiscuous; in others chastity and a fanatical hygiene are intrinsic to heroic bearing. I shall be interested to see how this turns out."

As shall I. I am not Edmar de Carvalho, as much as I wish I could be. I try to forget as he learned to forget, but what I wish to banish from my mind is the simple mundanity of my cell, and of my self within it. I try to forget the poem, though like him I have committed it to memory. With you I read it, as I first read it with him; with you I write it, as I first wrote it into my ideas of him, as I first wrote it into my ideas of myself. Each time, the newness of it brings me near his experience of one hundred forty-seven years' absence, ended at last in the presence of words. It is a glorious tale, and alone in my room I find a wild and fierce joy in the telling.

> Lusts of his body weakened his noble reserve
> He preyed on the women of his house. Wolflike
> He came in the night to the quarters, the preserve
>
> Of women. At last his debauches burst the dike
> They meekly tried to maintain, and angered they
>   turned
> To the giants for help. Our lord's head on a spike,
>
> They begged; his body on a pyre; his son exiled.
> These giants stood astride the women's wrathful
>   flood
> Grinning and stroking their beards, their senses
>   beguiled

By the scent of angry women's fiery blood.
We will come, they said as one, and free you; but
    first
We will have the noble seed that forms in the mud

Of your wombs. Each of the six women nearly burst
With the shame, but in turn they nodded and agreed
That their bodies' fruit should slake the giants' thirst.

The agreement thus struck, the six women took heed
That the lord should not visit them until children
Could be birthed, fed and weaned, and sent on
    goatherd's steed

To the shore where tall giants threw stones at the sky
In spiteful hope of bringing down the distant stars
And forcing the gods to yield their steely secrets.

"Why am I reading this?" Edmar de Carvalho asked finally.

I must stop at this question, to consider the moment at which it was asked. How long did it take him to ask? I do not know. What fears coursed through his mind, what uncertainties? They had told him to read, and he read; but they had not told him what for, and for all he knew, that was the one question he would not be permitted to ask. That he asked it tells more of his fortitude than I possibly could, and so I let pass my impulse to embellish, to filigree with detail and imagined emotion. Edmar de Carvalho considered the possible consequences, and he asked the question. I am cowed by his bravery.

————

"Why am I reading this?"

"Surely," said the blind jailer, "the balance of power in this situation is clear to you."

Clearer, thought Edmar de Carvalho, than perhaps it is to you. "You brought this from another planet," he said. "An artifact of a failed colony, I assume."

He had waited, and waited, and waited before making this assertion, being fairly sure that he was meant to know that much. The jailer's words "planet of origin" had clearly been intended to channel his thoughts in that direction.

"A reasonable assumption," the jailer said, as he had anticipated she would.

"A record," said Edmar de Carvalho. "Encoded, no doubt, by a literate outlaw as a last futile gesture." Emboldened by intuition, he guessed further. "The only record left."

A twitch at the corner of her mouth. Did she know the game he was (they were?) playing? The jailer said nothing. Edmar de Carvalho kept reading, certain she would have contradicted him if she thought he'd been wrong.

The women, all six, withdrew behind iron bars
They contrived a story of dreadful plague, called
    down
On women; made the lord believe they blamed his
    wars

Against their chastity; hid themselves in brown
Cloth and shaded rooms. Discord grew, and ugly
    words
Began to be spoken about six women's gowns

That grew looser as the lord's hands like vengeful
    birds
Pecked and tore his servants' hides. Still giggling
    gossip

Flew faster than the lord's blows; windy rumors
    whirred

Through rooms grown colder than a dead man's
    silver lips
Quieter than the last breath before winter dawn.
Six women whispered groans, six women arched their
    hips

And six children came, and as quickly six were gone.

I have no children. Of all the consequences of solitude, this is the most painful to contemplate. Edmar de Carvalho had children, if not of his body then of his deeds; I myself am among this issue. My solitude, conceived as an homage to him, becomes in this light yet one more instance of my inadequacy to his example. Like all who are grateful to live but do not bear children, I suffer the pain of not being able to reciprocate the gift given to me. Regrets are one of my few indulgences, and to palliate my regret I keep and continue this story. Each of us must accommodate our errors, and in spite of them find happiness.

    The lord's guest alone knew, the stripling foreign boy
    Washed up by a storm, amid weeds, like monsters'
        spawn

    Or windburned remains of a god's forgotten toy.
    Finding generosity in that house of secrets
    The boy who was not yet a hero knew the ploy

    And when the giants came, and cooling freshets
    Of loyal blood flowed over flagstone floors
    He lay in wait with stolen sword, and his regrets

Mounted with the number of bodies blocking doors.
At last a curious giant peered in, at last
The boy could act, and killing the giant make some
     poor

Recompense for the fallen house's noble past
That now blood-soaked began to burn, timbers
Fueled by giant's blood in a fiery blast.

The boy fled choking smoke, flames, falling embers.
Bodies caught like candles. Six women he found
Forgotten behind iron bars, and with them he
     clambered

Free of that falling house. Outside, they looked
     around
Hoping that other survivors would join them there.

"Telling, the ambiguity of the giants' portrayal," said Edmar de Carvalho.

"Explain."

"Are there giants on this planet? Physically large humanoids?"

The blind jailer did not answer him, and short seconds later the first interrogator entered the room. Edmar de Carvalho waited, savoring the forgotten sensation of being awaited. One hundred forty-seven years of speaking only to himself had taught him something about outlasting the patience of an interlocutor. The interrogator would speak soon enough, and Edmar de Carvalho soon enough would answer.

The interrogator's posture shifted, ever so slightly. "Of what value is this information to your task?"

Edmar de Carvalho nodded slightly. Understanding glimmered.

"If there are in fact giants on this planet, particularly giants who interact with the other sentient species who I assume forms the basis for this noble house, then the poem must be read in a particular way. If there are not, or you are uncertain, other readings obtain. It will be useful to me to know whether the giants are meant figuratively or as a literal representation of real biological entities." His mouth dry, Edmar de Carvalho reached for the cup of water he kept by his left hand.

Again the interrogator did not immediately respond. Edmar de Carvalho imagined the interrogator's words propagating through the aether: *How much do I tell him?* It took longer than he would have imagined for the answer to arrive, or perhaps his concentration was such that its ferocity simply curved time around the gravid silence in the white cell.

"It is reasonable to infer," the interrogator said, "that the giants here are representative of another culture, and that their physical stature figuratively represents an imbalance in relations of power."

In the pause following this pronouncement, Edmar de Carvalho realized that he had, however inadvertently, been teaching. Already the jailers—or whoever spoke through them—began to grasp figuration. He wondered if this recovered knowledge would propagate.

"Then you see," he said. "Clearly this culture has brought much of value to the people whom the heroic speaker has adopted as his own. Just as clearly, though, this bounty has come at an intolerable price. Extending the symbolic framework, one might understand the children as manifestations of a worry that the other culture has compromised the future of the civilization represented by the lord's household."

They lifted him away from the table, and sent him back to his cell.

My admiration for Edmar de Carvalho perhaps reaches its apex here, when with so much to say he is able to say so little. He must have known then.

I say "must have," and I fall back into the speculating,

deifying mob, and—you must understand this—*I enjoy the fall*. Indeed, at this moment fidelity to scholarly disinterest becomes impossibly difficult, something like Christian purity of spirit in a fallen world. Reading of Edmar de Carvalho, writing about him, I become preterite. Salvation recedes to the faintest horizons of abstraction.

In Purgatory, then, or even the outer rings of the Hell of hagiography, I tell the story the way it must be told. Like Edmar de Carvalho, I hold the rest of it away while I focus on those few moments in which I see cruxes, tangled matrices of desire and fear and dawning hope. Every fall is a forgetting, and at times such as this, when I feel his presence in the room—when I can even imagine his body, bony like mine, with rounded shoulders—I think I have forgotten properly. Perhaps, like him, I am learning to forget things in the way they must be forgotten in order to feel the connection that sustains us when the distance between bodies grows so great.

Something like the scene I have set down must have occurred, and Edmar de Carvalho, whose name I whisper like a charm under my breath, must have known. He must have seen the poem for what it was, and seen as well how close he skirted the edge of telling too much. In my room, so unlike his, I write, and am unworthy. It is a marvelous abasement.

Ash-faced, the lord's son, knees pressed into cold
    ground

And his eyes with hate reflecting the hellish glare
Cursed the boy: "You knew the giants would come.
    You
Knew the bargain these women made, knew that
    they would tear

The heart from this house whose beginnings memory
Cannot discern. I condemn you to wander with one
Of these women, and to watch the other five die.

Thus may you have regrets enough to sustain you
And divided love, since I have no family
Among whom to divide my own." With that, the son

Turned his broad back on them and left that land
 behind.
Six women and one boy wandered forsaken:
Such are giants' oaths, such the hero's first lesson.

Rolling from round horizons, bearing memories
Of his birth, the sea wind offers little relief.

These words too I say to myself: *The sea wind offers little relief*. Their truth, which is a function of the truth of the poem, aches in my memory, in my sense of duty to him. The line carries a meaning to me only because of the meaning it carried for Edmar de Carvalho; my reading of it is always, always a reading of him. At the end of these lines, the poet— the privilege of naming him belongs of course to Edmar de Carvalho—speaks for himself and for his hero. He doubles himself the way I must refrain from doubling myself. He is his own hero, while I can look on mine only from a great distance, squinting to make out a resemblance.

"It ends here?" Edmar de Carvalho looked up at the blind jailer, knowing the answer. The evidence of the last line proved what he had surmised before, and the knowledge hurt him.

Without turning her head she answered. "There is no more."

He mused. "The rhyme breaks apart at the end. I think he lost interest. He must have known the end was coming."

"The end of what?"

"Your speech is improving," he said, allowing amusement to distract him, to mask his thoughts. This close to escape, to atonement, he could not let his guard down. "That was the first time you've spoken that it hasn't sounded unnatural."

The next day a different blind jailer had taken her place. This was Edmar de Carvalho's latest lesson in the precariousness of his position, the proximity of telling too much, the cost of acting to preserve oneself. Unable to talk about the poem, he went back to his room and lay sleepless and tormented. What would they do to her, a young woman already blinded to perform her duties? Had she anticipated the moment when she would learn to speak too well, spent the hours listening to him mutter knowing that every communication, every unconscious absorption of his inflections and cadences, brought her closer to the end of her assignment? Of her life? Edmar de Carvalho wept, imagining his words like radiation, building up within her until she gave forth her toxicity as clear and beautiful speech.

When the jailers came for him the next morning he said to them, "I know what happened to your colony."

"Tell us," they commanded.

"I will not," he said. "And you cannot force me. We will trade."

The first jailer spoke. Edmar de Carvalho wondered if he was deliberately keeping his speech patterns rough, his vowels and diphthongs disproportionate. Perhaps he had learned from the fate of the blind woman who had guarded the text. Fresh guilt arose in Edmar de Carvalho, a feeling grown loathsome from long familiarity. He squeezed it ruthlessly back into the airless den of his conscience.

"What do you offer?" the first jailer said.

"I have your answer," answered Edmar de Carvalho. "I will deliver it to you when I am set down on the world where the poem was written. I am old, and I do not wish to die in this prison."

"What assurance do we have?"

"Neyaus is the name of a culture, is it not? Perhaps a race's name for itself. Certainly not imposed from without. It is not simply a female figure as it is represented in this poem."

They shut the door, and never again did Edmar de Carvalho look upon the text, save when he conjured it from its nook in the forgetting-place of his exemplary mind.

The sea wind offers little relief. The words recalled to him a conversation, one hundred and fifty years old. A disconsolate group of five, barefoot on a beach, escaping an academic conference, breathing fearfully the South Pacific air. Behind them the Sydney Opera House and the harbor, nothing like Rio's harbor; before them ocean, so much like Rio's ocean. The particulars of the conversation have escaped him, but Edmar de Carvalho remembers one of his co-conspirators saying something: *This, too, shall pass*, or some other weary sentiment born of resignation. The Assimilation has taken their sixth member, and the five know that their time has run out.

No, another says. *What if it doesn't?*

It is an argument they have had before, and the third joins. *Take the long view. The ocean is as close to eternity as a human can understand*, he says. *It will survive Assimilation. Something else will too, even if it's not us.*

Someone—Edmar de Carvalho himself? he does not remember—says: *True; but it does not help.*

A pause, a glance out, away from land, a bearded chin lifted and then dropping again. Words freighted with despondency. That they form the last line in the poem seems too improbable a coincidence; that the line recalls Edmar de Carvalho's name removes all possibility of accident.

It was more than exegesis. Edmar de Carvalho had experienced deprivation, and he had borne as best he could the anguish of treason and the sorrow of unfulfilled hope. The words on the table resonated in his mind, permeated his memories of what he had done before being imprisoned: *to wander with one, and watch five die.* Close enough. So completely did he drown in them that he concluded that they could mirror no experience other than his. A rigorous scholar might laugh at this conclusion, at the exercise of intuition unfettered by judgment and seemly disinterest; Edmar de Carvalho had, however, during his decades in prison lost the trick of scholarly rigor. In the words on the page he saw the speech and cipher of a life he had left one hundred forty-seven years before, the rebuke and exhortation of a friend long betrayed and dead. Even without the last line, he saw this.

It was his fortune, too, to be wrong about Neyaus in exactly the right way.

"Now you will tell us," the first interrogator said to him. Edmar de Carvalho looked at him, saw deprivation in the harsh lines of his face. Away from the aether's influence, the jailers began to look human to him again. He began to notice their faces.

This is why they did not search more thoroughly, he thought. Being neither convicts nor fanatics, they had no reason to suffer separation from the aether, and they could not bear the loneliness of themselves any more than a child in its amniotic ocean can withstand the stillness of its mother's heart. He thought he understood. Colonizing exile existed as an option because the Assimilated Worlds—Earth, Luna, Mars—were just civilized enough to renounce capital punishment, and just vindictive enough to demand a form of permanent sanction. No organized and Assimilated body had any intent of making a permanent foray beyond the insulating murmur of the aether to build on the foundations laid by spacefaring felons, and the aetheric infrastructure could not reach across interstellar distances.

Still, they had to monitor. Assumptions propagated through the aether, reinforced each other until they acquired the weight of fact, and became part of the collective axiomatic underpinnings of the Assimilated Worlds. One of those assumptions, rarely articulated, concerned the necessity of monitoring the exiled colonists. If it was perceived that they were allowed to simply disappear, much of the threat of exile disappeared; the possibility of surveillance and further exile, more than the reality of either, maintained the punitive illusion. Thus this pointless mission to investigate the ruins of a failed colony.

"Yes," said Edmar de Carvalho. "Now I will."

But he did not. Not exactly. He knew that the perfunctory surveillance would last only as long as Assimilation, and he did not believe that Assimilation could survive itself. Among the survivors on this world he would spread that belief. He would uproot Earth from the colonists' past and place it before them, within the grasp of their future.

"They have all died," he said. "I will stay here. I will discover for you the rest of the story."

It is the oldest choice: death or exile.

Every culture knows it and has enshrined it in myth, mortared it into the stalwart arches of literature. In this telling, it shapes itself thus:

A man fights for justice, which is always for this man the right to be only himself. He gathers about him a group of like-minded rebels, and their existence is their first disobedience. Secrecy is the next.

The group is caught, branded treasonous, made through guile to implicate one another. Convicted, they are offered the choice: death or exile. All choose exile, and are cut off from their peers as swiftly and surely as if their senses had been stricken from them and their bodies abandoned on a shore of brackish water and stinging flies.

Here is where this story is different. Some of this group choose to suffer their separation in the enforced solitude of incarceration. Others undertake a second exile, traversing the space between stars as if in the completion of that voyage lies the possibility of returning across the space between minds. Those who remain never learn which of their fellows stay, and which depart.

No records, save an elliptical fragment of epic poetry—a cryptic and desperate message—survive of the dispute that led to the collapse of the exile colony. It must have been another old story, told for the first time under this new sky: the story of powerful strangers, breasting the horizon with a cargo of knowledge and arrogance, failing to understand their impact on the place where they come to rest—and failing to understand the place's impact on them. The colonists suffered tremendous hardship. Each was cut off from the aether, and each carried the knowledge that this separation was his or her own fault, and most of them, unlike Edmar de Carvalho's co-conspirator, wanted nothing more than to return to its subsuming grace before they died. They knew, though, that this would never happen; they voyaged to lay the groundwork for a civilization that would never even arrive to excommunicate them again. Perhaps the stress of this is what finally, after decades of gradual differentiation, broke them apart into the two factions whose conflict survives in the poem.

Scholarly equilibrium reasserts itself. Dispassionate and careful, I tease possibilities from a stubbornly reticent record. I offer what follows as conjecture, untainted by the bias which has unfortunately colored so much of what has come before.

Perhaps the advance party, devastated by the conflict narrated in the poem, fell back on the paleolithic springs of tenacity that enabled humanity's survival. They had enough resources not to lapse into barbarity, but too few to attach any importance to their conscripted mission. They survived, and in the totalizing immersion of the impulse to survive, they forgot why they had fought amongst each other. They forgot, too, how deeply they had once desired to re-Assimilate.

Perhaps when the scout ships returned, they had simply learned how to let the planet forget them.

Perhaps it was some years after this forgetting that Edmar de Carvalho appeared.

"Which of them was it?" asks Edmar de Carvalho, as a last gesture to his charade of innocence. He is not free yet. They offer him the name he has expected. Stricken, he realizes that he has forgotten the face that went with it. He murmurs the name under his breath in a broken voice, the failure of his memory more, at last, than he can bear. *I should have gone,* he thinks to himself. *I was afraid, but I should have gone.*

Resolve gathers in him. He looks out at the desolate shore, the disorienting hues of sky and flower and stone. *I was unequal to this task,* he thinks. *I will be no longer.*

Somewhere are six women, and six children, and a lord's son poisoned by hate.

These sixes are of course myth. But the numbers may also be accurate. The same can be said of the account of Edmar de Carvalho's actions once the jailers left him to his sojourn: what persists are stories which may be true.

He found the colonists in small groups, violently divided and flung away from the remains of their first settlement where Assimilated scouts had recovered the poem. According to the descendants of these colonists, there were in fact six groups, but twenty-five centuries is ample time for redaction, for the revision of history to conform with myth.

Let us say there were six. Over the course of years, his body steadily failing, Edmar de Carvalho traveled between these groups. He sailed a jungle archipelago, trekked over mountains and along the coasts of three oceans. Where he found people, he listened to their stories and their grievances; then, gradually, he began to tell his own story. Some chose to listen. Others reviled him and drove him away. Still he persisted in his telling, allowing the force of his presence, his stature as witness and penitent and survivor, to work slow changes his words alone could not.

He asked after the poet, and found a gravesite—found, too, that mourning cleansed him of the worst of his guilt. I have done what I have done, he said to himself, and went on.

Then, finally, someone asked him if they might someday return.

Beneath rubble, lights still blink, powered by distant sources of energy. Under a regrown canopy of jungle, near an arc of red sandy beach and a limitless expanse of green and restless ocean, a sealed spacecraft performs minimal maintenance, keeping its siphons clear and manufacturing what it needs to continue functioning. Scored by hand into the ceramic cowling near its bay door, the name NEYAUS is obscured by creeping vines and opportunistic mosses.

Neyaus has not found Edmar de Carvalho. He has found her. This is the literal, denotative truth.

The poem, though, found him, and through the poem Neyaus has found her unformed hero. This is the exegetical truth, the truth of the aesthetic mind.

Etched under the word NEYAUS is a careful outline of Australia. Edmar de Carvalho understands: Sydney, Australia. Ney-Aus. Close after this understanding comes a burst of relieved laughter. A survivor's laugh, startling strange winged creatures out of the trees. *How very close I came*, he thinks as leaves fall around him. *If I had noticed sooner, would I have given it away?* Wrong in exactly the right way.

Edmar de Carvalho is not home. He will never be home again. He is not Adam, he seeks no Eve, this world is not an Eden. Here, though, he will find minds that have fallen far enough to desire, yet not too far to listen, and he will tell them what has befallen him. Already some few have asked the right questions, and more are listening to his answers. He will tell them why he made the choices he made. He will be frank about his failures, his betrayals, his fiery reawakening. From him they will learn the value of what he preserved within himself.

In the meantime, the three Assimilated Worlds will, unwittingly and each at its own pace, prepare themselves for his return.

He will not live to see it. Already he is old, and away from the Assimilated Worlds he will age more quickly. But one hundred forty-seven years of solitude has taught him something about turning inward. He knows the difference between an inner space that maintains the shape of the thinking self, and the greedy infinitude of Assimilation. Desiring a mind without horizon, Assimilated humanity created a negative space which drains them away from the world they no longer desire to inhabit, and when this negative space has absorbed a critical mass of human energy and intellect and desire, the inward spiral will be too tight and steep to arrest. When at last this space collapses upon them . . .

As it must . . .

Only then will the world be enough again.

Only then will the mind suffice.

Again I lose myself.

Again I forget that I write more than an exegesis of a poem, or a biographical meditation on a figure of historical importance. I write family history, and must not lose sight of that responsibility or the privilege that comes with it. Even so, I imagine Edmar de Carvalho tearing vines away from that name painstakingly etched into the cowling of an old spacecraft. I imagine him imagining the poet—the poet who had once been his friend, whose face he had forgotten. I imagine him imagining the poet who had been his friend dying after having written a history that had not happened yet, a poem chronicling a hero as yet unborn, an epic of the future rather than the past, of hope rather than nostalgic regret. An act of aesthetic revolution, yes—but more importantly an act of faith, as every poem must be.

I imagine Edmar de Carvalho imagining this, and I begin to know what it is to put oneself in the place of another.

Edmar de Carvalho disappeared into the ribonucleic white noise of the exile colony he adopted as his own. But first he brought them out of their forgetting. He found them, brought them together, held out before them the possibility of redemption and return he had seen in the fragment of a poem. I write because he left them both his wisdom and his dogged will, both learned too late in life to bring him anything but regret and forlorn hope, and because they survived to return, and because they stepped among the shards of Assimilated Worlds and rebuilt a human civilization. His legacy is no less titanic than that. Writing about it, safely ensconced in my pocket of history, I feel like a parasitic speck on his memory. I am ashamed of my luxury of introspection. I sorrow that I do not live in a time of heroes.

Another perspective exists, though. In the face of this sorrow, this shame, this clinging sense of unworthiness, I take a pleasure from this tale that I can only call transcendent. This pleasure, this sense that *from the absence of heroes emerges the beauty of my life's work*, far outweighs the deprivations of loneliness. It gives me what happiness I find, and that is enough. Perhaps the scholars are right that each hero's search is every hero's search, and that every hero's search is for himself. Abrogating my scholarly responsibility, writing myself into my ancestor Edmar de Carvalho, reading myself into the poem that has become the cornerstone of my culture, I fully understood—for the first time—what it meant to search for my name.

I have written this history, here on a planet, humankind's oldest planet, a palimpsest of suffering and ecstasy. Here there are oceans, and I have had occasion to feel the sea wind.

It seems to gentle me, and in its briny breath I scent the real distance between the experience of my life and the experience of writing about, and trying to understand, Edmar de Carvalho. On a strip of sand separating thousands of miles of land from thousands of miles of water, I understand distance.

SENATOR BILBO

"It regrettably has become necessary for us now, my friends, to consider seriously and to discuss openly the most pressing question facing our homeland since the War. By that I mean, of course, the race question."

In the hour before dawn, the galleries were empty, and the floor of the Shire-moot was nearly so. Scattered about the chamber, a dozen or so of the Senator's allies—a few more than were needed to maintain the quorum, just to be safe—lounged at their writing-desks, feet up, fingers laced, pipes stuffed with the best Bywater leaf, picnic baskets within reach: veterans all. Only young Appledore from Bridge Inn was snoring and slowly folding in on himself; the chestnut curls atop his head nearly met those atop his feet. The Senator jotted down Appledore's name without pause. He could get a lot of work done while making speeches—even a filibuster nine hours long (and counting).

"There are forces at work today, my friends, without and

within our homeland, that are attempting to destroy all boundaries between our proud, noble race and all the mule-gnawing, cave-squatting, light-shunning, pit-spawned scum of the East."

The Senator's voice cracked on "East," so he turned aside for a quaff from his (purely medicinal) pocket flask. His allies did not miss their cue. "Hear, hear," they rumbled, thumping the desktops with their calloused heels. "Hear, hear."

"This latest proposal," the Senator continued, "this so-called immigration bill—which, as I have said, would force even our innocent daughters to suffer the reeking lusts of all the ditch-bred legions of darkness—why, this baldfooted attempt originated where, my friends?"

"Buckland!" came the dutiful cry.

"Why, with the delegation from *Buckland* . . . long known to us all as a hotbed of book-mongers, one-Earthers, elvish sympathizers, and other off-brands of the halfling race."

This last was for the benefit of the newly arrived Fredegar Bracegirdle, the unusually portly junior member of the Buckland delegation. He huffed his way down the aisle, having drawn the short straw in the hourly backroom ritual.

"Will the distinguished Senator—" Bracegirdle managed to squeak out, before succumbing to a coughing fit. He waved his bladder-like hands in a futile attempt to disperse the thick purplish clouds that hung in the chamber like the vapors of the Eastmarsh. Since a Buckland-sponsored bill to ban tobacco from the floor had been defeated by the Senator three Shire-moots previous, his allies' pipe-smoking had been indefatigable. Finally Bracegirdle sputtered: "Will the distinguished Senator from the Hill kindly yield the floor?"

In response, the Senator lowered his spectacles and looked across the chamber to the Thain of the Shire, who recited around his tomato sandwich: "Does the distinguished Senator from the Hill so yield?"

"I do not," the Senator replied, cordially.

"The request is denied, and the distinguished Senator

from the Hill retains the floor," recited the Thain of the Shire, who then took another hearty bite of his sandwich. The Senator's party had rewritten the rules of order, making this recitation the storied Thain's only remaining duty.

"Oh, hell and hogsheads," Bracegirdle muttered, already trundling back up the aisle. As he passed Gorhendad Bolger from the Brockenborings, that Senator's man like his father before him kindly offered Bracegirdle a pickle, which Bracegirdle accepted with ill grace.

"Now that the distinguished gentleman from the Misty Mountains has been heard from," the Senator said, waiting for the laugh, "let me turn now to the evidence—the overwhelming evidence, my friends—that many of the orkish persuasion currently living among us have been, in fact, active agents of the Dark Lord. . . ."

As the Senator plowed on, seldom referring to his notes, inventing statistics and other facts as needed, secure that this immigration bill, like so many bills before it, would wither and die once the Bucklanders' patience was exhausted, his self-confidence faltered only once, unnoticed by anyone else in the chamber. A half hour into his denunciation of the orkish threat, the Senator noticed a movement—no, more a shift of light, a *glimmer*—in the corner of his eye. He instinctively turned his head toward the source, and saw, or *thought* he saw, sitting in the farthest, darkest corner of the otherwise empty gallery, a man-sized figure in a cloak and pointed hat, who held what must have been (*could* have been) a staff; but in the next blink, that corner held only shadows, and the Senator dismissed the whatever-it-was as a fancy born of exhilaration and weariness. Yet he was left with a lingering chill, as if (so his old mother, a Took, used to say) a dragon had hovered over his grave.

At noon, the Bucklanders abandoned their shameful effort to open the High Hay, the Brandywine Bridge, and the other entry gates along the Bounds to every misbegotten so-called "refugee," be he halfling, man, elf, orc, warg, Barrow-wight,

or worse. Why, it would mean the end of Shire culture, and
the mongrelization of the halfling race! No, sir! Not today—
not while the Senator was on the job.

Triumphant but weary, the champion of Shire heritage
worked his way, amid a throng of supplicants, aides, well-
wishers, reporters, and yes-men, through the maze of tunnels
that led to his Hill-side suite of offices. These were the largest
and nicest of any Senator's, with the most pantries and the
most windows facing the Bywater, but they also were the farthest from the Shire-moot floor. The Senator's famous ancestor and namesake had been hale and hearty even in his
eleventy-first year; the Senator, pushing ninety, was determined to beat that record. But every time he left the chamber,
the office seemed farther away.

"Gogluk carry?" one bodyguard asked.

"Gogluk *not* carry," the Senator retorted. The day he'd let
a troll haul him through the corridors like luggage would be
the day he sailed oversea for good.

All the Senator's usual tunnels had been enlarged to accommodate the bulk of his two bodyguards, who nevertheless had to stoop, their scaly shoulders scraping the ceiling.
Loyal, dim-witted, and huge—more than five feet in height—
the Senator's trolls were nearly as well known in the Shire as
the Senator himself, thanks partially to the Senator's perennial answer to a perennial question from the press at election
time:

"Racist? Me? Why, I love Gogluk and Grishzog, here, as
if they were my own flesh and blood, and they love me just
the same, don't you, boys? See? Here, boys, have another
biscuit."

Later, once the trolls had retired for the evening, the Senator would elaborate. Trolls, now, you could train them, they
were teachable; they had their uses, same as those swishy
elves, who were so good with numbers. Even considered as a
race, the trolls weren't much of a threat—no one had seen a
baby troll in ages. But those orcs? They did nothing but breed.

Carry the Senator they certainly did not, but by the time the trolls reached the door of the Senator's outermost office (no mannish rectangular door, but a traditional Shire-door, round and green with a shiny brass knob in the middle), they were virtually holding the weary old halfling upright and propelling him forward, like a child pushed to kiss an ugly aunt. Only the Senator's mouth was tireless. He continued to greet constituents, compliment babies, rap orders to flunkies, and rhapsodize about the glorious inheritance of the Shire as the procession squeezed its way through the increasingly small rooms of the Senator's warren-like suite, shedding followers like snakeskin. The only ones who made it from the innermost outer office to the outermost inner office were the Senator, the trolls, and four reporters, all of whom considered themselves savvy under-Hill insiders for being allowed so far into the great man's sanctum. The Senator further graced these reporters by reciting the usual answers to the usual questions as he looked through his mail, pocketing the fat envelopes and putting the thin ones in a pile for his intern, Miss Boffin. The Senator got almost as much work done during press conferences as during speeches.

"Senator, some members of the Buckland delegation have insinuated, off the record, that you are being investigated for alleged bribe-taking. Do you have a comment?"

"You can tell old Gerontius Brownlock that he needn't hide behind a façade of anonymity, and further that I said he was begotten in an orkish graveyard at midnight, suckled by a warg-bitch and educated by a fool. That's off the record, of course."

"Senator, what do you think of your chances for reelection next fall?"

"The only time I have ever been defeated in a campaign, my dear, was my first one. Back when your grandmother was a whelp, I lost a clerkship to a veteran of the Battle of Bywater. A one-armed veteran. I started to vote for him myself.

But unless a one-armed veteran comes forward pretty soon, little lady, I'm in no hurry to pack."

The press loved the Senator. He was quotable, which was all the press required of a public official.

"Now, gentle folk, ladies, the business of the Shire awaits. Time for just one more question."

An unfamiliar voice aged and sharp as Mirkwood cheese rang out: *"They say your ancestor took a fairy wife."*

The Senator looked up, his face even rounder and redder than usual. The reporters backed away. "It's a lie!" the Senator cried. "Who said such a thing? Come, come. Who said that?"

"Said what, Senator?" asked the most senior reporter (Bracklebore, of the *Bywater Battle Cry*), his voice piping as if through a reed. "I was just asking about the quarterly sawmill-production report. If I may continue—"

"Goodbye," said the Senator. On cue, the trolls snatched up the reporters, tossed them into the innermost outer office, and slammed and locked the door. Bracklebore, ousted too quickly to notice, finished his question in the next room, voice muffled by the intervening wood. The trolls dusted their hands.

"Goodbye," said Gogluk—or was that Grishzog?

"Goodbye," said Grishzog—or was that Gogluk?

Which meant, of course, "Mission accomplished, Senator," in the pidgin Common Speech customary among trolls.

"No visitors," snapped the Senator, still nettled by that disembodied voice, as he pulled a large brass key from his waistcoat-pocket and unlocked the door to his personal apartments. Behind him, the trolls assumed position, folded their arms, and turned to stone.

"Imagination," the Senator muttered as he entered his private tunnel.

"Hearing things," he added as he locked the door behind.

"Must be tired," he said as he plodded into the sitting-room, yawning and rubbing his hip.

He desired nothing more in all the earth but a draught of

ale, a pipe, and a long snooze in his armchair, and so he was all the more taken aback to find that armchair already occupied by a white-bearded Big Person in a tall pointed blue hat, an ankle-length gray cloak, and immense black boots, a thick oaken staff laid across his knees.

" 'Strewth!" the Senator cried.

The wizard—for wizard he surely was—slowly stood, eyes like lanterns, bristling gray brows knotted in a thunderous scowl, a meteor shower flashing through the weave of his cloak, one gnarled index finger pointed at the Senator—who was, once the element of surprise passed, unimpressed. The meteor effect lasted only a few seconds, and thereafter the intruder was an ordinary old man, though with fingernails longer and more yellow than most.

"Do you remember me?" the wizard asked. His voice crackled like burning husks. The Senator recognized that voice.

"Should I?" he retorted. "What's the meaning of piping insults into my head? And spying on me in the Shire-moot? Don't deny it; I saw you flitting about the galleries like a bad dream. Come on, show me you have a tongue—else I'll have the trolls rummage for it." The Senator was enjoying himself; he hadn't had to eject an intruder since those singing elves occupied the outer office three sessions ago.

"You appointed me, some years back," the wizard said, "to the University, in return for some localized weather effects on Election Day."

So that was all. Another disgruntled officeholder. "I may have done," the Senator snapped. "What of it?" The old-timer showed no inclination to reseat himself, so the Senator plumped down in the armchair. Its cushions now stank of men. The Senator kicked the wizard's staff from underfoot and jerked his leg back; he fancied something had nipped his toe.

The staff rolled to the feet of the wizard. As he picked it up, the wider end flared with an internal blue glow. He commenced shuffling about the room, picking up knickknacks and setting them down again as he spoke.

"These are hard times for wizards," the wizard rasped. "New powers are abroad in the world, and as the powers of wind and rock, water and tree are ebbing, we ebb with them. Still, we taught our handfuls of students respect for the old ways. Alas, no longer!"

The Senator, half-listening, whistled through his eyeteeth and chased a flea across the top of his foot.

"The entire thaumaturgical department—laid off! With the most insulting of pensions! A flock of old men feebler than I, unable even to transport themselves to your chambers, as I have wearily done—to ask you, to demand of you, why?"

The Senator yawned. His administrative purging of the Shire's only university, in Michel Delving, had been a complex business with a complex rationale. In recent years, the faculty had got queer Eastern notions into their heads and their class-rooms—muddleheaded claims that all races were close kin, that orcs and trolls had not been separately bred by the Dark Power, that the Dark Power's very existence was mythical. Then the faculty quit paying the campaign contributions required of all public employees, thus threatening the Senator's famed "Deduct Box." Worst of all, the faculty demanded "open admissions for qualified non-halflings," and the battle was joined. After years of bruising politics, the Senator's appointees now controlled the university board, and a long-overdue housecleaning was under way. Not that the Senator needed to recapitulate all this to an unemployed spell-mumbler. All the Senator said was:

"It's the board that's cut the budget, not me." With a cry of triumph, he purpled a fingernail with the flea. "Besides," he added, "they kept all the *popular* departments. Maybe you could pick up a few sections of Heritage 101."

This was a new, mandatory class that drilled students on the unique and superior nature of halfling culture and on the perils of immigration, economic development, and travel. The wizard's response was: "Pah!"

The Senator shrugged. "Suit yourself. I'm told the Anduin gambling-houses are hiring. Know any card tricks?"

The wizard stared at him with rheumy eyes, then shook his head. "Very well," he said. "I see my time is done. Only the Grey Havens are left to me and my kind. We should have gone there long since. But your time, too, is passing. No fence, no border patrol—not even you, Senator—can keep all change from coming to the Shire."

"Oh, we can't, can we?" the Senator retorted. As he got worked up, his Bywater accent got thicker. "We sure did keep those Bucklanders from putting over that so-called Fair Distribution System, taking people's hard-earned crops away and handing 'em over to lazy trash to eat. We sure did keep those ugly up-and-down man houses from being built all over the Hill as shelter for immigrant rabble what ain't fully halfling or fully human or fully anything. Better to be some evil race than no race at all."

"There are no evil races," said the wizard.

The Senator snorted. "I don't know how *you* were raised, but I was raised on the Red Book of Westmarch, chapter and verse, and it says so right there in the Red Book, orcs are mockeries of men, filthy cannibals spawned by the Enemy, bent on overrunning the world. . . ."

He went on in this vein, having lapsed, as he often did in conversation, into his tried-and-true stump speech, galvanized by the memories of a thousand cheering halfling crowds. "Oh, there's enemies everywhere to our good solid Shire-life," he finally cried, punching the air, "enemies outside and inside, but we'll keep on beating 'em back and fighting the good fight our ancestors fought at the Battle of Bywater. Remember their cry:

"*Awake! Awake! Fear, Fire, Foes! Awake!*
"*Fire, Foes! Awake!*"

The cheers receded, leaving only the echo of his own voice in the Senator's ears. His fists above his head were bloated and mottled—a corpse's fists. Flushed and dazed, the Senator looked around the room, blinking, slightly embarrassed—and, suddenly, exhausted. At some point he had stood up; now his legs gave way and he fell back into the armchair, raising a puff of tobacco. On the rug, just out of reach, was the pipe he must have dropped, lying at one end of a spray of cooling ashes. He did not reach for it; he did not have the energy. With his handkerchief he mopped at his spittle-laced chin.

The wizard regarded him, wrinkled fingers interlaced atop his staff.

"I don't even know why I'm talking to you," the Senator mumbled. He leaned forward, eyes closed, feeling queasy. "You make my head hurt."

"Inhibiting spell," the wizard said. "It prevented your throwing me out. Temporary, of course. One bumps against it, as against a low ceiling."

"Leave me alone," the Senator moaned.

"Such talents," the wizard murmured. "Such energy, and for what?"

"At least I'm a halfling," the Senator said.

"Largely, yes," the wizard said. "Is genealogy one of your interests, Senator? We wizards have a knack for it. We can see bloodlines, just by looking. Do you really want to know how . . . *interesting* . . . your bloodline is?"

The Senator mustered all his energy to shout, "Get out!" but heard nothing. Wizardry kept the words in his mouth, unspoken.

"There are no evil races," the wizard repeated, "however convenient the notion to patriots, and priests, and storytellers. You may summon your trolls now." His gesture was half shrug, half convulsion.

Suddenly the Senator had his voice back. "Boys!" he

squawked. "Boys! Come quick! Help!" As he hollered, the wizard seemed to roll up like a windowshade, then become a tubular swarm of fireflies. By the time the trolls knocked the door into flinders, most of the fireflies were gone. The last dying sparks winked out on their scaly shoulders as the trolls halted, uncertain what to pulverize. The Senator could hear their lids scrape their eyeballs as they blinked once, twice. The troll on the left asked:

"Gogluk help?"

"Gogluk too *late* to help, thank you very much!" the Senator snarled. The trolls tried to assist as he struggled out of the armchair, but he slapped them away, hissing, in a fine rage now. "Stone ears or no, did you not hear me shouting? Who did you think I was talking to?"

The trolls exchanged glances. Then Grishzog said, quietly: "Senator talk when alone a lot."

"A lot," Gogluk elaborated.

The Senator might have clouted them both had he not been distracted by the wizard's staff. Dropped amid the fireworks, it had rolled beneath a table. Not knowing why, the Senator reached for it, eyes shining. The smooth oak was warm to the touch: heat-filled, like a living thing. Then, with a yelp, the Senator yanked back his hand. The damn thing *definitely* had bitten him this time; blood trickled down his right palm. As three pairs of eyes stared, the staff sank into the carpet like a melting icicle, and was gone.

"Magic," said the trolls as one, impressed.

"Magic?" the senator cried. "Magic?" He swung his fists and punched the trolls, kicked them, wounding only their dignity; their looming hulks managed to cower, like dogs. "If it's magic you want, I'll give you magic!" He swung one last time, lost his balance, and fell into the trolls' arms in a dead faint.

————

The Bunce Inn, now in the hands of its founder's great-granddaughter, had been the favored public house of the Shire-moot crowd for generations. The Senator had not been inside the place in months. He pleaded matters of state, the truth being that he needed a lot more sleep nowadays. But when he woke from his faint to find the trolls fussing over him, he demanded to be taken to the Bunce Inn for a quick one before retiring. The Senator's right hand smarted a bit beneath its bandage, but otherwise the unpleasant interlude with the wizard seemed a bad dream, was already melting away like the staff. The Senator's little troll-cart jounced through the warm honeysuckle-scented night, along the cobbled streets of the capital, in and out of the warm glows cast by round windows behind which fine happy halfling families settled down to halfling dinners and halfling games and halfling dreams.

The inn itself was as crowded as ever, but the trolls' baleful stares quickly prompted a group of dawdlers to drink up and vacate their table. The trolls retreated to a nearby corner, out of the way but ever-present, as bodyguards should be. The Senator sat back with a sigh and a tankard and a plate of chips and surveyed the frenzy all around, pleased to be a part of none of it. The weight of the brimming pewter tankard in his unaccustomed left hand surprised him, so that he spilled a few drops of Bunce's best en route to his mouth. *Aah*. Just as he remembered. Smacking foam from his lips, he took another deep draught—and promptly choked. Not six feet away, busy cleaning a vacant table, was an orc.

And not just any orc. This one clearly had some man in its bloodline somewhere. The Senator had seen to it that the Shire's laws against miscegenation had stayed on the books, their penalties stiffened, but elsewhere in the world, alas, traditional moral values had declined to the point that such blasphemous commingling had become all too frequent. This creature was no doubt an orc—the hulking torso and bowlegs, the flat nose and flared nostrils, the broad face, the slanting eyes, the coarse hair, the monstrous hooked teeth at the corners of the mouth—but the way the orc's arms moved as it stacked dirty plates was uncomfortably manlike. It had genuine hands as well, with long delicate fingers, and as its head turned, the Senator saw that its pupils were not the catlike slits of a true orc but rounded, like the pupils of dwarves, and men, and halflings. It was like seeing some poor trapped halfling peering out from a monstrous bestial shell, as in those children's stories where the hero gets swallowed whole by the ogre and cries for help from within. The orc, as it worked, began to whistle.

The Senator shuddered, felt his gorge rise. His injured hand throbbed with each heartbeat. A filthy half-breed orc, working at the Bunce Inn! Old Bunce would turn in his grave. Catching sight of young Miss Bunce bustling through the crowd, the Senator tried to wave her over, to give her a piece of his mind. But she seemed to have eyes only for the orc. She placed her hand on its shoulder and said, in a sparkling gay voice: "Please, sir, don't be tasking yourself, you're too kind. I'll clean the table; you just settle yourself, please, and tell me what you'll have. The lamb stew is very nice today, and no mistake."

"Always pleased to help out, ma'am," said the orc, plopping its foul rump onto the creaking bench. "I can see how busy you are. Seems to me you're busier every time I come through the Shire."

"There's some as say I needs a man about," Miss Bunce said, her arms now laden with plates, "but cor! Then I'd be busier still, wouldn't I?" The orc laughed a horrid burbling mucus-filled laugh as Miss Bunce sashayed away, buttocks swinging, glancing back to twinkle at her grotesque customer, and wink.

At this inauspicious moment, someone gave the Senator a hearty clap on the back. It was Fredegar Bracegirdle, a foaming mug in his hand and a foolish grin on his fat red face. Drink put Bracegirdle in a regrettable bipartisan mood. "Hello, Senator," Bracegirdle chirped, as he clapped the Senator's back again and again. "Opponents in the legislature, drinking buddies after hours, eh, Senator, eh, friend, eh, pal?"

"Stop pounding me," the Senator said. "I am not choking. Listen, Bracegirdle. What is that, that . . . *creature* . . . doing here?"

Bracegirdle's bleary gaze slowly followed the Senator's pointing finger, as a dying flame follows a damp fuse. "Why, he's a-looking at the bill of fare, and having himself a pint, same as us."

"You know what I mean! Look at those hands. He talks as if someone, somewhere, has given him schooling. Where'd he come from?"

As he answered, Bracegirdle helped himself to the Senator's chips. "Don't recall his name, but he hails from Dunland, from one of those new, what-do-you-call-'em, investment companies, their hands in a little of everything. Run by orcs and dwarves, mostly, but they're hiring all sorts. My oldest, Bungo, he's put his application in, and I said, you go to it, son, there's no work in the Shire for a smart lad like yourself, and your dear gaffer won't be eating any less in his old age. Young Bunce, she's a wizard at these chips, she is. Could you pass the vinegar?"

The Senator already had risen and stalked over to the orc's table, where the fanged monster, having ordered, was working one of the little pegboard games Miss Bunce left on the tables for patrons' amusement. The orc raised its massive head as it registered the Senator's presence.

"A good evening to you, sir," it said. "You can be my witness. Look at that, will you? Only one peg left, and it in the center. I've never managed *that* before!"

The Senator cleared his throat and spat in the orc's face. A brown gob rolled down its flattened nose. The orc gathered its napkin, wiped its face, and stood, the scrape of the bench audible in the otherwise silent room. The orc was easily twice as wide as the Senator, and twice as tall, yet it did not have to stoop. Since the Senator's last visit, Miss Bunce had had the ceiling raised. Looking up at the unreadable, brutish face, the Senator stood his ground, his own face hot with rage, secure in the knowledge that the trolls were right behind him. Someone across the room coughed. The orc glanced in that direction, blinked, shook its head once, twice, like a horse bedeviled by flies. Then it expelled a breath, its fat upper lip flapping like a child's noisemaker, and sat down. It slid the pegboard closer and re-inserted the pegs, one after the other after the other, then, as the Senator watched, resumed its game.

The Senator, cheated of his fight, was unsure what to do. He could not remember when last he had been so utterly ignored. He opened his mouth to tell the orc a thing or two, but felt a tug at his sleeve so violent that it hushed him. It was Miss Bunce, lips thin, face pale, twin red spots livid on her cheeks. "It's late, Senator," she said, very quietly. "I think you'd best be going home."

Behind her were a hundred staring faces. Most of them were strangers. Not all of them were halflings. The Senator looked for support in the faces in the crowd, and for the first time in his life, did not find it. He found only hostility, curiosity, indifference. He felt his face grow even hotter, but not with rage.

He nearly told the Bunce slut what he thought of her and her orc-loving clientele—but best to leave it for the Shire-moot. Best to turn his back on this pesthole. Glaring at everyone before him, he gestured for the trolls to clear a path, and muttered: "Let's go, boys."

Nothing happened.

The Senator slowly turned his head. The trolls weren't there. The trolls were nowhere to be seen. Only more hostile strangers' faces. The Senator felt a single trickle of sweat slide past his shoulder blades. The orc jumped pegs, removed pegs: *snick, snick.*

So. The Senator forced himself to smile, to hold his head high. He nodded, patted Miss Bunce's shoulder (she seemed not to relish the contact), and walked toward the door. The crowd, still silent, parted for him. He smiled at those he knew. Few smiled back. As he moved through the crowd, a murmur of conversation arose. By the time he reached the exit, the normal hubbub had returned to the Bunce Inn, the Senator's once-favorite tavern, where he had been recruited long ago to run for clerk on the Shire First ticket. He would never set foot in the place again. He stood on the threshold, listening to the noise behind, then cut it off by closing the door.

The night air was hot and rank and stifling. Amid the waiting wagons and carriages and mules and two-wheeled pedal devices that the smart set rode nowadays, the Senator's little troll-cart looked foolish in the lamplight. As did his two truant bodyguards, who were leaning against a sagging, creaking carriage, locked in a passionate embrace. The Senator decided he hadn't seen that; he had seen enough today. He cleared his throat, and the trolls leaped apart with much coughing and harrumphing.

"Home," the Senator snapped. Eyeing the uneven pavement, he stepped with care to the cart, sat down in it, and waited. Nothing happened. The trolls just looked at one another, shifted from foot to foot. The Senator sighed and, against his better judgment, asked: "What is it?"

The trolls exchanged another glance. Then the one on the right threw back his shoulders—a startling gesture, given the size of the shoulders involved—and said: "Gogluk quit." He immediately turned to the other troll and said: "There, I said it."

"And you know that goes double for me," said the other troll. "Let's go, hon. Maybe some fine purebred halfling will take this old reprobate home."

Numb but for his dangling right hand, which felt as swollen as a pumpkin, the Senator watched the trolls walk away arm in arm. One told the other: "*Spitting* on people, yet! I thought I would just *die*." As they strolled out of the lamplight, the Senator rubbed his face with his left hand, massaged his wrinkled brow. He had been taught in school, long ago, that the skulls of trolls ossified in childhood, making sophisticated language skills impossible. If it wasn't true, it ought to be. There ought to be a law. He would write one as soon as he got home.

But how was he to *get* home? He'd never make it on foot, and he certainly couldn't creep back into the tavern to ask the egregious Bracegirdle for a ride. Besides, he couldn't see to walk at the moment; his eyes were watering. He wiped them on his sleeve. It wasn't that he would *miss* the trolls, certainly not, no more than he would miss, say, the andirons, were they to rise up, snarl insults, wound him to the heart, the wretches, and abandon him. One could always buy a new set. But at the thought of the andirons, the cozy hearth, the armchair, the Senator's eyes brimmed anew. He was so tired, and so confused; he just wanted to go home. And his hand hurt. He kept his head down as he mopped his eyes, in case of passers-by. There were no passers-by. The streetlamp flared as a buzzing insect flew into it. He wished he had fired those worthless trolls. He certainly would, if he ever saw them again.

"Ungratefulness," the Senator said aloud, "is the curse of this age." A mule whickered in reply.

Across the street, in the black expanse of the Party Field, a lone mallorn-tree was silhouetted against the starlit sky. Enchanted elven dust had caused the mallorn and all the other trees planted after the War to grow full and tall in a single season, so that within the year the Shire was once again green and beautiful—or so went the fable, which the Senator's party had eliminated from the schoolbooks years ago. The Senator blew his nose with vigor. The Shire needed nothing from elves.

When the tavern door banged open, the Senator felt a surge of hope that died quickly as the hulking orc-shape shambled forth. The bastard creature had looked repellent enough inside; now, alone in the lamplit street, it was the stuff of a thousand halfling nightmares, its bristling shoulders as broad as hogsheads, its knuckles nearly scraping the cobbles, a single red eye guttering in the center of its face. No, wait. That was its cigar. The orc reared back on its absurd bowlegs and blew smoke rings at the streetlamp—rings worthy of any halfling, but what of it? Even a dog can be trained, after a fashion, to dance. The orc extended its horrid manlike hand and tapped ashes into the lamp. Then, arm still raised, it swiveled its great jowly head and looked directly at the Senator. Even a half-orc could see in the dark.

The Senator gasped. He was old and alone, no bodyguards. Now the orc was walking toward him! The Senator looked for help, found none. Had the wizard's visit been an omen? Had the confusticated old charm tosser left a curse behind with his sharp-toothed staff? As the Senator cowered, heard the inexorable click of the orc's claws on the stones, his scream died in his throat—not because of any damned bebothered wizard's trickery, but because of fear, plain and simple fear. He somehow always had known the orcs would get him in the end. He gasped, shrank back. The orc loomed over him, its pointed head blocking the lamplight. The orc laid one awful hand, oh so gently, on the Senator's right shoulder, the only points of contact the fingertips—rounded, mannish, hellish fingertips. The Senator shuddered as if the orc's arm were a lightning rod. The Senator spasmed and stared and fancied the orc-hand and his own injured halfling hand were flickering blue in tandem, like the ends of a wizard's staff. The great mouth cracked the orc's leathered face, blue-lit from below, and a voice rumbled forth like a subterranean river: "Senator? Is that you? Are you all right?"

Sprawled there in the cart, pinned by the creature's gentle hand as by a spear, the Senator began to cry, in great sucking sobs of rage and pain and humiliation, as he realized this damned orc was not going to splinter his limbs and crush his skull and slurp his brains. How far have I fallen, the Senator thought. This morning the four corners of the Shire were my own ten toes, to wiggle as I pleased. Tonight I'm pitied by an orc.

TERRY BISSON

THE OLD RUGGED CROSS

ONE NIGHT BUD WHITE HAD A DREAM. IN THE DREAM, HE was hanging on the cross next to Jesus Christ, and the doors to Heaven opened wide, and a smiling little black girl in a starched white dress, the very girl he had raped and buried in the gravelly mud by the Cumberland River, welcomed him in.

Bud went to sleep a sinner, and woke up saved.

It so happened that the chaplain was on Death Row that very morning, counseling a Jehovah's Witness who couldn't, for religious reasons, be executed by lethal injection under the new Freedom of Religious Observance Act (FROA).

The scaffold or the electric chair? The condemned was having a hard time deciding. It was, he said, without a trace of irony, "the most important decision of my life."

The chaplain advised him to sleep on it. He had other things on his mind. The primer was dry on his 1955 Chevy 210 coupe, a Classic in anybody's book, and he intended to spend the evening sanding it again. It was ready to paint but he didn't have the money yet. $1225 for three coats, hand rubbed. You don't skimp on a Classic.

It was already almost noon. But on his way out of the tier, the chaplain passed by Bud's cell, and Bud called out, " 'Scuse me, Reverend."

The chaplain stopped. Here was a man who'd never had the time of day for religion or its representatives. All Bud did was watch TV. "What can I do for you, White?" the chaplain asked.

Bud told the chaplain his dream.

The chaplain held his chin in three fingertips, like a plum, and nodded as he listened. A plan was already forming in his mind. He reached through the bars and placed a hand on Bud's plump knee. "Are you sorry, then, for what you did?"

"You bet," said Bud. "Especially now that I know there is a Heaven, and I'll go straight there." He looked as pleased as if he had just discovered a dollar bill in a library book.

"I'll do what I can to help," said the chaplain. "Would you like to pray with me?"

That night instead of sanding his Classic, the chaplain made a phone call to his former professor at the Divinity School. "Do you remember a lecture you gave twelve years ago," he asked, "on the medical mysteries of Our Lord's Passion?"

"Of course," said the professor. "I give the same lecture every year."

"What if there was a way to actually watch it happen?" the chaplain said.

"Were," said the Professor, who also taught English Comp. "Watch what happen?"

"You know. The procedure and all. An actual crucifixion. What would it be worth?"

"To science or to religion?"

"Either, both, whatever," said the chaplain, who was beginning to wonder when the professor was going to get the point.

"It would be invaluable," said the professor. "It would be revelatory. It would settle once and for all the disputes over how long the crucifixion took, what was the actual cause of death, what was the pathology sequence. It would be marvelous. It would be worth a thousand pictures, a hundred thousand words; worth more than all the pious and vulgar—"

"No, I mean in dollars," said the chaplain.

"You have made an extremely impressive conversion," said the chaplain when he met with Bud the next morning, at 8:45. "I want you to meet with my old professor."

"How old?"

"Former professor," corrected the chaplain. "He's a professor of religion,"

"Professor of Religion!" said Bud, who had never realized there was such a thing.

"From my old, my former, divinity school," said the chaplain.

And Divinity School! It sounded like something good to eat.

After leaving Bud, the chaplain went two cells down, to see the Jehovah's Witness.

"Hanging," the young man said. He had apparently prayed all night. "The scaffold and the rope. Hemp and wood. It seems the most traditional."

"The hemp might be a problem," said the chaplain. (As it turned out, the wood was too.)

They prayed together and as he was leaving, as if it were an afterthought, the chaplain asked, "Who's the lawyer who handled your FROA suit? Can you give me his phone number?"

It turned out that he was a she. The lawyer lived in a condo overlooking the Cumberland River, only half a mile from the mud bank where the little girl Bud White killed had been found.

"A prisoner's case? I can't afford any more pro bono," she said. But when the chaplain told her that the professor was financing it through a grant, she was more receptive. When he told her about the TV interest, she was positively sympathetic. That evening the three of them had dinner together, on the deck of a restaurant in downtown Nashville.

The chaplain had the fiddler with fries. The lawyer had the jalapeño hush puppies. The professor had the crab cakes and picked up the bill. He was going to see Bud the next day.

Bud White was watching TV when the guard brought his visitor. Bud watched a lot of TV.

"Are you really a professor of religion?" Bud asked.

The professor assured him that he was. "And I'm here to hear about your dream."

Bud hit MUTE and told the professor about his dream. "Jesus nodded at me," he said.

The professor himself nodded. "Your dream was almost certainly a sign," he said.

Bud wasn't surprised. He had heard about signs.

"The only sure way to go to Heaven is to follow in the exact footsteps of Our Lord," the professor said.

Bud was confused. "Footsteps?"

"It's a figure of speech," said the professor, realizing he should be more precise, more literal in dealing with Bud. "What I mean is, go the way he went."

"Go," repeated Bud, looking around his narrow cell. The word had a nice ring to it. But then Bud remembered the dream. "Is it going to hurt?"

"I'm not here to bullshit you," said the professor, placing his hand on Bud's plump knee. "It will hurt some, that's for sure. But think of the reward."

Bud thought of the little black girl. Her face and hair were clean, but her dress was muddy. He closed his eyes and smiled.

"The first step is to sign these papers making the chaplain and I your spiritual advisers."

"I don't write very good," said Bud.

"I'll help you," said the professor, guiding Bud's hand. "Now let the chaplain and I worry about the details. But I can tell you this: Cumberland Divinity has agreed to pay for everything."

"Divinity!" There was that candy sound again.

The professor rose to go. "Any questions?"

"What about my mother?"

"I didn't know you had a mother."

"I haven't seen her since I was a little boy, but she was there in the dream."

It was hard for the professor to imagine Bud as a little boy. Maybe it was the beard.

"I'll see about it," he said.

"This is outrageous," said the warden. "It's preposterous. It's impossible."

"We are prepared to concede the first two," said the lawyer. "But not the third."

"He wants his mother to be there?" the warden persisted.

"As his spiritual advisers, we can require it under FROA," said the professor.

The warden frowned. "Oh, you can, can you?"

The chaplain shrugged apologetically. "Jesus's mother was there."

The lawyer put her attaché case on her lap. She unsnapped it but didn't open it. "We didn't want to trouble you with a whole separate FROA filing. We'd like to work this out between colleagues. Between friends."

"Friends?"

They were sitting in the warden's office, in front of the huge, half moon, barred window.

The lawyer leaned across the desk and presented the warden with her warmest (which was not as warm as his, and his was not warm) smile. "We needn't be adversaries," she said. "I am merely looking after my client's interest. You are merely obeying the law of the land. The chaplain and the professor here are merely fulfilling their spiritual responsibilities. None of us would choose what Bud White has chosen. But who would have chosen any of this?"

She waved a hand indicating the prison yard beyond the window. A few men lounged on rusted weight-lifting equipment, smoking cigarettes. Smoking was still allowed in the yard.

"I would have chosen it," said the warden. "In fact I did choose it. I dropped out of Law my second year and switched to Corrections."

"We're soul mates, then!" said the lawyer. "I dropped out of Police Academy to go to Law School."

"Ditto," said the professor. "I was studying for Ordination when I decided to get my Ph.D. instead, in Biblical History."

"Okay, okay," said the warden. He rose from his desk to signal that the interview was over. "I won't fight you on the mother, but I'm not sure we can do the cross."

"What's this Discovery Channel?" Bud's mother asked. "Hasn't anybody ever heard of ABC or NBC or even Ted Turner? What about Fox?"

"They didn't want it," said the professor.

"We tried them, in that order, as a matter of fact," said the lawyer.

"You should have come to me first," said Bud's mother, tipping a little more vodka into her Sprite.

"She's got a point," said the chaplain. He had positioned himself across the trailer so that he could see up her dress. "I say we cut her in for a full share."

"Cut me in? Just you try and cut me out! Who else is getting money out of this deal?"

"Other than the TV?" The lawyer tapped her attaché thoughtfully with a yellow pencil. "The professor and the chaplain split a stipend as Bud's spiritual advisers. I get my usual, plus a small commission on foreign rights. Oh, and the chaplain gets a finder's fee."

"Finder's fee? I gave birth to the sorry bastard!"

"It's only twelve-fifty," said the chaplain. "What say we make it twenty-five hundred and split it?"

The professor rolled his eyes, but it was only for effect. He had already decided to cut Bud's mother in.

"What about Bud?" she asked.

"What's Bud going to do with money?" asked the chaplain. "He would probably just leave his share to you anyway."

"My point exactly," said the mother. "Everybody else is double-dipping here."

"Oak? Does it say oak in the Bible?" asked the carpenter.

"Bud can't read the Bible," said the lawyer. "He must have got that from TV."

"It's probably the only wood he's ever heard of," said the chaplain. "There's not a whole lot about wood on TV."

"He's never heard of pine?"

"Historically," said the professor, "it should be cypress."

They were meeting in the prison shop, just off the yard.

"Cypress is out," said the warden. "Isn't it endangered or something?"

"I think that's mahogany," said the professor.

"Cedar's nice," said the chaplain. "The boy's mother likes cedar."

"He's not a boy," said the warden.

"Under FROA, Death Row prisoners have the right to die in a manner consistent with their religious beliefs," said the lawyer, reaching for her attaché case.

"We should rape him and bury him alive in a mud bank, then," said the carpenter, a trusty.

"Shut up, Billy Joe," said the warden. He looked from the chaplain to the lawyer to the professor. "How about plywood?"

"I've researched this whole procedure," said the professor, "and the one thing we *don't* need is a doctor."

"You don't, but we do," said the producer. "Under *Kevorkian*, we are only allowed to televise a suicide if a doctor is on hand to prevent unnecessary suffering."

"He doesn't look like a doctor," said the lawyer. "No offense."

They were sitting in the warden's office, under the large, barred, half-moon window.

"None taken," said the doctor. "I'm what they call a parasurgeon. I can stitch you up but I can't cut you open."

"It's not a suicide anyway," said the warden. "It's a state-mandated execution, perfectly legal. Totally legal."

"And what's this unnecessary suffering business?" asked the professor. "In a crucifixion, the suffering is part of the deal."

"It's the whole deal," said the chaplain.

"Making it, by definition, not unnecessary," agreed the lawyer.

"Last supper?" asked the warden. "Not a problem. That's on us, free of charge. Only we call it the last meal."

"He wants the Surf & Turf from Red Lobster," said the chaplain. "And he wants a long table, like in the frescoes. They must have showed the frescoes on PBS."

"Surf and Turf is technically two meals," said the warden. "The long table could be a problem, too. Unless it's in the corridor."

"What about the wine?" asked the professor.

"Wine's definitely going to be a problem," said the warden. "That's like the oak."

"We're trying to avoid a supplementary filing," said the lawyer, unsnapping her attaché.

"Maybe the Food Channel would pick up the cost of the Turf," suggested the mother. "Or the Surf."

"The Food Channel?" asked the warden. "When did they get in on this?"

"They're in the pool," said the producer.

"Scourging sounds okay," said Bud. It sounded sort of like deep cleaning. "But I don't like the part about the nails."

"The nails are an essential part of the experience," said the professor. He put his hand on Bud's plump knee and looked into his big, empty brown eyes. "Our Lord didn't shop around, Bud. None of this 'want this, don't want that' stuff for Him. You have to take it as it comes. Render unto Caesar and so forth."

Bud was confused. "Sees who?"

"And we've arranged the Last Supper," said the chaplain. "We're all going to be there. Me and the professor and the lawyer. Plus the producer and the doctor, and even the carpenter."

"I like the carpenter," said Bud. "What about my mother?"

"Her too. Turns out she likes lobster."

"I thought we agreed on plywood," said the professor.

"No go," said the carpenter. "New environmental regs. Something about the glue. Toxic."

He was fitting together two steel framing two-by-fours.

The lawyer tapped one of them with the longest of her long (and they were very long) fingernails; it rang with a dull ring.

The professor was skeptical. A metal cross? "What about the nails?" he asked.

The carpenter, looking pleased with himself, pulled three wooden squares from a shopping bag. "Butcher blocks," he said. "Drilled and ready to bolt on. Ordered them from Martha Stewart™ Online. And check this out—they're cypress!"

"Billy Joe, you're a wonder," said the warden.

The little girl's grandmother lived in a neat duplex on Cumberland Road, only a few blocks from the Cumberland River.

"According to the Victims' Families' Bill of Rights, you are entitled to attend and observe the execution," the lawyer said.

"But I would advise against it," said the chaplain. "It's going to be ugly and take a long time."

"Why is it going to be ugly and take a long time?" asked the little girl's grandmother.

The professor explained why it was going to be ugly and take a long time.

"We'll be there," said the little girl's uncle, a uniformed security guard at the Cumberland Mall, who was the last person (except for Bud) to see her alive.

"The guidelines say all deliberate speed," said the warden. "I think that means we have to start early."

It was noon on Friday. Bud's execution date was twelve hours away, at midnight.

The warden, the lawyer, the chaplain, the professor, the

producer, the doctor, and Bud's mother were in the yard, watching as the carpenter directed the four convict volunteers unloading the pile of stones that had been rented to make a small hill. Their names were Matthew, Mark, John, and John. The professor had chosen them from the prison's roster. He couldn't find a Luke. Each was to receive a magazine subscription and a hooded Polartec™ sweatshirt.

"Golgotha wasn't very high," said the professor. "It wasn't a hill so much as a mound, a pile of rubble. So this will do just fine."

"How long is it going to tie up the yard?" asked the warden.

"We will definitely be out of here by dawn," said the doctor.

"Dawn!" said the warden. "You're not intending to drag this out all night, are you?"

"It's supposed to be slow," said the lawyer.

"Can't be too slow," said the warden. "The state has guidelines. All deliberate speed is one of them."

"The whole point of this procedure is that it's slow," said the professor. "Excruciating is the word, as a matter of fact."

"I'm just asking you to speed it up a little," said the warden.

"There's no way we can speed it up without violating the fundamental rights of the petitioner," said the lawyer, reaching for her attaché case.

"Whatever," said the warden. "Can you give me an ETA?"

The lawyer turned to the professor. "What does the Bible say?"

"Our Lord took three hours," said the professor.

"Okay, then it's simple," said the warden. "We start at nine."

"Set another place for the Last Supper," said Bud's mother. "I invited a friend."

"You can't bring a friend," said the warden.

"She's my lesbian lover," said Bud's mother. "Protected under—"

She looked at the lawyer, and the warden realized that this entire scene had been rehearsed.

"Under the Domestic Partners Extension 347 of 1999," said the lawyer.

"She's never gotten the chance to watch anybody die," said Bud's mother. "Particularly a man."

"I had no idea you were a lesbian," said the chaplain, after the warden had left for his rounds. This was in the days when wardens still made rounds. The chaplain sounded disappointed.

"I'm not," said Bud's mother, with a wink, followed by a nudge. "I just wanted to make sure she got in. She's from the *Tattler*."

"That rag!?" exclaimed the professor.

"I tried to get the *Star* or the *Enquirer*, but they wouldn't return my calls," said Bud's mother.

"That's because Bud's not a celeb," said the doctor. "Wait till they start executing celebs, then they'll return your calls."

"They're already executing celebrities," said Bud's mother. "What about O J?"

"He got off," said the lawyer.

"Again?"

"They're paper," said the guard.

"Feels like regular cloth," said Bud, pulling on his orange coveralls.

"No wine?" asked Bud's mother.

"No wine," said the guard, who was doubling as the waiter. "And no smoking, either."

The reporter from the *Tattler* put out her cigarette.

"I don't smoke!" said Bud. He grinned. "And don't kiss girls who do!"

"Pass the sour cream for the baked potato," said the doctor. "It's better and better for you than butter."

"Pass the butter," said the professor.

"Bud gets served first," said the chaplain, who was sitting at the Condemned's right hand. "Bud, you want steak or lobster?"

"Both," said Bud.

"That looks good, but it's time to go," said the warden from the corridor. "Any last words?"

It was 9:05.

"What's the hurry?" asked Bud, helping himself to the last of the frozen yogurt. "I thought it wasn't till midnight."

"It's not, officially," said the guard, as he snapped the plastic shackles around Bud's feet. "But they asked us to bring you around early."

"The whole thing could take hours," said the warden. "We decided to try and get you up on the cross by ten at the latest."

"I don't know if I like that," Bud said, holding his hands behind his back for the cuffs.

"There's nothing not to like," said the professor. "It's a necessary precaution since with this procedure death's not instantaneous."

"It's not? I guess that's good, then," said Bud. Instantaneous sounded painful.

They walked two-by-two, except for Bud's mother, down the long hallway toward the door that led into the prison yard. The warden and the lawyer went first. Bud and the guard were right behind them.

A man in a rubber suit stood by the door. He was holding a tank with a short hose and a nozzle, like a paint sprayer.

"Who's that?" Bud asked.

"Remember, we talked about the scourging?" said the chaplain. He and the professor were right behind Bud. "That's why they gave you the paper coveralls."

"They don't feel right," Bud said. He had the feeling something bad was about to happen. He often had these feelings. Usually they were right.

"In order to duplicate the original procedure as closely as possible," said the professor, "there has to be a thorough preliminary scourging."

"So where's the whip?" the producer asked. He and the carpenter were next in line.

"It's going to be a chemical scourging," said the warden. "Whips are not allowed in Tennessee prisons."

The man in the rubber suit raised his mask, revealing himself to be the doctor. "This tank is filled with a powerful paint stripper," he explained. "It will traumatize the client before he is hung on the cross."

"Client," said the professor scornfully. "I can remember when the word was 'patient' "

The para-doctor ignored him and lowered his mask.

"Otherwise," said the chaplain, placing a hand on Bud's plump shoulder, "you could hang there for days."

"So let's have at it, then, boys," said Bud's mother darkly. She was the only one walking alone. The reporter from the *Tattler* had already gotten sick and gone home.

"Turn around, Bud," said the guard.

Bud turned around. The guard stepped out of the way.

The doctor sprayed a foam onto Bud's back and shoulders. For the first split second it didn't hurt. Then the paper soaked through and began to smoke.

Then Bud began to scream.

"Is this legal?" the producer asked the warden.

"Is what what?" Bud's screams made hearing difficult.

The producer repeated his question. The warden shrugged and nodded toward the professor. "Ask him. He's in charge from now until the actual MOE, or Moment of Expiration," he said.

"Is that legal?" asked the producer.

"Is what what?"

The producer repeated his question. "Check your Bible," said the professor, with an air of mystery.

"There's a threshhold requirement of religious authenticity," said the lawyer. "Otherwise none of this would be happening."

"Does that mean the client has been baptized?" asked the producer. Bud had quit screaming. He was rolling on the floor, which is hard to do in handcuffs, trying to get his breath back.

"You bet," said the chaplain, who had moved to the back of the line.

"You bet," said Bud's mother.

"You can't do that here," said the warden from the front of the line.

"Do what?" asked the chaplain and Bud's mother, in one voice.

"You two. That." They were holding hands.

"We lost the sound," said the little girl's uncle, who was watching from the Victims' Rights Closure Lounge on closed-circuit television. It was he who had found her, tracing her little doll to the muddy bank of the Cumberland.

Bud White had quit screaming. He was rolling on the floor of the corridor, trying to get his breath back.

"This ain't right," said the little girl's grandmother. Her name was Hecubah. The little girl had been named after her but hadn't liked the name. Her grandmother had always thought she would eventually come around, as children often do with unusual or Biblical names. But it was not to be, alas.

"We lost the sound," said the little girl's uncle. "Where's that guard?"

"That wasn't in the dream," said Bud. He was flopping like a fish on the cold concrete floor.

The doctor and the warden helped him to his knees. Then they handed him to the four convict volunteers, wearing rubber gloves, who dragged him through the door into the prison yard.

The rest of the party followed.

"Where's the cross?" asked Bud's mother.

A single steel upright stood at the top of a small hill of rubble.

The carpenter showed her the cross-piece, which lay on the ground at the foot of the hill. "It gets assembled as we go," he said.

"It's almost ten," said the warden. "Let's get on with this."

The chaplain didn't want to drive the nails.

"I'm a man of the cloth," he said. "Isn't the state supposed to be sending somebody?"

"They are," said the warden, "but she won't be here till eleven. She usually just inserts an IV."

"With any luck, we could be done by then," said the carpenter.

"Let's hope not," said the professor, under his breath.

"Bud's ready to go," said Bud's mother. "Why drag it out? My boy is eager to get into Heaven, aren't you, Bud?"

Bud was shaking his head and moaning. The convict volunteers were helping him out of what was left of his coveralls.

"And what is this?" asked the producer.

"It's a loincloth," said the professor.

"It's paper too," said the warden.

"Looks like a diaper to me," said Bud's mother.

"Here," said the carpenter, handing the doctor a nail gun. "Just pull the trigger. But get close. You don't want the nail flying out and hitting somebody. Somebody else."

"I've already done my bit," said the doctor, handing the nail gun to the professor. "I'm here to observe."

"Ditto," said the professor, handing it to the chaplain.

"Perhaps it should be a loved one," said the chaplain. He handed the nail gun to Bud's mother.

"No way," said Bud's mother. "He's mad enough at me as it is."

Bud was shivering even though October in Tennessee is rarely very cold. "I'm not mad at anybody," he said.

Nevertheless, Bud's mother handed the nail gun to the warden—who handed it back to the carpenter. "I'll owe you one, Billy Joe," he said.

Bud began to weep as the guard and the doctor laid him on his back over the metal cross-piece.

"Turn it up," said the little girl's uncle, who was watching from the Victims' Rights Closure Lounge.

"Don't you dare," said the little girl's grandmother.

The guard turned it up anyway. He was the only one allowed to touch the 44-inch Samsung; it was state property.

"He's weeping because the metal's cold and his back is raw," said the doctor. "From the scourging."

"Sounds like a cleanser," said the uncle. "Looks like a diaper."

"This ain't right," said the grandmother.

"Not through the hands," said the professor. "That's a common misconception. Through the wrists. Aim for the little hollow."

"Which little hollow?"

"That little hollow right there."

Bud looked away. He tried looking toward the ceiling, then saw the stars and realized he was outside. It was the first time he had seen the stars in six years. They looked as cold as ever. "I don't remember any of this from the dream," he said.

"That's why I'm here," said the professor. "To make sure it's all authentic."

"It's going to hurt but it's supposed to hurt," said the chaplain. "Try and roll with it, Bud; try not to—"

BANG!

The chaplain didn't get to finish. Bud's body twisted almost comically as he tried to reach toward the wrist that had just been nailed to the left chopping block. But the four volunteers held his right arm in place.

"Look away," said the carpenter. He was talking to Bud.

BANG!

"Let's take him up," said the professor to the warden, who nodded toward the four convict volunteers.

Matthew and Mark lifted the cross-piece over their heads and into the slot in the upright. Bud White was hanging from it. Meanwhile, John and John guided Bud's feet, which were still shackled together, toward the cypress block near the bottom of the upright.

Bud was screaming again. "I wouldn't have picked him for a screamer," said the warden. "Is that in the Bible? All that screaming?"

"How am I to know," said the professor. He was tired of the warden and his lofty attitude.

"Put the one over the other," said the carpenter, as Bud's feet were held against the lower block.

BANG!

Nailed in three places, Bud raised up and drew a breath, and screamed again.

"What's he smiling about?" asked Bud's mother.

"Probably just a reflex," said the chaplain, putting his hand, and then his arm, on her shoulder.

"I don't mean Bud," said Bud's mother. "I mean the professor."

"Wish they'd turn the sound up," said the little girl's uncle.

"You're done wishin'," said the grandmother.

She grabbed her youngest son by the arm and yanked him out of the Victims' Rights Closure Lounge, brushing past the producer, who was just entering.

"What's with them?" the producer asked the guard. He was carrying a plate of pimento cheese sandwiches. He had hoped to get a few shots of the family.

"Weak stomach," said the guard.

"Want a sandwich?" asked the producer. "Hate to see them to go to waste."

Bud was making a sort of honking sound. "Like a goose," said his mother.

"Or a car," said the chaplain. He had already shown her his Classic, newly painted, in the prison parking lot.

"It's 10:41," said the warden. "How long is this supposed to take?"

"Not less than three or more than four hours, if all goes well," said the professor.

The warden looked at his watch. "We have a shift change at eleven-thirty. That's less than an hour from now."

The watch, a Seiko, was a gift from his father-in-law, also a warden.

To breathe, Bud had to raise up on his feet. The nails made it painful; very painful; more painful than he had ever imagined anything could be.

Not that Bud was big on imagining things.

But the body's yearning to breathe, he learned, cannot be overriden, even by pain.

When he stood up was when he made the honking sound.

Stand, honk, breathe, honk.

His head turned from side to side.

"It looks like he's looking for somebody," the carpenter said.

"Who?" asked the professor.

"Bud."

"No, I mean who's he looking for?"

"Isn't that your department?" said the carpenter.

Bud was. Looking for somebody.

Somebody was missing.

"Professor," Bud said. "Professor!"

The professor looked up.

Bud raised up for air. Instead of honking, this time, he asked, "Where is He?"

"Who?"

"Jesus."

"Jesus Christ!" said the professor.

"He's not here in person, Bud," said the chaplain, reaching up to pat Bud's plump knee. "That was a long, long time ago."

"It's not required," said the lawyer.

Bud groaned and honked.

"Bud's like a lot of people," the professor said to the warden, "in that he takes things too literally."

Bud White groaned. He was supposed to be getting to heaven pretty soon.

He hoped Heaven wasn't anything like this.

He found he could still wiggle all his fingers but two.

From his high perch he could see the professor and the warden and the lawyer standing side by side.

The doctor and his mother and the chaplain stood right behind them.

The TV producer and the four convict volunteers, none of whom Bud knew, were milling around a small catering table.

Bud had never hurt so bad. When he had been shot, right before his capture, it had hardly hurt at all. The bullet had gone in and out of the flat part of his neck.

Bud's eyes filled with tears. He felt sorry for himself, and for everyone around him. They were all just flesh and bone, like himself. They were only alive for a few precious moments. Like the little girl herself.

"Bud? Bud White?"

He blinked away the tears and saw Jesus, hanging on the next cross, one over.

"Yes, sir?"

"You're in luck, Bud. See the gate?"

Bud looked up. The sky swung open, and swinging on it, there was a little girl in a muddy white dress.

She stuck out her tongue but Bud knew that she didn't hate him. Even though he had cracked her little neck with his hands, like a rabbit.

Her dress was muddy. The wind lifted it when she swung forward, and he could see her little blue panties.

She wore little gold shoes.

She stuck out her tongue again—just teasin'! Her lips said, "Bud White!" She took his hand, both hands, and pulled him up, not down, peeling him off the nails like a sticker.

Boy, did that hurt!

But it was worth it, 'cause—

"We could borrow a guard's club and crack his shins," said the doctor. "That way he couldn't stand up to breathe."

"The Romans often did precisely that," said the professor.

"They had great respect for quitting time. But when they went to do it to Our Lord, they found that he had already expired."

"We're in no hurry," said the new guard. "We're just starting our shift. We're good for the darnation."

"He means *du*ration," said the warden. "But shouldn't somebody check Bud? He's stopped honking."

Sure enough, Bud was silent. His big head drooped to one side.

"I don't like the diaper," his mother said. "And I never liked the beard."

"It was Bud you never liked," muttered the carpenter, who had grown to like Bud, a little.

"You watch your mouth," said Bud's mother. "When I want some stupid redneck opinion, I'll read the *Banner*."

"He's not raising hisself up anymore," said the chaplain.

"Him-self," said the professor.

The warden shook his watch, which had mysteriously stopped at 12:04. "Anybody got the time?"

It was 12:19, according to the producer. Amazingly, according to the professor, the re-creation had taken almost exactly the same time as the original Passion.

The Discovery Channel provided the ambulance as part of the deal. It pulled up in the yard. "You'd think whoever thought of a nail gun," said the carpenter, "would've come up with a better way to pull them."

He used a short crowbar which he called a "do-right." He had to use a block, since Bud's hands were soft. Hands get soft on Death Row. He gave one of the nails to Bud's mother, who wiped it off and put it into her purse. He gave one to the professor and kept the other for the warden.

The guards slid Bud into the back of the ambulance, feet first. He was headed not for a graveyard but an Autopsy Center.

"You want to ride with him?" the warden asked.

"No, no, no," Bud's mother said. "I'd rather ride with the chaplain. He's the spiritual adviser for the entire family, you know."

"What about the butcher blocks?" asked the producer.

"If you turn them over, they're still good," said the carpenter.

"I'll take one, too, then," said the professor. He was already planning where to send his paper. First he would mount the *précis* on the World Wide Web—a necessary first step these days.

"You can quit sulking, Luke," said the little girl's grandmother. Her youngest son was sulking because he had been dragged away from the Victims' Rights Closure Lounge.

"Yes, ma'am."

"And you can go to church with me tomorrow."

"Yes, ma'am."

The two of them were in her gray '97 Hyundai, heading east on the interstate, toward Nashville, where the grandmother taught, and still teaches, school. Sunday School, too.

A car passed them doing about eighty, also heading for town. A one-handed driver with a woman close by his side. A Chevy; a 1955 210 coupe, cherry red, three coats, hand rubbed.

A Classic in anybody's book.

ABOUT THE AUTHORS

TED CHIANG'S "Story of Your Life," in *Starlight 2*, won the Nebula Award and the Sturgeon Award. He previously won the Nebula in 1990 for his first published story ("Tower of Babylon"); the 1991 *Asimov's* Reader's Award for his second story ("Understand"); and the 1992 John W. Campbell Award for Best New Writer. A new novella, "Seventy-Two Letters," appeared in Ellen Datlow's anthology *Vanishing Acts* (Tor, 2000). He lives in the Puget Sound area.

STEPHEN BAXTER is one of the most prominent modern writers of hard SF. His novels have been published in the UK, the US, and in many other countries including Germany, Japan, and France. He has won the Philip K. Dick Award, the John W. Campbell Memorial Award, the British Science Fiction Association Award, the Kurd Lasswitz Award in Germany, and the Seiun Award in Japan. In 2000, his collaboration with Arthur C. Clarke, *The Light of Other Days*, was published by Tor. Due in 2001 are the novels *Manifold 3: Origin* and *Mammoth 3: Icebones. Time Out* has called him "the most credible heir to the hard SF tradition previously monopolized by Clarke and Asimov." He lives in England.

MAUREEN F. MCHUGH'S first novel, *China Mountain Zhang* (Tor, 1991), won the James Tiptree Jr. Memorial Award, the Lambda Literary Award, the *Locus* Award for Best First Novel, was a finalist for the Hugo and Nebula Awards, and was a *New York Times* Notable Book. In 1996 she won the Hugo for her short story "The Lincoln Train." Her *Starlight 1* novella "The Cost to Be Wise" was also a finalist for the Hugo and Nebula awards, and formed the basis of her third novel, *Mission Child* (Avon, 1998). Forthcoming in 2001 is her fourth novel, *Nekropolis*. She lives in Ohio with her husband and teen-aged stepson, and maintains a web page at http://www.en.com/users/mcq/.

COLIN GREENLAND is one of Britain's best-loved SF writers. His work has won awards there and in the US, has been broadcast on the BBC, and has been translated into many languages including Russian and Finnish. His last novel, *Spiritfeather* (Dolphin, 2000), was his first for younger readers. His next, *St. Clair's Light*, will be his first for people who think they don't like SF. He spends much of his time reviewing beer and choosing five-hundred-word stories for Adhoc (www.adhocity.com). He lives in Cambridge with his partner, Susanna Clarke.

SUSAN PALWICK is an Assistant Professor of English at the University of Nevada, Reno. Her first novel, *Flying in Place* (Tor, 1992), won the Crawford Award; she is currently working on her second novel, *Shelter*, also for Tor. Her recent short fiction has appeared in *Asimov's, F&SF, Xanadu 3, The Horns of Elfland, Not of Woman Born*, and on Scifi.com. Her story "G.I. Jesus" in *Starlight 1* was a finalist for the World

Fantasy Award; her story "Going After Bobo," in the May 2000 issue of *Asimov's*, was chosen for Gardner Dozois's *Year's Best Science Fiction: Eighteenth Annual Collection* (St. Martin's Press, 2001). She lives with her husband and three cats in Reno.

JANE YOLEN'S "Sister Emily's Lightship," in *Starlight 2*, won the Nebula Award and became the title story of her latest collection of SF and fantasy for adult readers, published by Tor in 2000. The author of over 200 books, mostly for younger readers, Yolen has been called "the Hans Christian Andersen of America" (by *Newsweek*), "the Aesop of the twentieth century" (by the *New York Times*) and most recently "the Tom Clancy of children's books" (by the owner of BookEnds in Warner, New Hampshire.) She is also the winner of another Nebula, a World Fantasy Award, and three Mythopoeic Society Awards, plus a slew of children's book prizes and two honorary doctorates. Her highly comprehensive web page is at http://www.janeyolen.com/. At home in both Massachusetts and Scotland, she is a gracious hostess but a lousy cook.

GREG VAN EEKHOUT'S short fiction has appeared in a small number of magazines and anthologies. His other published writing includes travel and entertainment articles, scripts for CD-ROMs, and T-shirt slogans for fictitious liquor companies. He lives in Tempe, Arizona, with his fiancée, an astrophysicist, and works as a multimedia developer and instructional designer at Arizona State University. His web page is at http://www.sff.net/people/greg/.

GEOFFREY A. LANDIS has won the Hugo and Nebula awards for his short SF. His first novel, *Mars Crossing*, appeared in 2000 from Tor, and his short story collection, *Impact Parameter (And Other Quantum Realities)*, will be published by Golden Gryphon in 2001. He lives in Ohio with his wife, the author Mary Turzillo, and works on advanced concepts at the

NASA John Glenn Research Center. His web page is at http://www.sff.net/people/Geoffrey.Landis/.

BRENDA W. CLOUGH spent much of her childhood overseas, courtesy of the US government. She lives in a cottage at the edge of a forest in northern Virginia, and writes novels, short fiction, and nonfiction. Her web page is at http://www.sff.net/people/Brenda/. Her latest novel, *Doors of Death and Life*, was published by Tor in 2000, and her most recent short work can be seen in the April 2001 *Analog*.

SUSANNA CLARKE says she draws inspiration from Jane Austen, Charles Dickens, Neil Gaiman, and G. K. Chesterton, pretty much in that order. She writes in England but is published in America—a place she is almost certain exists, though she has never been there. She feels happiest in the early nineteenth century but makes occasional forays into the seventeenth and eighteenth. The curious reader can find her stories in previous *Starlights* and in Ellen Datlow and Terri Windling's fairy-tale anthologies. She is working on her first novel, *Jonathan Strange and Mr. Norrell,* and lives with her partner Colin Greenland in the medieval city of Cambridge.

MADELEINE E. ROBINS'S short fiction has appeared in *F&SF, Asimov's,* and various anthologies. Her first fantasy novel, *The Stone War* (Tor, 1999), was a *New York Times* Notable Book; her next novel, *Point of Honour,* forthcoming from Tor in 2002, explores the question of whether it is a truth universally acknowledged that a young lady in search of her fortune must be packing a piece. She lives in Manhattan with her husband and two daughters, and her web page is at http://www.sff.net/people/madrobins/.

D. G. COMPTON was born in London in 1930. After many years as a writer and publisher's editor in England, he has settled in Portland, Maine. His many critically acclaimed SF novels include *Chronocules* (1970), *Ascendancies* (1980), and *The Continuous Katherine Mortenhoe* (published in the US as *The Unsleeping Eye* and later reissued in the UK as *Deathwatch*), which was filmed by the French director Bertrand Tavernier in a version starring Harvey Keitel and Max von Sydow. Astute readers may see a connection between this new short story and Compton's recent involvement in Maine's November referendum on a Death with Dignity bill similar to Oregon's; the bill was narrowly defeated.

CORY DOCTOROW won the John W. Campbell Award for Best New Writer in 2000. His first story collection is forthcoming from Four Walls Eight Windows. *The Complete Idiot's Guide to Publishing Science Fiction,* co-written with Karl Schroeder, appeared as part of the popular "Idiot's Guides" series in summer 2000. He is co-founder of openCOLA (http://www. opencola.com), an open-source software project that will make the world safe for cool stuff. His remarkable web page is at http://www.craphound.com. Originally from Toronto, he lives on the road, and is the most wired individual in the entire world.

ALEX IRVINE'S first novel, *A Scattering of Jades*, is forthcoming from Tor. His short fiction and poetry have appeared in or are forthcoming in *F&SF*, *Asimov's*, *Hitchcock's*, and *Lady Churchill's Rosebud Wristlet*. He has published criticism on Sean Stewart, James Morrow, and H. G. Wells. He is working on a second novel, and lives in Massachusetts with his wife, Beth, and two dogs. His web page is at http://www.du.edu/~airvine/.

ANDY DUNCAN made his fiction debut in 1996 with "Liza and the Crazy Water Man" in *Starlight 1*. Since then, his stories have appeared in *Asimov's, Event Horizon, Realms of Fantasy, Weird Tales*, and Stephen Jones's *Best New Horror* series, and his work has been shortlisted for the Hugo, Nebula, Campbell, and International Horror Guild awards. His first collection, *Beluthahatchie and Other Stories*, was published in October 2000 by Golden Gryphon Press. Other recent fiction includes "The Pottawatomie Giant" at Scifi.com, and a new *Asimov's* novella, "The Chief Designer." He lives with his wife, Sydney, in Tuscaloosa, Alabama, where he teaches creative writing, literature, and composition at the University of Alabama. His web page is at http://www.angelfire.com/al/andyduncan/.

TERRY BISSON's 1990 story "Bears Discover Fire" won the Hugo, Nebula, Sturgeon, and *Locus* awards. His novels include *Talking Man* (Arbor House, 1986), *Fire on the Mountain* (Morrow, 1988), *Voyage to the Red Planet* (Tor, 1990), *Pirates of the Universe* (Tor, 1996), and *The Pickup Artist* (Tor, 2001). His short fiction is collected in *Bears Discover Fire and Other Stories* (Tor, 1993), and *In the Upper Room and Other Likely Stories* (Tor, 2000). Other recent books include the e-text *Numbers Don't Lie* (ElectricStory) and *On a Move* (Litmus), a (hardcopy) biography of Mumia Abu-Jamal. His web page is at http://www.terrybisson.com/. He lives in Brooklyn, New York.

ACKNOWLEDGMENTS

For ongoing support of the *Starlight* series, my thanks to many essential people at Tor Books, including but hardly limited to Claire Eddy, Tom Doherty, Linda Quinton, Irene Gallo, Beth Meacham, John Klima, and the late Jenna Felice. For intrepid help with untold numbers of submissions, thanks to Soren de Selby and Velma Bowen. For dozens of hours of computer support, thanks to Erik V. Olson.

And for everything, as ever, thanks to my wife and colleague, Teresa Nielsen Hayden.

—PNH